"Mama mia, let's escape! Let's fall in love! Let's eat chicken parmesan, fettuccine Alfredo, *and* Bubba's down-home barbecue without gaining a pound. It's all possible when we hang out with Bella Rossi in *Fools Rush In*. Janice Thompson's first installment in the Weddings by Bella series is a fun, welcome distraction from life's boredom and stress. You'll fall for Bella's D.J. even faster than she does. And you'll root for the Rossi and Neeley families as they break down cultural barriers and rush toward each other, arms wide open. No fools, they!"

Trish Perry, author, *Beach Dreams*
and *The Guy I'm Not Dating*

"From the Lone Star state, where everything is supersized, Janice Thompson brings us the larger-than-life story of Bella Rossi and her transplanted Italian family. I fell in love with the Rossi clan, a delightful collection of quirky characters who feel as passionate about their pizza as Texans do about chili. Add a hunky cowboy with a slow Southern drawl, and you've got a recipe for one terrific story. Polish up your line-dancing skills and get ready for a boot-scootin' good time with *Fools Rush In*."

Virginia Smith, author, *Stuck in the Middle*

"Janice Thompson is a master storyteller who draws her readers into the tale along with the characters. From page one of *Fools Rush In*, I felt as if I were Bella's best friend, sitting down with her over cups of Italian cappuccino while she told me the latest happenings in her zany family. One of my top picks for 2009, *Fools Rush In* earns a permanent place in my library."

Ane Mulligan, editor, Novel Journey

"Janice Thompson's gift for writing humorous, romantic tales proves true once again in her book *Fools Rush In*. The story unfolds on Galveston Island, where Bella Rossi, a wedding planner of Italian descent, meets D.J. Neeley, a Texan through and through. Such a blending produces a joyous, fun-filled adventure for readers, whose lives will surely be richer for the time they spend at Club Wed in *Fools Rush In*."

Nancy Jo Jenkins, author, *Coldwater Revival*

"*Fools Rush In* is a charming tale about stumbling upon love and finding a bit of your true self along life's journey. Wedding planner Bella Rossi bounds from one crazy situation to another in this fun read that makes you grateful for the truly important things in life—a loving family and a strong faith. Like fine seasonings in rich gravy, Janice Thompson skillfully blends in several insightful moments to distill truth in a meaningful way."

Megan DiMaria, author, *Searching for Spice* and *Out of Her Hands*

Weddings by *Bella*

BOOK ONE

Fools Rush In

A NOVEL

Janice Thompson

Revell

a division of Baker Publishing Group
Grand Rapids, Michigan

© 2009 by Janice Thompson

Published by Revell
a division of Baker Publishing Group
P.O. Box 6287, Grand Rapids, MI 49516-6287
www.revellbooks.com

Printed in the United States of America

Library of Congress Cataloging-in-Publication Data
Thompson, Janice, 1959–
    Fools rush in : a novel / Janice Thomspon.
        p.   cm. — (Weddings by Bella ; bk. 1)
    ISBN 978-0-8007-3342-1 (pbk.)
    1. Single women—Fiction. 2. Weddings—Planning—Fiction. I. Title.
PS3620.H6823F66 2009
813′.6—dc22   2009015690

Published in association with MacGregor Literary Agency.

In memory of my stepfather, Billie Moseley,
a true-blue Texan,
who is currently residing in heaven . . .
and likely still wearing his boots

Prologue

If Uncle Lazarro hadn't left the mob, I probably wouldn't have a story to tell.

Okay, so he wasn't actually *in* the mob, he only sold vacuum cleaners to a couple of guys who were. In the '70s. In Atlantic City, New Jersey. Before I was born.

But still, mob ties are mob ties, right? And we Rossis certainly know how to take a little bit of yeast and puff it up into a whole loaf of bread—which means we've managed to elevate Uncle Lazarro's story to folklore status. And why not? As my mama always says, "A little extra spice never hurts the sauce, just gives it more flavor."

Depending on who you ask, it was a Damascus Road experience that did it. Uncle Lazarro swears he was blinded by a bright light that drove him backward to the ground, just like the apostle Paul in the book of Acts.

My Aunt Bianca, God rest her soul, told the story a little differently. In her version, Uncle Lazarro was hit by a bus on a city street late at night while walking home from a bar in a drunken stupor. She said the headlights came at him like two glowing snake eyes just before the kiss of death. She always exaggerated her s's when she said the word *ssssnake*, which made the story more exciting.

Afterward, Aunt B. would lift her tiny silver crucifix to her lips, give it a kiss, then roll her eyes heavenward and mouth a silent prayer of thanks to the Almighty—not just for sparing her husband's life, but for returning his sanity and his religion.

Regardless of whose story you believed, Uncle Lazarro ended up at the Sisters of Mercy hospital in Atlantic City, where the nuns got ahold of him and led him to the Lord. He called it a "come to Jesus" meeting, and his eyes filled with tears every time he spoke of it.

According to my pop, my uncle gave up selling vacuum cleaners that same night. From what I hear, he was never quite the same . . . and neither was anyone else in my family. Funny how one event can change absolutely everything. In our case, it set the wheels in motion for the whole Rossi clan to end up in the most illogical of places—Texas.

Transitioning my story from the East Coast to the humid South would be impossible without mentioning my uncle's love for pizza. It's one of a million things we have in common, particularly when it comes to deep-dish, heavy on the pepperoni. He's also keen on coffees, especially the flavored ones with the foam on top. So when he came up with the idea to move to Galveston Island in the late '80s to open Parma John's—a pizzeria featuring the ultimate in Italian coffees—everyone took the news in stride.

Likely, my parents were intrigued by Lazarro's suggestion that they join him in this new venture. My pop, heaven help him, has always been lactose intolerant. I'm still not sure what motivated him to follow after this mozzarella-driven

Pied Piper. Probably just his overwhelming love for his older brother. Love and loyalty—these have always been powerful opiates in the Rossi family. I've found them to be both a blessing and a curse.

How my uncle settled on Galveston Island is another story altogether, one that involves the untimely passing of my beloved Aunt Bianca, may she rest in peace. Upon her deathbed, she mumbled these strange and startling words: "Toss my ashes into the Gulf of Mexico." At least we *think* she said the Gulf of Mexico. My mother insists she must've meant Galva Messio's, her favorite shoe store. Then again, my mama is always looking for an excuse to shop.

Regardless, the entire Rossi clan ended up in Texas, a far cry from Atlantic City not just in miles but in personality. Transplanting the whole group of us—three adults and five children—was no small feat. And the little things nearly proved to be our undoing. For example, I spent the better part of my elementary years figuring out how to transition from "you guys" to "y'all," something I thought would never come naturally. Now I can "y'all" with the best of 'em.

Turns out Galveston Island was the perfect place to grow up and the ideal setting for a family business. In fact, it turned out to be *such* an ideal setting that my pop, probably weary with the whole cheese thing, decided to open a business of his own—Bella's Wedding Facility.

And that's pretty much where my story begins.

1

Mambo Italiano

To be twenty-nine and single in an Italian family is one thing. To be twenty-nine and single with a wedding facility named after you is quite another.

From the day my father opened Bella's, I knew I would never marry. I had enough working against me already. Legs as skinny as Uncle Lazarro's walking cane. Interfering family members, who sabotaged every relationship I ever attempted. Now this. What were the chances someone would actually propose to a building's namesake?

Bella. My pop said he chose the name because I was such a beautiful baby. His face always lit up when he told the story of the first time he laid eyes on me in the hospital nursery. "What a vision of loveliness, bambina!" he would say. "All wrapped up like a piggy in a pink blanket with those big brown eyes peeking out . . . You were every papa's dream!" Of course, he could never finish the tale without shouting "Bellissimo!" and kissing his fingertips with dramatic flair.

I always loved that story.

My mother, known for her brutal honesty, opted to reveal the truth in the trickiest of ways—by showing me photographs. Not only was I the homeliest baby on Planet Earth, my bald head appeared to be oddly misshapen. No wonder they kept me wrapped up like a sausage. They were afraid I'd scare the neighbors.

I'm told by Aunt Rosa—Mama's older sister—that the head thing got better as I aged—kind of like a melon coming into season. And my hair, a mop of long, dark curls, eventually covered up any remaining imperfections. Still, I never completely trusted my father's stories after that. So when he announced his retirement from Bella's a couple of months ago, I wasn't quite sure I believed him.

Only when he added "Bella will take over as manager, and we will all work for her!" did I take him seriously. But why in the world would he pick me of all people—a melon-headed spinster with skinny legs and a penchant for pepperoni?

In spite of my reservations, I eventually came to terms with my new position, even looked forward to the challenges ahead. Right away, I came up with the idea of changing the name of the facility, opting for something modern and trendy. I chose Club Wed, hoping it would draw clients from the mainland for one of our advertised themed weddings. Country-western. Medieval. Hawaiian. Forties Swing. You name it, I planned to offer it.

Only one problem—I'd never actually *planned* a themed wedding before. We Rossis had only hosted traditional ceremonies and receptions. And now, with less than two weeks before my first Boot-Scootin' bridal event, I found myself in a world of trouble. I needed a deejay who knew a little something about country-western music, and I needed one yesterday.

I did what came naturally when in a jam—picked up the phone and called my best friend, Jenna. She answered on the third ring, breathless as always.

"Parma John's, we deliver."

I couldn't help but smile as I heard her voice above the strain of a familiar Dean Martin song. I started to say more, but she continued on before I could get a word in.

"Would you like to try our special of the day—a large Mambo Italiano pizza with two cappuccinos for only $17.95?"

"Skip the cappuccino. Let's go straight for the cheesecake," I said.

"Bella?" She let out a squeal. "Is that you? Why didn't you stop me?"

"I love it when you give me the spiel. Makes me feel special. And hungry."

"You *are* special." She let out an exaggerated sigh, and I could almost envision the look on her face.

If I didn't know her better, I would think she was schmoozing—trying to bamboozle me into buying the Mambo Italiano. But Jenna was the real deal, "a friend that sticketh closer than a brother," as the Bible would say. Or, in this case, closer than a vat of melted mozzarella.

I explained my predicament. As I started to ask for her help, she put me on hold and never returned. I listened to three rounds of "Mambo Italiano" before finally hanging up. Some things were better handled in person.

After a hurried good-bye to my parents—who were scouring the World Wide Web for a great deal on a European vacation—I raced out of the door, hoping to find the deejay of my dreams. Only when I reached the driveway did I realize I had company. Precious, my Yorkie-Poo, circled my feet, trying to weasel her way into both my car and my heart.

"Oh no you don't," I scolded. "This is a canine-free catastrophe I'm facing."

Three minutes later, I found myself belted into the front
seat of my SUV, headed out onto Broadway with a Yorkie-
Poo—whose disposition did *not* match her name—wrapped
around the back of my neck like a lumpy mink stole. Some
battles just weren't worth fighting.

We made the trip to Parma John's in record time. As I
pulled onto the Strand—Galveston Island's historic shopping
and business Mecca—a sense of wonder came over me. The
cobblestone sidewalks put me in mind of an earlier time,
before the 1900 storm that had taken the lives of so many.
And to think the historic buildings were still standing after
the recent devastation of Hurricane Ike—what a testimony!
Somehow, the two-story brick buildings along the Strand had
proven to be as stalwart as most Galvestonians.

I parallel parked next to the sidewalk, not far from the
Confectionery, one of my favorite places. Inside, children
nibbled on taffies and licked the edges of ice cream cones.
I'd spent countless hours in there as a child. Didn't hurt that
Uncle Laz had befriended the owners. In fact, he'd made his
presence known throughout the district, often giving away
pizza and coffees to his fellow merchants at no cost. One
thing—maybe two—could be said of my uncle above all others. He knew how to win over people, and he had the strongest
work ethic of anyone I'd ever met. Next to Rosa, of course.
She lived with us and worked round the clock to keep us all
fed. She worked from sunup till sundown most days, rarely
complaining.

Making my way past several of the shops, beyond the
throngs of flip-flopping tourists, I finally landed in front of
Parma John's. Seeing the sign out front still made me smile.

Though I'd been young at the time it went up, the love and care that went into it would remain with me forever—the same love and care that went into the design of the shop and the creation of the foods and coffees on the menu.

Stepping inside, I found the shop filled with a larger-than-usual crowd, particularly for a Monday. No wonder Jenna had left me hanging. Likely, she was up to her elbows in sauce and sausage and would hardly remember I'd called in the first place.

I slipped Precious into my oversized purse, then noticed the sound of teenagers' voices raised in song. How Uncle Lazarro got these high schoolers hooked on Dean Martin was beyond me, but they seemed to have the lyrics to "Mambo Italiano" down pat. I found the choice of music quite clever. My uncle should've considered a career in marketing.

Or wedding planning.

Surely, if someone in my gene pool could come up with a themed pizza, I could carry through with a themed wedding, right?

I caught a glimpse of my older brother, Nick, and gave him a wave. My baby brother, Joey, buzzed around cleaning tables but managed to flash a warm smile my way. I hollered out, "Hey, Professor," and his cheeks flushed. No doubt he was tired of the name family members had given him after he'd acquired his associate's degree at Galveston Community College. Others in the family teased Joey—all five foot five of him. His long ponytail and tattoos set him apart from the others, but I secretly favored him. Who could resist such a kindhearted nature? And that servant's heart! Wow. We should all have a heart like that.

As predicted, I found Jenna behind the counter, helping with the pizza prep. She looked up as I approached, and a dazzling smile lit her face. Until she heard Precious yapping from inside my purse. "You can't bring that little demon in here," she scolded.

"She's no demon," I argued as I pulled the handbag a bit closer.

Precious chose that moment to let out a growl. I peeked inside the purse, and she bared her teeth at me. I quickly closed her back inside, then turned to my best friend with a forced smile. "She's getting better."

"Sure she is." Jenna shook her head. "You're in denial, Bella. That dog needs a therapist. And why you would bring her in here—"

"Shh."

"Do you want the health department to shut us down?"

"I'll only be a minute," I whispered. "I just need your help with something."

"If your Uncle Laz gets wind of this, he'll fire me." Her eyes grew large, and I couldn't help but laugh. My uncle would never fire Jenna. Next to my brother Nick—who now managed the place—Jenna worked harder than any of his employees.

I watched my best friend's expression change immediately as she took in my new blouse. "Oooh, pretty. That color of green looks great against your olive skin."

She dove into a dissertation about her pale self, and I listened without comment, as always. Could I help it if the girl had been born with red hair and freckles and skin as white as the gulf sand? To be honest, I found her enviable. What I wouldn't give to have her petite frame. And those perfectly shaped legs! Where could I go to find a pair of those? Frankly, I thought Jenna was about the prettiest thing I'd ever seen, especially if you factored personality into the mix.

Still oohing and aahing, she brushed the flour off her hands, then reached out to touch the sleeve of my blouse. "See now, you can get away with wearing this style. You're tall enough to pull it off. But me . . ." Off she went again, on a description of her too-short stature and her inability to wear decent clothes as a result. I'd never really considered myself tall—five foot seven wasn't Goliath, after all—but Jenna apparently did.

Precious let out another growl, and I shifted gears, ready to get to work. "Thanks, but I'm not here for fashion advice. I've got a problem. A real problem."

"Oh, that deejay thing?" She turned back to her work. As she ladled sauce onto a large circle of dough, she added, "You need someone with country-western experience?"

"Yes." I shifted the purse to my other shoulder, hoping Precious would remain still and quiet. "Do you have any ideas?"

"What happened to Armando?" she asked as she spread a thick layer of chunky white mozzarella. "He's a great deejay, and I'm sure he could handle any type of music."

I sighed as she mentioned my middle brother's name. "He's in love."

"So what?"

"So . . ." I reached over the counter to grab a pepperoni and popped it in my mouth. In between bites, I explained, "He's moved off to Houston, never to return again."

"Oh, come on. You know how he is. He'll be back in just a few weeks. His relationships never last that long. He only dated me for nine days, remember?"

"You were both in junior high at the time," I reminded her. "Besides, I don't have a few weeks. Sharlene and Cody are getting married in less than two weeks, and they've got their hearts set on a country-western theme, complete with line dancing and the Texas Two-Step."

"Sharlene and Cody? Do I know them?"

"Nope. They're both from Houston. And that's the goal here, to draw in customers from the mainland. But if I can't pull off even one wedding on my own—and let's face it, I've never done a themed wedding before—we're going to have to close the facility." My heart twisted inside me as I spoke the words. I didn't want to disappoint my parents. For that matter, I didn't want to disappoint *me*. I needed to make this thing work—and I would, with God's help.

As we chatted about my problem, an incoming pizza customer—a twentysomething construction-worker type—made his way to the counter with a cell phone pressed to his ear. His skin glistened, and his damp shirt carried that "I forgot to put on my deodorant this morning" aroma. I stepped aside to give him the floor. He carried on an animated conversation with the person on the other end of the line, one that didn't appear to be ending anytime soon. I could see Jenna waiting for an opportunity to take his order, but finding a spot might be difficult.

Finally his speech slowed a bit, and my best friend, ever the savvy one, jumped right in with a polite, "Can I help you?"

He put the person on the phone on hold a moment and glanced her way with a wrinkled brow. "Um, sure. I'll have the, um, the . . . that Mambo thing. With the frappuccinos."

"The Mambo Italiano—our spicy sausage pizza—with two large *cappuccinos*?" she corrected him.

"Yeah. Whatever." While pulling cash from his billfold, he dove back into it with the person on the other end of the phone. I wasn't deliberately listening in, but my antennae went straight up into the air as I heard him mention something about a deejay.

After he hung up, I couldn't wait to ask. "Did you say deejay?"

The guy turned to me with a quizzical look on his face. "Yeah."

I reached into my bag, nearly forgetting the dog until I bumped up against her and she let out an aggravated yip. I came up with an ink pen. Reaching for a scrap of paper, I added, "And he works here—on the island?"

"Well, yes, but . . ." The guy rubbed his whiskery chin and gave me a funny look.

"Would you mind giving me his number?"

"I guess not." With a shrug, the confused stranger glanced at his cell phone. He squinted to read the number, then said it aloud. I scribbled it down with relief washing over me.

"And would you say his work is good?" I shoved the pen back into my purse.

"Oh, he's the best on the island." He slipped his phone into the back pocket of his jeans and narrowed his eyes, perhaps trying to figure me out. "He comes highly recommended. I've seen him in action several times over, and his clients have never been disappointed."

"And how is he with country-western music?" I posed the most important question of all. Whoever I hired would have to know his stuff in this area. Heaven knew I didn't.

"Country-western music?" My new hero shrugged. "It's his favorite. How come?"

"Oh, just curious." I reached out and shook his hand, adding, "Mister, I think you might've just saved my life."

"Really?" As he reached up to swipe a hand through his

thick blond curls, his cheeks reddened. "Go figure. I just came in here to order a pizza."

"No, you came in for far more than that," I explained in a whisper. "I believe this was a divine appointment."

"Divine appointment," he repeated as if trying to make sense of the words. He reached to pick up the two cappuccinos Jenna had prepared for him. I heard him muttering the words again as he made his way to a nearby table.

I gave Jenna a "Go God!" wink, then turned toward the door. I'd nearly made it when Uncle Lazarro's voice rang out from the kitchen.

"Don't you let me catch you bringing that dog in here again, Bella."

"Yes sir!" I gave him a playful salute, then, with a spring in my step, headed out to face the rest of my day.

2

Just in Time

The people in my family have always leaned heavily on the old saying, *"Finché c'è vita c'è speranza*—as long as there is life, there is hope."* I heard it countless times while growing up. Whenever things looked bleak—say, a relative in the old country was stricken with a fatal disease or one of my brothers left the top off the milk jug—Aunt Rosa would clutch her wrinkled hands to her sagging chest and cry out: *"Finché c'è vita c'è speranza"* in a voice laced with pain. Her Italian accent, still rich after all these years in the States, came naturally. The agony in her voice . . . a little more rehearsed. I'm pretty sure I caught her practicing in front of the bathroom mirror once, though she flat-out denied it.

In spite of Aunt Rosa's antics, the familiar saying brought comfort on a chaotic day like today when I needed to believe, needed to hope.

I made the journey home from Parma John's in a more positive state of mind. A worship song played on the radio, further lifting my spirits. If I could have raised my hands in praise, I would have. I wanted to thank the Lord for answering my prayer so quickly and efficiently. Glancing up, I noticed the sky above seemed bluer now that my troubles were behind me. The clouds whiter. The grass greener. Yes, I would surely pull off this wedding—with help from on high.

"Finché c'è vita c'è speranza." As long as there was life, there was hope. And as long as there was hope, there was a chance my new deejay would sweep in and save the day before this Boot-Scootin' bridal extravaganza got under way. Heaven knew I couldn't do it without him. And it was heaven I leaned on now—more than ever. A gentle reminder in the lyrics to the worship song was all I needed to convince me I could trust God to see me through this, and any other difficult experience.

Cruising down Broadway with the afternoon sun blazing high in the sky, I fumbled around with my right hand in my oversized Balenciaga handbag—a Christmas gift from my ex-boyfriend, Tony DeLuca—all the while keeping my left hand on the steering wheel. Not an easy trick with an ill-mannered pooch wrapped around my neck.

It took a few seconds of scrambling, but I finally came up with the phone. Now, to locate the deejay's number. I nudged my fingers into the pocket of my jeans and eased out the scrap of paper. Seconds later, safely pulled up to a red stoplight, I made the call.

Four rings later, the guy's voice-mail recording kicked in. "Hey, you've reached Dwayne Neeley. Sorry I can't get to the phone. Leave a message and I'll get back to you."

Dwayne. Only he'd pronounced it *Duh*-wayne. Interesting how the name matched his over-the-top Texas accent . . . which, to my way of thinking, proved to be a little too heavy on the twang. Maybe I could get him to tone it down a bit before the big day. Then again, he did have that nice bass sound to his voice. Crowds always loved that. I know I did. In fact, I loved it so much that I missed the changing of the light. The guy behind me gave a gentle reminder with a toot of his horn that green, at least on Galveston Island, still meant "go."

Startling to attention, I forged ahead down the busy street, leaving a message as I went. "Hi there." Speaking in my most businesslike voice, I continued, "I'm looking for a deejay. My name is Bella Rossi, from Bella's wedding facility on Broadway." I caught the mistake and corrected it. "Er, Club Wed on Broadway in the historic district. If you're interested in a great paying job weekend after next, please give me a call at 409-555-0402."

I hit END and tossed the phone into my purse, then leaned back against the seat. Well, tried to lean back, anyway. My rotten-tempered pooch let out a yip, and I found myself offering a rushed apology to the world's most self-absorbed canine. Precious indeed.

Oh well. No time to worry about that right now. No, right now I had a job to do. Having never before planned a wedding with a country-western theme, I had my work cut out for me. Though I'd spent most of my growing-up years in Texas, I'd never been into the whole cowboy-meets-cowgirl scene, and I'd certainly never line danced. Strange, I know. But in our family, it was the mambo all the way. Or one of Aunt Rosa's famous country folk dances.

Still, I would pull off this themed wedding or die trying.

Hmm. Nix the latter.

I pulled the SUV into the driveway, startled to find my aunt chasing a neighbor boy with a broom in her hand. This wasn't the first time I'd caught her in such an aggravated state. Last time, however, it was Uncle Laz on the other end of the bristles.

I stepped out of the car to watch all of this go down just as Rosa hollered, *"Gli dai un dito e si prendono il braccio"* to my mother. I knew the meaning, of course: "Give them a finger and they'll take an arm." Fully translated: "Give them an inch and they'll take a mile." Still, I couldn't imagine what the neighbor kid had done to deserve this.

The boy turned back and shouted, "Watch out, people! That old lady is crazy!"

I wasn't sure I could dispute him, though Rosa was usually tearing into Laz, not neighbor kids. With Laz, she was on equal footing.

Rosa, my mother's oldest sister from Napoli, and Lazarro, my father's pizza-loving older brother, had an understanding. They would go on hating each other until the day they died.

There were mixed stories regarding the origin of their feuding. Something about Frank Sinatra having a better voice than Dean Martin was all I'd been told. Oh, and Rosemary Clooney. Somehow she factored into the mix. At any rate, the bickering—both in rapid-fire Italian and rough-hewn English—had gone on for nearly sixteen years, and frankly, I'd had enough.

But today Aunt Rosa seemed content to chase the neighbors, not Laz. Though she did it with the usual amount of gusto. Her salt-and-pepper hair—more salt than pepper these days—was a fright. And her plumper parts—mostly around the midsection—seemed to lag behind a bit as she ran. Then again, the support hose and heavy black orthopedic shoes probably gave her an added advantage. I could almost see her gaining on the kid.

Precious scrambled out of my arms and down onto the ground, where she shot off after the boy, probably thinking him to be a burglar. Her frantic yaps filled the air, adding to the chaos. I called out to her, but she paid no attention. Nothing new there.

My mama—still regal and slender at fifty-seven—stood on the porch, shouting out to my aunt in Italian, "Rosa, *lasciare il ragazzo solo*. Leave the boy alone." Either Rosa didn't have her hearing aid turned up, or she simply didn't care to listen. The stubborn sixtysomething continued on around the side of the house, broom slicing through the air as she hollered out to the kid in Italian. Poor little guy. Probably never knew what hit him.

I looked up at my mother with a grin. "Rough afternoon?"

She swept a perfectly manicured hand through her dark hair, then turned to me with an exaggerated sigh. "You have no idea."

"But I've only been gone an hour." I climbed the stairs up to the veranda to join her. "What could have possibly happened in that length of time?" The cool afternoon breeze off the gulf provided a momentary relief from the mid-June heat. It caught a piece of my long, curly hair and whipped it into my face. I pushed it away and continued in her direction.

"I'm not sure you want to know."

She proceeded to fill me in, whether I wanted to know or not. Apparently the kid had turned our veranda and front steps into a skate park, maneuvering his board back and forth, up and down, until Aunt Rosa, who'd been baking bread inside the house, finally snapped.

A shiver ran down my spine as I contemplated what *that* must've looked like.

25

"She confiscated the skateboard," Mama explained. "Said she's not giving it back until she gets a written apology—in English and Italian."

"Oh dear."

"Yeah. But the kid wouldn't go down without a fight. Said his daddy's a lawyer."

"Uh-oh. The new family across the street?" I glanced across Broadway at the beautiful historic home recently restored. We'd watched them move in just the day before. Tens of thousands of dollars in antiques and other fine furnishings had given us plenty to talk about over dinner last night.

"Yes, the Burtons. So much for making a first impression."

"Man. I really hoped to get off on the right foot with them."

From what I'd heard through the grapevine, Bart Burton planned to run his office out of his home. Knowing that made me feel better about the fact that we ran a business along Broadway. Not that the neighbors were complaining, necessarily. The area boasted dozens of beautiful historic homes, many used for residential purposes, others used for business. There was a nice mix of both. But having another businessman close by might draw in clients. I hoped. Unless he was a divorce attorney. Hmm. I'd have to check into that.

Mama tried to pick up where she'd left off, but the sound of Andrea Bocelli's rich tenor voice interrupted her. My cell phone. I prayed it was the call I'd been waiting on.

"Sorry, Mama." I reached to open the slender pink phone. "My deejay awaits."

"Deejay?"

After a nod in her direction, I mouthed the words, "I'll fill you in later," then answered with a tentative "Hello?"

"Bella Rossi?" The same twangy voice greeted me, though slightly deeper than I'd remembered. I felt myself captivated by this Texan at once. Surely he was tall and brawny with a five o'clock shadow. I could envision him now in his boot-cut jeans and starched button-up shirt. To complete the picture—cowboy hat and boots, naturally.

"Yes?" I finally managed as my imagination got itself under control.

"I'm returning your call. Something about a job at your wedding facility."

"Yes, thank you for calling back so quickly."

"No problem. I would've called sooner, but I had the music turned up and didn't hear the phone."

"Understandable." Even now I could hear an unfamiliar melody in the background. More twang-twang. Perfect.

"I'm working a job on the west end of the island for the next few weeks," he explained. "But I can probably swing a second gig, as long as it's not time consuming."

"Just one day's work. The last Saturday in June." After a second thought, I threw in, "Though, if you do a great job—and I'm sure you will—we could probably talk about more opportunities in the future."

"Sounds great."

Trying not to gush, I added, "I'm looking for a pro, and you come highly recommended." I didn't want to carry the flattery too far, not knowing his capabilities, but a little enticement never hurt.

"Well, thank you for the opportunity. I've only been on the island a few months. Folks down here are mighty friendly."

Yep. The voice was definitely growing on me. I could almost picture him now, standing off to the edge of the crowd, microphone pressed to his lips as he urged folks to take one more spin around the floor.

"Where are you from, *Duh*-wayne?" I couldn't resist.

"Splendora."

Okay, so he had me there. "Never heard of it."

"Small town about an hour north of Houston. Off Highway 59. Tucked away in the trees."

He dove into a detailed explanation of small-town life in the piney woods of east Texas, but I only half heard what he had to say. His lyrical voice pulled at me, like the tide urging my heart out to sea. Still, I'd better stop myself before proposing marriage to this total stranger.

"I'd like to meet with you in person at my facility to talk more about the job, if you're available tomorrow."

"Sure," he said. "What would be a good time for you?"

Remembering my bride and groom would arrive at six the following evening for a final planning session, I responded with, "What about 5:15?"

"Not a problem. I'll see you then."

I proceeded to give him the directions, then we ended the call. Seconds later, Aunt Rosa came sprinting around the side of the house, a long string of Italian words flowing in the breeze and a half-crazed Yorkie-Poo yapping at her heels. The boy was nowhere to be seen, but that didn't stop Rosa from carrying on with a vengeance. She'd paused long enough to pluck a few tomatoes off the vine in Uncle Laz's garden. I could almost see the look of horror on Laz's face now. No one messed with his garden. Surely Rosa didn't plan to pelt the kid with the tomatoes, right? Nah, she was probably just trying to save herself a trip before cooking dinner.

With the dog so stirred up, I couldn't make out everything

my aunt said, but I managed to decipher a bit of it. Something about a lawsuit against the neighbors. Or maybe it was a lawsuit *from* the neighbors. I couldn't be sure. I gave Mama a shrug and headed off to the house, far more important things on my mind.

3

Fools Rush In

As I entered the house with Precious in my arms and started
up the stairs, a familiar Frank Sinatra tune greeted me. As
Ol' Blue Eyes crooned across our piped-in PA system, I found
myself caught up in the words. One thing could be said of
the Rossi household—we never lacked for music. Variety,
yes. Music, no.

My sister appeared at the top of the stairs, dressed in a
luscious pair of jet black capris and the prettiest hot pink top
I'd seen in ages. Amazing strappy sandals, luscious handbag,
lots of bling around the neck and the wrists. Yep, I'd raised
her right.

"Hey, Bella." Her thick, dark hair bounced off her shoulders as she took a couple of steps toward me.

"Sophia. You look great." I offered up a little whistle as I
took her in. In so many ways, my younger sister resembled
my mother, right down to the manicured nails and tattooed
eyeliner. I got a little wistful about the fact that her head—

underneath those cascading locks—was perfectly rounded. This I knew for a fact, having seen it myself when she was born. Sure, I was only six at the time, but my baby sister's bowling ball perfection had made the headlines, at least in the Rossi family.

"Thanks." She released an exaggerated sigh. "I was supposed to have a date this evening, but it fell through."

"Oh no." I hated to say that Sophia struggled in the date department, but something always managed to go wrong.

"Yeah." She sat down on the top step and groaned. "That means I have to have dinner with the family tonight."

"Hey," I argued, "nothing wrong with that."

The roll of her eyes let me know her take on the matter.

Just then, Dean and Frankie, my brother Nick's boys, came bounding down the stairs dressed in shorts and swim goggles. Odd, since we didn't have a pool. Dean, the chubbier of the two, had something in his hand that looked like an electronic game of some sort. I couldn't be sure. He called out a threat to his brother, and they nearly knocked me down as they blew by.

"Slow down, Deany-boy!" I called out. He paused just long enough to glare at me for calling him by the dreaded nickname, then picked up his pace once again.

"Stop running in the house!" Sophia shouted as the boys reached the bottom of the stairs. They disappeared into the living room. She turned to me with yet another groan, followed by an explanation. "They've been awful this afternoon. I took them to Stewart Beach, and the lifeguard kicked us out."

"What did they do this time?"

"Well, apparently they were wreaking havoc in the men's room. No idea what all they did, but it was enough to get us ousted from the place. And I don't think they want us to come back. That's a huge problem because the summer just started. Seriously, how am I going to keep them busy? I'll go crazy if we have to stay at home."

"There are plenty of other beaches on the west end of the island," I offered. "Jamaica Beach, Pirate's Beach . . . and you could always hit one of the pocket beaches out near the state park. They're more secluded anyway. Not as many people for the boys to annoy."

"Like that would stop them."

"Well, if you don't like the beach idea, take them to Moody Gardens or the waterpark. Or Seawolf Park to see the submarine. They love that."

"Yes, but I don't." She pushed a loose hair out of her eyes. "Being confined with those two boys inside a submarine is not exactly my idea of fun." She paled at the very idea.

I couldn't blame her for complaining, really. Watching our oldest brother's kids over the summer holidays while he and his wife were working at the restaurant was taking its toll on her. I saw the fine lines in Sophia's brow where wrinkles were beginning to form. Pretty soon they'd be permanently etched there. The wrinkles, not the boys.

"I can't wait for school to start." In true Rossi form she leaned her forehead into her outstretched palms and began to dramatize in Tex-Italian about what a difficult life she led.

Please. The girl was in her twenties, still lived at home with her mama, and . . . Wait. I was describing my own life.

Precious, who'd managed to behave herself for the past thirty seconds, took Sophia's ranting as some form of a threat and started that low growl thing in the back of her throat. My sister looked up in alarm, and the dog shifted into an attack stance. The six-pound monster didn't come across as terribly intimidating to me, but this one move was enough to cause Sophia to rise to her feet. Her eyes widened in fear.

With hands clutched to her chest à la Rosa, she muttered, "That dog is evil."

I wrapped my little angel in my arms, prepared to argue the fact, when her growl morphed into a full-fledged barking fit aimed at my sister.

"We need an exorcist," Sophia said. "I'm calling for a priest."

"But we're not Catholic," I protested. "And neither is the dog." No indeed. The Rossis—at least those under sixty— were all of the Methodist persuasion. Rosa and Laz still clung to their Catholic roots, but the rest of us had made the switch years ago during a local Methodist revival. I couldn't speak for Precious, of course. Based on her actions, I'd have to conclude she had not yet been won to the Lord. But I was working on it.

"That mongrel needs help." Sophia dove into a lengthy speech about the various demon spirits currently residing inside my dog, and I did my best to remain calm. While our local Methodist congregation had a multiplicity of ministries, I seriously doubted they catered to canines, even those in need of spiritual help. Not that it mattered. I would prove my pup's innocence to everyone, sooner or later.

Still Sophia continued on, ranting and raving.

"Enough about the dog already." I managed to get Precious under control, gave my sister a polite nod, then eased past her and continued on my way to my room. As we parted ways, I was pretty sure I heard her say something about joining the witness protection program to get away from our nutty family.

Settling down onto my bed, I kicked off my shoes and reached for my notepad, the one I'd carried around for days. With Sharlene and Cody arriving tomorrow evening for their final meeting, I had little time to wrap up my plans. Precious sat at the edge of my bed, still panting from her earlier escapades. It must take a lot out of a dog to be so disobedient.

Going over my list, I noted a couple of discrepancies. We'd need to tweak the menu a bit. No problem there. Jenna and Uncle Laz would be catering the event, and they were the best in the business, hands down.

Next I turned my sights to the decor. Sharlene had been specific. She wanted a cowboy boot theme—both in the ceremony and at the reception. Her colors? Red, white, and blue, of course. With yellow roses in abundance. I'd balked at the idea. At first. But it was growing on me. This was a true-blue Texas event, after all. And the week before the Fourth of July, no less. We had to do it right. Not an easy task, what with everything being so last minute and all. I only hoped my jumbled nerves wouldn't get in the way as I attempted to pull off my first themed wedding—in a hurry!

I rolled over on the bed, still clutching the notepad. Precious curled up next to me, finally opting to behave. Giving her a tender rubbing behind the ears, I begged her to change her evil ways, lest I turn her over to her former owner, my ex-boyfriend.

The tiniest sigh escaped my lips as I contemplated Tony DeLuca. Much as I'd tried to love him, I couldn't. Still, he was perfect—at least in my mama's eyes. Came from just the right Sicilian family. Spoke fluent Italian, with just the right lilt in his voice. On top of all this, the man was gorgeous, as in Hollywood gorgeous. Dark hair, deep brown eyes, tanned skin, perfect physique. Plus he had a knock-you-down wardrobe and always looked like he'd just stepped out of a magazine. He happened to be related to the best tailor in town—a real advantage for a man who stood only five seven. One thing was for sure, Tony DeLuca could shop. I'd give him that much.

These days I found myself hoping he'd start shopping for a new girlfriend—soon.

At least he could afford to spend money on clothes and grooming supplies. He had an amazing job. I wanted a man who wasn't afraid to work, to get his hands dirty. Not that I wanted Tony—at least, not anymore. No, three years of dating the wrong man had shown me exactly what I *wasn't* looking for.

Not that Tony was a bad guy. Not all bad, anyway. Okay, he spent a little too much time in front of the mirror. He was what Pop called a diva-dude. And then there was the clothing issue—mine, not his. Tony insisted on picking out my clothes—everything from casual wear to fancy. He also encouraged me to wear makeup around the clock, even when no one was looking.

Why he cared so much about my appearance was a mystery. Pride, perhaps? Anyway, no matter how much makeup I wore, I'd never be as pretty as Tony, so what was the point in trying?

I'd rarely used the words "high maintenance" to describe a guy, but there really was no other way to say it. Tony was high maintenance. I'd put up with it for three years, then finally cracked. A girl needed to pull her hair up into a ponytail once in a while without hearing about it. And who cared if I skipped the mascara every now and then?

Still, Tony was a great guy. Just not the guy for me.

I thought again about Sharlene, the bride-to-be. Though

we were nothing alike physically—her long blonde hair, curvy figure, and bright blue eyes set us worlds apart—we were kindred spirits. We both longed for the same things. Of course, she longed for them set to the tune of a Rascal Flatts song, and I preferred mine with an Andrea Bocelli melody lingering in the background, but other than that, we were just alike. We both wanted love. We both wanted the happily ever after. And we both wanted it now.

I closed my eyes for just a minute, allowing sleepiness to take hold. Maybe a little nap would do me good before dinner.

It didn't take long to drift off. For some strange reason, I dreamed of a pizza-loving cowboy, one with a special anointing from on high to drive demon spirits out of badly behaved little dogs . . . one who didn't care if I wore makeup or fancy clothes. In other words, I dreamed of my ideal man, my cowboy. Only, I hadn't *known* I wanted a cowboy. Until now.

The sound of slamming doors roused me from my slumber. I could hear a myriad of voices rising up from the bottom floor, and the comforting smell of garlic and oregano filled the house. My mouth watered at the possibility of what awaited me downstairs. Surely Aunt Rosa was working her magic.

A smile rose at the memory of my aunt—straight off the plane from Napoli—complaining that our Galveston home had only one kitchen. "Every decent Italian home has at least two!" she'd informed us. Pop had promised to build on a second, but so far that hadn't happened. I wasn't holding my breath.

After taking a few minutes to freshen up, I made my way to the kitchen, ready to greet the family, pushing all cowboy images out of my mind once and for all.

Oddly, I found Tony standing near the stove, pressed squarely between Aunt Rosa and Uncle Laz, who appeared to be having it out. I almost missed him through the crowd.

Hmm. He might not be my cowboy, but it certainly looked like he needed my help. I took a few tentative steps through the throng of people—my mother, father, brothers, sister-in-law, and nephews—to come to his aid. Along the way, I shot a "why did you have to go and invite him?" look to my mama, who returned it with a rehearsed smile. Would her matchmaking attempts never end?

I drew near to Tony, and the familiar, yummy scent of his cologne sent my nostrils flaring. Crazy how a smell could drive you to your knees. I finally managed, "Hey." Not brilliant, but it would have to do for an opener.

Tony turned to face me, his eyes widening as he took in my new blouse. "Bella, you look beautiful."

Do not let him get to you. Do not let him get to you.

"Thanks. You look great too." I eased him away from my feuding relatives. "What's up with the two of them?"

"Ah. Well, it seems your Uncle Laz bought a new CD today and wanted to play it during dinner. *The Best of—*"

"*Dean Martin*," I finished. *Say no more.*

"Yeah." Tony nodded, and his rich, coffee-brown eyes twinkled in true DeLuca style. "But apparently Rosa's got her heart set on something different."

Above the din of voices, I now took note of the music playing overhead. "Fools Rush In." Ironic.

"Ol' Blue Eyes." We spoke the words together, then laughed.

"He's the best," Tony said with a shrug.

I put my finger over my lips and pulled him a few inches farther away from my uncle, who continued his passionate rant. "Just don't let Laz hear you say that, okay? The last time, Rosa came after him with a wooden spoon in her hand. You should've seen the marks on his arms."

"Well, Rosa insists she makes a far better chicken piccata when Sinatra is singing."

"Mmm. Is that what I smell?" I worked my way back over to the stove for a quick peek. Yep. The bubbling sauce wafted up, overwhelming my senses. I closed my eyes and inhaled, hurled backward in time to Rosa's first meal with us, sixteen years ago when she'd arrived straight off the plane from Napoli. After a moment's pondering, I removed the top from a huge kettle, eyeing the thick minestrone soup inside. "Primo."

Still, I knew there had to be more. My nose led me to take a quick peek in the oven below. Sure enough, I discovered three beautifully twisted loaves of Rosa's homemade garlic bread. Could life get any better than this?

Looking around the room at this loud, wacky family of mine, I had to conclude . . . it couldn't.

Unless you happened to factor in a boot-wearin' cowboy spinning a sappy country tune.

4

Ain't That a Kick in the Head?

The following morning, Aunt Rosa ranted and raved about the new neighbors and their threats to take us to court if the skateboard was not returned forthwith. She refused to return it, naturally. Until she got her apology in both English and Italian, the boy would never skate again. My mother's words, *"E buona notte al secchio,"* echoed around the house. I'd heard the expression all my life, of course: "And good night to the pail." Loosely interpreted, it meant, "That's that! There's nothing more I can do."

For the better part of an hour, my mother pleaded with her sister to give in, but Rosa would not relent. Visions of lawsuits filled my mind, but I pushed them away. I had enough to think about, after all. I put together a list of questions for the bride-to-be, went over the items we'd have to rent for the reception, and spent every moment in between daydreaming about my new deejay.

At 4:30 that afternoon, I headed next door to the beautifully renovated Victorian home now known as Club Wed. My home away from home. My proving ground.

At straight-up five o'clock, a noise from outside caught my attention. An engine. From the sound of it, a pretty big vehicle had pulled into the driveway. Probably Eugene, our UPS guy, making a delivery. He'd become a regular fixture around our place.

I glanced out of the window, my sights falling on a black Dodge 4x4 complete with chrome, mud flaps, oversized running boards, and those big tires that looked as if they were made merely to be recycled as multiperson flotation devices. Not unusual in Texas, but more than a little out of place in our neck of the woods. I held my breath as the door swung open and Dwayne Neeley stepped out.

"Whoa." My imagination hadn't done him justice.

Tall. *Check*.

Brawny. *Check*.

Five o'clock shadow. *Check*.

I stopped checking after that, worried I might lose track of the reason for his visit. He drew a bit closer, and I took note of the fact that Sophia—who'd been sitting on our veranda next door—was now on her feet, giving him a solid once-over.

Watch yourself, girl.

As Dwayne ambled up the drive, the pointed toes of his boots moving in perfectly timed steps, my heart seemed to beat along in sync. After a few seconds of staring at his broad shoulders and rugged good looks, I sprinted to the front door, pausing only to double-check my appearance in the front-hall mirror before stepping out onto the veranda. Once there, I did my best to look calm and unassuming.

A smile lit my cowboy deejay's handsome face as he

climbed the stairs to meet me on the porch. My, but the boy was tall.

"Dwayne Neeley?" I managed.

"The one and only."

He extended his right hand. I took his hand but found it difficult to focus, because now that we were within hand-shaking distance, something else stood out, something that totally threw me. His clothes were . . . well, dirty. And he had that same wet-puppy smell Nick's boys always got when they'd been playing in the summer sun too long. And I was pretty sure he had . . . sawdust? . . . in his hair.

"Nice to meet you." I gripped his hand and focused on his eyes. Blue. Riveting. Perfect against the tanned cheeks and hair the color of the sand on East Beach—kind of a darkish blond. Completely out of place with the wardrobe. "Come on in."

Dwayne flashed a smile and made a quick apology before we entered. "So sorry about the way I look. I came straight from work."

"Oh, um, no problem." Frankly, I'd never considered the fact that spinning tunes was such dirty business, but I didn't waste his time asking about it. Instead, I led him inside and offered to give him a grand tour of the facility so we'd have a little more time to get to know each other before talking business.

I kept a watchful eye on him as we walked side by side through the various rooms. His smile, warm and engaging, drew me in. And his voice, every bit as deep as he'd sounded over the phone, only added to the attraction. On top of all that, Dwayne Neeley proved to be a nice guy. A really nice guy.

After a few minutes in the air-conditioning, the wet puppy

smell disappeared altogether. And the sawdust in the hair was growing on me too. Gave a whole new meaning to the term *dirty blond.*

As I led him from room to room, I told the story of how my father had worked to renovate the place from a home into a wedding facility. Doing so brought back memories I'd almost forgotten, of how we'd labored together to tear down walls, hang trim, and paint in beautiful muted shades of gold. We'd given the whole place an old-world feel, one that met with even Rosa's hard-to-earn approval.

All along the way, Dwayne commented on the beautiful architecture, pausing to examine the carvings in the wood trim around the doors in the chapel. "Great craftsmanship."

"Thanks. My pop loves to work with his hands."

"Me too." He paused, then looked around in curiosity. "So, which room will I be working in?"

I led him to the ballroom where the reception would take place, and he let out a whistle as he looked at the chandeliers and other decor. "I'd be scared to touch anything in here."

"It is pretty, isn't it." I looked at the room through new eyes, trying to imagine how a stranger might take it in for the first time. "You should see it when it's full of people having a great time. The lighting in this room is just right, and once the candles on the tables are lit . . ." I stopped myself before going on. Didn't want to wear the guy out. He wasn't here to talk about decor, after all. He'd come to discuss music, nothing more.

I led him to the sound system where I'd watched Armando perform his deejay duties for years. "What do you think of this? Pretty impressive, huh?"

"Wow." He ran his fingers across the knobs with a stunned look on his face. "This is some setup."

"My brother Armando is a pro. And if you think this is great, you should see the sound system he put in our house next door. Just last night at dinner . . ." I dove into a lengthy story about the Frank Sinatra/Dean Martin fiasco that had transpired during our last meal together. I deliberately skipped the part where my ex nearly started a riot by stating that he preferred contemporary Italian music to the old-school standards. I shivered even now remembering how Laz and Rosa had responded to *that*.

"So, you live next door?" After a nod from me, Dwayne chuckled. "At least you don't have to drive far to get to work." A hint of a smile graced his lips, then he looked me straight in the eye with a "let's get to business" look. "And speaking of work, I guess we should talk about why I'm here. What exactly did you have in mind?"

"Oh, well, I—" Just then the sound of tires squealing against the pavement interrupted our conversation. I took a peek out of the front window, stunned to see Sharlene's Lexus in the drive. Yikes. I flashed Dwayne a frantic look. "My clients are early. Would you mind joining us while we meet, and I can fill you in after they leave? Or maybe we can work it in during."

Dwayne glanced at his watch. "I guess that would be okay, but do you think it will take long? I'm driving back to Splendora tonight to have dinner with my parents. My brother is barbecuing."

"I'm sure we won't be long." Hmm. To be fair, I really needed to give the bride and groom all the time they needed. "Just stick with me and then I'll fill you in. And thanks, by the way."

A moment later the bell above the front door jangled, and Sharlene's voice rang out. "Yoo-hoo! Anybody home?"

Her fiancé's laughter—already familiar after our last visit together—filled the lobby. I met them with Dwayne at my side.

Sharlene took one look at my bohunk of a deejay and stopped dead in her tracks. Her gaze shifted back and forth between the two of us, her pink-lipsticked smile widening in suspicion. "Who do we have here?"

"Sharlene, Cody, this is Dwayne Neeley." I deliberately minimized his first name to one syllable in an attempt to maintain professionalism.

"*Duh*-wayne!" Sharlene grabbed his hand. "My brother's name is *Duh*-wayne. Great to meet you. Where are you from?"

When he responded with "Splendora," a jolt of electricity ricocheted around the room.

"My grandparents live in Splendora," Cody said. "My grandpa's the pastor at the Full Gospel Chapel in the Pines. He's the one performing our ceremony."

"No joke? Pastor Higley?" Dwayne's face lit up.

"Yep." Cody nodded. "Ed Higley. That's my grandpa."

My deejay's smile brightened at this news. "I grew up at that church. My parents still attend. Do the names Dwayne and Earline Neeley mean anything to you?"

"Sister Earline?" Cody said. "The pianist?"

"The very same one."

"Sure, I know who she is," Cody said. "Though, to be honest, *all* of the women at that church stand out in my mind." He paused and then grinned. "I've only been to my grandpa's church a handful of times in recent years, but I always thought they should've named it the Full *Figured* Chapel in the Pines, myself."

Dwayne erupted in laughter, and a humorous conversation

44

ensued surrounding the size of the women at that particular house of worship.

"I know what we should do!" Sharlene's eyes lit up. "We'll ask your mama to play the piano at our wedding! We've been looking for a pianist."

"Well, I'm sure she'd be honored, if she doesn't already have plans," Dwayne said with a nod. "She's got a portable keyboard. And she plays a mean wedding march."

"Oh, wonderful!" Sharlene clasped her hands together. "If she agrees, we'll send a wedding invitation to your whole family. That includes you too, Dwayne, of course."

"Well, of course," I explained. "That's what I was about to tell you. Dwayne is the—"

"I think it's a great idea," Cody said. "It'll be old-home week."

Another lively conversation followed. Within minutes, Dwayne, Sharlene, and Cody were best friends. Turned out they had more than names and families in common. They'd all gone to A&M. Go figure. Looked like *I* was the outcast, not my deejay. Still, I couldn't help but marvel at how God had orchestrated all of this. Perhaps, if all went well at this wedding, Dwayne would agree to stay on and deejay the next. And the next.

In an attempt to steer this ship in the right direction, I cleared my throat. "Everyone ready to start?"

"Sure, honey." Sharlene took me by the arm, whispering in my ear that Dwayne was the handsomest thing she'd ever seen, next to her own fiancé, of course. Forcing the edges of my lips not to betray me, I led them all into my office, where we all settled into plush wingback chairs.

I glanced over at Dwayne with an apologetic shrug. I hadn't planned to make the poor guy sit through a meeting with the bride and groom, but now that we were all buddies, maybe he wouldn't mind. Besides, I'd make this up to him later by upping his pay. If he stuck around.

We dove into a detailed discussion about the upcoming wedding, and the minutes ticked by. Make that hours. Several times I noticed Dwayne glancing at his watch. I also observed—through the window—the sun setting off in the west.

Still, Sharlene continued on, making several changes to our earlier plans. She discussed, at length, the country-western decor, and then shifted her attention to the food. Barbecue, of course. At this point, Dwayne offered his brother's help. Turned out "Bubba" was a barbecue aficionado. Wouldn't be a bad idea to include someone outside my own family on this one, I reasoned. After all, Laz and Jenna had never attempted a Boot-Scootin' barbecue before and would probably appreciate the help.

After that, Sharlene and Cody expressed their preferences for centerpieces—cowboy boots filled with yellow roses and silk bluebonnets tied off with red, white, and blue bandanas. I bit my tongue—literally—and we plowed forward, finally turning our discussion to the music.

Clasping my hands together, I turned to Dwayne. "Well, it looks like we've hit on a subject that involves you." I gave him my warmest smile. "Let's talk about the music."

Sharlene and Cody turned to face Dwayne with puzzled looks on their faces.

"Oh, is that the missing piece to this puzzle?" The bride-to-be's face lit in recognition. "I get it. You must be our—"

"Dwayne is your deejay!" I interjected, then turned to my boot-wearing cowboy with another smile, grateful he'd stuck around to talk about the most important thing of all.

But he didn't say anything. Didn't have to. The frantic look in his eyes let me know at once that something had gone terribly wrong.

"Well, it makes perfect sense that you'd choose a career in music, what with your mama being a pianist and all." Sharlene flashed a warm smile in Dwayne's direction, then pulled a piece of paper out of her purse. "I wrote down all of our favorite songs," she said. "Including the one we'd like to use for our first dance." She looked at Dwayne with a dreamy-eyed look. "We're huge Martina McBride fans."

"And Kenny Chesney," Cody said. "Hope you have some of his music."

"I, uh, well, sure I do." Dwayne looked like he might be sick, and my stomach suddenly felt plenty queasy too.

With great animation, Cody and Sharlene shared their great passion for country-western music, the hub of their reception—the one thing that pulled everything else together. I listened to them carry on, but I couldn't get over the feeling of nausea that gripped me every time I looked into Dwayne's wide eyes.

I managed a silent *E buona notte al secchio*, knowing I was sunk. Finished. Finito.

Still, my cowboy said nothing. Oh, he occasionally nodded and responded with a "yes" when asked if he knew a particular song or another, but beyond that, he kept his thoughts in his head. I had a feeling I'd be thanking him later.

Just as the shadows of the evening nearly darkened the room, the bride- and groom-to-be stood to their feet and offered their good-byes. I walked them to the door, gave Sharlene a hug, then turned back to Dwayne, whose cheeks blazed redder than the sauce on the Mambo Italiano special.

He flashed an accusing look my way as he stammered, "W-what in the world just happened here?"

"Y-you're a deejay." The words were really more question than statement.

"Yes. I'm a D.J." He raked his fingers through his sawdust-filled hair. "Dwayne Neeley Jr."

E buona notte al secchio!

Everything faded to black.

5

Make the World Go Away

There's nothing like waking up on the floor with half a dozen frantic family members hovering over you to make you wonder what you missed while you were out.

Through the dizzying haze, my mother's perfectly made-up face came into focus. She rocked back and forth at my side as if mourning my death. Aunt Rosa stood near the front door, clutching her rosary and crying out to every available saint. And my father—whose voice could be heard above the din as he called 9-1-1—paced the room, his heels clacking against the thick, wood-planked floor. My brother and sister-in-law stood nearby, praying at Indy 500 speed, while their boys hovered off to the side, wide-eyed and silent. Precious sat on my chest, lamenting in slow, high-pitched doggy wails.

I shook off my grogginess and tried to focus on Uncle Lazarro, who leaned over me, wailing, "*Ritornare*, Bella! Return to us!" His garlic-laced breath jolted me back to reality. Who needed smelling salts with relatives around?

I blinked hard and tried to speak but couldn't. What in the world had happened? Had I died? If so, this certainly answered any lingering questions about my dog's salvation.

My gaze shifted from person to person as I tried to make sense of it all. Were these perhaps angels sent to usher me into God's holy presence? If so, the Lord had an interesting sense of humor.

Through the sepia-toned fog, I noticed my sister's red-rimmed eyes. She clutched the hand of someone who definitely qualified as angel material—a handsome cowboy with a five o'clock shadow and sawdust in his hair. Who was that again?

Ah yes. As the world came into focus, I remembered . . . everything. *Duh*-wayne. *Duh*-wayne who *wasn't* a deejay.

Nope, I hadn't died, though I suddenly wished I had.

Seconds later I managed to get my lips to move, though no sound escaped.

"I think she's trying to tell us something!" My mother's words echoed against the slick floor, magnified a hundred times over in my already ringing ears. Everyone drew near. So near, in fact, that I could scarcely breathe.

"What is it, Bella?" My father's tear-stained eyes locked on to mine.

"Yes, what are you trying to say?" Mama clutched my hand.

"I'm . . . trying . . . to . . . say . . ." I squeezed my eyes shut and willed the shrieking in my ears to halt so I could finish the sentence. "I'm trying to say . . . it's so *loud* in here I can barely hear myself think."

As I pushed the dog aside and struggled to sit up, everyone in the place broke out in wild celebratory applause. Lazarus himself would've been impressed by the reception. Aunt Rosa dropped to her knees in the open doorway and ushered up her praises in Italian with palms extended heavenward. My mother clasped her hands together at her breast, tears flowing, and my father told the 9-1-1 operator I'd been resurrected, then began to dance a little jig with Deany-boy and Frankie. Even my normally dignified sister shouted an uncharacteristic, "Praise the Lord!" The dog took to yapping with vigor, then snatched *Duh*-wayne's pants leg in her teeth, pulling it this way and that.

Had they really thought I was a goner?

"Oh, Bella, my Bella!" My mama's lyrical voice rang out. "If not for this wonderful man"—she pointed to Dwayne—"we might have lost you." She dove into a lengthy explanation of how "this angel sent from God" had come to the house to fetch them and how they'd all come running to my rescue. To hear her tell it, I might never have awakened if not for all of them.

I ran my fingers through my matted hair and wiped the drool from my chin, horrified at what I must look like. "I just fainted." I tried to shrug it off. "It's really not that big of a deal. People faint every day."

"Did you hear that? No big deal!" Uncle Lazarro reached for his walking cane and struggled to stand. "Bella has tasted death and lived to tell about it." He wobbled to his feet and gazed down at me with newfound admiration in his eyes. "You must tell us of your experience."

My experience?

"Yes, what did you see while you were in heaven?" my mother asked. "Was there a white light?"

"A long tunnel?" my sister-in-law asked.

"A heavenly choir?" my father queried.

"Well, I do remember a light," I mumbled. When they all

gasped, I pointed up to the chandelier with a giggle. "And I'm pretty sure there was a choir, but man, were they off-key."

No one seemed to get the joke except Dwayne, ironically. He drew near and extended his hand with a smile. I sighed as I took it and allowed him to help me to my feet. As we stood there—the two of us—surrounded by so great a cloud of witnesses, I couldn't help but think I'd better make introductions, and fast.

The next ten minutes were spent doing just that. When you come from a family as large as mine, the getting-to-know-you part takes time. And when you come from an *Italian* family, it takes even longer. It's not, "Meet my Aunt Rosa." It's "Meet my Aunt Rosabella Donata Savarino from Napoli, the best cook on Galveston Island, known for her homemade sauces and unquestionable love of Frank Sinatra music." And so on.

Dwayne nodded politely as each new person was introduced, but I couldn't help but wonder what was going through his head. Did he have as many questions for me as I did for him?

After meeting the relatives, my mother sang Dwayne's praises for another five minutes, then promptly did what any good Italian mama would do—invited him to stay for dinner. Great. Dinner and a show. What more could a cowboy from the piney woods of east Texas ask for after a hard day's work?

"I, uh . . ." He gazed at his watch. "I was supposed to be in Splendora a half hour ago for a barbecue with my family."

Yikes. That was my fault. I mouthed the words, "I'm sorry," and offered up a shrug.

"No big deal." He flipped open his cell phone and punched in a number. "Just let me make a call, and then I'll join y'all next door."

"Y'all," Sophia whispered in my ear as she linked her arm through mine. "Did you hear the way he said 'y'all'?" Her eyes filled with wonder. "That voice of his . . . it's hypnotic. I could swoon."

"Mm-hmm." I shrugged. What more could I add, really? That he'd sound even better with a microphone in hand? That I'd be willing to pay double if he'd reconsider and save my neck?

The others headed off to our house, but Sophia tugged at my arm and whispered, "Let's wait for Dwayne. Don't you think that's the polite thing to do?"

"Well, of course." Now that I'd already made such a vivid first impression, why not wow him with my politeness?

Dwayne ended the call and turned to us with a smile. "Looks like I'll be having barbecue another night. So, what's for dinner?"

Sophia's eyes lit up as she listed the items on tonight's menu: "Eggplant parmesan—my personal favorite, rosemary chicken, and Tuscan meringue with fresh berries."

His eyes widened, and I could almost see his mouth watering. "Never heard of half that stuff," he admitted, "but it sounds mighty good."

I tried to envision a meal with Dwayne seated next to me. Surely we'd both feel awkward if we didn't clear the air first. I let out a lingering sigh, ready to face the music—pun intended. "Before we go over there, I think we should talk. We need to get to the bottom of this."

"Yes." He nodded and let out an equally impressive sigh.

"Bottom of what?" Sophia asked. Her gaze ping-ponged back and forth between us.

I would fill her in later. Right now there were problems to solve. I did my best to avoid looking directly into Dwayne's gorgeous blue eyes as I presented my case. "When I called and asked you to come work for me, I said I was looking for a deejay."

"And I am a D.J."

"Yes, but I *specifically* told you I needed to hire you for a gig at a wedding facility. What did you think I meant?"

He shrugged, a look of confusion clouding those beautiful eyes. "You said that I came highly recommended. The only folks who know me—know my work—are my boss and a few of the other construction workers on the west end of the island, where we've been rebuilding homes damaged during Ike. So I figured . . ."

I couldn't help but slap myself in the head as the realization hit. "You thought I was hiring you to do construction work at the wedding facility?"

"Well, yeah. That or repair work from the storm. And when you started showing me around the place—talking about the architectural design and all that—it just made sense. It wasn't until Sharlene and Cody showed up—"

"Wait. Who are Sharlene and Cody?" Sophia looked back and forth between the two of us, her brow wrinkled in apparent confusion. "I'm having trouble keeping up."

Dwayne and I spoke in unison. "They're the bride and groom."

"So, let me get this straight." Sophia turned to face me. "You're coordinating a wedding and need someone to handle the music." When I nodded, she asked, "Why can't Armando do it, like always? He'll drive down from Houston, I'm sure of it."

"He's in love." I groaned, then leaned against the wall in defeat. "But even if he falls out of love in the next two weeks—which is somewhat likely considering his history—he doesn't know the first thing about country-western dancing, and neither do I. And I promised Sharlene and Cody a Boot-Scootin' wedding."

"I see." Sophia now added a deep sigh, and we all stared at one another in silence.

"I'm going to be a failure before I even get started." I slid down the wall and plopped onto the floor, fighting back tears. Then, with great vibrato in my voice, I choked out a lengthy sermon about how my life as I knew it was about to come to an end. How my parents would never get to take their European vacation. How my mistakes would drive our family to financial ruin.

All the while Sophia stared at me like I'd lost my mind. Dwayne, however, gazed down at me with compassion in his eyes.

"Well, shoot," he responded after hearing my discourse, "I know just about everything there is to know about country music. Got the largest CD collection of anyone I know. Tim McGraw. Garth Brooks. Carrie Underwood. Tricia Yearwood. You name it, I've got it. And I've got even more on MP3."

He rambled on, and I looked up at him, feeling more hopeful than before. "Really?"

"Sure. And I can Texas Two-Step with the best of 'em. Don't have the foggiest idea about your brother's equipment in there, and I sure don't know nothin' about speaking into a microphone, but I guess I could give it a try . . . if you think it'll help."

My heart lurched, and I stared into his gorgeous blue eyes through my tears. Was he just saying that because a blubbering wedding coordinator sat on the floor at his feet, begging for mercy?

Probably. But who cared? If D.J. wanted to become a deejay, who was I to stop him?

We made our way across the lawn, though I moved slowly. The past hour had really done a number on me. But, oh, the number my family was about to do on Dwayne! He had no idea what he'd just stumbled into.

Once in the house, I excused myself to check my appearance. After making sure the drool lines were gone, then touching up my lipstick, I entered the dining room to find everyone seated. Dwayne smiled at me as I took the empty seat next to him.

"Let's pray." Pop extended his hands, and we all clasped hands while he prayed—in fluent Italian. When he finished, Dwayne looked at me and mouthed, "Wow." I had the feeling it was the first of many "wows" to come.

Within seconds the whole table came alive with conversation, some in English, some in Italian. The noise level grew to its usual ear-piercing level as Rosa dished up the food. Through the chaos of sounds, I managed to whisper a quick "You okay?" to Dwayne.

He nodded, then leaned my way to whisper, "So, can I ask a question?"

"Sure."

"Do *all* of you live here together? In one house?"

"Well, not all." I pointed to Nick and Marcella and their boys. "My oldest brother and his wife live a few blocks away with Frankie and Deany-boy." I turned my gaze to Joey with a smile. "Joey's my baby brother. He still lives at home. And so does Sophia, my baby sister. And Aunt Rosa and Uncle Laz and Mama and Pop and me. And sometimes my brother Armando, when he isn't in love. He happens to be in love right now, so you won't be meeting him tonight."

"I see." Dwayne grinned as he stabbed his fork into the

rosemary chicken and cut off a piece. "Must be a pretty big house. I've only got one brother, and we grew up in a double-wide." He shoveled down a bite, and his eyes grew wide. "Man, this is great stuff."

I laughed as I took a bite, then whispered, "If you really want to win over the family, tell Rosa that."

"I will." He took another big bite, then washed it down with a drink of tea. Turning to Rosa, he said, "Ma'am, I've gotta tell you, this here's the best chicken I ever ate. You should open your own restaurant. I'd come for dinner every night."

The table grew silent, all parties gazing at him admiringly.

"See, Bella," Mama said with a wink, "I *told* you he was an angel. First he raises you from the dead, then he compliments Rosa's cooking."

My aunt beamed from ear to ear, then rose from her seat and walked to our side of the table. She took Dwayne's face in her hands, kissing him on the right cheek and then the left. The boy's face turned as red as the Roma tomatoes in Laz's garden. Not that I blamed him. I wanted to ask what he was thinking. Did he want to sneak out of the front door and head back to Splendora?

No, from the looks of things, he just wanted seconds of the rosemary chicken. And Rosa, as always, was happy to oblige.

6

Simpatico

The following afternoon I slipped into my SUV and headed over to Patti-Lou's Petals, my florist shop of choice. As I backed out of the driveway, I telephoned Jenna, ready to tell her the whole sordid tale. If anyone would get a kick out of the deejay misunderstanding, she would. And I felt sure she'd have a fit when she heard I'd fainted in front of a real cowboy. If Laz and my brothers hadn't already told her. A shiver ran down my spine as I contemplated their possible renditions of the story.

Jenna answered on the fourth ring, breathless as always. "Welcome to Parma John's. We deliver." I tried to spit out a "hello," but she forged ahead, as always. "Want to share a pizza with a friend but can't settle on the topping? You're keen on pepperoni, he's got his heart set on Canadian bacon? Why not try our Simpatico special—a large hand-tossed pizza, split down the middle with your choice of toppings on either side. Now you can both be happy for just $14.95."

"Well, if I had someone to share it with, I might be happier," I said with a laugh. "In the meantime, how about sharing some tiramisu and a great chat with an old friend?"

Jenna giggled. "Bella, we've got to figure out some kind of a signal or something, so I know it's you."

"It's called caller ID. Just look down at the phone in your hand."

She groaned. "Who has time for that?"

A giggle escaped me as I pulled the car out onto Broadway. "I told you, I love the spiel. It always inspires me."

In fact, today's message motivated me more than usual. Maybe I should get Uncle Laz to come up with a phone message for Club Wed, something equally as clever. I could just hear it now: "Thank you for calling Club Wed, Galveston Island's premier wedding facility. Having trouble settling on a theme for your big day? You're a little bit country, he's a little bit rock and roll? No problem. Try our Simpatico special. We'll split the chapel down the middle, filling each half with the appropriate decor. All for one low price."

"Bella, are you there?"

"Oh, yeah." The strains of a Dean Martin tune playing in the background pulled me back to reality. I couldn't help but giggle again. "Just got lost in my thoughts."

"Ah. So . . . I heard about last night, how you landed belly-up on the floor with the whole Rossi clan praying you back to life."

I didn't even try to stop the groan. "Who told you?"

"I heard it from your mama . . . the first time. She stopped by to pick up an espresso on her way to a meeting at the opera house. She only had time to give me the cut-and-dried version. I think Laz could've done the story justice. Unfortunately, he's been up to his eyeballs in vendors today and hasn't had time for a conversation."

"Please don't ask for his version." I groaned again. "He thinks I died and went to heaven."

"From what I hear, you did." Jenna laughed. "Sophia said that deejay of yours *is* a little slice of heaven."

"You talked to Sophia too?" I squeezed my eyes shut in preparation for the inevitable.

"She stopped by this morning to grab a cappuccino. Said she needed the caffeine before dealing with Nick's boys. So, tell me about this guy."

"I'll come by the restaurant in a couple of hours, and we can talk then." I rounded the corner onto Main Street. "But don't get any ideas about Dwayne. He's just a cowboy from Splendora."

"Hey, I have cousins in Splendora. Maybe they know him."

"From what I can tell, everyone knows everyone up there. But let's talk later. Right now, I'm headed to the florist's shop to order twenty-two dozen yellow roses."

"Wow."

"Yeah. Don't ask. But I'll be there soon enough."

We ended the call, and I pulled into the parking lot of Patti-Lou's Petals. Through the plate-glass window I could see Patti-Lou, a perpetually single fiftysomething who'd been planning her wedding since childhood. Unfortunately, the petite bleach blonde had yet to locate Mr. Right, but she kept her plans in a three-ring binder in the top drawer of her desk, just in case. She'd updated the particulars several times through the years—after all, weddings had changed a great deal since the '70s. She would marry . . . one day.

I contemplated our common fates. Patti and I were far too

much alike. Two single business owners, never finding true love. One in her fifties, the other in her late twenties. Each working to make other people's dreams come true, never giving a thought to her own happiness.

I exhaled, letting go of the tension that had suddenly mounted. No time to think about my ailing love life right now—I had a wedding to plan.

Entering the shop, I paused to draw in a whiff of the familiar intoxicating aroma. *Flowers, glorious flowers!*

"Smells delicious in here. Better than Aunt Rosa's garlic bread." With my eyes closed, I stood in silence, just breathing in, out, in, out, with steady, successive breaths.

Patti-Lou looked up from her work and laughed. "Bella, you've really got to get a life."

"Hey, I have a life!" I opened my eyes and gave her my best "cut it out" look. "That's why I'm here, in fact." Drawing near the counter, I looked around at some of the new arrangements. Pointing to a unique red, white, and blue arrangement, I nodded. "Very Fourth of Julyish."

"Yeah, I've got to stay on top of the holidays. You'd be surprised at how many people purchase flowers in the weeks leading up to Independence Day." She stood and wrapped me in a warm embrace. "But you didn't come in here to talk about that. What can I do you for?"

"I know this is last minute, but I'm hoping you can forgive me for that."

Her eyebrows elevated as she said, "Spill it."

"I'm here to order roses for my first ever Boot-Scootin' bridal event." I beamed with pride, knowing that as a fellow business owner, she would understand my enthusiasm.

"That's awesome." Patti-Lou reached for a pad and pen. "So your themed wedding ideas are grabbing some attention."

"Of course! Did you ever doubt it?"

"Never." She flashed an encouraging smile. "So, what's it gonna be? And when? Early August, I hope. Or even late August. Not sure I can pull off something before that."

Hmm. I'd better handle this carefully. "This bride and groom just signed on a couple of weeks ago, and I didn't get the paperwork on their flowers till last night."

"What's the date?"

I hesitated to tell her, knowing she'd likely panic. "The last Saturday in June."

She shook her head. "Nope. No can do."

Time for a little enticement. "Before you say no, this is going to be a huge moneymaker for you. Twenty-two dozen premium yellow roses for the reception and chapel, to start with. And we'll need more than that for the bouquets and corsages, so prepare yourself."

She stared up at me in disbelief. "Twenty-two dozen?"

"Yep. And spare no expense. Get the very best. We're talking about a bride and groom with cash to spare, and they want the prettiest yellow roses we can find. Oh, and bluebonnets."

"Can't get real ones."

"I know, I know. Silks will do. But now let's talk cowboy boots."

"Cowboy boots?"

"Yes, there are going to be twenty tables of eight—not counting the head table and parents' tables—and she wants boots for centerpieces at each, loaded with the roses and bluebonnets, with red, white, and blue bandanas tied around them."

Patti rolled her eyes. "Please."

"Hey, the bride always gets what she wants."

"At least she found a man." A lingering sigh from Patti-Lou left us both speechless for a moment as we contemplated our common fates. Would either of us ever get to pick out flowers for our big day? Would we design centerpieces and quibble over the details?

To break the somber mood, I spoke the magic words: *"Finché c'è vita c'è speranza."*

"As long as there is life, there is hope," she echoed. "I remember." After a brief pause, she reached for a slender, cylinder-shaped glass vase. Holding it up for closer examination, she asked, "Think this'll fit inside a cowboy boot?"

"I think so."

"Okay, well I've got plenty of these in the back room. Want me to provide the boots, or will you take care of that? I don't exactly have a country-western store on speed dial."

"Hmm." Hadn't thought about that. Maybe Dwayne could point me in the right direction. Or maybe . . . A fabulous idea struck. I could get them off eBay. That certainly made more sense than buying them new, after all. And that way we'd end up with a variety of boots in all shapes and colors.

After I settled the issue, Patti-Lou agreed to provide the flowers for the event. I breathed a huge sigh of relief, and we dove into a long chat about Sharlene's floral needs. By the end of it all, I could tell that dollar signs had replaced Patti's eyeballs. I could almost hear the "cha-ching" as she blinked, and I sensed her gratitude for the order.

She looked up with contentment written all over her face. "This is going to cost a pretty penny, ya know."

"Yep. Call this number." I slipped her Sharlene's daddy's business card. "He'll give you a credit card number. And don't be afraid to shoot high. This is a Texas oil man."

"Is he single?" She looked up with hope in her eyes.

"Focus, Patti-Lou."

She sighed, then reached for a notepad to write everything down. "You know, if you keep bringing me business—and I know you will—I'm going to have to hire someone to help out around here. Be thinking on that, will you?"

"I will."

We wrapped up our conversation, and I left the shop in a happy frame of mind, ready to visit with Jenna. As I reached the car, my cell phone rang. I looked down at the number, and my heart skipped a beat. Dwayne.

"Hello?"

"Bella, is that you? Dwayne Neeley here."

"Yes, it's me." *The same one who groveled at your feet just last night.* "What can I do for you?"

"I just wanted to let you know that Bubba's in. He'll help with the barbecue."

Bubba? Who's Bubba? Oh yes, the brother. I did my best not to let my voice give me away as I repeated, "Bubba's in. Got it. Tell him we're expecting 160 guests, and give him this number." I reeled off the phone number for Parma John's. "Have him ask for Lazarro Rossi or Jenna Miller. They're the official caterers. They'll be the ones providing the meat and so forth."

"Will do." Dwayne chuckled. "Oh, and I talked to my mama. She's happy to play the piano. Thrilled, in fact. She's been aching to get back to Galveston ever since the storm hit. Says this'll give her a chance to clamp eyes on the place—and the people—she's been praying for."

"Wonderful! Tell her the island is on the mend, but not to expect everything to be up to par just yet. And I'll pass the word on to Sharlene that we now have a pianist."

Dwayne paused, then spoke in a tentative voice. "Hey, I

just wanted to apologize. I feel mighty bad about what happened last night."

"*You* feel bad?" Was he kidding?

"Well, sure. Ain't every night my knee-jerk reaction to something knocks a woman to the floor."

"Ah. Well, don't worry about that. It wasn't your fault. Besides, I think everything's going to work out fine." I glanced at my watch and gasped. Four forty? Had I really spent more than three hours in Patti's shop? "Say, Dwayne . . ."

"Call me D.J."

"D.J." I tried not to smile as I spoke his name, but found it impossible. "How do you feel about pizza?"

"Pizza? Love it. Why?"

"When you get off work, could you stop by Parma John's on the Strand? My treat. There's someone I'd like you to meet." Boy, would Jenna get a kick out of this cowboy!

"Sounds great. I'll be there around 5:15."

"See you then."

I ended the call and leaned back against the car seat, whispering the words, "He's a little bit country. I'm a little bit Italian."

Simpatico!

7

With My Eyes Wide Open

By the time I arrived at Parma John's, I'd almost cleared my nostrils of the scent of flowers. Good thing, because with the Wednesday Simpatico special going on, the pungent aroma of pepperoni might've proven deadly in combination.

I found the restaurant overflowing with teens. Most were gathered around tables with red and white checkered tablecloths, eating humongous slices of pepperoni/Canadian bacon pizza. Still others were seated at the bar. Their shrill voices zigzagged around the room, causing my ADD to shift into overdrive. I strained to make out the song playing overhead. Ah yes. "Simpatico." God bless Uncle Laz. He had this "let's merge the music with the pizza" thing down to a science. And all to the tune of a Dean Martin song. Some things would never change.

Nick greeted me with a nod, and I smiled in response. My older brother looked more like Pop every day, right down to the receding hairline and broadening physique. Marriage had put quite a few pounds on him. His midsection had broadened significantly over the years, thanks to Marcella, a brilliant cook. In fact, she was brilliant at most everything. I'd never met anyone so creative. And thoughtful. She'd turned my wild and woolly brother into a decent family man. And now that he'd hit his midthirties, I could almost envision him taking over Parma John's one day. Not that I was ready to boot-scoot Uncle Laz out of the way anytime soon. I just saw life for what it was—ever-changing.

Off in the distance, Jenna worked behind the counter to fill an order. She glanced my way and welcomed me with a nod of her head. I inched my way through the crowd, beyond the cute young couple making eyes at each other—*Don't get too excited, honey, this teenage fantasy that you're actually going to marry that football player is just that, a fantasy*—past the table filled with pimply-faced boys bent over their handheld video games—*Boys, you will one day rule the world*—to the register.

Jenna turned my way after wrapping up with her customer, wrinkled her freckled nose, and shouted an exuberant, "You're here!"

From back in the kitchen, Uncle Laz flashed a warm smile. "Tell her about your time in heaven, Bella."

"Yeah." Jenna leaned her elbows on the counter and whispered, "Tell me about this deejay of yours."

After an Academy Award–worthy sigh, I told her the whole thing, right down to the part where I'd groveled at *Duh*-wayne's feet.

"So, you won him over with your acting skills?" she asked.

"Trust me, I wasn't acting." I sighed. "I've got to make a go of this wedding facility, Jenna. My parents are counting

67

on me. Sharlene and Cody are depending on me. Everything hinges on me."

"No, Bellissima," my uncle called out from the kitchen. "Everything hinges on the Lord. Don't forget that! He is the potter"—Laz tossed a soft lump of pizza dough into the air and twirled it around before catching it—"and you are the clay."

"I know, I know. And I guess it's just my pride speaking, but I don't want to fall flat on my face, especially with so many people looking on."

Jenna's lips curled up, and a girlish giggle escaped. "Remember the time you did that in tenth grade, when you tried out for the drill team?"

"Jenna, I was speaking figuratively."

"Still, remember how funny—"

"Jenna!"

"Oh, and what about that time we were playing tennis and you tripped over the net? That was hysterical. Remember, Kevin Yauger took your picture and put it in the yearbook?"

How could I forget? Could I help it if I was a little klutzy? Awkward, even? Did Jenna have to point it out to anyone and everyone? Next thing you knew, she'd be telling total strangers about my misshapen head and talking about all the guys who'd broken my heart in high school. Maybe she'd even throw in the part where Jimmy Peterson told my entire ninth grade class that my face didn't match my name. Of course, that was back in the days of pimples and braces.

"You'll do fine, Bella." Uncle Laz's voice rang out again, jarring me back to the present, where at least a few people believed in me. I appreciated his confidence in my abilities but wondered if I would ever feel the same way about myself.

More often than not, I *did* fall flat on my face. Symbolically, anyway. Which left only one part of my anatomy visible to a watching world.

No, this wasn't the first time I'd doubted my abilities. For example, there was the time I ran for president of the junior class and got only ten votes. Turns out Jenna had voted five times. And then there was the time I tried out for a part in a school play, only to be told I would be better off working backstage. Were my acting skills really that bad? Worst of all, though, was my choir audition. The pained look on the director's face still haunted me, along with the words "tone-deaf," which still resonated in my ears. He had suggested I take a creative writing class. Unfortunately, writing didn't turn out to be my bag either.

"Bella?" Jenna said. "Have we lost you?"

I turned back to her with a sigh, but her attention had shifted away from me. Her mouth gaped open, and for a moment I could practically see all the way down to the girl's tonsils.

"B-Bella!"

"What?" I attempted to make sense of her sudden lack of concern about my problems.

"Take a look at that one, will you." She gestured toward the door with a dreamy-eyed look on her face, and I turned, surprised to see D.J. standing there, looking a bit like a fish out of water. His gaze darted to the left and the right, but he apparently couldn't see me through the crowd. Not that I minded. No, I needed the extra time to stare at his broad shoulders and handsome face.

I didn't even try to stop my grin as the words slipped out. "Oh, he's early."

"Th-that's your guy?" Jenna's gaping mouth still proved

problematic. I wanted to reach over and close it manually, but I thought she might slap my hand. Instead, I turned to face D.J., hoping he wouldn't notice my gawking friend and flee for his life.

Overhead, Dean Martin's voice crooned something about love. I felt my cheeks heat up in both anticipation and embarrassment as D.J. shuffled my way, the pointed toes of his boots moving in synchronized steps with the song's meter. No sawdust in his hair today. A plus, what with Jenna meeting him for the first time and all. But those eyes . . . From the moment those marble-blue babies locked into mine, I found myself deaf, dumb, and blind to everything else around me.

Or maybe just dumb. What was it about this cowboy that suddenly prevented me from speaking in complete sentences? I finally managed a wobbly "H-hey, *Duh*-wayne." Shame washed over me at once. *Tell me I did not just make fun of his name out loud!*

Apparently he didn't notice. Fascinating. A wide-as-Texas grin lit his face as he countered with his opening line. "Pinch me to prove I'm awake."

"E-excuse me?" I gave him a curious look.

"Oh . . ." His face turned deep red, and he raked his hand through his hair. "Sorry. I'm distracted by the music. Just quoting the lyrics. They struck me as funny."

Heavens, if that man didn't look amazing with flushed cheeks and sawdust-free hair. Made me want to pinch *myself*, just to prove *I* was awake.

Straining to hear the music above the noise of the crowd, I quickly realized that "Simpatico" had been replaced with another tune.

"Oh, that's 'With My Eyes Wide Open,'" I said. "It's one

of my uncle's favorites. Of course, anything by Dean Martin makes Uncle Laz smile."

"Funny how music can have that effect on a person," D.J. said. His eyes took on a faraway look. "I grew up listening to down-home country music. Mostly stuff from *Hee-Haw*."

"*Hee-Haw*?" This was a new one to me. I'd have to look it up on the Web.

"Sure, it's an old TV show," he explained. "My dad watched it when he was young and got me hooked when the VHS collection came out. There's some priceless stuff on that show. Great comedy. Amazing old-style country music. Guitar-pickin'. Lots of gospel. That's my mama's favorite."

Should I mention that I didn't know *Hee-Haw* from a hoedown? That my only experience with country music was an occasional song playing overhead at the grocery store? That the theme seemed pretty universal—someone always got drunk and cheated on someone else?

Nah. I simply smiled and said, "I see." Perhaps I would . . . with time.

Jenna hovered around us like a UFO coming in for a landing. "Did I hear something about *Hee-Haw*?" she asked, her voice a little more animated than necessary.

"Yep." D.J. flashed a now-familiar grin, one sure to snag my best friend's heart and send her sensibilities reeling. "I'm a fan. What about you?"

"Oh, I'm a fan all right." She gazed into his beautiful blue eyes, but I had a pretty strong suspicion she wasn't talking about the television show. Or music. No, my friend had something else on her mind, something altogether different. Should I remind her that she was practically engaged? That her boyfriend was working offshore to earn enough money to pay for their yet-to-be-announced wedding? The one she'd promised I could coordinate?

Startling to attention, I made introductions. "D.J. Neeley, this is my best friend in the world"—*even when she's making a total goober of herself*—"Jenna Miller."

He gave a polite nod, and Jenna gestured for us to take our seats at the counter.

"I hear you're from Splendora," Jenna said as she went back to work scrubbing the already clean countertop.

"Sure am. Born and raised."

"I wonder if you know my cousins—Jimmy John Taylor and his little brother, Beau." She lifted the sponge and gave him an inquisitive look.

D.J.'s beautiful blue eyes lit with excitement at the revelation. "I've known Jimmy John since we were kids. Played on the same baseball team in high school. Beau was a little younger, but he was light-years above most of us, academically speaking."

She tossed the sponge aside and gave D.J. another pensive once-over as she added, "Yeah, he works for NASA now."

"No joke. Well, don't that beat all."

For a moment, I thought I saw a hint of jealousy in D.J.'s eyes. Just as quickly, it passed.

Was this a new side to my deejay? Was he a small-town boy wishing he could make something of his life, like Beau? Had D.J. strived for bigger things only to end up on Galveston Island, doing construction work?

Thankfully, my brother Nick interrupted my thoughts when he stopped by to shake D.J.'s hand. "You survived having dinner with the family last night, and now you're back for more? That speaks volumes. Most people can only take our family in small doses."

"Hey, I enjoyed it." D.J. gave him an unpretentious smile.

"Well, hey, what's not to like?" I said, hoping the conversation would shift.

Joey appeared as if by magic and extended his hand to shake D.J.'s. I couldn't help but wonder what the handsome cowboy thought about my eclectic baby brother. Joey was quite a contrast to the other men in the family—his short stature and dark, curly ponytail set him apart. And the tattoos got almost as much attention as his mustache and goatee. Not that D.J. seemed to notice. He quickly engaged my brother in easy conversation about one of his tattoos—two nails overlapping each other to form a cross.

Flexing his upper arm, Joey explained, "I got this one after I started doing street ministry with our church. It's a great conversation starter."

D.J. gave it another look. "No doubt. It's great."

The chatter must've summoned Uncle Laz, who joined us from the kitchen. He nodded in D.J.'s direction. "Glad to see you survived Rosa's cooking."

"Oh?" D.J. looked my way, clearly confused.

I simply shrugged. "My uncle would like you to think he's the only one in the family with any culinary skills. But don't give him an inch on this one, okay? He'll take a mile."

Laz scowled at me, but I knew he meant no harm. We did this sort of harmless bantering all the time.

"Rosa's great with pasta and breads, but the boss does make a mean pizza," Jenna threw in. "Best I've ever tasted anyway."

Uncle Laz raised his ladle in the air and exclaimed, "*Segreto nella salsa*. And I've told you not to call me 'the boss.'"

D.J. looked at me again.

"Secret's in the sauce," I whispered. "But it's not much of a secret these days." I stopped short of explaining that Laz didn't like to be called "the boss" because it had too many negative connotations.

"Hush now, Bella." Laz gave me a warning look, followed by a wink.

"As for the rest of the family, well, we're a little, um . . ." Nick shrugged, and I could almost read his mind. *Crazy? Nutty?*

"A little what, Nicholas?" Uncle Laz countered, raising his ladle again. "Better watch yourself, boy. God put you in this family, and he can just as easily take you out."

"Spoken like a former mobster," Nick whispered.

"I heard that." Laz raised his voice above the pitch of the music, plenty loud enough for everyone on Galveston Island to take note. "And for your information, I was never in the mob."

Nick decided this was his cue to do his near-perfect impression of Don Corleone. He quoted a couple of familiar lines from *The Godfather*, then ended with an over-the-top rendition of Brando's famous line, "I'm gonna make him an offer he can't refuse." I had to give it to him—my brother was a dead ringer for the infamous mob boss. Er, make that a good match.

D.J. smiled as my brother wrapped up his act. "Right, right. *The Godfather*. Saw that movie once on cable."

"Just once?" We all turned and stared at him. *The Godfather* movies were a staple in the Rossi home. We owned both the VHS and DVD versions of every one.

"Nick memorized the first movie in high school," I explained, "but please, whatever you do, don't get him started. He'll quote the whole thing."

Nick turned to D.J. and shrugged. "I'll stop. But talk to me later. There are a few things you might want to know about Laz's ties to the mob if you plan on sticking around."

"So, mob ties?" D.J. turned to me again.

"Let's just say he has a connection," I said.

"Two connections," Nick corrected me.

"Who are they?" D.J. directed his question at anyone who might provide an answer.

My uncle sighed. "Since you must know, I once sold vacuum cleaners to Salvadore Lucci and Benigno Damiano—two very, um, *influential* men back in the day." Laz's eyes suddenly filled with tears. "I led Benigno to the Lord in '95 just before he passed."

"What about Salvadore?" D.J. asked.

Laz's jaw tightened. "We haven't spoken in over five years. I've done all I can to reach out to him, but he wants nothing to do with me or my faith, so I must leave him in the Lord's hands." At once, Uncle Lazarro bowed his head and offered up what I knew must be a prayer.

D.J. must've picked up on his enthusiasm. "I'll be praying for him too," he promised. I looked into his eyes to check his level of sincerity. No problem. The guy would really pray for mobster Salvadore Lucci to come to the Lord. Wow.

At this news, Uncle Laz's eyes lit up with joy, and he offered us a pizza on the house. "I just thought Bella's guest might be hungry," he explained, turning back to his work.

"Oh, yes sir. Thank you." D.J. grinned. "Thank you all. You've all been mighty polite."

"Yep. You've figured us out," Nick said. "We Rossis are a polite bunch." He punched me in the arm, and I countered with a wallop to his belly. Never one to be outdone, Nick offered a dramatic reaction, bending over at the waist and groaning as if I'd done him mortal harm. He rose with a smile and gave me a wink. "Gotta go." He leaned over and gave me a kiss on the forehead, then shuffled out the door, singing "With My Eyes Wide Open."

I shuddered, thinking of D.J.'s likely reaction to all of this. Did he think he'd stumbled into a badly written scene from a yet-unreleased *Godfather* sequel, perhaps?

He turned back to me, putting my mind at ease. "Our families are as different as night and day, that's for sure. But in some ways they're just alike. Doesn't seem to matter where you're from, family dynamics are pretty much the same everywhere you go."

Well, amen to that. I could rest easy. This was a man who got my family.

"Might be fun to get them together," Jenna suggested. "East meets west."

"More like city meets country," D.J. explained. "Or better yet, the Grand Opera meets Grand Ole Opry."

Hmm. My mama was a sponsor of Galveston's illustrious Grand Opera, so I had that part figured out. But Grand Ole Opry? I'd have to do a little searching on the Web to figure out that one. Regardless, Jenna seemed to get it. She giggled, then blazed a white smile.

Sure, why not show off those newly whitened teeth, girl-friend? You've got nothing better to do.

Time to shift gears. Get this train back on track.

"Laz and Jenna cater all of our big events," I explained to D.J., trying to keep my focus on the conversation at hand. "They're the best in the biz." I nodded back toward the kitchen where Laz was working.

"Don't ever let Rosa hear you say that," Laz hollered from the kitchen. "You know how she is."

"How they *both* are," I whispered to D.J. He responded with a knowing look, and I raised my voice to add, "Anyway, she's pretty sensitive when it comes to cooking. And with good right. She's very good at what she does."

"Humph." Laz turned back to his work.

I had to smile, thinking of the rivalry between the two. Might be fun to watch them in a showdown sometime. No telling who'd come out on top. Rosa could make some mean classics, and my uncle had a passion for fresh foods, as proven by the garden that consumed over half of our backyard. Of course, his distaste for all things related to Rosa meant she was rarely allowed to root around in his veggies. The man would drop his false teeth if he knew she was hurling his Romas at the neighbors.

D.J. continued the conversation, oblivious to my ponderings. "Bubba's looking forward to meeting you both when he helps with the barbecue at the wedding."

"Bubba?" Through the window leading to the kitchen, Laz looked up from his pizza making and gave me a curious look. Oops. Had I forgotten to tell him he'd be receiving assistance from Bubba, the barbecue extraordinaire from Splendora, Texas? Perhaps now would be a convenient time. I filled him in on the particulars, and he seemed to take the news in stride. After the hyperventilating passed, anyway.

"Speaking of barbecue reminds me of something." Uncle Laz slipped our pizza into the oven, then joined us once again. "I've been trying to come up with a barbecue-themed pizza for months now. I think the customers would really love it."

"What's stopping you?" D.J. gave him a puzzled look.

"Can't find the right song."

"What do you mean?"

"All of his daily specials have a Dean Martin song as a

basis," I explained. "He's into themed specials. We've done a lot of searching but just can't come up with the right song for a barbecue pizza."

"Hmm." D.J. didn't look convinced. "I wouldn't mind taking that on as a project, if you'd agree to let my brother help come up with the recipe for the pizza."

"Son, you've got a deal." Laz extended his hand. "And here's another thing . . ." With a twinkle in his eye, he turned to me. "If you come up with the perfect song, I might just let you date my niece."

"Uncle Lazarro!" I literally felt the color drain from my face, and for a moment I thought I might faint. Again.

Only when I heard D.J. say, "Well, I'll work double hard then," did I snatch my first breath of fresh air. I flashed what I hoped would look like a coy smile, and he winked.

Okay then. This put a whole new spin on things.

I basked in the glow of this new possibility for approximately seven seconds. That's exactly how long it took my ex-boyfriend, Tony, to make it from the front door of the restaurant to the counter where we all sat. He saw the gleam in my eye, and I realized I'd been caught with my hand in the cookie jar.

Oh, but what a cookie jar!

I couldn't stop the giggle that rose up. I wanted to holler, "Yee-haw!" but stopped short, suddenly confused. Was it *yee-haw* or *hee-haw*?

Oh, what difference did it make? With D.J.'s hypnotic blue eyes staring into mine, only one thing mattered. I needed someone to pinch me—and quick!

8

You Belong to Me

Mama always says, "*A mali estremi, estremi rimedi*—desperate times call for desperate measures."

As my gaze shifted back and forth between D.J. and Tony, I realized I'd fallen on desperate times. But what could I do? D.J. didn't know Tony from Adam, and Tony . . . well, Tony looked like he didn't really care to know D.J. at all—outside of a boxing ring, anyway.

Tony pulled up a chair, sat as close to my stool as possible, and muttered a stiff, "Hey, Bella." Though he spoke to me, his gaze never left the handsome deejay sitting on my left. As he raked his fingers through his thick, dark hair, unspoken words shot out of my ex's eyes: "Hey, cowboy, did I just catch you flirting with my girlfriend?"

Only, I *wasn't* his girlfriend. Hadn't been for weeks now. When would he get it?

I managed one word: "Tony."

Jenna, coward that she was, decided she'd better get back

to work in the kitchen. Laz, never one to miss out on anything exciting, leaned his elbows onto the counter and stared us down, as if he anticipated dueling pistols to be whipped out at a moment's notice. *Duh*-wayne sat there with a loopy smile on his face, completely oblivious.

First things first. I'd better introduce Exhibit A to Exhibit B. That way, at least D.J. would know the name of the man who'd pummeled him when the police asked for information.

"D.J. Neeley, this is Tony DeLuca."

"Pleased to meet you." D.J. nodded with sincerity etched on his handsome face.

Alrighty then. Exhibit A was doing just fine. On to Exhibit B.

"Tony, this is D.J. from Splendora," I explained. "He's the deejay for the upcoming country-western themed wedding I told you about."

"Ah."

I'd never known Tony to be short on words. In fact, I'd never known any Italian man to be short on words, so the sudden gap in the conversation made me nervous. I prayed D.J. wouldn't fill in the empty space by telling Tony this was his first gig. I could only imagine what *that* would do to the conversation. I could already read Tony's mind as it was.

Thankfully, Jenna came to my rescue with our fresh-from-the-oven Simpatico special and a cheerful, "Howdy, y'all!" The twang was probably meant to impress D.J., but he seemed to take it in stride.

As she placed the steaming pizza in front of us, Tony's face lit up. "You remembered!" He turned to me with newfound confidence in his expression. "Simpatico! I love Canadian bacon and you're crazy about pepperoni!"

True. But his theory that I'd ordered the pizza with him in mind was flawed. First, I had no way of knowing he'd be stopping by today, and second—somewhere between the Canadian bacon and the pepperoni—he'd completely left D.J. out of the equation.

I bit my tongue, waiting to see how a cowboy from Splendora might respond to being snubbed.

"Oh, look." D.J. pointed at the pizza. "Here's a piece that has a little of both. Think I'll take that one." He snagged it with an ever-widening smile, one that showed off his strategically placed dimples.

Ah, compromise. It was the stuff relationships were made of. Good relationships, anyway.

I grinned as I reached for a piece of pepperoni pizza, then kept a watchful eye on Tony as he grabbed one loaded with Canadian bacon. With our mouths full, we couldn't exactly quarrel, so the next few minutes gave me plenty of time to pray in silence that things would end well.

"So, what do you think of the pizza, D.J.?" Laz asked after he'd scarfed down a couple of pieces.

"Aw, it's great." My cowboy deejay responded with that deep bass voice I'd quickly grown to adore—the same voice Sharlene and Cody's wedding guests were sure to love. "But then, any real pizza tastes good to me. I usually just buy the frozen ones from the grocery store."

I half expected the overhead music to come to a grinding halt and for the crowd to fall silent at this public confession. D.J. nibbled away, never knowing what he'd said, but I could tell Uncle Laz's breathing had grown shallow. Not a good sign. No one ever used the words *frozen pizza* in his presence.

Tony gave D.J. a look that said, "Are you kidding, or what?"

and Jenna, drawing on her cowardice once again, announced she had to wait on some incoming customers.

"Young man." Laz stared D.J. down. "A few minutes ago, I thought you might be capable of coming up with a name for our new barbecue pizza. Now I'm not so sure." He paced back and forth. "I must rethink this proposition. Something has to be done. But what?"

"W-what do you mean?" Confusion registered in D.J.'s eyes.

"I'm going to have to see you in action."

"Excuse me?" D.J. shook his head. "In action? Are you talking about construction work?"

"No."

"That deejay thing? 'Cause I'm a little new at—"

"I'm talking about pizza making, cowboy," Laz explained. "Roll up your sleeves. There's going to be a duel."

"A . . . a duel?"

"Between you and Tony here."

Tony almost choked on his Canadian bacon. "W-what?"

"A pizza bake-off," Laz said. "The winner wins the right to name the barbecue pizza."

I sighed with relief when he didn't add, "And the winner gets to date Bella." I didn't want Tony to think for one minute that this had anything to do with me. Our Simpatico days were over.

"B-but I've never made a pizza in my life," D.J. stammered. "Wouldn't even know where to start." I could read the fright in his eyes. Who could blame him? My invitation hadn't included the words, "Bring your dueling pistols." I'd simply asked him to come for some pizza.

I decided to throw in my two cents' worth. "You're not playing fair, Laz."

"All's fair in love and war." My uncle gave me a wink. "Now, as soon as you boys are done eating, wash up and meet me in the kitchen. We've got some baking to do."

Tony, born and raised by an Italian mama, swaggered into the kitchen minutes later. D.J. followed along behind him, looking exactly like I felt—deflated. He glanced back at me as if to ask, "How did I get here?" and I shrugged. Some families had dueling pistols. Ours had dueling pizzas. What could I say?

Still, I couldn't help but feel bad for the poor guy. One day he was a happy-go-lucky construction worker humming a country tune to pass the time. The next, he was a pizza-making deejay with a Dean Martin mandate hanging over his head.

I rose from my barstool and tagged behind the others into the oversized kitchen, where Joey slaved away. He looked over at D.J. with a "Hey," then at Tony with an "Uh-oh" and moved over a bit to continue his work.

Uncle Laz pulled out a batch of freshly made dough and a couple of containers of homemade sauce, then leaned against his cane as he made an announcement. "Gentlemen, you are free to use anything you find in this kitchen. I don't care what kind of pizza you make—just come up with something edible. Forty-five minutes from now, one of you will be crowned the winner and will earn the right to name the barbecue pizza."

I took note of Tony's puffed-out chest—a familiar sight. And I saw the wrinkles in D.J.'s brow—also familiar by now.

"May the best man win!" Laz exclaimed. Then he turned to Jenna and me and said, "Ladies, out of the kitchen."

"But—" I said.

"No buts."

I returned to my seat at the counter and watched through the opening leading to the kitchen. Tony slipped on an apron over his dress shirt and began to move at lightning speed, spreading his dough across the large pan, then ladling on ample amounts of sauce. He laid it on thick—the silent bragging, not the sauce.

D.J., on the other hand, looked at the dough as if it were some sort of alien being. Finally, likely intimidated by Tony's speed, he took it in his hands and began to spread it out on the pan. Okay, so it didn't quite reach the edges, but who cared, really? No one said the pizzas had to be shaped perfectly, they just had to taste great.

Tony started cooking up a pan of sausage on the stove, and the whole room filled with a tantalizing aroma. This would be hard to beat. I watched as D.J. reached for a skillet. He ambled over to the refrigerator, returning with a pound of hamburger.

Hamburger?

He fried it up in the pan, then lightly simmered some onions on top.

By now, Tony had covered his pizza in large lumps of fried Italian sausage. To that, he added ham, pepperoni, anchovies, and an ample spread of black olives. Yummy.

I watched with fear and trembling as D.J. added cayenne pepper to his meat and onion mixture. He spread it out on top of the pizza, then looked at Laz, dead serious as he asked, "You got any pinto beans 'round here?"

"Pinto beans?" Jenna and I looked at each other, dazed. Who put pinto beans on a pizza?

Laz nodded. "My pinto bean soup is the best on the island. I always keep them on hand." He pointed to the supply cabinet in the back of the room. D.J. returned moments later with a can of pinto beans. He drained the juice and covered the spicy meat and onion mixture with the tiny brown beans. Certainly didn't look very appetizing.

"Got any jalapeños?" he asked.

My eyes widened. Man. Talk about one spicy pizza!

Uncle Laz brought him a couple of fresh jalapeños, and he took to chopping them, then placed the thin slices atop his meat, onion, and bean mixture.

My gaze shifted to Tony, who'd taken the block of mozzarella and started slicing ample amounts to seal the deal on his Italian lover's delight. My mouth watered as I watched those pieces slide into place. I could almost imagine them bubbling away in the oven. Nothing tempted me more than mozzarella. Well, other than cheesecake. And tiramisu. And one very handsome deejay who now had a puzzled expression on his face.

"Do you need something?" I asked.

He nodded, then looked over at Laz and asked, "Where's the real cheese?"

"Excuse me?" Uncle Lazarro gave him an incredulous look. "*Real* cheese? *This* is real cheese." He lifted the block of mozzarella, and for a moment I thought he might hurl it D.J.'s way. Thankfully, that did not happen.

"No, where's the orange stuff?" D.J. asked.

I wanted to turn and run from the building.

"Did he just say orange stuff?" Jenna whispered.

I groaned my response. If things kept up, I'd never get to date my handsome cowboy.

Uncle Laz went to the walk-in refrigerator and came out with a container of shredded cheddar. "This is the only orange cheese we've got in the place. I usually put it on the salads."

"Perfect!" D.J. grabbed it and covered the top of his pizza.

Now, I'd seen plenty of pizzas in my day, but none that looked like the one in front of me. Funny thing—both Tony and D.J. beamed with delight as their concoctions went into the oven.

We filled the next few minutes with pleasant-enough conversation, but my scrambled thoughts got in the way. I couldn't explain why it was so important to me that D.J. make a good impression on Laz, but it was. And it had nothing to do with pizza.

Fifteen minutes later, two bubbling pizzas emerged from the oven. I had to admit, they both looked tantalizing. To my surprise, D.J. went back to the refrigerator and returned with a bag of shredded lettuce, which he sprinkled atop his pizza. After that, he added a couple more handfuls of grated cheddar, then diced a tomato and sprinkled the bright red pieces around on top. What had started out as a dull-looking pan of pizza suddenly looked like a feast for the eyes.

To add that final touch, D.J. placed a hefty dollop of sour cream in the center of it all, jabbed a jalapeño in it and stepped back to examine his work. He crossed his arms at his chest, and the little dimples that appeared let me know he was pleased with his work. I didn't blame him. I could see exactly where he was headed with this new idea of his, and I liked it—a lot.

Jenna jabbed me. "I get it," she said. "Taco pizza. Cool."

"No. Taco pizza . . . spicy." D.J. gave her a wink.

Jenna turned several shades of red, and her eyelashes fluttered—just like they always did when embarrassment got the better of her.

"Looks wonderful. Don't know why I didn't think of it myself." Laz turned and looked around the restaurant, assessing the crowd. "We'll choose a couple of customers to be our round-one judges. Then you ladies will judge round two. I'll make the final decision."

I looked into D.J.'s eyes and saw the satisfaction written there. Funny. My construction-working deejay cowboy might just turn out to be a top chef as well. Was there anything the boy couldn't do?

The crowd swooned over both pizzas, but amazingly, the taco pizza won out. Jenna and I took our seats, ready for a nibble. I felt Tony's gaze on the back of my neck as I bit into his traditional Italian pizza. *Delicioso!*

D.J. gave me a lopsided grin as I bit into his concoction. The first bite took me by surprise. Something about the cold lettuce, cheese, and tomato atop the hot, spicy ingredients really did something to my palate. And that little touch of sour cream was just right. If I closed my eyes, I could almost see myself nibbling away on a taco.

"Mmm." Jenna looked up at me, surprised, then whispered, "Tony's going to kill us."

I nodded, thinking of my mama's words: "*A mali estremi, estremi rimedi*—desperate times call for desperate measures." I glanced up at Laz with an unassuming smile. "We, um, love 'em both. So the decision's up to you."

Uncle Lazarro bit into a slice of Tony's pizza and gave him a thumbs-up. "Excellent, son. You can come to work for me anytime."

Like that would happen. Tony? In a kitchen?

Next it was D.J.'s turn. Laz took a hesitant bite of the pizza, then looked up with excitement in his eyes. "This one surprises me."

"In a good way I hope, sir," D.J. said.

"Yes." Laz wolfed down the rest of the piece, then licked

his lips. "Where did you come up with the idea for this? It's brilliant."

"Well, every day out on the construction site, a trailer pulls up with the words *Tacos Sabrosas* written on the side. I love their homemade tacos. Just figured I'd use those same ingredients on my pizza. See if it would work."

"Worked like a charm," I said with a nod.

D.J. shrugged. "Yeah, but I think it might be a little better if we add some cornmeal to the pizza crust to give it a truer flavor. And I think some homemade salsa would be great, or at least a little pico de gallo." He turned to Laz. "What do you think?"

"What do I think?" My uncle lifted his cane in the air and exclaimed, "We have a winner! D.J. has earned the right to name the barbecue pizza." He took another bite of the taco pizza and grinned. "But first things first! This taco pizza must be added to our menu today. What should we call it?"

"Oh, I know!" I could barely contain my excitement. "Didn't Dean Martin have a song called 'South of the Border'?"

"Never heard of it." Tony's voice hinted of ridicule.

"Let's look it up on the Web," Jenna suggested. Seconds later, thanks to the computer in the office, we had our answer.

Uncle Lazarro looked as if he might explode with joy. "Praise God! South of the Border it is." He turned to D.J. "You've done it, boy. You've created a new pizza and earned the right to name another."

Tony glanced at his watch. "Whoa. Look at the time. It's almost seven. I've got to go."

I saw the defeated look in his eyes and felt a little sorry for him, but I didn't know how to make things better.

I settled on, "Great job, Tony," which Jenna echoed.

As soon as Tony left, D.J. rose from his chair and stretched. "I guess I'd better get on out of here too."

"Yeah, it's a long drive to Splendora," Jenna said.

"Oh, I live here on the island." D.J. quirked a brow. "Guess I should've mentioned it sooner. I go back up to see my parents at least once a week, but mostly I just go to my condo and crash after working all day."

"Where's your place?" Jenna asked.

"I found a great one-bedroom not far from 61st and the seawall a few weeks back."

"Wow. Busy area," I said. *But close!* My heart practically danced with joy at the fact that he lived nearby.

I followed him to the door and thanked him—for everything. "Sorry. I didn't plan to bring you here to put you to work. Seems like I keep doing that."

"No problem." He leaned in a bit closer—so close I could smell the jalapeños on his breath. "I had a blast. Learned a lot too." He gave me a pensive look. "I have a feeling I'm going to learn a lot from you, Bella." He reached with a fingertip and brushed a loose hair off my face. Something about his touch sent a tingle all the way down to my toes.

We both stood in silence for a moment. Well, unless you counted the sound of Dean Martin's voice crooning "Simpatico" overhead or the chatter of the customers. I finally broke it with a comment. "Just think, we never even got around to discussing the wedding."

"Just means we'll have to get together again . . . real soon." He flashed a dimple-lit smile, and my heart jumped for joy.

He wants to see me again!

"Well, if today was any indication, I have to wonder what our next meeting's going to be like."

"Won't matter, as long as you're there," he said. With a wink, D.J. turned to leave.

I couldn't be sure, but I think he took a slice of my heart with him.

9

Young at Heart

Aunt Rosa has never been one to let go of a grudge. Take, for example, the time Uncle Laz planted himself in her self-designated seat at St. Patrick's Catholic Church and refused to move. It took several nuns and a very patient priest to convince her that she could hear the Mass just as well from a different pew. And then there was that episode with the dry cleaner. Sure, they'd accidentally given her favorite blouse to another customer, but . . . picketing the store? Petitioning the neighbors to do the same? I still shivered at the embarrassment that had caused.

Based on the past, I knew this thing with the neighbor kid wouldn't just fade away. Rosa had the tenacity of a bulldog. She would not relinquish the boy's skateboard until she got what she wanted from him, and I had a feeling he wasn't going to bend any time soon.

I struggled with the idea of getting involved. A part of me wanted to sneak across the street and work out some sort of deal with the Burton family—after properly introducing myself, of course—and part of me wanted to see the boy treat Rosa with the respect she deserved. What was wrong with kids these days, anyway?

What I did not want to see happen, especially with the wedding coming up, was an unnecessary feud between our families. We had enough excitement going on without involving the new neighbors. No, I needed peace and quiet—and I needed it to last until after Sharlene and Cody's wedding had boot-scooted on by.

On Thursday morning, I approached my mother as she took her seat on the upholstered vanity stool in her bathroom, preparing to put on makeup. This process usually took the better part of the morning, so I knew we'd have time for a good, long chat.

"Any word from the Burtons?" I asked as I sat on the edge of the oversized Jacuzzi tub. Precious sprang up and down like a yo-yo, so I reached down and scooped her into my arms.

Mama pulled her jet black hair back with a headband and shook her head as she responded. "I'm going with the 'no news is good news' philosophy. I'd rather assume the best than to worry." She pulled the lighted makeup mirror close and examined her freshly scrubbed face in its reflection. The magnification made her pores look like dots of sand on the beach.

"Don't you think she's being a little stubborn?" I said. "Shouldn't she just let it go?"

Mama, who more often than not agreed with me on issues related to Rosa, gave her response in Italian: "*Ogni medaglia ha il suo rovescio.*"

"Right," I responded. "I know there are two sides to every coin, but not in Rosa's world. In her world, all coins are one-sided." I wanted to throw in "And they have Frank Sinatra's face imprinted on them" but thought better of it.

I watched as my mother used an expensive three-in-one facial cleanser and exfoliation system. She rubbed it into her skin in tiny circles, then lathered it up and rinsed all remnants away. After dabbing her skin dry, she applied her moisturizer, then dabbed on some eye revitalizer, a skin-tightening gel, and a new wrinkle reducer she'd just purchased from her beauty consultant.

Now came the fun part. The makeup.

Mama fumbled around in her makeup bag, finally coming up with her concealer stick. Then, like Michelangelo painting the Sistine Chapel, she went to work on her face. Every day the task grew a bit more time consuming, but talk about precision! And necessary precision at that. In spite of good genes, her face had finally started to show signs of aging.

Still, I thought Mama's post-makeup look was pretty impressive. Not that she would dream of going out in public without all of the powder and paint. She'd just as soon show up for choir practice at the Methodist church wearing only her slip. Some things were simply inconceivable.

A few minutes later, as she slathered on ample amounts of liquid foundation, a noise outside interrupted our conversation. I looked out the window and watched a wrecker pull up to the curb. Something in my expression must've alarmed my mother.

"What is it, Bella?" She turned away from the mirror to gaze at me.

"I'm not sure." I tried to give it a closer look, but from this distance I could barely make out the logo on the side. "It's a wrecker. I have no idea why it's—"

She never even gave me a chance to finish before springing to her feet. "You don't suppose . . ."

"What?"

"I told Rosa to park her car on the street this morning so that Sophia could back out of the driveway," Mama explained. "Do you think the new neighbors . . . ?" Her voice trailed off, but I could see the fear in her eyes.

"Surely not. They wouldn't have one of our cars towed out of spite. Would they?"

Mama sprang from her seat, clutched her bathrobe tightly around her, and headed toward the bathroom door. I quickly ushered her back into place in front of the mirror and told her I'd take care of it myself. There's something about a half-made-up face that can be pretty alarming.

I sprinted down the stairs with Precious on my heels, reaching the door at the same moment the bell rang. "Lord, please let this end well," I whispered. Reaching down to snatch up the dog, I opened the door. "C-can I help you?"

An extremely tall twentysomething male with rough-around-the-edges features greeted me. "Hey."

"Hey."

Precious—likely intimidated by his size and his deep voice—began that low growl thing in the back of her throat, and I swallowed hard, praying she would keep her cool. I needed to talk this guy out of towing Rosa's car.

He glanced at a paper in his hand and then said, "I'm lookin' for Bella Rossi."

There was something about the way he pronounced Bella— *Bay*-luh—that made a nervous laugh rise up. Who was this guy? He had a familiar look about him. And that voice—that deep, hypnotic voice . . .

I leaned to the right and strained to read the logo on the

side of the wrecker. From here I could almost make it out. If he'd just move a little to my left . . .

The stranger pulled off his cap and ran his fingers through sandy-colored curls. "D.J. said something about barbecuin' for a wedding. Told me to stop by here before meetin' up with him for lunch."

Welcome, Bubba!

I threw open the door and ushered the towering hunk-a-Bubba inside, trying to figure out why D.J. hadn't called to give me a heads-up on his brother's unexpected visit.

As these thoughts swirled around in my brain, Mama came bounding down the stairs wearing a pair of navy slacks and a mismatched yellow blouse. She still wore her cloth headband but had somehow found the time to apply a smidgeon of blush. However, she had missed something pretty important—her usual rose-colored lip liner and lipstick. Without any color on her lips, she came across a bit ghostlike in appearance. Not that I had much time to contemplate the fact. My mother, who rarely got worked up, took one look at Bubba and went into a panic.

"Please don't take our car," she pleaded. "We promise never to do it again."

"Take your car?" He scratched his head, looking back and forth between us. "Why would I want to—?"

"This whole thing has been a terrible misunderstanding." She used her hands to talk, as always. "I'm sure we can work it out peacefully."

"Mama, relax." I nodded in her direction. "This is D.J.'s brother. He's here to discuss the food for Sharlene and Cody's wedding. We're not being towed."

"Oh, thank God." My mother dropped into a chair and began to fan herself with her hand.

Rosa chose that moment to enter the room. She took one look at Mama and the scolding began. "Imelda! Go upstairs and put on your lips."

I wanted to disappear into the woodwork. Of all the times for my aunt to deliver a line in English.

My mother ran her index finger along the edges of her mouth, then with a horrified look on her face, she rose from her seat and raced toward the stairs.

"She's fast on her feet," Bubba observed, slipping his cap back on.

"We're from Jersey," I explained. "Everything's faster up there."

"Yeah, but everything's *bigger* in Texas," he countered.

"No doubt about that." I looked up, up, up into his blue eyes—eyes that mimicked his older brother's in every conceivable way. "So, um, you've come to talk about the wedding? Maybe we should go next door to Club Wed and—"

I never got to finish because Rosa interrupted me. "You like Frank Sinatra, young man?" Her eyes narrowed as she gave Bubba a solid, albeit suspicious, once-over.

"Oh, yes, ma'am," Bubba responded. "My dad was in the Navy, so *Anchors Aweigh* is one of his all-time favorite movies. I grew up watching it. And I love that one song . . . something about being young."

"'Young at Heart'?" Rosa's eyes lit up as she quoted the title of her favorite song.

"Yeah, that's the one."

"Come with me to the kitchen. Are you hungry?"

"Well, I'm supposed to eat lunch with D.J. in an hour or so, but I guess I could . . ." His voice trailed off as Rosa took him by the arm and led him to the kitchen. One thing about

Italian women—our timing might not be great, but we sure knew how to feed our men.

Only, Bubba wasn't our man. He was our caterer. Sort of.

Flustered, I tried to stop my aunt in her tracks. "Rosa, Bubba's here to work."

She turned to look at him, her brow wrinkled. "Bubba?" After a moment's pause, she added, "What's your real name?"

"Excuse me?" He looked perplexed at best, but who could blame him?

"When they don't call you Bubba." Rosa spoke with determination. "What do they call you?"

"Oh, Lucas."

"A good Bible name. Are you Catholic, boy?" She squinted and dared him to answer otherwise.

"No, ma'am." He pulled off his cap and ran his fingers through his hair again. "I'm from Splendora."

I bit my tongue to keep from laughing.

"Methodist, then?" Rosa asked. "Like Bella and her father?" As always, she tripped over the word *Meth-o-dist*. No doubt she still found it hard to believe my parents had converted. And strange that she'd only mentioned Pop. Mama had switched to the Methodist church just after we moved to Galveston, right alongside my pop and us kids. Perhaps Rosa still held out hope that her baby sister was suffering a temporary lapse in judgment.

"Meth-o-dist?" Bubba gave her a curious look. "Um, no, ma'am. I attend Full Gospel Chapel in the Pines. We're independent charismatic."

"Independent charismatic." She spoke the words slowly as if trying to make sense of them.

"Yes." He slipped his cap back on. "Our services are very

. . . lively. Some of our members take to dancin' when the Holy Ghost falls on 'em."

"Well, for heaven's sake." Her eyes narrowed as she pondered this bit of news. After a moment, a smile lit her face. "You're practically Catholic! St. Patrick's hosts a dance for the young people every Saturday night." She nodded, as if that settled everything. "And how wonderful that you're named after Saint Luke—the good doctor."

"Oh, trust me, ma'am. I ain't no saint." Bubba looked more than a little embarrassed. "And I sure ain't got no medical degree."

"Never you mind all that." She reached for an apron. "Just let me put this apron on you, Lucas. Then take a seat on that barstool. I'm making ravioli today. You can help me. I'll feed you a big breakfast first to get your strength up."

Like a pup on a leash, he stood in silence while she tied an apron around his waist. Then he plopped down on the nearest barstool and watched her work. Within minutes, the strains of "Young at Heart" filled the room.

My thoughts were as scrambled as the eggs Rosa whipped up shortly thereafter. Bubba had come to talk about Sharlene and Cody's wedding. We needed to get to it. But how? With Rosa in the mix, we would never get any work done.

Not that my barbecue aficionado seemed to mind. He paid close attention as she gave her ravioli-making instructions, even going so far as to add, "Wow, I can't wait," when she finished. I could tell from the look on his face that he really meant it. Clearly he and D.J. were both alike in this area. They seemed to be genuinely good people who put the needs of others above their own. Who could argue with that?

Rosa smiled and patted his hand. "We will start on the ravioli *after* you eat breakfast," she explained. "So get busy."

I put Precious down, then reached for my cell phone to call Jenna. She answered on the third ring. "Thank you for calling Parma John's."

"Hey girl, I have a favor to—"

"You've got your heart set on Mexican food? He's in the mood for pizza?" she interjected. "Why not try our South of the Border special—a taco pizza for two. It's spicy and delectable with just that right kick. Hot meets cold in this amazing new dish from Parma John's, Galveston Island's premiere pizzeria. And speaking of hot, why not add two espressos to your order for an additional four dollars."

Wow. For a minute I didn't know what to say. Somewhere between the ravioli, the scrambled eggs, and the South of the Border special, the world had gone crazy.

"Hello?" I heard Jenna say. She sounded agitated. "Is anyone there?"

"Look at the caller ID, Jenna," I managed.

"Bella!" She giggled. "What do you think of the new pitch? Laz came up with it this morning."

"I think it's . . ." *Deep breath, Bella.* "I think it's great. You guys are really fast. But I'm calling for a different reason." I filled her in on the news du jour, and she gasped.

"Bubba's at your house right now?"

"Yeah. I'm about to call D.J. to see if he can meet us here for half an hour during his lunch break. Do you think you and Laz can slip away? We really need to talk about the food for the wedding. It's coming sooner than you know, and I'm getting nervous."

"Yes, but do we have to do this today? I can't imagine leaving during our busiest time of day, especially with our new South of the Border special selling like hot tortillas."

"Jenna. Just half an hour. Marcella's there, right? I promise, you can go right back to work after."

She sighed. "I guess she can take care of things for a few minutes, if you think it's that important. And Nick and Joey are both here too."

"It is. I've got to get this wedding under control."

Even as I spoke the words, my heart plummeted to my toes. Reality set in. I'd forgotten to order the cowboy boots for the centerpieces! I'd have to take care of that after handling one more very important matter.

After ending my call with Jenna, I telephoned D.J. I felt pretty sure my opening line would deliver a punch. "I know you're going to think this is crazy," I explained, "but Rosa has put Bubba to work in our kitchen making ravioli."

"Well, he's in his element then," D.J. said with a hint of laughter in his voice. "My brother's a mighty fine cook. He took a blue ribbon at last year's Houston Livestock Show and Rodeo for his brisket, and his ribs are the best in south Texas."

"Mmm. You're making me hungry for barbecue."

"Well then, I'll have to take you up to meet my folks when this wedding shindig is over. Maybe for the Fourth of July. We always have a ton of people over."

"Oh?"

"Yeah, we spend the day eating brisket and watermelon and playing chickenfoot."

Chickenfoot? I didn't have a clue what that meant but decided not to show my ignorance. If the boy wanted me to play chickenfoot, I'd play chickenfoot. And I'd eat a truckload of barbecue, as long as I could do it with D.J. sitting at my side.

Snapping to attention, I remembered the reason for my call. "Can you meet at my house at noon?" I asked. "You guys can have lunch here. We really need to talk about this wedding. Hopefully it won't take long, and that way we can kill two birds with one stone."

D.J. readily agreed, and I hung up, feeling my first glimmer of hope all day.

Then I remembered the cowboy boots.

Excusing myself from the kitchen, I grabbed my laptop. Finding eBay was the easy part. Locating twenty used boots was a bit harder.

Crazy thing about eBay—you have to bid on items. I didn't have time for that. I needed my cowboy boots, and I needed them now! Still, what choice did I have?

Flying into action, I found a multiboot collection with only twelve hours of bidding left. Bidders weren't always winners, so I overshot my estimate, then used the company credit card to secure my place in line. Sharlene's dad could pay me back later.

Afterward, with Precious on my heels once more, I joined Rosa and Bubba in the kitchen. My aunt had rolled out the dough for the ravioli and was explaining the process in detail. Bubba seemed to be an apt pupil. Would wonders never cease?

I'd just opened my mouth to ask, "How's it going?" when my father plodded into the room in his boxers and undershirt. Nothing like greeting the company in style. I started to make introductions but never had the chance. Pop took one look at our very tall guest and whistled.

"You play basketball, boy?"

Bubba turned to him with the same crooked grin I'd seen on D.J.'s face. "Yes, sir. Played for three years at Splendora High."

"When you're done in here, let's go outside and shoot some hoops."

Well, terrific. Ravioli and a basketball game.

My father exited the house through the back door, never knowing—or caring—who exactly he'd be shooting hoops with. Or the fact that he'd be playing in his underwear.

My mother joined us—fully made up and looking like a queen in clothes that now matched perfectly. Quite a contrast to Pop, and an odder contrast still to the stocky, un-made-up Rosa, who worked with abandon in her flour-covered apron.

Welcome to the Rossi family.

Just then the music changed. "Strangers in the Night" came on. Rosa stopped her work, her eyes filling with tears. "I love this one," she whispered. "It's the song Ol' Blue Eyes is going to sing to me when I get to heaven."

For a moment, the entire room was at a standstill as a lone tear trickled down my aunt's wrinkled cheek. She closed her eyes and began to rock back and forth, as if dancing with an imaginary partner.

With perfect timing, Bubba extended his hand and asked, "May I have this dance?"

Her eyes flew open at once, and a look of wonder came over her. When she nodded, he swept her into his arms, and the two of them began to waltz around the room to the melody of the familiar Frank Sinatra tune. I felt pretty sure my aunt could die right then a happy woman. I might just offer to go with her, to avoid some of this embarrassment.

I observed the action in front of me in a state of disbelief. Rosa sang along with Frank in a voice as clear as crystal, a look of sheer contentment on her face. Bubba joined in, singing in perfect harmony. Who would've known hunk-a-Bubba, the barbecue aficionado, was a vocalist? I filed the information away, in case I ever needed someone to sing at Club Wed.

Mama opened the fridge and pulled out a Pellegrino, then took a seat on a nearby barstool with her ankles delicately crossed, looking every bit the royal lady. And Pop . . . through the kitchen window I caught a glimpse of him in the driveway, still dressed in his undergarments, setting up the portable basketball hoop in preparation for his game with our new guest.

I shot an urgent prayer heavenward, pleading with the Almighty to help me. How and when had things spiraled out of control? Was there any returning from the abyss?

From the looks of things, I had my work cut out for me.

10

Little Did We Know

Jenna and Uncle Laz arrived at five minutes to twelve, just as my father coaxed Bubba outside to shoot a few hoops. Mama had managed to convince him to put on a pair of slacks—Pop, not Bubba—and the two guys took turns aiming at the basket. Seemed odd, my five-foot-nine father standing next to someone of Bubba's stature, tossing the basketball around.

Jenna took one look out of the kitchen window at D.J.'s younger brother and froze in her tracks. I'd seen her flabbergasted before, but never to this extent. "W-who is that?" she whispered.

"Bubba Neeley, D.J.'s younger brother."

"Mama mia." Her green eyes widened, and she leaned a bit closer to get a better look. "That's our barbecue guy?" She grabbed a loose red hair and began to fidget with it. I'd never seen her this flustered before.

"Yes, but Jenna, you're practically engaged," I reminded her. "Remember David? Your boyfriend?"

"I . . . I know." She kept a watchful eye through the kitchen window as Bubba sank another shot. "He's . . . he's . . ."

"He's offshore. Working to earn money so he can ask you to marry him."

"No, I meant . . ." Jenna leaned her elbows on the counter and focused all her attention on Bubba. "Wow, he's really tall."

"No, David isn't tall."

"David? Hmm?"

Good grief. I'd already lost everyone else to the craziness. Now Jenna?

"Quando il gatto non c'è il topo balla." Laz's animated voice rang out as he observed the expression on Jenna's face. "When the cat's away . . ."

"The mice will play," I finished. "But this is one mouse who needs to stay focused." I glared at Jenna. She shrugged, then gazed back at Bubba, her eyes wider than the pepperoni on the Simpatico special. With her cheeks flushed pink like this, her freckles were even more pronounced.

Laz peeked out the window. "So that's the barbecue guy?" He huffed. "Doesn't look like much of a cook."

Jenna watched in rapt awe as Bubba shot the basketball through the hoop for the umpteenth time. "Oh, I don't know . . . looks like he's cookin' to me."

Laz rolled his eyes.

"Why so cynical today?" I asked. "You probably never thought D.J. could make a pizza, and now that South of the Border special is your main attraction!"

"Humph." He glanced at Rosa. "Speaking of which, what's for lunch?"

"Ravioli." She pointed to the stove with a confident look on her face. "Bubba helped. He's really something."

With another grunt, Laz opened the cupboard and pulled out a box of antacids. After filling a glass with water, he dropped in a tablet and waited. It fizzled up and he gulped it down, then let out an exaggerated belch. Lovely.

Rosa turned back to her work, muttering under her breath in Italian.

Just then the doorbell rang, and my heart shifted into overdrive. *D.J.!* I tried not to look too anxious as I made my way to the front door. As it swung wide, I gazed into the beautiful eyes of the world's most handsome carpenter-turned-deejay. His smile sent my heart into a flutter. And those broad shoulders! The man belonged on the cover of *Tool Time* magazine.

Unfortunately, Precious chose that moment to go into attack mode. I scooped up the ornery pooch and did my best to get things under control before stepping out onto the veranda. When the yapping stopped, I brought D.J. up to speed. Number one: Bubba had made Rosa's day by singing and dancing with her. Number two: His culinary skills were quite good, particularly where ravioli was concerned. Number three: He could shoot a mean basket. Number four: He'd won over my father—no small task.

To prove my final two points, I led D.J. around the side of the house to the far end of the driveway, where Pop and Bubba continued on with their basketball game. Bubba hollered out a greeting, then dribbled the ball our way and passed it to D.J., who took a random but perfectly aimed shot.

"Two points!" we all shouted as it slipped easily through the hoop.

Looked like both of the Neeley boys *were* cookin' today. And boy, I decided as I fanned myself, were they ever generating heat.

Pop leaned over and put his hands on his knees, panting. I

hated to say he was out of shape, but . . . well, he was out of shape. "I'll be back in a minute, boys," he explained. "Got something I want to show you."

As he limped toward the house, I turned to the Splendora duo and shifted the conversation to the upcoming wedding. D.J. and I made plans to meet with Armando on Saturday afternoon. Thank goodness my brother had agreed to come back for a couple of hours and show D.J. how to work the soundboard. Bubba promised to chat with Laz and Jenna about the barbecue over today's lunch. We'd iron out the details of Sharlene and Cody's big day in no time. Looked like things were really moving along!

Rosa interrupted our chat with a vivacious *"Venite a mangiare!"* which she hollered out of the kitchen window. Nothing new there.

Still, our guests couldn't seem to figure out her meaning, so I filled them in. "She's saying, 'Come and eat.' Lunch is ready."

"Ah." Bubba nodded. "It's ravioli time."

"Right. And it's better not to keep her waiting," I whispered. "She gets cranky if the food turns cold." I reached for the basketball and headed toward the back door, then led the way into the kitchen, where I placed the ball on the counter. My father joined us, holding yet another basketball, this one a brighter orange.

I pondered his logic, especially in light of his earlier limp. "Hey, I thought you were done playing."

"I am. Just wanted the boys to see my prized possession."

He tossed the ball Bubba's way, and Bubba let out a whistle as he read the signature. "Hakeem Olajuwon? Wow."

"Impressive." D.J. drew close to look at it. "Hakeem the Dream."

"Hakeem the Dream?" Rosa looked at him with confusion etched in her brow. "Who's that?"

All of the men in the room turned to her at the same time, and for a moment I thought there might just be some sort of mutiny. So what if Rosa had never heard of the great Hakeem Olajuwon, former star player for the Houston Rockets? Was it her fault she didn't follow basketball?

"Hakeem Olajuwon," Pop repeated, perhaps thinking she hadn't heard him correctly. "Two-time NBA champion, 1994 MVP, and all-time leader in blocked shots."

Rosa snatched the ball from Bubba's hands and placed it next to the other one on the counter. "In my kitchen we eat. We don't talk sports."

"Yes, ma'am." Bubba hung his head, duly chastised.

He looked around for a place to sit, and I watched with fear creeping over me as he landed in the chair next to Jenna. My friend, usually talkative and bubbly, seemed nervous and quiet. I didn't know what to make of her bug-eyed silence.

Thankfully, Mama shattered the awkwardness with her usual premeal admonition to my father. "Take your pill, Cosmo."

"Oh yeah." Pop rose from his seat and went to the cupboard, where he pulled out a familiar bottle. After swallowing down a lactose-intolerance tablet, he sat at the table, eyes wide as he took in the cheesy meal. As always, he bowed his head to pray, and the rest of us followed suit. The prayer—filled with heartfelt praises for all the Lord had done—brought a sense of stability to the proceedings.

After his emotional amen, the real chaos began. After a little provoking from Uncle Laz about the proper way to barbecue a brisket for the upcoming wedding, a near-argument ensued. I tried to listen in but found myself staring at D.J.

out of the corner of my eye instead. What great fortune! I'd shared a pizza with him yesterday and dinner with him the night before. Now, here he sat at my table, eating ravioli. The handsome Splendora cowboy had boot-scooted into my life—hopefully to stay.

At my feet, Precious let out a whimper. I slipped her a tiny piece of ravioli on the sly. D.J. caught my eye and gave me a wink. Thankfully, he didn't give me away. Just one more thing we had in common. He tolerated my dog. Perhaps one day he'd even learn to love her. I hoped.

Jenna, who hadn't uttered a word, finally managed some small talk. "Where are Sophia and the boys?" She directed the words at me, but her gaze never shifted from Bubba.

"They're at the Museum of Natural Science in Houston," I explained. "Field trip. She tries to keep the boys busy as much as possible."

"Wow. She's brave." Jenna's eyes widened.

"Tell me about it." I could only imagine the stories Sophia would have to tell when she arrived home. Then again, I might have a few stories of my own, the way things were going. I begged my heart to stop fluttering and turned my attention to the food once again.

"Could you pass the tomato sauce?" D.J. nodded toward the huge bowl in the center of the table. When everyone grew silent, he looked my way. "Did I say something wrong?"

"It's gravy, son," Laz informed him. "When you're at Parma John's, you can call it what you like. We use the word *sauce* on our menu to appease the customers. But inside the walls of the Rossi home, it's called gravy. Nothing more, nothing less."

"Gravy?" I could practically hear the wheels clicking in D.J.'s head. "But I thought gravy was brown. Or white. You put it on potatoes or rice. Or some of my mama's homemade biscuits."

"Not in this family," Rosa informed him. She lifted the bowl of thick red gravy and passed it his way. "This is the best gravy you'll ever eat."

"Humph." Laz grunted and took another bite. I hoped he'd keep his opinions about Rosa's cooking to himself today.

After settling his dispute with Laz, D.J. took several more bites of food, then proclaimed it the best food he'd ever eaten, adding, "If I ate like this every day, I'd put on some serious weight."

I had to smile. "My aunt likes to joke that people leave her table ten pounds heavier than when they arrived. And that's especially true when she makes meatballs."

The conversation shifted to talking about Rosa's amazing cooking skills, and I noticed Laz's silence. When would these two ever stop their squabbling over who cooked a better meal? Why not just combine efforts and keep the peace?

Rosa served up double portions and wouldn't let us rest until we'd all eaten ourselves silly. We shoveled down the food, bit by tasty bit. The ravioli was great, but Rosa's homemade bread really made the meal, as always. I hoped to one day learn her secret. In the meantime, I redirected the conversation to talking about food for the wedding.

After lunch, Pop rubbed his extended belly and turned to D.J. and Bubba. "Want to shoot a few more hoops before you go?"

"Well, sure." D.J. looked more than a little pleased at that idea.

Laz decided to spend a few minutes in his garden before heading back to work. He disappeared with a basket in hand, hoping to find a few ripe tomatoes.

Pop snatched one of the balls from the counter and made his way back outside with D.J. and Bubba on his heels. Jenna and I followed closely behind. My father, who appeared to have caught his second wind, moved amazingly fast. Still, D.J. managed to outscore him, though he was somewhat apologetic about it. Minutes later, my father—looking weary and a bit flustered—took a flying leap upward and tossed the ball toward the basket. It hit the rim, shot to the ground, and landed hard on the driveway, then shot upward again. After several bounces, it began rolling toward the street.

At that same moment, Mama appeared, holding the other basketball in her hand. "Cosmo, what are you doing playing with that signed basketball? Shouldn't you be using this one?"

A shock wave rippled through us. The ball rolling toward the street was my pop's pride and joy.

Bubba went running after it, shouting all the way, and D.J. followed closely behind. They bounded into the northbound lane, where a woman in an SUV missed D.J. by only a few inches. I let out a cry, and Rosa, who'd only just joined us, made the sign of the cross and called out to St. Joseph, patron saint of protection.

I somehow managed to make it from the driveway to the curb in seconds, but I found myself trapped by a slew of oncoming vehicles. Standing behind Bubba's wrecker, I readied myself to make my move. I watched in horror as an older-model sedan caught the ball with the edge of its rear right tire. It shot straight up in the air—the ball, not the car—then traveled across the grassy median and landed on the southbound side of Broadway, where it continued rolling, faster than ever.

I cried out, "Be careful!" then squeezed my eyes shut.

"I've got it!" Bubba raced across the second lane of traffic, landing in the yard across the street. Just as he reached for the ball, which had rolled to a stop near the sidewalk, a familiar-looking kid in shorts and a T-shirt snatched it.

Yikes. The Burton boy. He gave the ball a solid once-over, smiling as he realized what he held in his hand. "Cool! Hakeem the Dream!"

As I drew near, Bubba held out his hands and, true Southern gentleman that he was, flashed a smile at the kid, oblivious. "Thanks for your help."

"Help?" The boy gave him a quizzical look, clutching the ball. "You're kidding, right? Possession is nine-tenths of the law." He rolled the prize around in his hands. "My dad's gonna love this. He's a collector, you know."

"'Scuse me?" D.J. narrowed his eyes.

The Burton boy scowled before repeating himself. "I said, 'Possession is nine-tenths of the law.' And you're trespassing on our property, by the way."

"Technically I'm standing on the sidewalk," D.J. informed him, the level of his voice now intensifying. "And so are you."

The kid scooted back onto the grass and gave him a "what are you going to do about it?" glare. He held on to the ball like a dog with a bone.

"Give it up, kid." Bubba reached out to take the ball, but the Burton boy took another giant step backward.

"Who's gonna make me?"

"I'm gonna." Bubba took one step onto the grass.

I shook my head. "Don't do it," I warned under my breath. "It's not worth it."

"But that ball's worth—" Bubba clamped his mouth shut, apparently not wanting to give the kid any more fodder.

"Worth a lot of money, huh?" The Burton boy gave it a once-over. "Enough to buy a new Plan B?"

"Plan B?" I'd like to give him a Plan B.

"What are you talking about?" D.J. asked.

The kid's jaw tightened. "Plan B. My skateboard of choice. To replace the one that crazy old lady stole from me."

My jaw tightened at the words *crazy old lady*, but I managed not to respond. How dare he say such a thing! I crossed my arms at my chest and stared the kid down. Two could play at this game.

"First of all, she's not a crazy old lady. If you'd give her half a chance, you'd know that. Besides, you provoked her. Second, she didn't steal your skateboard. You were on our property. Possession is nine-tenths of the law, remember?"

The kid's demeanor changed right away. "Hmm. Well, when you put it like that . . . Tell you what. I'll make you a deal." His eyes narrowed as he said, "I'll trade."

"Trade?" My aunt hadn't agreed to give up the skateboard, but surely, considering the circumstances, she'd come to her senses and work out a deal. Right?

"One basketball for one skateboard," the Burton kid said with a nod. "We'll just call it even. And I'll talk my dad into dropping that lawsuit he's planning to file."

Please. You're not fooling me.

Just then, Rosa came sprinting across Broadway, broom in hand, Italian threats streaming from her mouth. Her wind-whipped hair, gray on black, made her look a bit like Cruella de Vil . . . from the neck up, anyway. The apron-covered day dress, sagging support hose, and black orthopedic shoes created a completely different image. Still, as she ranted and raved, I gave up on my plan to prove her sanity.

The boy took one look at her and took off running. She

started off after him, the shoes giving her an added advantage.

"Rosa, you don't want to end up in jail!" I called out as she crossed over onto his property line. That stopped her cold. She planted both feet on the sidewalk and shouted in lyrical Italian as the kid headed into his house, Pop's basketball in hand. So much for thinking they might be willing to strike a deal.

Bubba pulled off his cap and scratched his head. "I ain't never seen a kid talk to adults like that before. That boy needs a serious comeuppance."

"No kidding," D.J. agreed. "But I somehow doubt he'll ever get it. Something tells me he runs the show over there."

"No doubt," I said quietly.

We stood there in silence for a few minutes, hoping the little thief would return. No such luck. We eventually made our way back through the early afternoon traffic to our front yard. The conversation vacillated between contacting the kid's parents and letting him keep the basketball. Both options left me feeling nauseous—especially when I saw the look in Pop's eye as he shuffled up the drive and into the house.

As soon as we reached the veranda, D.J. glanced at his watch, and his eyes widened. "It's ten after one. I have to get back to work."

"Me too," Jenna said. "We've been gone way too long."

As D.J. turned to leave, something caught my attention. A black limousine pulled into our driveway and came to an abrupt halt just a few yards away from us.

"Are you expecting company?" I asked Mama.

"No. I don't know who that is. But what a car!"

A tall and stately driver, dressed in a black tuxedo, white dress shirt, and black bow tie, climbed out of the driver's seat.

His dark moustache and neatly edged goatee complemented his formal attire. He tipped his cap to us, then opened the back door of the limo and reached inside, coming out with something rather large covered in a colorful cloth. My mind reeled at the possibilities.

The well-dressed stranger approached our sweaty crew with the contraption in hand and posed his opening question. "Is there a Mr. Lazarro Rossi here?"

My uncle hobbled his way forward, cane in hand. "I am Lazarro Rossi."

"Ah. Very good." The fellow smiled and introduced himself as Joe Barbini. "We meet at last. Mr. Lucci speaks of you often."

"Salvadore Lucci?"

A gasp went up from everyone in the family as Uncle Laz's old friend was mentioned. I watched as my uncle's eyes filled with tears.

"Yes, sir." Mr. Barbini nodded. "I'm sorry to tell you Mr. Lucci has suffered a stroke and will be in rehab for several months."

"Oh no! Poor Sal!" Uncle Laz shuffled about with his cane in hand, moaning in passionate Italian about how he had failed his friend on a thousand levels. How a better man would have won Sal to the Lord by now.

Mr. Barbini listened intently and nodded politely until Laz reached the end of his speech. "Mr. Lucci has asked that Guido stay here with you. Until he recovers, that is."

"Guido?" Uncle Laz's brow wrinkled.

Mr. Barbini pulled the cloth away to reveal an ornate cage with the most exquisite green and red parrot inside. As soon as the bird came into view, a string of curse words escaped his beak, followed by an ear-piercing, "Go to the mattresses!"

"What in the world?" I took a step toward the cage but stopped in my tracks as Guido lifted his leg and made a noise that sounded just like a machine gun going off.

Aunt Rosa let out a bloodcurdling scream and looked as if she might faint, which sent D.J. rushing to her side. God bless that cowboy from Splendora.

The noise finally stopped. For a moment, no one moved. Mr. Barbini, looking more than a little embarrassed at the bird's behavior, finally broke the silence. "My apologies. Guido's had a long drive from Atlantic City. Carsick, you see. Now, I'm not making excuses for his behavior, but I'm sure he's exhausted. And he doesn't do well with change. Never has."

"Am I to understand you drove all the way from Atlantic City in a stretch limo . . . to bring us . . . a bird?" My mother turned to him with a look of horror on her face.

"Yes, that's right." Mr. Barbini nodded, as if that made perfect sense.

"But, I'm confused." Uncle Laz gave the parrot a careful once-over. "Why did you bring him here, of all places?"

The limo driver set the birdcage on the veranda and cleared his throat. "Mr. Lucci explained that you've always been like a brother to him. You're the only one he trusts."

We all turned to face Laz. His eyes welled up with tears once again.

Mr. Barbini hoisted a large bag of bird food out of the limo and placed it on the veranda step, alongside another bag labeled Supplies. Then he pulled an envelope from his coat pocket and handed it to my uncle. "I believe you will find what you need inside. Instructions for Guido's care. His feeding schedule. Prescriptions for allergy medications. Those sorts of things. Oh, and he's overdue to have his wings clipped again. You might want to take care of that before he takes off flying."

"Feeding schedule? Allergy meds? Wings clipped?" I scarcely had time to get the words out before the fellow tipped his cap, climbed back into the limo, and backed out of our driveway. From inside the cage, Guido continued to chatter, this time repeating the words, "Wise guy."

I happened to catch D.J.'s eye and had to wonder what the poor boy was thinking. Would he run as fast as he could from this nutty family of mine? Head back to Splendora to give the folks at his church a list of prayer requests about the crazy people he'd met in Galveston?

My handsome deejay turned to me with an engaging smile, and all of my fears dissolved in an instant.

"Gotta go," he whispered. I could almost see the sadness in his eyes. He slipped an arm around my waist and gave me a comfortable hug—a sure sign he wasn't going anywhere for long. I wanted to melt in his arms, to spend the rest of my day staring into those baby blues. Instead, I returned the hug, then watched as he and Bubba ambled down the driveway side by side.

"Mama mia," Jenna whispered once again.

I responded with a quiet, "Amen to that!"

11

That's What I Like

Life is full of curious coincidences. I call them *bada-bing, bada-boom moments*. Those strange coincidental times. Take, for example, the time my oldest brother, Nick, ran a red light and sideswiped a woman driving a brand-new Mazda Miata. They ended up married six months later, and subsequently produced two of the most spoiled children on Planet Earth. And then there was the time Mama and I drove to the airport to pick up Aunt Rosa, only to find her in police custody. Who knew she was a dead ringer for a murder suspect back in Napoli?

Yes, the Rossi family had surely seen its fill of coincidences, large and small. And lately I'd started to wonder if these so-called ironies were truly accidental, or if the Lord just had a quirkier sense of humor than I'd imagined. Did heaven cry out, "Bada-bing, bada-boom," every time something coincidental happened? If so, then the angels who'd been assigned to my care must be plenty busy of late.

On Friday morning I awoke thinking of the recent ironies in my life. Specifically, I pondered the whole D.J./deejay thing. What were the chances a man's name would create such lovely chaos? And what were the chances these unpredictable twists of fate would continue?

At 8:30 I faced my first coincidence of the day as I stood in the doorway of Laz's bedroom, staring at Guido's cage. How ironic that Sal Lucci, a man with dubious connections, would send his unholy parrot all the way from New Jersey to live with a Christian friend in Texas. Surely the Lord had a hand in this.

I looked at Guido, perplexed. Though beautiful on the outside, he certainly needed a lot of work on the inside. Could Laz handle it? Did he really have it in him to nurture our new fine-feathered friend?

"What are you thinking, little bird?" I asked. "Do you think you're ready for life in the Rossi household?"

Just then, Guido opened his beak and warbled out the first line of "That's Amore." I'd been hearing it all morning. How Uncle Laz had managed to teach the bird so much in such a short time, I couldn't say. I had my suspicions he'd done it just to torment Rosa. After all, there were only so many times a day you could hear a parrot squawk, "When the moon hits your eye like a big pizza pie" before snapping like a twig. Of course, after wrapping up his new song-and-dance number, Guido continued to add his "Go to the mattresses!" addendum, and then always threw in a round of faux machine gun fire. The bird had a real knack—I had to give it to him.

Laz had promised to "get this bird walking the straight and narrow in no time." And now, as I stood in his doorway, gazing at the brilliantly colored parrot, I almost thought it possible. As if to prove me wrong, the ornery bird let a string of curse words fly—words that had never before been used in the Rossi household. Well, with the exception of that one time when Uncle Laz hid in the broom closet and scared Aunt Rosa right out of her false teeth.

With a sigh, I turned and headed down the stairs, ready to get to work. Club Wed called, and I must answer.

For whatever reason, focusing on the wedding proved to be problematic. I wanted to think about D.J. About his beautiful eyes. About his lanky walk. About that mesmerizing voice, buff physique, tall stature, and winning smile. I did not want to work.

"Mama mia!" What a challenge! How would I ever get any work done?

At 10:00 in the morning, just an hour or so after arriving at the wedding facility, I faced my second coincidence of the day. It started with an unexpected phone call from someone with a 713 area code. Houston.

I answered with my most professional voice. "Thank you for calling Club Wed, Galveston Island's premiere wedding facility. This is Bella. How may I assist you?"

The bubbly female voice on the other end of the phone practically oozed excitement. "I'm Marian," she said. "And I've heard such wonderful things about you from my friend Sharlene Billings." The vivacious young woman went on to explain that her boyfriend, Rob, had just proposed, and they were interested in the medieval wedding package.

"We go to the Renaissance festival every year," she explained, "and I love dressing in the costumes. I've always dreamed of a Camelot wedding. And isn't it *so* cute that my name is Marian? Rob always calls me Maid Marian. Adorable, right? So, we just *have* to have a medieval ceremony. We've got our hearts set on it." She went on to gush over the amazing coincidence that had caused our paths to connect. She found it ironic that one of her best friends in the world had recommended a facility that happened to specialize in—of all things—medieval weddings!

So did I. Would this be a good time to mention that I'd never actually coordinated one before? That the idea had just sounded good on paper? That I'd advertised something with confidence, without ever actually having pulled one off?

Nah. Instead, I opened my book, and we set the plans in motion.

"Do you have a date yet?" I asked.

"Nothing solid, but we're looking at the first Saturday in October." She giggled, and I could almost envision the smile on her face. "Is that date available?"

"It is. Are we looking at a morning, afternoon, or evening event?"

"Oh, evening. I think a Renaissance-themed wedding will be beautiful in the moonlight."

"Perfect. Evening it is. Depending on the number of guests, you could get married indoors in the chapel or outside in the gazebo. Which would you prefer?"

She giggled again. "Neither, actually. We have a friend in the acting business, and he knows someone who works with set design. We'd like to build a castle, if you don't mind."

"B-build a castle?" I scribbled that down but could hardly believe it.

"If the property is big enough," she added.

Marian went on to describe the castle in detail, then began to tell me her dreams for the ceremony. The groomsmen (knights in shining armor) and the bridesmaids (ladies-in-waiting) would be dressed in appropriate medieval attire, supplied on the bride's end. And all music, decor, food, etc., would have that distinct Renaissance flavor. Just thinking about it got my already overactive imagination reeling. I could see the cake now—a towering castle with a moat. And the food! What fun Laz and Jenna would have, preparing an authentic medieval meal.

After swapping the necessary information, Marian promised to send a check to cover the cost of the deposit, and I thanked her profusely for the business. As we ended the call, I offered up a prayer of thanks to the Lord for another ironic confirmation that he did, in fact, see me as the right candidate for the job. I could almost hear the heavenly "bada-bing, bada-boom" now.

Around noon, my third coincidence reared its head. It started with what appeared to be a normal phone call from my brother Armando. I answered with my usual, "Hey, bro. What's up?"

"Just wanted to let you know that I'm headed home," he responded.

"Right. Tomorrow afternoon," I said. "To teach D.J. how to use the soundboard."

"No." Armando paused. "Coming home . . . for good. Just called Mama this morning and asked if I could have my old room back. Till I find my own place, I mean."

"Wow." Now, I must admit, a week ago I would have jumped up and down at this news. Back then I'd needed a deejay. But now, with the entrance of Dwayne Neeley Jr. into my life, God had filled that empty slot.

Or had he? How could I possibly tell my brother he couldn't have his old job back, especially when he was the only one who knew how to run the equipment?

"What happened to your girlfriend?" I asked. "What was her name? Julia?"

"She, um . . ." He groaned. "Do we have to talk about her?"

"Well, no. I guess not."

"Let's just say we had a little misunderstanding."

I knew all about Armando's misunderstandings. They usually involved some pretty young thing in a short skirt. Someone other than whomever he happened to be dating at the time.

"But weren't you working for Julia's father?" I asked. "I thought you loved your new job." Maybe, if I played my cards right, I could talk him into staying in Houston awhile longer, even with girlfriend #863 out of the picture.

"He fired me. See, there was this girl who worked in the office with me. She was always hitting on me . . ." He went on to tell a not-so-convincing tale of how he'd been falsely accused of romancing the wrong female. How it had all been a huge mistake. Not *his*, of course. He hadn't done anything wrong, naturally. But now that he'd been victimized in such a public and humiliating way, he felt it would be best to come back home to Galveston. To the family. No doubt he wanted the safety of his family nearby—so that when Julia's father showed up with a shotgun, he could hide behind the rest of us. Wouldn't be the first time.

Was it awful to admit I didn't want him to return so quickly? If he showed up now, it would spoil everything. But how could I tell him that without hurting his feelings? Looked like I had a few decisions to make—and quick. We ended the call, and I spent some time trying to collect my scattered thoughts related to Armando, D.J., and the upcoming wedding. Surely the Lord had an answer to this mess.

At 1:30 in the afternoon, I faced my fourth coincidence of the day. Thanks to a miscommunication with the eBay boot owner, I'd somehow bid on—and won—forty pairs of used cowboy boots. According to the congratulatory email I received, my payment of $800 plus tax had been charged to my Visa card, along with an additional ninety-eight dollars in expedited shipping charges. The boots, which currently belonged to a woman in Lubbock, Texas, would arrive tomorrow.

I must admit, I thought the email was spam. At first. But after a bit of scrambling on my part, the truth surfaced. There was no turning back. I was the proud owner of eighty cowboy boots. Sure, I could charge Sharlene's father for twenty of them, but who would pay for the rest once the credit card bill came in?

As I pondered this dilemma, the fifth coincidence of the day occurred. At exactly 2:15 in the afternoon, a power outage took out the electricity along Broadway. My computer screen fizzled to black, and the AC in the wedding facility came to a grinding halt.

"No way! Why now?" I moaned.

I tried to busy myself with phone calls and paperwork . . . for a while. But with the temperature rising, I could only stand to stay put so long. Frustrated, I finally called Jenna to see if the restaurant had been affected. The minute I heard the strains of "Volare" playing in the background, I realized they were still going strong.

Jenna greeted me in her usual chipper voice. "Thank you for calling Parma John's."

"Hey, girl. I—"

"Having a rough day? Need to lighten the load? Parma John's has a pizza that will lift your spirits without adding extra pounds. Order our Volare special—a light and airy thin-crust pizza made with low-fat mozzarella—and we'll throw in a complimentary Caesar salad, made with our homemade low-calorie dressing. Let the Volare special fill you up without weighing you down, for only $17.95."

Wow. There was clearly no power outage at Parma John's.

"Jenna—" I started.

Her squeal nearly deafened me. "Bella! I'm so glad you called. The strangest thing just happened." She went on to describe her most recent coincidence in detail—how Bubba had just called and would be arriving at the shop within minutes to talk more about the food prep for the wedding. How she'd hardly slept a wink since meeting him. How his coming to the shop must be a God-thing.

Bubba in Galveston two days in a row? Didn't he work with his father in Splendora?

Determined to prevent my best friend from making a rash mistake—à la Armando style—I made a quick decision to head down to Parma John's. So off I went to the land of low-fat, thin-crust pizza lover's delight—a land where blue-ribbon barbecue chefs and nearly engaged redheads pondered the what-ifs of ill-fated romance.

I walked in the door of the pizzeria and immediately started humming "Volare," which played overhead. Funny how I never got tired of the songs that went along with each day's special. Neither did the customers, for that matter. I'd caught many singing along. And now for the first time, I actually paid attention to the lyrics. Dean Martin, in that sultry voice of his, crooned something about flying away to the clouds to get away from the maddening crowds. Seemed appropriate, especially in light of the influx of people at Parma John's. Not that I wanted to escape, at least not yet. No, I'd come to save my friend from ruin.

Once again the song distracted me. I found myself smiling

as I heard "Just like birds of a feather, a rainbow together we'll find." My thoughts shifted at once to Guido. Then, just as easily, they swung to D.J. In spite of our differences, he and I *were* birds of a feather, and I felt sure we'd eventually find both the rainbow and the pot of gold at the end . . . especially if these coincidences kept up.

But first I had to figure out what his younger brother was doing spending so much time with my vulnerable best friend. I made my way to the counter, where Jenna stood bug-eyed across from Bubba, drinking in his every word. From the looks of things, she'd had one too many. The poor girl could hardly walk a straight line. I'd never seen her in such a state. Were she and Bubba two birds of a feather?

"Jenna tells me you two have been best friends since junior high," Bubba said, flashing a smile my way.

"Mm-hmm."

Instead of looking my way, Jenna continued to stare at him. "Bubba, I think that story you told me about your best friend in elementary school was so cute. Anyone would be lucky to have your friendship."

"Well, thanks." As he swallowed some soda, his cheeks turned crimson.

I settled onto a barstool near them, determined to get to the bottom of this. How did they know so much about each other?

I spent the next hour trying to figure that out. Turned out Bubba had spent nearly two hours at the restaurant already—most of that time gabbing with Jenna. And it looked like they still had a lot to talk about.

By the end of the conversation, I'd pretty much decided these two were destined to marry and have at least a dozen children. I only had to wonder if Bubba would sweep my best friend off to Splendora-land, where she would convert from the staid life of a Methodist to the somewhat more rambunctious independent charismatic. Would she raise a passel of children in the piney woods of east Texas? Would she return to the island occasionally to show off her brood all decked out in cowboy attire, clutching blue ribbons for hog calling from the Houston Livestock Show and Rodeo? If so, how would I adapt?

Overcome with the image, I forced myself to sing "Volare" to lift my spirits above the madness going on in my overactive imagination. What the Lord chose to do with Bubba and Jenna was his business, not mine. Mostly.

Coincidence number six proved to be one of the happiest of the day. My cell phone rang at 5:17, just as I headed out the door of Parma John's. I recognized D.J.'s voice right away.

"Hey, you!" I said, not even trying to disguise the joy in my voice. "What's up?"

"Well, hey Bella." The momentary silence that followed concerned me a little. "I, um, must've punched the wrong number. Meant to call Bubba."

Bubba. Bella. I could see how it could happen. But on a day like today, with so many other ironic things transpiring? Likely the Lord had guided D.J.'s finger to this heavenly misdial.

"My brother Nick and his wife Marcella invited Bubba to dinner," I said. Should I mention that they'd invited Jenna too? That Bubba and Jenna would probably be engaged by the night's end, the way things were going? That Jenna's poor boyfriend, who worked offshore, had no idea his fiancée-to-be had fallen head over heels for D.J.'s baby brother?

Nah. Better skip all that.

D.J. laughed. "Bubba's always had a knack for winning folks over. He's got a great personality."

He's not the only one in the Neeley family with an amazing personality.

"It's hard to believe we've only known him a couple of days," I said. *And harder still to remember I haven't known you much longer.*

Silence rose up between us, and then D.J. said those magic words, the words that caused me to believe this coincidence was almost too good to be anything other than divine intervention. "So, what are you doing tonight?"

"Who, me?" I played it cool. "Oh, just hanging out with the family, I guess. Maybe watching a DVD with Sophia. How come?"

"Well, I was thinking . . ." He went on to describe his plan. He could swing by and pick me up around seven. We could go to a great little steakhouse that had just opened on the seawall. One he'd actually played a role in building. Wow. The boy could grill a steak *and* build the restaurant to serve it in. Pretty impressive.

I agreed to be ready at seven. When I got home, Sophia, excited by my news that D.J. and I were going out, helped me choose an appropriate outfit. I settled on a gauzy teal blouse and snazzy dark jeans, which Rosa had lightly starched and creased. Sophia then loaned me her favorite necklace and earring ensemble and advised me on hair and makeup.

I finished at exactly 6:55 and stood in front of the mirror, gazing at my reflection. Though I normally questioned nearly everything about my appearance—my unruly curls, my skinny legs, my too-pointy nose, I had to admit she'd done a good job of transforming me.

Sophia stood back and whistled her approval. "You're gonna knock his socks off."

"Really?"

"Really." She gave me a warm hug and then whispered, "You deserve the best, Bella. You really do. That D.J.'s a keeper."

My heart swelled at her words of kindness. Now, if only we could locate a "keeper" for Sophia as well.

D.J. arrived at seven on the dot and stared at me as if he'd never seen me before. Perfect reaction. I'd sufficiently wowed him. And I found myself so wowed by his appearance in a dress shirt and dark slacks that I could hardly say hello without stumbling over the word.

My gaze shifted up to his handsome face, then up again.

"Wow, you've done something with your hair." The sandy-colored waves had been perfectly tamed.

"Yeah." He shrugged. "Thought it might make me more presentable."

I wanted to say, "You're more than presentable, regardless," but decided not to. Frankly, I was too distracted by his tan. The sun had kissed both his cheeks and the tip of his adorable nose. The coloring in his face accentuated his blue eyes. They drew me into their grasp and refused to release me. Until he took my hand in his and kissed it. Then I very nearly stopped breathing.

"You look beautiful today, Bella," he whispered.

I wanted to respond, but the words stuck in my throat. Did he really think my face matched my name?

We said our good-byes to the family and headed over to his massive Dodge 4x4. Its sheer size took my breath away. Seemed just right for a man with a presence as big as D.J.'s.

"Your chariot awaits!" he said.

I had to laugh, because his words reminded me of the upcoming medieval wedding. "Thank you, kind sir!"

I took his extended hand and tried to get into the oversized cab. Scrambling up inside proved to be difficult but not impossible. And once inside, I felt like the queen of the world. Or at least the queen of Galveston Island.

As we made our way down Broadway toward the seawall, I peered down at all of the other vehicles below. Riding in a truck this size was a real power trip. Reminded me again of the lyrics to "Volare"—the part about flying up to the clouds. Sitting here with my deejay cowboy next to me, I felt like I'd been transported above the madness, just as the song suggested. I was floating, flying, reeling. A girl could get used to this. In fact, as I peeked at D.J. out of the corner of my eye, I realized there were a great many things a girl could get used to.

"So, tell me about this place we're going to," I said.

He flashed a smile. "It's called the Prime Cut. It's a pretty high-end beef eatery. The guy who owns the place is an old friend of mine named Mark. He lives in Kingwood, not far from my parents in Splendora. He's determined to help Galveston get back on her feet and thought this new restaurant would be just the ticket."

"And you helped build it?"

"I did." D.J. grinned. "We wrapped up the job last month. Mark threw a great party to celebrate. I'm sorry you missed it."

"Me too."

"They've got the best steaks on the island," D.J. added. "You've got to trust me on this."

My mouth started watering right away. Suddenly I could hardly wait to get there.

Coincidence number seven truly caught me off-guard. D.J. and I had just ordered our steaks, and I sliced a big, juicy piece and popped it into my mouth. He chose that moment to tell a funny story about his brother, and somehow the chunk of steak went down the wrong way and lodged itself in my throat.

At first I didn't panic. Then, when I realized I couldn't force the piece up or down, I started that frantic wave that so often accompanies near-death choking experiences. The waiter came running, but D.J. nudged him out of the way. My cowboy hero pulled me out of my chair, and with the whole restaurant looking on, he performed the Heimlich maneuver with the precision of a trained EMT. The piece of steak dislodged immediately and shot across the room, landing in a woman's water glass. She jumped to her feet with a shriek and proceeded to pitch the glass from the table as if it were a snake, soaking the man across from her.

"I–I–I . . ." I tried to apologize, but words wouldn't come, at least not yet. Finally I managed a weak, "Sorry!"

After several gasping coughs on my part, the shaking kicked in. I thought for a second I might faint, but D.J. held me upright. Locked in his secure embrace, I didn't care that fifty-plus strangers stared at me as if I'd put on the show of the century. I'd lived through the incident. That was really all that mattered. Well, that, and the realization that God, in his amazingly unique way, had propelled me directly into D.J.'s waiting arms.

Not that I was blaming God for choking me, necessarily. No, I had to fault D.J. for that. He'd chosen the wrong moment to tell a funny story. But what a lovely coincidence.

Now, as I stared into his baby blues, the trembling in my body slowly dissipated. He drew me close and placed a gentle kiss on my forehead. For the first time, I noticed the tears in his eyes.

"You scared me to death," he whispered.

My deejay cowboy gazed at me with such tenderness, I thought my knees might buckle. Blame it on the lack of oxygen from nearly dying, but as D.J. leaned toward me to place a kiss sweeter than tiramisu on my lips, heaven and earth collided. I felt myself floating above the clouds once again, only this time I didn't want to return to earth. In fact, it didn't matter if my feet ever touched down again.

As the kiss intensified, I closed my eyes, given over to the passion of the moment. Who cared about the crowd? Who cared that I'd just made a fool of myself? All that mattered was this man, this moment. And in that moment, as I melted in his embrace, I'm pretty sure I heard a heavenly "bada-bing, bada-boom!" along with the stirring of angels' wings overhead.

And that's exactly when coincidence number eight occurred.

Just as D.J. and I came up for air, I caught a glimpse of someone familiar out of the corner of my eye.

Tony DeLuca . . . approaching with fire in his eyes.

12

Who's Sorry Now?

The morning after my run-in with Tony DeLuca, I received a UPS delivery—one that was destined to change my life forever. I'd never seen so many cowboy boots in my twenty-nine years on Planet Earth. And thanks to a glitch—the address on the Visa card being my home address and not the wedding facility—the boots arrived on the doorstep of the Rossi home. There would be no hiding this mistake from my very large and overly intrusive family.

Naturally, Pop and Joey were working in the yard, weeding the front flower gardens. Marcella had just dropped off Nick and the boys before heading to the restaurant to help Jenna, so the gang was all there. My brothers looked up, stunned, as Eugene, our regular UPS guy, started unloading the boxes. Marcella dropped off Nick, then headed to the restaurant to help Jenna. Deany-boy and Frankie were up to their usual tricks, tormenting the driver as he tried to unload the forty boxes. He took it all in stride . . . at first. However, after a few trips back and forth to the truck, I could tell his patience was wearing thin. I called for Rosa, who bribed the boys with an offer of Italian cream cake. They did not refuse.

Within seconds, I felt the cloud of curiosity settle over the Rossi clan. One by one they all joined me on the veranda to watch Eugene as he continued to unload his truck. The barrage of questions kicked in, but I fended them off. There would be plenty of time later to explain my little faux pas. For now, I simply nodded and smiled and acted as if I'd ordered all eighty boots on purpose.

Everyone looked on in a daze. To say the Rossis were unfamiliar with cowboy boots would be putting it mildly. Maybe my brothers had worn a pair or two over the years. I couldn't say. But the rest of us were boot virgins. We didn't know one brand from another. However, with the pictures on the front of most boxes, we could see the incoming product just fine. We saw black boots, brown boots, pink boots, and red boots. We saw boots with animal skins, boots with buckles, and boots with intricate detailing. We saw pointed-toed, square-toed, and rounded boots. We saw traditional Western boots in black, fancy rodeo boots in turquoise, and buckaroo boots in yellow and rust. I'm pretty sure I even saw a goatskin boot in the mix, and another hand-designed appliquéd model unlike anything I'd ever seen before.

More than anything else, though, I saw Eugene frazzled and exhausted. The afternoon heat caused beads of sweat to rise up on his forehead, but he continued on, as if bringing eighty boots to a family of wedding facility owners on Galveston Island was an everyday thing.

When Eugene finished—approximately fifteen minutes after arriving—Rosa brought him inside, as always, and offered him a large glass of iced tea and a slice of cake. He thanked her and even accepted a second glass of tea before heading off to his next delivery. After he left, we all stood in the front hallway, staring at the boxes.

"So, what are you going to do with all of these?" Uncle Laz turned to me with a worried look on his face. "You didn't buy them to wear, did you?"

"No. I, um . . . hmm. I'm going to use some of them for the wedding." Forcing my voice to sound more confident, I added, "Sharlene wants boots on the tables. For centerpieces." Hopefully that would be enough to satisfy them.

Wrong.

"Boots on the tables?" My mother's elevated eyebrows showed her take on the idea. "But there are only twenty tables, right? What will you do with the rest?" Her gaze shifted to the rows of boxes, and I could see her mentally counting them.

"Well . . ." I sighed. "Sharlene and Cody are getting married outside in the gazebo, so I'll use several for decoration. You know . . . around the perimeter? They'll be perfect."

"Hmm." Mama just shook her head. "I can't imagine it."

"I can see how you might use a few," Rosa said. "But what about the rest?"

When I shrugged, they all stared at me in abject silence. No doubt everyone in the Rossi clan thought I'd lost my mind. They'd given me Club Wed to run, and I'd turned it into a country-western theme park. How would I ever redeem myself from this fiasco? If I could've two-stepped out of the room, I would have done it right then and there. Instead, I stood in silence, trying to think of something brilliant to say.

Uncle Laz reached for a box that contained a pair of traditional Western boots. He opened it and gave a whistle. "These are really nice." Pulling one from the box, he added, "And they're just my size."

"Uncle Lazarro." I shook my head, hoping he'd take the hint.

He shrugged, then pushed the box back in place. "I'm just saying . . ."

"I've never worn cowboy boots before," Sophia admitted as she perused the boxes. "Have you?"

"Nope." I'd tried on a pair back in high school but found them hot and uncomfortable. Couldn't see what so many of my classmates saw in them, though they seemed to be all the rage in Texas.

"Don't see what all the fuss is about," Marcella agreed. "And some of these . . ." She picked up a box of orange and brown boots with a look of disgust on her face. "Well, they're just hideous. Who would wear something like this?"

"Right. I know." I shrugged.

"And some of these look like they've been worn before," Mama added, opening one of the more beat-up boxes for a peek inside.

"Yes. I bought them all secondhand."

She immediately dropped the box and stepped back as if a snake had bitten her.

A few minutes later I managed to convince everyone that I had things under control.

Rosa went off to finish cooking lunch, and Mama joined her, no doubt to talk about me behind my back. Likely she had a psychologist on speed dial. And who could blame her? Laz lingered with me a few minutes, looking in the various boxes, and Pop disappeared into the living room to watch television with the boys.

As I stared at the scene in front of me, I tried to figure out what to do. Sure, I'd sounded confident in front of the others. But was I?

Some of the boots really could be used as decor for the actual ceremony. I'd certainly ordered enough yellow roses to put together a few lovely boot-themed floral arrangements around the outside edges of the gazebo. And perhaps an idea for the rest would come after pondering the matter awhile. In the meantime, I decided to stack the boxes according to usability. Those appropriate for table centerpieces and/or other decorating on the left, everything else on the right.

I'd no sooner chosen the twenty boots for the reception than Rosa called out, *"Venite a mangiare."*

No one ever balked when the "come and eat" call went out. The boys rushed from the living room, almost knocking me down. As they plowed on ahead of me, I deliberately hung to the back, trying to work up the courage to talk to Armando alone. D.J. would arrive in a couple of hours, after all, ready to learn the soundboard. Could I convince my brother to give up the reins just this once? Perhaps if I played the "baby sister is crazy about a big, handsome cowboy" card, he might be swayed.

Hmm. Better wait until after he'd had some of Rosa's good home cooking.

We arrived in the kitchen, and Armando immediately took note of the birdcage in front of the big bay window. Rosa had covered it with a lace-trimmed cloth, but that didn't stop my curious brother from sneaking a peek inside. When he lifted the lace trim, Guido hollered out, "Wise guy!"

"We have a bird?" Armando dropped the cloth and stared at me.

I sighed. "We have a bird. If you want the details, ask Uncle Laz."

Armando went to do just that, and I turned to my aunt. "Rosa, what's up with that white fabric over the cage?"

"Ah." She nodded, her eyes narrowing to slits. "Prayer cloth."

"Prayer cloth?" Somehow I couldn't imagine Guido holding a prayer meeting inside the cage, so I lifted the edge of the lace and peeked inside. Immediately he released a string of expletives. I dropped the cloth back into place and shrugged.

"I took one of your great-grandmother's handkerchiefs to Father Espinosa, and he prayed over it," Rosa explained. "It's been blessed."

"A blessed handkerchief?"

She explained in fluent Italian her theory that the bird wouldn't dare commit a sin as long as he stayed underneath the covering of the blessed hankie. I lifted the edge again, and "Go to the mattresses!" rang out. I let the cloth fall back into place, and Guido grew silent.

Hmm. Seemed to be working. But how long could you keep a bird covered? And was he really feeling the effects of the hankie, or was he just scared of the dark? To test the theory once more, I lifted the edge of the lace. Guido hollered, "Wise guy!" Tossing the cloth back down, I noted his silence. I turned to my aunt, amazed. Maybe she was on to something here.

I felt a little like Guido as the family shared lunch together. I needed someone to pull up the corner of my protective covering so I'd have the courage to say what needed to be said to Armando. After the meal, as he, Pop, Nick, Joey, and Uncle Laz accompanied me to the courtyard area of Club Wed, I managed to catch his ear. Pulling him behind the others, I asked, "Hey . . . favor."

"Favor?" He stopped and looked at me. "What is it?"

"Remember I told you about D.J.?"

Armando smiled. "Yes. I heard the story from several different people, actually. I can't believe you actually fainted. I've certainly seen my share of swooning women, but no one's ever fainted on me before."

"Stop it." After slugging him in the arm, I continued. "Anyway, he's coming at two. I still haven't told him you're back."

"Why not?" When I didn't answer right away, Armando gave me a knowing look. "Aha. I see. Bella's in love."

I felt heat rise to my cheeks immediately. "Well, I wouldn't say it's love, exactly. I haven't even known him a week. But he's pretty amazing, Armando, and I want him to stick around. So, could you . . ."

"Back off? Disappear?"

"Not that exactly. Just make him feel . . ."

"Needed?" My brother gave me a warm smile, then slipped an arm around my shoulder. "I'll make him feel so needed, he'll think we can't do this without him."

I didn't say anything, but in my heart I wondered if I *could* pull off this wedding without D.J. He epitomized country-western to me. In fact, I'd probably never look at another cowboy boot without thinking of my sawdust-wearin', slow-drawlin' deejay.

"He's bringing a ton of country-western CDs," I said. "So you guys will have to decide which songs are appropriate for the reception. Sharlene's already given me a list of the main songs—for the father-daughter dance and that sort of thing. But the rest will be up to D.J. And you, of course."

"Of course," he echoed. Then he gave me a wink. "I'm a team player. Nothing to worry about here."

"Mm-hmm." Glancing at my watch, I gasped. Was it really ten after one? We had less than an hour to get the courtyard whipped into shape before the man who now captivated my thoughts arrived.

Pop and Laz put together a plan for the gazebo, which needed a fresh coat of paint. Nick, Joey, and Armando went to work on the mowing, edging, and so forth. I had to chuckle, watching the three of them together. There were never three more different brothers. Nick—all two-hundred-plus pounds of him, the stable but quirky fatherly figure. Joey—smaller, tattooed to the hilt, and gentle as a lamb. And Armando—the not-quite-responsible-yet romantic who tended to put his wants and wishes above those of others. I had to give it to the Lord—he'd done a remarkable job of putting every personality type in our family.

Determined to stay focused, I walked the aisle, trying to imagine how I might use some of the leftover cowboy boots to enhance the country-western ambiance. Hmm. Maybe a few along the edges of the gazebo. The rest . . . well, the rest I would keep packed away for a future date. No point in overwhelming the guests.

After a few minutes of pondering, I went to work helping Joey in the garden, pulling weeds. He told me in a hushed voice about a girl he'd met at the restaurant. Norah. From the shimmer in his eye, I had to conclude she must be something pretty special.

By the time 2:00 rolled around, I looked like a mess. I'd somehow backed into the wet paint and had a stripe across my back. And fifty minutes in the afternoon sun had me soaked to the bone. I could feel the makeup slipping down my face, and my wet hair stuck to the back of my neck. Pulling it back, I wound it in a knot atop my head. Still, that did nothing to counteract the wet puppy smell that now emanated from every pore.

And my shoes! My beautiful sandals were covered in grass clippings and mud. I'd just decided to make a quick trip to the house to clean up and change clothes when I heard the scrape of D.J.'s tires as he pulled into the driveway of Club Wed.

"Oh no." I couldn't possibly make it to the house without D.J. seeing me. Now what?

"What's wrong?" Armando looked my way, a crooked smile on his face. "Afraid this guy's going to see you for who you really are?"

"I just . . ."

"Listen, Bella." Nick drew near. "You need to let him see you like this. Trust me, if you marry him, he's going to see you in far worse shape." He dove into a story about Marcella's less-than-perfect appearance first thing in the morning, and I punched him.

"Who said anything about marrying him?" I gritted my teeth. "And besides, when I get married, I don't plan to look like this. Ever. Early morning, late at night, or anytime in between."

Apparently my brothers—now looking and sounding more like the three stooges—found great humor in that one. I felt pretty sure folks on the mainland heard their laughter.

D.J. chose that very moment to approach with a stack of CDs in hand. He took one look at me and grinned that crooked grin of his, the one that melted me like butter. "Now that's what I like to see." His gaze swept over me. "A girl who's not afraid to get her hands dirty."

My fears dissolved immediately, and I was transported back to our date at the Prime Cut, where I'd looked—or maybe just felt—like a million bucks. Before the choking incident, anyway. Seemed no matter how hard I tried, I still came off looking like a goober. Oh well.

Armando drew near and whispered in my ear, "So, this

is Prince Charming, eh?" then nudged me with his elbow. I jabbed him and then forced a smile. Better make introductions.

"D.J., this is my brother Armando."

"Oh yeah, the deejay, right?" I saw my cowboy's expression change right away. Was that disappointment in his eyes, or relief?

"I'm home, but, um . . ." Armando stumbled over his words. "I'm going to need a lot of help with this wedding Bella's coordinating. Don't know much about country music. And besides"—he slapped D.J. on the back—"you've got a great speaking voice. The guests will love that, so I'll just run the sound, and you can call the show. How's that?"

"Well . . ." D.J. removed his cap and ran his fingers through his hair. "I suppose that's fine. Just show me what to do and I'll do it. If you're sure."

"I'm sure." Armando gave him a confident nod.

I looked back and forth between my brothers and the man who'd so recently swept me off my feet. Looked like they were all the best of friends. So far, anyway. But if I knew my ornery brothers, the peace would last only so long. Before long they'd be up to tricks, and D.J. would be boot-scooting out of my life. Just like Craig Harrison, who dated me briefly my senior year of high school. And James Kirkpatrick, the guy I'd dated in college. They'd both left—not because of anything having to do with me personally, but because they found my family too . . . overwhelming. Only Tony had stuck around—too long, actually.

I swallowed hard. The very thought of losing D.J. brought the sting of tears to my eyes. As I gazed up at him, I thought, *I've fallen . . . and I can't get up.* Not that I wanted to. No, I wanted to hide under the prayer cloth I'd knitted over my heart and force the real world to go away forever. *Stop it, Bella. Don't let your anxieties get the best of you.*

Pushing aside all worries about how I looked or smelled, I gave D.J. a reassuring smile, then led him inside the wedding facility to the reception hall. Armando tagged along on our heels, making wisecracks in my ear, just like he used to do when we were kids. The ribbing went on until we arrived at the soundboard, where my brother kicked into deejay gear. He turned on the system, reached for a microphone, and took the stack of CDs from D.J.'s hand. "Once we decide what songs we're going to use that night, I'll turn them into MP3 files. Put them in one folder in the right order."

"Sounds great. But hold that thought." I headed off to my office for a notepad and a pen. As I passed by the mirror in the foyer, I did a double take at my reflection. Man. I needed a bath. And a fresh coat of makeup. And a new outfit. And a trip to the hair salon.

On the other hand, D.J. had already seen me looking and smelling like this and hadn't seemed to mind. Knowing that put me more at ease than ever. I couldn't help but think of how different D.J. was from Tony in that respect. Tony would have sent me to the shower at first whiff.

After a quick stop in my office, I returned to the reception hall with my notepad in hand, ready to get down to business. I found the guys seated together in front of the soundboard, talking about the ins and outs of the equipment. D.J. had that sort of paralyzed look on his face that came when you were venturing into uncharted territory.

As I pulled over a chair and sat near him, I tried to look relaxed. Excited, even. "You're gonna be great at this. I can feel it in my gut." My confident smile would surely win him over.

"Really?" He gazed at me with deep worry lines between his brows. "Cause all I feel in my gut is nausea."

"Let's start at the top." Armando turned to D.J. with a confident nod. "Let's get this show on the road." At that point, my brother—God bless him—helped us lay out the order of events, and even gave D.J. a few key lines to memorize to help the evening transition more smoothly from one thing to another. They went over everything—introducing the bride and groom as they made their entrance, passing the microphone to the pastor to pray over the meal, setting up the couple's first dance together as husband and wife, the father-daughter dance, and so on.

Finally the moment came for D.J. to take the microphone. I could hear the nerves in his voice at first, but after a few minutes, he sounded like himself. Only better. Something about that deep voice amplified through the sound system made my palms sweat. Sure, he was working off a script now, but knowing him, he'd get the lines down before the big event.

Eventually convinced he could actually pull this off, D.J. relinquished the microphone to my brother. We spent the rest of the afternoon doing something I'd never envisioned myself doing—listening to country-western music. I had to admit, the songs—at least the ones D.J. suggested—weren't as stereotypical as I'd imagined. In fact, there wasn't one song in the bunch about people getting drunk and cheating on each other. Looked like my cowboy had discriminating taste. Good taste, even.

As the guys shifted from one CD to another, I leaned back in my chair, notepad and pen in hand. Every time we would hear a song that might work for the reception, I scribbled down the title. Before long, we had over two hours' worth of music picked out. I could hardly believe it. A couple of the songs had such a great rhythm, I could barely sit still. Surely the ballroom floor would come alive with two-steppers when those were played. Several of the other songs were tender and filled with words of love. I closed my eyes and let the words sink in. In my mind's eye, I could see myself in D.J.'s arms, dancing the night away.

Who knew? I'd not only fallen for a cowboy, I'd fallen for his country-western music, to boot. Pun intended. Maybe I'd just never given it a chance before. Funny.

Looking at D.J., I realized there were a lot of things I'd never given a chance before.

A sigh rose up as I imagined myself, like Guido, peering out of the bars of my far-too-small cage. Lifting the cloth. Peeking out at the world around me. Discovering new and somewhat frightening worlds. Just as quickly, that old gripping sensation took hold of my heart. I wanted to get beyond my fears of failing—fears that went all the way back to high school. Who cared if I couldn't sing? Or act. Or play tennis. Did it really matter that I'd failed in my one attempt to run for office? Or that my name didn't match my face? Or that my boyfriends found my family overwhelming?

No, those things were behind me. Now, I wanted to walk on water. Wanted to dance to a country song. Wanted to lift my arms and praise! But could I? I'd lived one way for so long, I could hardly imagine anything else.

As another twangy tune filled the room, D.J. looked my way. I couldn't quite read the expression on his face. Maybe he could hear my thoughts. *Can you learn to love me, just as I am? With my hair in a ponytail? With no makeup on? With all of my flaws?*

He flashed the warmest smile I'd ever seen, and my heart

felt comforted. Maybe D.J. saw my insecurities, my fears. Maybe he knew God still had a lot of work to do in my life before I'd be good girlfriend material.

Or maybe, just maybe, he saw beyond all that and simply wanted to flirt with the wedding coordinator instead of rehearse for the big night.

I did my best to relax . . . and let him.

13

Walk on By

On Monday morning I awoke with a splitting headache. In spite of the pain, work beckoned, so I dressed, haphazardly slapped on a bit of makeup, and headed next door to Club Wed. I could feel the bags under my eyes weighing me down. They, like my heart, felt the pull of gravity. On the way, I sipped a cup of coffee, my idea of a nutritious breakfast. I'd be hard-pressed to find anyone in the Rossi family to disagree.

As I made my way across the manicured lawn, I pondered the words from yesterday's sermon. Reverend Woodson's topic du jour—"Walking the Walk"—still had me reeling. His words about authentic faith had painted me into a proverbial corner. Specifically, when he said, "Bella Rossi, you need to *be* who you say you are, and *do* what you say you're going to do," guilt had risen up inside me like a mound of foam on top of one of Uncle Laz's famed lattes. I had to wonder if the Lord above had flashed a heavenly spotlight over my head and whispered, "Preach this sermon just for her. She's not going to get the message otherwise."

Okay, so the good reverend hadn't really called me by name in front of the congregation, but he might as well have. Certainly felt like his words were directed at me, anyway, and they'd cut me to the core.

But what could I do about it? Something about being put on the spot—even internally—forced me to reexamine my motives and actions of late. Sure, I'd told people I was a woman of faith who, with God's help, could whip the wedding facility into shape in no time. But I hadn't been living it. I'd managed to convince others I had it all together, but on the inside I quivered like a half-baked cheesecake.

My thoughts drifted back to that life-altering sermon. What struck me as ironic—beyond the pastor's passionate words—was something he'd done at the end of the message. He'd lifted the hem of his pants and exclaimed, "These boots are made for walkin'!"

Now, who knew Reverend Woodson wore cowboy boots? You could've heard a pin drop in the congregation at that revelation—at least in the Rossi section. Just one more coincidence to add to my ever-growing list.

And now, thanks to the soul-jarring sermon, I had boots on the brain. Eighty of them, to be precise. I could just see it now. After my untimely demise—likely caused by stress related to this wedding—my tombstone would read, BELLA ROSSI, KIND BUT DENSE—SHE HAD MORE BOOTS THAN COMMON SENSE.

It was time to put my money where my mouth was. To stop pretending I had it all together when I really didn't. Time to be real. Genuine. I'd start by confessing the eBay debacle to my father. Surely he could help me come up with a plan. Maybe I could turn around and resell the excess boots, redeeming the money. Maybe I could even make a little extra cash in the process. Hopefully before the Visa bill arrived.

Not that I really had time to be buying or selling anything at the moment. No, I needed to focus on Sharlene and Cody's big day, just five days from now. I stared at the wedding facility and sighed. If only the weight of the world didn't rest on my shoulders. If only my parents could take their European vacation without wondering if I'd drive the family business into the ground. If only . . .

Pushing the thoughts away, I remembered Uncle Laz's words: "Everything hinges on the Lord. Don't forget that! He is the potter and you are the clay."

Funny. The only thing that felt like clay this morning was my feet. I stared down at them and tried to imagine what they'd look like with boots wrapped around them.

Nope. Couldn't fathom it.

I forced my attention back to the project at hand. A country-western themed wedding. A boot-scootin' heyday. This morning I needed to finalize plans with Joey (who would serve as photographer), double-check the guest list, and take care of a few other details.

But first things first. As I entered the wedding facility, I noticed the postman had already dropped off the mail. I glanced through the envelopes, perplexed when I found a tiny Priority package addressed to Lazarro Rossi. The return name was Bro Pockets, with an address in Shreveport, Louisiana. Why had it been delivered to the wedding facility instead of next door or the restaurant? An accident . . . or did Laz have something to hide?

I picked up my cell phone and gave him a call. Upon hearing of the delivery, he came rushing over—rushing being a relative term. Laz moved pretty slowly these days, particularly if there were stairs involved. He eventually joined me in the office of Club Wed, where he took the package in his hands and tried to sneak out the door before I could begin my first round of questioning.

"Wait." I made it to the door before him and closed it so he couldn't make his intended getaway. "What's the big secret? What's in the package?"

His cheeks reddened. "Oh, nothing."

"Uncle Laz . . ."

He sighed, then dropped into a chair. "Forget about it. It's really not that big of a deal. Nothing to get all worked up about."

"Mm-hmm." I took my seat and waited. "'Fess up. Who's Bro Pockets?"

"Bro Pockets?" He looked at the return address label as if trying to make sense of it, and then said, "Oh, I see. They've abbreviated it. That's *Brother*. Brother Pockets."

"Brother Pockets?" I racked my brain to figure out why that sounded so familiar. Suddenly it came to me. "Wait a minute. You don't mean Brother *Phillip* Pockets, the televangelist scam artist, do you?"

"Well, I—"

"Tell me you didn't send that man any of your hard-earned money." I knew enough about the guy to know he'd scammed thousands of elderly folks out of their pensions, all in the name of religion. Jenna and I had joked about his "fill up pockets" name, to be sure. But I never dreamed anyone in my family would succumb to his twisted tactics.

Laz shrugged and shifted the package from one hand to the other.

"Uncle Lazarro." I placed my hands on my hips and stared him down. "What have you done?"

He released a sigh. "Look, I'm worried about Sal, that's all. And Guido too."

"Guido?" Somehow I'd never figured him to play a role in this story.

"I'm going to make a new bird of him. Or, rather, the Lord is going to make a new bird of him."

"Laz, what in the world are you talking about?"

My uncle leaned forward with tears in his eyes. "Sal never wanted anything to do with the gospel before his stroke. Never. And trust me, I tried to approach the subject from every conceivable angle. Ran into a brick wall every single time. But now he's entrusted Guido to me. I have no idea how long I'll have the little guy, but I truly believe the Lord has given me an opportunity to teach an old bird some new tricks."

"Such as . . ."

"I figure if I can get him to give up his old ways—let go of the bad language, forget about the questionable phrases, and so forth—then I can retrain him. I'll teach him a few Scripture verses and a couple of praise choruses before I have to send him back to Sal. Get it? Then Guido can do the work of winning my old friend to the Lord." Laz leaned back in his chair, a satisfied look on his face.

"So Guido is going to become a missionary? You're going to send him back to Atlantic City to witness to Sal?" I leaned back in my seat, ready to hear this explanation.

"Exactly. After I've anointed him with Brother Pockets's miracle-working oil." Laz held up the package. "When I called to place the order, one of the telephone prayer partners joined me in a prayer of agreement."

"I see. And just how much did you pay for this oil?" I stared at the little package in stunned disbelief.

My uncle's gaze shifted downward. "Well . . ."

"Uncle Laz."

"Okay, look. I paid extra for the double anointing package. It's concentrated. Made by monks who live in a monastery in a remote mountainous region."

"Of Shreveport?"

"Yes. The sole purpose of their order is to grow the olives, then produce the oil using the same process in the Old Testament. Afterward they pray over every bottle individually before it's sent out. Isn't that an amazing story?"

"To say the least." I shook my head. "How much?"

"What?"

"How much did you spend on the oil?" I bit my lip, preparing myself for his answer.

"Well . . . $49.95 plus overnight shipping."

"Uncle Laz!" I ripped open the package and stared at the tiny bottle inside. "Surely you jest." I opened the bottle, poured out a few drops, and sniffed. Immediately I regretted it. "This isn't olive oil. Look at the color. It's corn oil with some kind of cheap perfume in it." I let out a sneeze, and my eyes filled with tears. Unable to handle the overwhelming smell, I closed the bottle and held it out to my uncle. "It reeks. What were you thinking?"

A lone tear trickled out of the corner of my uncle's right eye and rolled down his wrinkled cheek. He ran his fingers through thinning gray hair, then rose to his feet, using his cane. "I was thinking that my friend is going to die without knowing the Lord if I don't do something." He reached a trembling hand my way and snatched the bottle from me before pacing the floor. "Maybe this wasn't the best idea. I don't know. Sounded pretty good at the time. I just know I have to do something. And what can it hurt? I'll pray with Guido tonight before bed. Anoint him head to toe—er, beak to claw."

"And tomorrow he'll be a changed bird?"

"Maybe. Stranger things have happened."

"Mm-hmm." I happened to glance down at my uncle's feet as he paced, noticing, for the first time, a familiar pair of cowboy boots. "Hey." I looked up at him. "Where did you get those?"

"Oh, um, these? I, um, I've had them for a while now."

"Since Saturday, perhaps?"

"Oh, I, well . . ." He squirmed, and I noticed the tips of his ears turn red. "I found them . . ."

"In the front hall?"

His gaze shifted. "Maybe."

"You're not going to pull that 'possession is nine-tenths of the law' thing, are you?" I asked. "'Cause if you are . . ."

He waved a hand in the air. "I just thought it would be fun to try them on. I've never worn cowboy boots before. I'll give them back, I promise."

"Before the wedding?"

"Of course. Don't you trust your old Uncle Laz?"

I glanced at the bottle of anointing oil and sighed as I contemplated my rebuttal. On the other hand, how could I—a girl who'd accidentally ordered eighty cowboy boots from a total stranger—possibly judge my uncle for a seemingly unreasonable purchase? His heart was in the right place, after all.

"Have a look at this." He lifted his pants leg to reveal an intricate design on the back of the boot. "These boots have got to be worth a pretty penny. How much did you pay for them?"

"Twenty bucks." I stared a bit closer, realizing the truth. The boots were beautifully made. Great quality. Exquisite leather detailing. I'd never seen anything quite like them. Had heaven just dropped an unexpected gift in our laps?

"Hang on a second." I reached down and lifted the boot, looking for the name of the manufacturer on the bottom. Lanciotti. The boots were made in Italy? Another coincidence? I promised myself I'd look up the name on the Internet when things slowed down.

Laz glanced at his watch and gasped. "Ten thirty? Jenna's probably wondering where I am. Gotta go." He gave me a half smile, snatched his package from Brother Pockets, and headed toward the door. At the last minute, he turned back. With tears in his eyes, he whispered, "Keep praying for Sal, Bella. *Finché c'è vita c'è speranza.*"

I looked at him with the sting of tears in my eyes and echoed, "As long as there is life, there is hope." Somehow just speaking the words put everything in perspective. This wasn't about Brother Pockets or a parrot. This was about Uncle Laz and his good friend. This was about moving Sal toward the same life-changing encounter with God my uncle had experienced. Minus the bus, of course.

Laz gave me a wink, then headed home, anointing oil in hand. I had a feeling I'd be hearing more about Guido later, and I also felt sure the whole Rossi house would reek of cheap perfume before day's end.

I could fault Uncle Laz on a number of things, but one thing was for sure—he certainly understood what it meant to be an authentic Christian. His boots—albeit stolen from the front hallway—were made for walkin'. He'd made that plain. In fact, I imagined he'd be willing to walk all the way to Atlantic City if he thought it would help Salvadore Lucci find the Lord.

I felt ashamed when I realized I'd questioned my uncle's actions. On the other hand, could he really rehabilitate a cantankerous parrot and turn him into an evangelist? Only time would tell.

In the meantime, I had a few projects of my own to tend to. Determined to "walk the walk," I turned back to the wedding plans.

14

Pennies from Heaven

On Tuesday afternoon, as the south Texas temperature climbed into the upper nineties, the air conditioner at the wedding facility went on the fritz. I tried to reach Mama, who was up at the Opera House, putting together programs for an upcoming performance. Nothing new there. She'd been caught up in the world of opera ever since I could remember.

When Mama didn't answer, I tried Rosa. Her voice sounded strained as she whispered, "Hello?"

"Aunt Rosa, it's Bella. I—"

"Bella, I can't talk right now. I'm at St. Patrick's. We're in the middle of a Bible study on the epistle of James."

"Oh, sorry, I just wanted to—" I never got to finish. She hung up on me.

I groaned, then snapped my phone shut while I tried to figure out what to do. And though I hesitated to do it, I eventually telephoned my father, interrupting his fishing trip with Deany-boy and Frankie.

"Pop, I hate to interrupt, but—"

"Bella, hang on! I've got a live one on the line. Give me a minute to reel her in!" His voice faded, then I heard him holler out something to the boys about fetching a net. He returned to the phone moments later, breathless but happy. "It's a redfish, Bella! She's a beauty! Looks like we're having fish for dinner."

"That's great, but—"

"What do you think, boys?" I could tell he'd turned his attention back to Deany-boy and Frankie. "Grilled or blackened?"

Their excited voices rose and fell as the signal on the phone cut in and out. I groaned. At this rate, we'd never get the AC fixed. "Pop, I need you." After a long pause, I hollered, "Pop!"

He finally came back on the line. "What is it, Bella Bambina? What does my girl need?"

I explained the air conditioning dilemma, and he agreed to call a repairman and get back with me. Half an hour later, he called back to let me know the repairman—a guy named Pete—couldn't come until tomorrow.

I didn't mind. Not really. But I had to get out of the building before the heat fried my few remaining brain cells. Because I had a few wedding-related items to pick up at Walmart on the seawall, I headed off for some time alone.

The traffic on Broadway was more troublesome than usual. Tourist season was at its peak, after all. And when I reached the seawall, the situation did not improve. Not that I really minded. No, with the windows down and the salty breeze in my face, I felt at home, traffic or no traffic.

A thousand things rolled through my brain as I headed west toward Walmart. I found myself thanking God, not just for my quirky family and my new love interest, but for Galveston Island, my home. Well, my home since New Jersey.

Though I rarely talked about it, I loved just about everything to do with living on the island. In spite of her many storms, she was a survivor. I could relate to her tenacity, her unwavering spirit. And the people! Seemed no matter how many times they faced the ravages of the sea, they returned to rebuild. Talk about backbone!

I gazed out across the waters, taken in by the waves. How calm they seemed now, but how quickly they could be riled up. On a peaceful day like today, I could almost envision moonlit strolls on the beach. The misty breeze off the gulf in the morning. The seagulls, white with gray wings, as they dove into the water for bits of food. The sound of tourists' voices as they chased the shallow waves along the shoreline. The majestic colors of the sun setting over the water.

More than anything, I loved the pull of the waves. They did their usual back-and-forth thing, day in and day out. Sometimes I felt the pull of the sea more than I admitted. I knew what it felt like to be tugged back and forth, and there were times I wanted to just release myself to the unknown, to allow something new and exciting to pull me to an unknown place. That's why running the wedding facility got under my skin so much. Organizing weddings . . . well, that was my "unknown place," and I loved it.

I passed the condominiums at 61st and the seawall where D.J. lived and tried to imagine what his place looked like. Had he chosen country-western decor? Was it a typical bachelor pad with black leather sofas and empty walls? At the rate things were going—both of us so busy—I'd never find out.

Since our meeting on Saturday with Armando, we'd only had snatches of conversations by phone. Was it possible to miss someone I'd known only a week?

As if to remind myself he was more than just a figment of my overactive imagination, I reflected on his kiss that night at the steak house. Oh, what sweetness! I'd never known such a fireworks moment . . . until Tony had walked in on us. Then we'd experienced fireworks of a completely different kind.

Not that it mattered. I could handle Tony's glares and snide remarks. With D.J.'s arms wrapped around me, I'd felt safe, secure. I'd also felt completely comfortable—a fact that still surprised me, in light of the fact that we barely knew each other. I wanted to relish that comfort and yet step out into the vast unknown of this new relationship all at the same time.

As I drove, I glanced to my left. The mighty Gulf of Mexico beckoned. Tourists—the bread and butter of Galveston Island—lined the beaches, and their colorful umbrellas dotted the beige sand. How long had it been since I'd been out in the water? Seemed strange to live on an island surrounded by water on every side and never venture out into it. People drove all the way from north Texas and beyond to visit my hometown. Why couldn't I take a few minutes and let the waves toss me to and fro?

Oh yeah. Because I was too busy running a wedding facility. And planning for a country-western themed wedding. And boot shopping. And falling in love.

Ah, love! I chewed on that idea as I pulled my SUV into the parking lot of Walmart. Leaning my head back against the seat, I closed my eyes and thanked God for the cowboy he'd dropped into my life. What an unexpected but wonderful surprise.

My cell phone rang, startling me. My mother spoke with

such emotion, I hardly recognized her voice. "Bella, the neighbors are at it again."

"What?" I sat up straight. "The Burtons?"

"Yes."

"What've they done?"

"When I arrived home a few minutes ago, I found a letter typed on legal stationary taped to our front door."

"What?"

"Yes, and it was a very firm letter, demanding the return of the skateboard. It's really specific about what will happen if we don't. They're going to file a lawsuit."

"A lawsuit? What kind? That's ludicrous!"

"I don't know, but the letter threatened to sue us for every penny we're worth. We could end up in court, Bella. We could lose our home, the wedding facility—everything."

She shared her thoughts on what this could ultimately mean for our family, and I trembled with anger. "They don't stand a chance, Mama. The kid was on our property, plain and simple." After a few seconds, I added, "But don't you think Rosa's had enough now, anyway? Maybe she can just take the skateboard back across the street and they'll come to their senses. Give back Pop's basketball."

"I wish." Mama shared Rosa's thoughts—that the Burtons were just bluffing. I hoped she was right.

As I hung up the phone, anticipation hovered over me like the morning fog. I hated to see my mom so worked up, especially now, just before the big day. I headed into Walmart and made my purchases, pondering the Burtons and their threats. What could I do, if anything, to hold them at bay until after the wedding?

At 3:45 I wrapped up my business on the west end of the island and headed to Parma John's. Laz had purchased the briskets for the wedding and wanted me to have a look-see. I also needed to chat with Jenna about several other things related to the menu—the appetizers and the side dishes, to be precise. I wanted to make sure she had a handle on everything. I couldn't shake the overwhelming feeling that something might go wrong. Was I capable of pulling off an event-free event? Probably not. But with the Lord on my side, I would give it my best shot.

I entered Parma John's to the sound of "Pennies from Heaven." I knew the song well. Laz had come up with the Tuesday meatball pizza special, stating that meatballs had always been his pennies from heaven. They were, after all, round in shape and had served to fill his pockets with real coins.

Locating Laz and Jenna proved more difficult than I'd expected. I found my uncle in the freezer, his teeth chattering as he took inventory of his meat supply. Jenna, it turned out, had called in sick. I'd have to check on her later. In the meantime, Uncle Laz agreed to visit with me about the wedding details, even Jenna's part.

Over the next hour or so, he and I put together a detailed plan of how the wedding reception would go. Bubba would bring his smoker from Splendora and start cooking the briskets on the morning of the wedding. He and Laz would create an authentic outdoor fire pit, hanging the big pot of beans over it to cook. Bubba had assured me his mama's recipe for southwestern beans would knock my socks off. Jenna had agreed to put together the potato salad as well as a host of barbecue-themed appetizers. Rosa would bake and decorate the wedding cake, and everyone would meet at the wedding facility midafternoon, in plenty of time to set up before the 7:00 event.

Funny, sitting next to Uncle Laz, listening to the calm in his voice, I almost felt we might actually pull this thing off. Almost.

By the time we wrapped up our conversation, I found myself hungrier than ever. Thankfully, Laz picked up on my hints for food and ordered up a meatball pizza on the spot.

I'd just shoveled the first piece into my mouth when a familiar voice rang out behind me. I turned—pizza sauce smearing across my left cheek—to see D.J. standing beside me.

"Here. Let me get that for you." My handsome cowboy reached for a napkin and wiped my cheek, his eyes sparkling all the while.

I swallowed the mouthful of pizza and stared at him, overcome with joy. "Hey. I didn't expect to see you today."

"Same here. I just stopped by to pass on some information from Bubba about the barbecue. Sure didn't know you'd be here. I would've stopped off at my place and showered first."

"Why?" Sure, the boy had sawdust in his hair and reeked after too much time in the sun, but how could I argue with perfection?

Just then, Laz's booming voice rang out in a forced twang. "Well, hello, cowboy. What brings you down here to our neck of the woods?" Somehow the twang-twang just didn't work coming from an elderly Italian man. Still, I had to give my uncle credit for trying.

D.J. stuck out his hand. "I'm here to talk to a man about a barbecue. Do you have a few minutes?"

"For you? Anytime!" Uncle Laz gestured for D.J. to sit at a nearby table, then started to join him, but not before he lifted the hem of his pants and showed off his new boots. "What do you think of these, cowboy? Not bad, eh?"

D.J. let out a whistle. "Man. Where in the world did you get those?" His eyes widened. "I've seen 'em in pictures, sure, but never in person. Can't believe you're wearing them to work."

Laz's bushy eyebrows nearly joined in the center. "Wearing them to work? Why shouldn't I?"

I tried to play it cool, but my insides started to sweat. "You've seen boots like that before?"

"Have I!" D.J. laughed. "You're funny, Bella. Everyone has seen Lanciottis. They're the most expensive boots on the market. A new pair costs upward of eight thousand dollars." He turned to my uncle again. "And with the detailing on yours, I'd say even more than that. Not that I'm trying to be nosy."

"W-what?" I managed. This had to be some sort of joke. Either that, or the boots on Uncle Laz's feet were knock-offs. Surely.

D.J. scrutinized my uncle's feet. "Yep. These are crocodile. I've only seen a few in my life, but none like these. Leastways, not in person. At the rodeo we sometimes catch a glimpse of a Lanciotti, but not in this price range."

I'd seen my uncle shaken before, but nothing like this. With the help of his cane, he staggered to the chair opposite D.J. and took a seat. The boots came off immediately.

"What are you doing?" my stunned hunk-of-a-deejay asked.

"Getting rid of the evidence." Uncle Laz shoved the boots my way. "The Lord isn't going to answer my prayers if I'm wearing stolen boots. Take them back, Bella. I don't want 'em."

I couldn't help pondering the fact that he'd been willing to wear twenty-dollar stolen boots. Just not expensive ones?

Still, there I stood in Parma John's, holding eight thousand dollar boots in my hand. Boots I'd purchased for a song on eBay. I quickly explained how and where I'd acquired them to D.J., and he let out a whistle.

"Has to be a mistake. Let me check the imprint on the bottom." We leaned in closer and read the word LANCIOTTI aloud. "They're the real thing all right." D.J. put the boots on a chair, and we all stared at them as if they'd grown horns.

"So now what?" I asked.

"Possession is nine-tenths of the law," Joey said as he passed by. "You could sell them and make a lot of money. That's what I'd do."

I had to admit, the idea had flitted through my mind, if only briefly. I could earn enough off one pair of boots to pay the Visa bill, and then some. Still, if these boots were the real thing—if they were worth thousands of dollars—I could no more sell them than Aunt Rosa could give up cooking. My gut told me I needed to contact the owner to let her know of the dilemma. Surely she would rejoice at the news. And even though I'd be losing a bundle of money, my conscience would be eased. I'd sleep better. Hopefully.

As we pondered this startling news, a string of curse words rang out from the kitchen. D.J. looked that direction, a stunned look on his face. "What in the world?"

"Wasn't me!" Nick stuck his head through the window and groaned. "And if you want the truth, I'm getting sick and tired of taking the blame for Guido's sins." My brother went off on a tangent, talking about Uncle Laz's attempts to lead the ornery parrot down the straight and narrow.

When Nick's conversation lapsed, D.J. looked my way, confusion in his eyes. Clearly he'd missed a few key points, so I decided to fill him in.

"Uncle Laz ordered anointing oil from the televangelist Phillip Pockets."

"Brother Pickpocket?" D.J. took our laughter in stride as he added, "That's what Pastor Higley calls him. He's warned everyone in the congregation to stay as far away from that guy as possible. Honestly, anyone who would scam others in the name of Christianity . . ." D.J. dove into a lengthy dissertation about the evils of leading the flock astray.

"Well, I can't judge the man," Laz said, "but his oil didn't exactly have the desired effect, so I'm writing a letter of complaint to the monks in Shreveport."

"Wait. What happened?" D.J. shook his head, clearly confused.

"I anointed Guido beak to claw, but he, um . . ." Uncle Laz's cheeks reddened.

"Turns out the parrot is allergic to the perfume in the oil," I explained.

"Yikes." A look of compassion came over D.J.'s face. "Do I even want to know what happened next?"

"I had to call the vet." Laz sighed. "Poor little guy was dropping feathers all over the place."

"He's on an antihistamine now, so that helps," I explained. "But it'll be a long time before Guido forgives us for what we've done to him. And with him missing so many feathers, he's a bit odd-looking."

My uncle shrugged. "I just can't give up on him," he said. "To do so would be to give up on Sal, and I'll never do that. Not till he comes to know the Lord." His eyes filled with tears.

"I think you're amazing." D.J. nodded in my uncle's direction. "It's admirable to hear you're going to such efforts to lead someone to the Lord. I think we all have a lot to learn from you."

A holy hush fell over our little group as we pondered his words. In spite of Laz's unique attempts, his heart was in the right place.

"I just hope Guido's feathers grow back before I have to ship him home to Sal." Laz rose to his bootless feet and made his way back to the kitchen. "Otherwise he's liable to send someone to Galveston to pluck a few of my feathers. So keep those prayers coming!" My uncle disappeared into the back.

D. J. turned my way with a smile. "Sounds like I've missed a lot over the past couple of days." He reached to brush a loose hair from my face, and I smiled at his touch. His hand lingered a moment, and he gazed into my eyes. In that moment, everything else faded away. Oh, I vaguely heard "Pennies from Heaven" playing in the background and heard the voices of the customers. But all I saw—all I ever wanted to see from this point forward—was the love pouring from D. J.'s eyes. Startled by this revelation, I froze in my tracks.

D. J.'s hand cupped my cheek, and he leaned in to kiss the tip of my nose.

"I saw that," Joey said as he passed by again. "Watch yourselves, kiddos. No PDA."

"PDA?" D. J.'s brow wrinkled as he asked, "What's that?"

"Public displays of affection," I explained. "In our family, there's no PDA till you're married. Or at least engaged." Almost immediately I realized what I'd said. I wanted to slap a hand over my mouth for speaking the word aloud. Hopefully D. J. wouldn't see that as some sort of signal that he needed to drop to one knee and offer me a ring. From the look in his eyes, he might be willing to do so at any time.

"So, um . . . let's go back to talking about the bird before I get myself in trouble with your brothers. Tell me more about Guido."

"Well, he's loopier now more than ever since he's been drugged," I said. "Flying into things and acting even more peculiar than before, if that's possible. That's why he's here today. Laz wanted to keep a close eye on him."

"Poor Guido."

"Yeah. Even Rosa's sympathetic to the cause. I caught her talking to him. And she prays over him too, you know."

"Oh?"

"Yeah, it's funny." I leaned in to whisper the rest. "This is the first time I've actually seen Laz and Rosa work together on a project. Neither will admit it to the other, but they're both on the same team on this one. They'll figure it out soon enough. And who knows . . . maybe Guido will give up his evil ways."

"Turn over a new feather?" D.J. laughed.

I shrugged. "Maybe. Stranger things have happened."

"Yes, stranger things have happened." The light in his eyes made up for the sudden silence. I had a feeling the boy was thinking about how we'd first met. After a few seconds, he spoke up. "Hey, what are you doing tomorrow night?"

"Tomorrow night?" I allowed my mind to roll forward to tomorrow. "Hadn't thought about it. I've been so consumed with this wedding."

"It'll do you good to take some time off. My mom's invited me up for dinner tomorrow evening, and I was hoping I could talk you into going with me. She's making chicken-fried steak—my favorite."

"O-oh?" Did I dare take time away from my wedding plans? Would everything crater if I took an evening off? And didn't I have enough stress without meeting his family during this chaotic week?

After silence on his end, I added, "I really don't know if

I could take time away before the big day." Surely he would understand. Right?

As my hunky cowboy's smile faded, I could've slapped myself. D.J. was taking a critical step forward in our relationship, and here I stood blowing it. The wedding would go on whether I took an evening off or not.

D.J. wanted me to meet his mama. I would meet his mama. He wanted me to eat chicken-fried steak. I would eat chicken-fried steak.

Even if it meant the stress of this wedding caused me to fall apart in the process.

15

Walkin' My Baby Back Home

On Wednesday afternoon, with Mama and Sophia's help, I scrubbed the wedding facility from top to bottom. By 4:00 the wood floors in the reception hall gleamed, the chandeliers sparkled, and the linens had all been washed. I stood back and surveyed the place, trying to imagine it filled with people. Line dancing. Eating barbecue. Laughing. Nibbling slices of cake. Sipping cups of punch. Congratulating the bride and groom.

Yes, I could see it all now. This wedding would come off without a hitch, and the whole Rossi clan would breathe a collective sigh of relief.

Feeling more confident than I had in days, I wrapped up my work and headed home to shower and dress for my date—if you could call a trip to Splendora for chicken-fried steak with Earline and Dwayne Neeley Sr. a date.

D.J. arrived promptly at 5:15. As the doorbell rang, Precious went into one of her typical Yorkie-Poo frenzies. Panic set in, though it had nothing to do with the dog. The moment had arrived at last. I would head off to Splendora-land to meet the Neeleys face-to-face. If I could've located the bottle of Laz's anointing oil, I might've smeared some on my heart. Instead, with a forced smile and a determined attitude, I opened the door to the man of my dreams.

D.J.'s five o'clock shadow gave him that down-home Texas look I suddenly found so appealing. I took one look at the boy and remembered why my heart had gotten tangled up with his in the first place. I wanted to holler "Yee-haw!" and reach for a pair of those boots in the front hall. Instead, I found myself wrapped in his arms as he placed a gentle kiss in my hair.

"No PDA," Pop said with a wink as he entered the foyer.

D.J. stepped back and extended his hand. My father took it, and the two dove into a lengthy conversation about the weather while I tried to still my heart. But oh, heaven help me! How could I? In that moment, as I watched my old-school father and my new-school love interest exchanging pleasantries, I could almost forget about our families' differences. Almost. I had to wonder if a cheesecake-loving Italian girl from Galveston could really merge worlds with a chicken-fried-steak-lovin' cowboy from Splendora. I guess if I wanted to find out, God would have to lead the horse to water. Or, in this case, take the Italian girl to the piney woods of east Texas.

As D.J. pointed his truck north on Interstate 45, I asked him to tell me anything and everything about his parents and his brother.

"Well, let's see now." He appeared to be thinking of where to start. "My family is originally from Tennessee."

"Wow. What part?"

"Knoxville. My dad's been in the auto repair business for as long as I can remember." He sighed. "I used to work with him, but I really don't have what it takes to be a mechanic. Bubba, on the other hand . . ." D.J. went off on a tangent about his baby brother's skills under the hood, as well as his many certifications. "'Course, Bubba's good at just about everything he does," D.J. said with a smile. "He won all sorts of singing contests as a kid."

"No way."

"Yep. And his barbecue's the best in town. I'm not just saying that because he's my brother." D.J. looked my way. "You ever been to the Houston Livestock Show and Rodeo?"

I shook my head. "No. I was supposed to go with Jenna a couple of years ago, but at the last minute she got sick and we had to cancel. I think we were supposed to see Martina McBride or someone like that."

"Well, it's a fabulous event," D.J. said. "And every year my brother competes in their big barbecue cook-off."

"Oh, I've seen those on the Food Network," I said.

"Then you know what the jackpot looks like."

"Are you saying Bubba won?"

"Well, in the rib category, anyway. And he came in second in brisket. He's pretty amazing."

"Sounds like you and Bubba are really close." I sighed.

"Why the sigh, Bella?" He looked my way with concern in his eyes.

"Oh, I don't know. I guess if I only had one sibling, there would be time for a really deep relationship. There are so many of us, sometimes it's hard to keep up with what everyone's doing." I paused a moment to think about that, then turned back to him with a smile. "But enough about that. Tell me more about your family."

For the rest of the ride, he did just that. Turned out most of their extended relatives had either passed on or lived elsewhere. D.J.'s parents had planned to have a large family, but complications from Bubba's birth had prevented his mother from having any more children. She still mourned the loss but found her solace in a strong relationship with the Lord and in her local Full Gospel church, where she'd acquired some fame as a gospel-style pianist. She'd raised her boys to believe in God, country, and hard work.

"I think you'll like my mama," he said with a smile. "Can't wait for you to meet her. And vice versa."

"Me too."

As the conversation lapsed, I couldn't help but think of my own mother. She'd given birth to five children, and the ensuing chaos of raising a houseful of hooligans quickly followed. Spoiled hooligans, no less. Our family reunions consisted of rambunctious relatives, an overabundance of rich foods, and arguments before night's end. Never a dull moment in the Rossi household. Would the Neeleys be put off by our craziness when the families met face-to-face the night of the wedding rehearsal? Would they mind that their son had fallen for a girl who'd never even been to Splendora, Texas? Who couldn't line dance to save her life? Who—gasp!—attended the Methodist church? I whispered a prayer that they would somehow see beyond any differences and sweep me into the fold.

As we approached downtown, D.J. turned onto Highway 59, continuing the drive north. I drew in a deep breath, knowing we'd just come to the proverbial fork in the road. My world as I knew it ended at the intersection of Interstate 45 and Highway 59. Beyond that point lay the vast unknown. An undiscovered galaxy. A place I'd never pictured myself traveling. Could I really trust God with the things I couldn't see or control?

My breathing escalated, but I did my best to slow it back down as I pondered these things. *That's what faith is all about, Bella. Deep breath, girl.*

We sat in evening traffic until we reached the Kingwood area, north of Houston. Then suddenly the terrain changed. The forest seemed to grow up on both sides of the freeway. Beautiful green pines stretched majestically toward the sky.

"Oh, D.J.! This is amazing."

"Yep." Just one word, but it spoke volumes.

Our conversation quieted, and I breathed in the unexpected beauty of my unfamiliar surroundings. I felt as if we'd slipped off into a green wonderland, where ribbons of late afternoon sunlight danced through the green needles of the sturdy pines. The whole thing reminded me of a fairy tale, something with animated characters dancing to beautifully scored music. But never mind the dwarves and magic mirrors. Skip the choreography. I just hoped this story would wrap up with the classic happily-ever-after ending.

Shaking off my daydreams, I shifted my attention back to the road. D.J. exited the freeway and turned onto a side street. We crossed over railroad tracks and wound our way down a country lane. The trees enveloped us on both sides now, casting shadows of their limbs onto the road below. I couldn't remember when I'd ever seen anything so pretty. Or so awe inspiring. The whole thing was breathtaking.

D.J. made a couple more turns, and we finally came to a stop in front of a double-wide trailer with the most colorful garden I'd ever seen.

"Wow." I stared in silence.

"Mom's really into azaleas," he explained.

"They're amazing." I drew in a deep breath and prayed as he came around to my side of the truck to let me out. Half of me wanted to stay put, and the other half just wanted to get this over with.

My feet touched down on the ground, and he leaned over to plant a gentle kiss on my cheek, then whispered, "Don't be nervous."

"M-me? Nervous?"

"Mm-hmm. You're shaking."

"Oh." A few calming breaths did the trick.

Within seconds, the front door swung open, and a man who looked like an older version of D.J. appeared with a broad smile on his face. "So, the prodigal has returned?"

"I've returned." D.J. grinned.

"Well, good thing we killed the fatted calf then. Should I call for the neighbors? Throw a welcome-home party? Try to locate your brother?"

"Nah."

The boisterous man bounded down the wooden stairs and wrapped his son in a fatherly embrace.

D.J. responded with a boyish grin. "Dad, this is Bella Rossi." He slipped an arm around my shoulders, and I reveled in the comfort of his touch.

"Bella." Mr. Neeley's warm smile put me at ease right away. I extended a hand in his direction, trying to hide my nervousness. He shook it, then gave me a welcoming hug. "I'm Dwayne Neeley."

Duh-wayne. His pronunciation took me back to my first phone conversation with D.J. Had it really only been a week ago? Felt like I'd known him for years.

"Nice to meet you," I said.

"Glad you could join us tonight, Bella." Mr. Neeley gave me a pat on the back, then released his hold on me.

I looked into the man's sparkling eyes and felt at home right away. Still, many things about him surprised me. D.J.'s dad wore a button-up Western-style shirt and dark jeans. And boots, of course. But it wasn't really his clothing that captured my attention. No, something else altogether drew me in. The man had picture-perfect hair. I'd never seen anything like it. Not a strand out of place. Perfect color—brown with shimmers of gray shining through. Perfect design—parted on the side and neatly combed. Impressive.

"My baby boy is home!" A female voice rang out, and I realized D.J.'s mama had joined us. I shot a glance her way, nerves taking hold. Ah, so the boys got their looks from their father. Still, Earline Neeley had a great "mama" look about her, and genuine kindness radiated from her sparkling eyes. Now this was a woman I could love. I just hoped she felt the same way about me. And my wacky family.

"You must be *Bay*-luh." She wrapped me in an embrace, and her chest—which reminded me a bit of our family's two basketballs, only softer—nearly swallowed me whole. I sucked in my breath and waited for the hug to end. Turned out Earline was a professional hugger.

Finally, just about the time I thought I'd pass out from lack of oxygen, she stepped back and examined me from head to toe. "Well, if you aren't about the prettiest thing I've ever seen. C'mon in here, *Bay*-luh, and have a seat. We're fixin' to eat."

She ushered me inside, and within minutes we sat together at their handcrafted oak table. Dwayne Sr. prayed over the food, and then we dove in. Earline's chicken-fried steak was the best I'd ever eaten in my life.

I must've appeared a little bug-eyed as I ate, because D.J. glanced my way and laughed. "Enjoying that?"

"Mm-hmm!" I shoveled another bite into my mouth, then paused, realizing the impression I must be giving. Noticing the others seemed to be eating at about the same pace, I dove back in. "These mashed potatoes are *so* creamy." I took a bite and closed my eyes, sheer ecstasy setting in.

"Well, thank you, honey." Earline's cheeks flushed pink. "I can whip up taters in my sleep."

At that moment I had the strangest picture flash into my mind. I could just see Aunt Rosa and Earline in the kitchen together, peeling taters. Side by side. The Rossis and the Neeleys. We were destined to unite. Of course, with Aunt Rosa involved, there would be the usual bantering over which was better—mashed or fried—but by the end of the meal, we'd all be one big, happy, well-fed family. Right?

D.J.'s voice interrupted my thoughts. "Say, where's Bubba?" he asked his mother. "I thought sure he'd be here tonight."

"Haven't seen him all day," Earline said with the hint of a smile playing on her lips. "I suspect he's with that gal he met down in Galveston."

"W-was her name Jenna?" I knew the answer even before asking, of course.

"Yes, that's it." Earline grinned. "I dare say Bubba is down-right twitterpated."

"Mm-hmm." Well, this explained why Jenna had called in sick yesterday and today. A little white lie, perhaps? A secret date with Bubba Neeley?

"He's one-over for her," Earline continued. "Never seen the likes of it. But I've been praying for my boys since they were knee-high to grasshoppers that God would bring just the right girls to be their wives. So why should I be surprised when it happens? No sir. Not surprised a bit."

176

Earline promptly gave me a wink, and I felt my stomach lurch. Was she trying to tell me I was the one for D.J.? The one she'd prayed for all these years? The wink told me yes, but my fears said a feeble no.

Turning my attention back to the food, I enjoyed the last of my mashed taters and chicken-fried steak. Oh, what a fascinating trip this was turning out to be!

At ten minutes to seven, just after serving up hefty portions of banana pudding, Earline rose to her feet. "We need to get on the ball, folks. Church starts in ten minutes. Won't be much of a worship service if the piano player's missing." She gave me another wink.

"Church?" I looked at D.J., surprised by this news. He hadn't mentioned anything about visiting his parents' church tonight. Did we really have time, what with the long drive back to Galveston and all?

He flashed a "Sorry about that" look, and I responded with a sympathetic shrug. I didn't mind, really. No, if it made Earline happy, it would make D.J. happy. And if it made D.J. happy, it would ultimately make me happy. So, off to church we went.

D.J. and I followed along behind his father's truck until we came to a tiny wood-framed church on concrete blocks just a few blocks from the Neeley home. The sign out front read FULL GOSPEL CHAPEL IN THE PINES. I could hear a steady drumbeat coming from inside, along with the repetitive strum of an electric guitar. Our Methodist congregation boasted an organ and a piano, but with the exception of the youth department, we wouldn't know what to do with a set of drums. Not that I minded the drums here. No sir. I loved the idea of a rousing song service, especially in such a quaint church tucked under the canopy of these beautiful pines. And besides, this would serve as a nice distraction from the chaos of late. Perhaps the Lord was calling me away to a quiet place with him.

Or not so quiet. The music escalated, and the sound of women's voices—laughing, talking, and squealing in delight—filled the air.

Following along behind D.J., I climbed up the rickety wooden steps and entered the small foyer, where a row of larger-than-life women greeted me with enthusiastic hugs. I met Sister Twila, Sister Jolene, and Sister Bonnie Sue. Though everyone referred to the buxom trio as sisters, I had a feeling they weren't related. And they *definitely* weren't nuns. No, the eclectic wardrobes convinced me of that. Well, that and Sister Jolene's beehive hairdo.

The worship service turned out to be different from any I'd ever experienced. I recognized a few of the choruses, but they had a distinctive Southern gospel feel to them. While I was accustomed to a rather High Church form of worship, this certainly had its appeal. All around me, men and women swayed to the rhythm and raised their hands in joyful praise.

Through the crowd of upraised arms, I sneaked a peek at Earline, who played the piano with reckless abandon. Some folks were just born with a gift from on high, and this woman was one of them. Leaning forward, eyes closed, she allowed the music to flow through her fingertips. And talk about fast! Earline had the Jerry Lee Lewis anointing, for sure.

Now that I'd seen D.J.'s mother in action, I had to wonder if he had any musical abilities, anything that would help him in his new role of deejay. As if in answer to my question, he began to sing. I turned in rapt awe as the most beautiful bass voice I'd ever heard pealed forth. Wow. The boy could sing. And then some. I did my best to warble along, but to be honest, Guido could carry a tune better than I could. Determined not to get frustrated, I closed my eyes and focused on worshiping, reminding myself that all the Lord asked of me was a joyful noise. I happily obliged.

The tempo of the music changed to something really lively, and everyone clapped along. I did my best to join in, but my ADD got the better of me when Sister Jolene took to dancing in the aisle, her exaggerated hairdo bobbing this way and that. Before long, Sister Bonnie Sue joined in, her bright pink dress swaying in the breeze. Then Sister Twila kicked up her heels and did a jig that reminded me a bit of Rosa and her Italian folk dances. By the end of the song, I literally felt the sway of the wood-framed building. It shifted back and forth on its concrete block foundation as the larger-than-life trio worshiped the Lord with their whole hearts and every ounce of strength.

But I didn't mind. On the contrary, I found myself in a different place spiritually as I witnessed such intense, heartfelt worship. I had to wonder what Aunt Rosa would think of all this. If given the chance, would she join the trio of sisters, turning in happy circles and lifting her arms to the heavens, or would she steal their seats when they weren't looking?

Before I could give this idea any more thought, Pastor Higley, a slightly chubby, balding man, rose to begin the Bible study. Just then—to my great horror—my cell phone rang. I felt my cheeks heat up as everyone turned to face me. The pastor waved his hand my way. "Don't worry about it, sister. Just give 'em a warm hello from all of us and invite 'em to Sunday service."

I started to ignore the call but then recognized the number as Sharlene's. Worming my way out of the pew, I muttered my apologies to D.J. and answered the phone as I hit the aisle. "Hang on a second, Sharlene," I whispered.

Pastor Higley went back to teaching as I reached the back

of the aisle. Heading into the tiny foyer, I exhaled. "Sorry. I was in church."

"Oh, I'm so sorry!" She went into a lengthy dissertation about how she'd forgotten it was Wednesday night. About how the days had all been running together. After a few minutes she stopped to ask, "Wait a minute. Where are you?"

"In church," I repeated.

"Is that Pastor Higley's voice I hear in the background? Cody's grandpa?"

"Well, I, um . . ."

"Are you at Chapel in the Pines?"

"Maybe."

"Girl, are you dating that handsome cowboy? Our deejay?"

She let out a whistle, and I groaned before responding. "Well, if you can count a Wednesday night church service as a date, I guess you could say that. Oh, and we went out for dinner last weekend. I choked on a piece of steak, and he saved my life by performing the Heimlich maneuver."

"No way."

"Yes way."

"Well, thank God you're still among the living." Sharlene laughed. "I need you too much right now. Promise not to do anything crazy between now and the dress rehearsal on Friday night, okay?"

I glanced back in the church as the trio of full-figured sisters hollered out a resounding "Amen!" then turned my attention back to Sharlene.

"I promise to be careful, but that's about it. When it comes to slipping over the edge of crazy, I've already done it." I dove into the story about the eighty boots, then told Sharlene all about the D.J./deejay misunderstanding, but reassured her that everything would go well on her big day now that D.J. and Armando were working together. After that, I shared my heart about the wedding facility, even going so far as to tell her about my fears and concerns that I'd run my family's business into the ground. All the while, I heard Pastor Higley's voice in the background as he talked about trusting God with your problems.

At the end of the conversation, Sharlene—the bride-to-be, the one I should be encouraging—offered to pray with me. Ironic, but her prayer corresponded with the one going on in the little chapel. In fact, the words were pretty much the same as her future grandfather-in-law's. She prayed that I would find peace in the middle of my storm and that God would have his way, even if it meant moving me out of the way.

The service ended, and Sharlene must've picked up on the fact because she said she had to go. I whispered a quick "Thanks for praying me back from the abyss" as a crowd of folks rushed me in the tiny foyer.

D.J. headed my way with a concerned look on his face. "Everything okay?"

"Yeah. The bride-to-be." I offered a "you know how brides can be" smile, and he responded with a nod, though I doubted he had a clue.

"Is she falling apart at the seams?"

No, but I am.

In that moment, as I stared into D.J.'s sympathetic eyes, the shocking truth set in. I'd fallen in so many ways, and not just in relation to the wedding. I'd tumbled head over heels for D.J. Neeley, and there was no returning from the depths. This little Italian girl was . . . what was that word Earline had used again?

Ah yes—I was twitterpated.

16

Please Don't Talk about Me
When I'm Gone

On Friday morning I stayed in bed later than usual. Precious, usually ready to go outdoors at the crack of dawn, slept peacefully at my side. I did my best not to wake her. I needed time to absorb everything that had happened over the past few days. The wedding preparations. The boots. D.J. The neighbor kid. Earline's piano-playing abilities. Pastor Higley. Dwayne Sr.'s perfect hair. The trio of sisters at Chapel in the Pines.

Maybe D.J. had it right when he said the coming together of our two families would be more than east meets west. More than city meets country. To merge my life with his in any way, shape, or form would mean a whole new perspective . . . on pretty much everything. Food. Automobiles. Worship. You name it.

Not that I really minded. No, I'd fallen hard and fast for the boy and would do just about anything within reason to cement this relationship. But did I have it in me to move to the country and take up gospel singing? Could I ask the sisters for dancing lessons? How would the Neeleys feel about Precious, my somewhat less-than-perfect canine companion? And how would my mama take the news that I was moving to the country?

But, was I moving to the country? I closed my eyes and tried to envision myself living in Splendora. My flower garden filled with azaleas. My kitchen sink loaded with dirty dishes after feeding my man his daily portion of the fatted calf. My newer, simpler wardrobe and hairdo. My cowboy boots. My brood of children.

Don't get ahead of yourself, Bella.

Knowing the workload that lay ahead, I spent a few minutes curled up in bed, praying. Then I reached for my Bible and allowed peace to flow over me as I read several comforting verses. I resolved myself to a new way of thinking. This wedding would be great. The food would be great. The reception would be great.

But only if I crawled out of bed and got to work.

After showering and dressing in a cute pair of jeans with a button-up yellow blouse, I telephoned Parma John's to ask Uncle Laz a catering question. I was greeted with Jenna's enthusiastic spiel about the Volare special. She quickly put my uncle on the phone.

After Laz answered my questions about the southwestern beans—which he and Bubba were determined to cook outdoors over an actual chuck-wagon-style campfire—I headed down to the kitchen to find Aunt Rosa hard at work on the wedding cake. Sharlene and Cody had chosen Italian cream cake, my personal favorite. The cream cheese frosting made it a bit harder to decorate, but knowing Rosa, she didn't mind a bit. She would pull off the most beautiful cake anyone had ever seen.

"Come, Bella." My aunt gestured for me to sit on a barstool as she pulled one of the larger layers of cake from the oven and tested it with the prongs of a fork. "Let's talk."

"But I . . ." I wanted to argue. Wanted to tell her that I didn't have time for a chat, that work beckoned. On the other hand, Rosa rarely asked for a private audience. So I took a seat and found myself telling her all about my adventures of Wednesday night. When I reached the part about the dancing sisters, she stopped her baking and looked at me, stunned.

"Well, that's different."

"That's the thing, Rosa," I explained. "There are so many things about D.J. and his family that are different. But different isn't a bad thing. It's just . . . different."

She smiled at me and took a few steps my way. As she gently laid a palm on my cheek, Rosa spoke in hushed Italian. "Go after your heart, Bella. Even if it takes you to new and different places."

A holy calm came over me at her words, and my eyes filled with tears. I'd never seen this side of Rosa before. Her tender words startled me. And to be totally honest with myself, I'd never truly followed my heart. Oh, I'd followed my mama's advice and dated Tony. I'd listened to Pop and taken over the wedding facility. In fact, I'd pretty much always done what was expected of me. But I'd never really stepped out on my own. Never taken a chance like the one I was now taking with D.J. Never followed my heart into the vast unknown.

Maybe that's why I was so scared. I was facing something . . . different.

My aunt's eyes narrowed. "When I left my friends back in Napoli to come here, to America, I questioned my decision a hundred times," she said. "But it was the right thing to do. After Mama died, my sisters were the only family I had left. And all of you children, of course. So I came here. And I've never regretted it. Oh, it was hard at first. I wanted to go back home half a dozen times. But I've been able to watch you and your brothers and sister grow into beautiful people, and now I'm here to see the little ones grow up too." Her eyes filled with tears, and I realized for the first time what a sacrifice she'd made, leaving her homeland to come here. "You can trust God with the changes you go through, Bella," she whispered.

Mama chose that moment to walk into the kitchen and took Rosa's tenderness for something more.

"Are you all right, Bella?" She rushed to my side. "Has something gone wrong with the wedding?"

"N-no." I shook my head and embraced Rosa. "Not at all. In fact, everything is going according to schedule."

"Something else, then?" Mama looked back and forth between us. "Something to do with the neighbors?" She dove into a heated discussion about the letter she'd discovered on the door, and I sighed. So much for relaxing today.

"What ever happened with that?" I asked. "Do you think they're serious about filing a lawsuit?"

Rosa scowled as she muttered, *"Tutto fumo e niente arrosto."*

"All smoke and no fire? What do you mean?" I stuck my finger in the bowl of cream cheese frosting, and she slapped it away. "You think they're bluffing?"

"Yes." She gave a firm nod. "They're all talk but no action. I don't believe a word of it."

"What makes you think they're not serious?" I asked.

"What sort of people tape a letter to your door instead of

185

sending it in the mail?" she asked. "Especially something as important as a lawsuit. I don't believe a word of it."

"But it was on legal stationery." Mama's eyes reflected her concern. Of course, Mama was the sort to get overly concerned about most everything. She'd turned worrying into an art form.

The more Rosa explained her bluffing theory, the more my mother relaxed. By the end of our discussion, I could almost feel the Spirit of God breathe peace over the room.

Then Bubba and Jenna stopped by.

I thought about asking my friend the obvious question— "So, how's David, your soon-to-be-fiancé?"—but didn't. No, looking into my best friend's eyes, I was almost ready to forgive her for pretending to be sick this week.

Then the coughing fit began. Her face turned pink, then red with embarrassment as she finally managed to catch her breath.

"You really are sick!" I said.

My face must've conveyed too much joy at this revelation because she looked at me, stunned. "Well, you don't have to be so happy about it." After blowing her nose, she added a stuffy, "I'm miserable. Summer colds are the worst. If Bubba hadn't asked for my help with this campfire thing, I would've stayed at work. Or at home in bed, even. But I hate to say no to people. Always have."

"Aw, thanks." Bubba shrugged as he turned to her with a loving glance. "I guess I could've done it without her, but . . ." He didn't finish. He didn't have to. The boy was twitterpated.

She looked up at him with red-rimmed eyes and smiled. For a moment, time stood still. I half expected a Sinatra song to chime in overhead in perfect time. These two were hopelessly hooked on each other, whether they wanted to admit it or not. Jenna would have a lot of explaining to do when David arrived home.

Bubba's words jolted me back to attention. "I'm just here to get the campfire site started," he explained. "Want to show me where you want it?"

With Mama and Jenna tagging along, we made our way to the far side of the Club Wed property, which we'd deemed Bubba's cooking station. I'd managed to get the city of Galveston to allow for the campfire, but not without some finagling on my part. I just prayed we wouldn't burn the whole place to the ground in the process.

Passing the gazebo and perfectly lined chairs, we located the ideal spot on the south lawn. "I thought I'd set my smoker up right here," Bubba said. "And the campfire can go right there." He pointed at a level spot without any grass. "It's away from the trees, so there's no real fire hazard." I watched as Bubba made a U-shaped perimeter using large rocks, which he said he'd purchased at a local lawn and garden store. He placed a large, flat rock at the rear of the fire pit, explaining, "This one will act like a chimney, pushing the smoke up and away from the guests."

"That's a relief."

"Now, for the kindling." Bubba filled the area inside the rocks with bits of wood and crumpled paper, layer upon layer. Then he stepped back and examined his work. "After tonight's rehearsal, I'll set up the pot and get the beans to soaking. Then I'll be back first thing in the morning to get the smoker fired up and the briskets to cooking."

"What time in the morning?" Mama asked. "We could help you, if you like."

"Oh, five-ish."

"Five-ish?" we all repeated.

"Well, sure." He slapped his thigh and laughed. "Takes all day to smoke the briskets and cook the beans. You want this to taste good, right?"

"Sure. Of course." I wanted it to taste good, but I'd never pondered the fact that the neighbors might awaken to the tantalizing smell of barbecue.

Not that it really mattered. Folks along Broadway were accustomed to merging business with personal life. Our home sat in the shadow of the historic Moody Mansion and the Aston Villa, after all—two of the top tourist sites in the city. Our neighborhood boasted the perfect blend of business life and residential life merged into one. Still, a five a.m. barbecue might be a bit over the top.

"Bubba knows what he's doing, Bella." Jenna sneezed and went into another coughing fit before adding, "He's done this for years."

"At the rodeo cook-off, I hear." I smiled his direction, hoping to bring encouragement.

"Yep. A couple of friends usually help me. We make a nice team. And my dad's shop, Shade Tree Mechanics, is our sponsor. We call ourselves the Shade Tree Cookers."

"They've won lots of blue ribbons," Jenna said with pride. "I've seen the pictures." She proceeded to tell a rip-roaring story of Bubba's adventures at the Houston Livestock Show and Rodeo, but she lost me somewhere between the ribs and the brisket.

Since when did Jenna care about the rodeo? Or meat, for that matter. The girl could barely tolerate tiny pieces of pepperoni on a pizza, let alone hefty slabs of beef and pork, which she now described in detail with a broad smile and enthusiastic ring to her voice. Surely someone had cast a spell on her. Maybe David would have the magic potion necessary to awaken her . . . when he returned home from his ventures offshore.

Bubba interrupted my ponderings. "I'll be staying at D.J.'s place tonight," he explained. "He'll come with me in the morning to get things started. And just so you know, he'll be around most of the day keeping an eye on things while I head up to Parma John's to see if Jenna and Laz need my help with the side dishes. Hope that's okay."

"Oh, sure." I felt my cheeks warm and saw the look of understanding in Jenna's eyes. She knew me well. I couldn't hide my crush on D.J. any more than she could hide hers on Bubba. Our shared glance spoke a thousand words. I could almost hear *"Finché c'è vita c'è speranza"* now—"where there is life, there is hope."

Hope. Funny how my life had been infused with it over the past week and a half. And now, standing here with my soul sister, I knew she sensed it too.

Not that I had time to be standing around. Glancing down at my watch, I gasped. Eleven thirty? Where had the morning gone? I had a thousand things to do between now and this evening's rehearsal.

With my nerves twisting themselves into a bundle, I headed inside the wedding facility to tie up all the loose ends.

17

Memories Are Made of This

Later that afternoon, about two hours before the wedding rehearsal, I walked through every room of the wedding facility one last time, just to make sure I hadn't overlooked anything. After seeing to the details in the reception hall, I turned my attention to the garden, specifically the gazebo where the wedding ceremony would take place.

If it didn't rain.

Yikes. Reality hit head-on. Glancing up at the skies, I pondered the fact that I'd forgotten to worry about the weather. Forgetting to worry was a novelty in our family, something that happened rarely. Despite Uncle Laz's constant quoting of "Be anxious for nothing," I often found myself fretting over this or that. And this afternoon was no different. While I hadn't given any thought to the weather, today's anxieties were focused on the inevitable meeting of the Rossis and the Neeleys, which was set to take place at 5:30 p.m. Visions of the Hatfields and the McCoys danced around in my head.

At 5:07 the doorbell rang, and I braced myself.

Pop answered the door, this time wearing a pair of slacks and a proper shirt. Mama had dressed him for the occasion. She stood behind him, a bright smile on her face. As the door opened, I could see her mentally taking in Earline, who wore a floral skirt, button-up blouse, and white sandals. Dwayne Sr. looked pretty spiffy in a pair of crisply ironed blue jeans and freshly pressed Western shirt. And boots. Of course. And D.J. had never looked finer. His beautiful eyes twinkled as he glanced my way.

Somehow I doubted Earline paid much attention to my wardrobe, though I'd paid particular attention to my attire this evening. She took one look at me and swept me into the folds of her abundant chest. "Oh, *Bay*-luh, it's so wonderful to see you again!" She finally loosened her embrace and turned to my mother. "And you must be Mrs. Rossi. We just love your daughter. And I'm sure we're going to love the rest of you too!"

"Well, thank you." My mother had just offered up a nod when Earline grabbed her for a powerful hug. "Oh my. Well, I . . ." Her voice drifted off as Earline's overwhelming bosom swallowed her up.

I saw the fear register in Uncle Laz's eyes as he watched this interaction. He took several steps backward, away from potential harm. Couldn't say I blamed him.

After a few seconds of chatter, I ushered everyone inside to the living room. Before taking a seat on the sofa, Dwayne Sr. approached Pop with a broad smile. He extended his hand. "*Duh*-wayne Neeley. Nice to meet you."

Pop shook the man's hand and grinned. "Cosmo Rossi. Nice to meet you too." He gestured for Mr. Neeley to sit, which he did with a smile. Within seconds they were best friends, talking about everything from cars to motorcycles to gas prices.

The initial "getting to know you" went better than expected, especially when Rosa offered to show Earline her state-of-the-art kitchen. I'd never seen two happier women. Even Mama joined in, chatting leisurely about recipes. Since when did my mother care about cooking?

Shortly thereafter Pop initiated a tour of our hundred-year-old home. Earline oohed and aahed over the various decorating choices, which brought a huge smile to my mother's face. And Dwayne Sr. admired the house's intricate Victorian woodwork. When they reached the master bedroom, Earline practically swooned. "This bed is divine."

Mama grinned. "It was my parents' in Italy. There's quite a story as to how we got it here." She began to tell said story, and before long, all of the women were sitting on the bed, gabbing like girlfriends. Then Rosa and Mama decided it was time to show off the paintings in the hallway, which their father had done.

D.J. and I lagged behind, holding hands as we walked together from room to room. "They seem to be getting along pretty well," he whispered at one point.

"Yes, so far so good." Still, I did have to wonder when the dam would break. When Aunt Rosa would dive into an argument with Uncle Laz, scaring everyone to death. Or when Pop would insist they head outdoors for an impromptu basketball tournament.

At quarter to six we all headed next door to the wedding facility, and I took a final look around the outdoor area where tonight's wedding rehearsal—and tomorrow's actual ceremony—would take place. The white wood-slatted chairs would look beautiful decked out in covers and sashes, but that was a job for tomorrow. Tonight we just had to get through a makeshift ceremony.

I'd taken the time to write everything down. The order of service. The special music Earline would play as the bride and groom lit the unity candle. The vows. Everything.

I watched in awe as Bubba and Jenna showed off the fire pit. My best friend couldn't seem to focus on anything but Bubba, but who could blame her? He was tall, rugged, and handsome, wasn't he? And I'd never met anyone kinder than the Neeley boys. They certainly put most of the guys I'd known to shame. Yes, these cowboys were getting harder to resist by the minute.

Glancing over at D.J., I smiled. He offered up a wink, then helped Bubba unload the smoker from the back of their flatbed trailer.

Yes, things were really going well. I could finally start to relax.

Sharlene and Cody arrived promptly at six, along with the others in the wedding party. The bride-to-be radiated joy, but the poor groom-to-be looked like he might be sick at any moment. I whispered quietly in his ear, "You're going to do fine. Take a deep breath."

For the first time, I met Sharlene's father face-to-face. The handsome south Texas oilman had that "this is my only daughter and she's got me wrapped around her little finger" look on his face from the get-go. Not that I minded. Neither did Patti, who arrived at ten after six to finalize her floral plans. Though she'd spent the better part of the last few days whining about her singleness, Patti-Lou shifted gears the moment she realized Sharlene's father wasn't wearing a wedding ring. She found an excuse to gravitate to his side and never left.

At 6:30, under skies as clear as cut glass, I gathered the troops for the rehearsal. The groom and groomsmen were lined up inside the gazebo, along with Pastor Higley. D.J.'s mom sat at the electric keyboard, playing Pachelbel's "Canon in D." I marveled at her skill as her fingertips danced across the keys. At my cue, the five bridesmaids sashayed down the aisle. Off in the distance, I made eye contact with Sharlene, who gave me a confident wave before she slipped an arm through her daddy's for their walk down the aisle.

Just then I heard a gasp from Patti-Lou, who stood at my side. The music came to a grinding halt as she cried out, "Wait! The bride isn't supposed to participate in her own rehearsal! That's a Southern tradition!"

"She's right!" Earline called out. "What if the pastor accidentally marries them tonight? It'll put a damper on tomorrow's ceremony."

Everyone chuckled, and I thought about her words. Some Southern women still followed this old tradition of replacing the bride for the rehearsal, so I looked at Sharlene, curious as to her reaction. "What do you think?"

She offered a shrug in response. "That's fine. I'm a true Southern belle, so I don't mind abiding by tradition."

"Looks like we need a bride then." Pastor Higley looked around, noting that all of the others—outside the family, anyway—were already in the wedding party. Finally, he looked at Patti-Lou with a nod. "Will you do the honors, young lady? And Mr. Billings, once you reach the front of the aisle, you can go ahead and stand in for your future son-in-law for the rest of the service."

"I'll be happy to," Sharlene's father agreed.

I couldn't tell if Patti's near-swoon came as a result of being called a young lady or from the fact that she would get to walk down the aisle on the arm of one very handsome widower. Either way, she practically sprinted to the back of the aisle and took Sharlene's place on Bob Billings's arm. After a scrutinizing glance, I had to admit they made a nice couple. Had Patti-Lou finally found her man—at a wedding rehearsal, no less? Another bada-bing, bada-boom moment, perhaps?

D.J.'s mom started the wedding march once more, and the couple moved confidently down the aisle. The sight brought tears to my eyes. Just as they neared the gazebo, I heard the strangest sound. Almost sounded like . . . fluttering. Then . . . what was that—squawking?

With the piano music going on, no one else seemed to notice. I shifted my gaze this way and that, trying to figure out if we had a bat on the loose, perhaps. No, thank goodness. I didn't see anything that resembled a bat.

As the music drew to a close, Pastor Higley took his place and began to lead everyone through the rehearsal. I wanted to pay attention. Honestly, I did. But the oddest bit of chattering to my left now had me completely distracted. I turned and looked up into the far rafters of the gazebo, stunned to see a near-featherless Guido. He sat perched in the oddest of places, just above Pastor Higley's head, swaying to and fro. The loopy parrot appeared to be muttering something at first, then stopped and stared at me with the oddest look on his face.

No no no! I vaguely remembered something the limo driver had said about having Guido's wings clipped. We hadn't had time to figure that part out yet. And now . . .

I stared up, praying in silence that he would not move an inch or utter a single, solitary sound from this point forth. He seemed to pick up on the warning shooting from my eyes. I'd never seen the bird so quiet. Or so wobbly. Must be the antihistamines at work. Guido tipped this way and that, nearly falling on Pastor Higley's head on several occasions. Only my prayers seemed to keep him planted in place.

Fortunately, the service progressed rapidly, and before long the pastor wrapped up with, "I now pronounce you husband and wife. You may kiss your bride."

Poor Patti-Lou. I could read the disappointment in her face as Bob Billings skipped the kiss and turned her around to face the congregation. Earline began to play the recessional music. The faux bride and groom headed down the aisle at a steady pace.

For whatever reason, Guido chose that particular moment to make his presence known to the masses. He let out a piercing shriek, followed by a lengthy stream of particularly foul words. Or would that be "fowl" words?

Pastor Higley glanced up in time to see the parrot take flight, heading to his left. "Watch out, Earline!" he called out. "We're under attack!"

As if to prove him right, Guido landed on top of the keyboard, cried out "Go to the mattresses," and began his machine-gun routine.

Everything after that seemed to happen in slow motion. I vaguely remember Earline fainting. And I'm pretty sure D.J.'s dad—a former military man—dove forward to catch her as she tumbled from the piano bench, shouting something about being under enemy fire.

Perhaps sensing his fear, Guido swooped down on Mr. Neeley and landed on top of his head. Mr. Neeley let out a scream, and the parrot—probably spooked—took to flight once more, but not before delivering a string of words that would've made a sailor blush. In Guido's beak was a hairy blob of something indistinguishable. Horrified, I looked at Mr. Neeley, realizing his hair had gone missing. In its place, a shiny, bald head.

Off to my left, Patti grabbed Sharlene's father by the hand, and they took off running across the courtyard, headed for the safety of the indoors. And Sharlene ran squealing into Cody's outstretched arms.

From out of nowhere, Aunt Rosa appeared, looking even stranger than usual with a pair of bright orange cowboy boots on her feet and a broom in her hand. She began to chase after Guido, calling out to him in Italian. Something about cooking him up for dinner.

Laz stumbled along behind her, using his cane as a potential weapon—not against Guido but against Rosa. His cries, "Leave that bird alone, you old fool. He's not hurting anyone!" rang out against the cacophony of other sounds.

Through the chaos, I looked over at D.J. as he rushed to his mother's side and knelt in the grass to try to revive her. Bubba soon joined him, and the whole Neeley family took to praying aloud for the Lord to intervene. Earline woke up for a moment, started screaming and flailing her arms, took one look at her bald husband, and then promptly passed out again.

After giving up on Aunt Rosa, Uncle Laz hobbled over on his cane and knelt at Earline's side, pulling something from his pocket.

"Laz, don't!" I called as I recognized the familiar bottle of stinky oil.

Ignoring my pleas, he doused her forehead, then began to pray in Italian that the Lord would raise her from the dead. Seconds later, much to my surprise, Earline sat straight up, smiled at the crowd, and asked what had happened.

"It's a miracle!" Laz proclaimed. "She's been resurrected!" Tears flowed down his cheeks, and he knelt in the grass with hands extended heavenward, praising the Lord for allowing him the honor of witnessing a miracle.

Convinced she'd truly been raised from the dead, Earline rose to her feet and began a celebratory dance that would've made the Full Gospel sisters proud. Her triumphant chorus of "Praise the Lord! Thank you, Jesus!" filled the air, adding a whole new flavor to what had just transpired. Her husband, bald but likely happy to be alive, swept her into his arms. They helped Laz to his feet and thanked him for the role he had played in ministering to them.

At that moment, Guido—likely exhausted after his capers—landed on a chair in the front row with Mr. Neeley's toupee in his mouth. I grabbed it, tossed it D.J.'s direction, and then snatched the featherless bird in my hands, muttering, "You're not going anywhere," to quiet him down.

As everyone looked my way, I offered up a lame smile and tried to come up with something brilliant to say. After a few seconds, I finally managed to squeak out, "Well, I think that went pretty well, don't you?"

18

Let's Be Friendly

Crazy dreams always seem to follow particularly stressful incidents in my life. For instance, after I skipped out on a couple of classes in college, nightmarish dreams plagued me for years. The Technicolor replay was always the same. I would wake up, look at the alarm clock, and realize I'd overslept. Then I'd spring into action, shimmy into my clothes, and run across the campus, hairy-scary, in search of my class. Only, I could never find my class. Instead, I spent the entire hour roaming from building to building, completely lost.

And then there was the near-naked dream. I couldn't recall dreaming it as a child, but after a particularly traumatizing event as a teen—one in which I'd bared my soul to a good friend in school, only to have her share the story with the masses—I'd repetitively dreamed that I showed up at school wearing only my underclothes.

On the night before Sharlene and Cody's wedding, I had the near-naked dream. My, what a dream! Surely it was one of those pizza-induced nightmares. In this version, I stood in front of the congregation at Chapel in the Pines dressed in Aunt Rosa's slip, insisting I couldn't possibly dance without my clothes on. The craziest part of all was that no one seemed to notice my lack of clothing. My vulnerability, though completely obvious to me, seemed to elude them.

Sister Jolene grabbed me by the hand. "C'mon, Bella! Don't worry about the choreography! Just let the Spirit move you!"

I tried a few tentative steps as Earline banged out a rousing melody on the piano off in the distance. When the music stopped, a bald Dwayne Neeley Sr. stood before the congregation with microphone in hand.

"I stand before you today to ask your forgiveness," he said, his shiny head bowed low. "For years I've lied to you about my hair—or, rather, the lack thereof. Can you find it in your hearts to forgive me?"

As a mighty chorus of yeses rose from the congregation, Earline began to play once more, and we all took to dancing again. On and on I danced, completely oblivious to the crowd. Through the window I could see Bubba with his big meat smoker. The pungent aroma of barbecue beef filled the air.

I'd barely had time to consider its ramifications when I heard a squawking sound off in the distance, then some familiar lyrics. "When the moon hits your eye like a big pizza pie . . ." I glanced around, looking for Guido, as everything faded to sepia tone.

And that's where the dream ended.

Only, it didn't. The drowsiness slowly lifted, but from the safety of my bedroom, I could definitely hear Guido chirping away in the next room. He had both the lyrics and the melody to "That's Amore" down pat. And just as in my dream, the distinct smell of barbecue filled the air. I closed my eyes and drew in a deep breath, realizing Bubba really was outside, preparing for tonight's Boot-Scootin' barbecue extravaganza. I tried to imagine how wonderful it would taste. At the wedding. The one I hoped and prayed I could still pull off after last night's chaotic rehearsal.

In the midst of my reverie, a rap on my door gave me a jolt. My mother peeked inside with a wider-than-usual smile. "Ready for the big day, Bella Bambina?"

I smiled as I pondered her nickname for me, the one she used only in very special circumstances. Just as quickly, the smile faded. Thinking back on last night's fiasco, I wanted to pull the covers over my head and hide for a week or two.

"Come on now." She approached the bed and smiled at me. "Surely you're not going to let a little thing like what happened last night keep you from moving forward. Things happen, Bella. Things happen."

Yes. Things happened. To me. A lot. Strange things. Things that didn't happen to anyone else I knew. And I had the oddest feeling stranger things lay ahead. So staying under the covers might just be my best option.

"Laz feels terrible about letting Guido out of his cage," Mama said with a sigh. "He didn't mean any harm. He said he thought the fresh air would do the poor little bird good."

"The poor little bird?" I just shook my head, unable to think of anything sensible to say.

"Aw, c'mon, bambina. Forgive and forget. That's what we're called to do. And today is a new day, after all."

After a few more words of reassurance from my mama, I started to feel better about my life and its strange coincidences. She left the room, and I took the time to reach for my Bible, determined not to let yesterday's events determine today's attitude. So what if everything had crumbled around me last night? So what if D.J.'s parents thought I was a nutcase? There were worse things, right?

I stumbled from Scripture to Scripture, finally landing on just the right one: "Be anxious for nothing, but in everything, by prayer and supplication, make your requests known." Laz's favorite verse resonated once again, and I finally felt a sense of relief sweep over me. Still, how could I lay down every anxiety? The way things were going, I'd lay one down and another one would pop up. I felt like my life had morphed into a never-ending arcade game with no win in sight.

Clutching the Bible, I closed my eyes for some alone time with God. I prayed for the bride and groom, that their day would be perfect. I prayed for my parents, that they'd be able to rest easy and enjoy the day. I even offered up a special prayer for Guido. And for Sal. That done, I offered up a quick prayer that the Neeley family would see fit to forgive me for last night's bizarre and unexpected antics.

After praying, I rose from the bed and showered, then dressed for the day in some cute shorts and a Galveston-themed T-shirt. I'd be changing later tonight into a denim skirt and Western shirt, one I'd purchased especially for this occasion. Jenna had even loaned me a hat, though I wasn't sure I could bring myself to put it on.

Only one thing remained undone. I stared down at the pair of cowboy boots I'd selected from the front hall batch. They were cute, I had to admit. Brown leather against pink. They matched my pink country-western shirt and had a great boot-scootin' feel about them. But, cowboy boots? Could I really do it?

Just for fun, I slipped them on, then primped a bit in front of the full-length mirror. Sophia chose that moment to stick her head in the door. "Hey, Bella, can I borrow your—" She never finished the sentence. Instead, her gaze shifted to my feet. "You're wearing boots."

I shrugged. "Don't know if I can do it tonight, but I'm trying them on for size. Gotta see if they fit."

"They do. It's just like Cinderella."

"What?"

"You know. If the boot fits . . ."

"Then the Texas cowboy version of Prince Charming will sweep me away to wedded bliss?"

She nodded and reality hit. These boots symbolized a lot more than just a country-western themed wedding. If I committed to wear them, I'd be making a statement. I was ready for change. Ready to embrace something new. Different. Ready to Texas Two-Step my way into D.J.'s arms.

If he still wanted me after Guido had stolen his father's hair.

Sophia continued to stare, worry etched in her brow. "I'm not sure the boots go with your shorts, though."

She left the room, and I took off the boots and set them to the side, reaching for my sandals. There would be plenty of time to contemplate the boots later.

As I entered the hallway, I heard Guido's raspy voice ring out from inside Uncle Laz's room. I rapped on the door, and he answered with a look of chagrin on his face. "Bella, about last night—"

I put my hand up. "No. Don't worry about it. What's done is done. Today we start fresh."

"Guido has something he wants to tell you." Laz took me by the hand and practically dragged me across the room. "Go ahead, Guido, tell her."

The featherless bird warbled out something that almost sounded like, "Sorry, Charlie!" and I had to laugh.

"Did you teach him that?"

"We worked on it till after midnight. It's the least I can do."

With outstretched arms, Laz pleaded silently for my forgiveness. I slipped into his embrace and heard him praying over me in Italian, asking the Lord to bring peace. To grant my every wish on this fine day. And to make the wedding facility a success.

I stepped back and brushed the tears from my eyes. "I love you, Uncle Laz."

"Love you too, kiddo." He planted a kiss on my cheek, then glanced at his watch. "I'm supposed to be at the restaurant, helping Jenna and Marcella. But I'm going to stop off next door and see how those Neeley boys are doing with the barbecue first."

"Me too. I'll be over there in a few minutes."

He headed off on his way, and I stopped to chat with my mother, who sat on the stool in her bathroom, going through the usual morning makeup routine. She took more time than usual this morning—probably needing to erase the worry lines from last night.

At exactly 9:30, I headed downstairs to catch up with the boys next door. I'd almost made it to the bottom of the stairs when the doorbell rang. My heart flew into my throat when I saw D.J.'s mom standing there. Visions of Mr. Neeley's toupee in Guido's beak flashed through my memory, and I squeezed my eyes shut, wishing I could somehow have a do-over. Had Earline come to give me a piece of her mind, perhaps? Was she hoping to dissuade me from dating her son? Or had she decided to ask us to pay for the damages to her husband's hair?

Ushering her inside, I once again offered profuse apologies for Guido's behavior, hoping my heartfelt words would win her over. She shushed me, then reached into her purse to pull out a stack of bright pink CD cases, which she handed me with a relaxed smile as she offered up an explanation. "A couple of months back, Pastor Higley preached a series called 'Taming the Tongue.' After some prayer on the matter, I decided Guido needed to hear the sermons. They're arranged according to date, so they should be easy to follow. And the topics are most assuredly appropriate."

I stared in disbelief as she flipped through the six CDs, which she promised would change Guido's life forever. Was I the only one who hadn't yet climbed on the "let's get Guido saved" bandwagon? Was the Lord trying to send me a message? Was it really possible to rehabilitate a bird and thereby minister to his owner?

"You just give this situation to the Lord, Bella," Earline said with an affirming nod. "He cares for the birds of the air and the fish of the sea. And he loves you even more. And by the way . . ." Her eyes filled with tears as she finished. "I think you're just wonderful, darlin'. Don't you fret one little bit about what happened last night."

Relief swept over me, and I reached to give her a hug.

After releasing me from her embrace, Earline reached into her purse and pulled out a tiny slip of paper. Pressing it into my hand, she said, "Memorize this Scripture. Trust God for a new season."

I opened the paper and read, "The flowers appear on the earth; the time of the singing of birds is come. Song of Solomon 2:12."

I glanced back at Earline, curious as to its meaning. She gave me a wink, and I had the strongest feeling the verse—at least her interpretation of it—had nothing to do with Guido. No, Earline was trying to tell me something altogether different. She somehow recognized the fact that the Lord was shifting me into a new season.

Suddenly, reality hit again. Like Guido, I'd spent my whole life in the confines of a tiny little cage—aka the Rossi clan. I knew little outside the realm of my own family. But now, with D.J. in the picture, the Lord was symbolically opening the door to my little cage and asking me to spread my wings and fly a little. Could I? Would I?

A girlish giggle rose up as I pictured myself flying straight into D.J.'s arms.

Earline chose that moment to wrap me in another motherly hug, one that felt quite comfortable. She finally released her hold, and I saw a glimmer of tears in her eyes again. "I'm headed next door to check on my boys," she announced. "Want to come with me?"

"Do I ever!"

We followed our flared nostrils to the brisket on the far side of the lawn. Bubba stood to the side of the fire pit, stirring the massive pot of southwestern beans. I gave an admiring whistle, which caught his attention. "This looks great, Bubba. I feel like I'm on the wagon train, waiting for my chuck wagon supper."

He smiled his response. "Well, that's high praise, Bella. Thanks." His cheeks flushed pink. Actually, they'd been pink all along. It was ninety-five degrees outside, after all. Still, he didn't look bothered by that fact.

For the first time, I noticed his apron with the words SHADE TREE COOKERS on the front, and the tagline SPLENDIFEROUS BARBECUE FROM SPLENDORA, TEXAS, underneath. I couldn't help but smile, especially when D.J. appeared at my side.

He slipped his arm around my waist, and I melted into his embrace.

"You're still speaking to me?" I whispered.

"Well, of course." He looked baffled. "Why wouldn't I be?"

I started to give him a list of all the reasons he should turn and run all the way back to Splendora, but I stopped myself short. I did somehow manage to squeak out a weak response. "For starters, my bird stole your dad's hair. And then there's the part where my uncle raised your mother from the dead."

At this, D.J. laughed long and loud, and I breathed a sigh of relief. *Well, at least he's got a sense of humor about it.*

"My dad and that toupee." D.J. grinned. "We've been trying to talk him into going without it for years now, but his pride wouldn't let him. Likely this'll do the trick. And as for Laz raising my mother from the dead, well, I should be thanking him. We witnessed a miracle, you know." D.J. gave me a wink, and my heart melted.

"I don't know how to thank you," I whispered, leaning my head against his shoulder.

"You're doing just fine." He pulled me a bit closer and placed a few tender kisses along my hairline.

Uncle Laz appeared and muttered a teasing "Hey, no PDA, you two," and D.J. and I each took a small step back. My uncle shifted his attention to the fire underneath the beans, and his pleasant demeanor took a turn for the worse. "It's not hot enough." He spoke to Bubba like one would scold a child. "Those beans are going to be half-cooked if we don't get a better flame going."

"No, sir. It's fine like it is." Bubba's response was more Southern gentleman than harried chef. "This ain't my first rodeo." He added a playful wink.

When Laz gave him a curious look, D.J. offered an explanation. "He's just saying he's done this dozens of times before, Mr. Rossi. You've got nothing to worry about."

"Yeah." Bubba nodded. "The coals are nice and white, just like they need to be. And I've banked them, so they're plenty hot." He pointed at the bottom of the pit to prove his point.

Laz grunted, then went over to the smoker to check the meat. I looked at Bubba apologetically and shrugged. "He's used to being the one in charge. Sorry."

"No problem. I understand."

A plume of smoke rose from the open smoker just as my uncle's voice rang out again. "I think this brisket is getting dried out. Come and have a look."

To his credit, Bubba didn't respond right away. Instead, he drew in a deep breath, then walked over to the fifty-five-gallon drum smoker. After a quick look inside, he assured Laz everything was moving according to plan. "I've kept the temperature at 220 since five this morning. We're in great shape. The food will be cooked perfectly, I promise."

Laz muttered, *"Troppi cuochi guastano la cucina,"* under his breath. I knew the translation, of course: "Too many cooks spoil the broth." But I said nothing. Instead, I offered the Splendora team an encouraging smile and thanked them for their hard work. Laz took that as his cue to head back to Parma John's to help Jenna with the appetizers and side dishes.

The rest of the afternoon sailed by. I found myself strangely calm as the undeniable presence of God swept over me, removing any lingering anxieties. After giving the facility a thorough once-over, I made sure the linens on every table were spotless and wrinkle free. Then I spent some time fuss-ing over the head table, all the while trying to imagine what it would look like once the bridal party was seated. That done, I set out the chafing dishes and the punch bowl and checked our ice supply.

At 3:00, I watched with trepidation as Mama and Aunt Rosa carried the wedding cake into the reception hall and pieced the layers together. That done, Rosa touched up a couple of spots with the cream cheese frosting, then pulled out the decorating tips, and the party began. My, but that woman could make a simple cake look like something out of a magazine. Using perfectly white buttercream, she added her own unique reverse shell technique around the edges of each layer, then began to place some intricate scrollwork on the sides of each cake. Maybe one of these days she would teach me her tricks.

We all laughed when Mama added the cake topper—one Sharlene had specially selected with a cowgirl bride lassoing a cowboy groom. Sometimes a picture really does paint a thousand words. We stood back and examined the whole cake, now complete. I gave a little whistle, and Mama nodded.

"It's a little uneven on the back," Rosa said, walking around the table. "But I don't think anyone will notice."

"Uneven? Rosa, it's perfect."

Why did she always insist on seeing her flaws, not her achievements? What had caused her to be this way? After a moment of thinking about it, I had to conclude we were two peas in a pod. I usually noticed my flaws before my achievements too. Interesting.

I turned my attention to Patti-Lou, marveling at her handiwork as she put together the centerpieces. My, but those boots looked spiffy filled with gorgeous yellow roses and bluebonnets, all capped off with red, white, and blue bandanas. Yes, the whole thing was coming together—hee-haw style. Before long, the room would be filled with happy guests, wishing the bride and groom many years of marital bliss.

At 5:00—completely convinced everything was under control—I headed home to change into my cowgirl gear. Afterward, as I stared at my reflection in the mirror, I could hardly believe the transformation. I'd truly morphed into a real, honest-to-goodness Texan, from the tips of my boots to the top of my head.

My head. Hmm. I'd forgotten to put on Jenna's hat. Could I really do it? Would I look like a goober in a hat? Slipping it on my head, I felt like a character in an old Western. Striking a pose in front of the mirror, I pretended to draw a pistol. Pointing my index finger straight ahead, I drawled, "This town ain't big enough fer the both of us. So yer gonna hafta get on outta town, mister."

Of course, my sister chose that very moment to peek her head in the door.

"Bella?" She looked at me as if she wasn't quite sure it was me. "Laz and Jenna are here with all of the appetizers, and they're having trouble with one of the chafing dishes. Jenna needs to talk to you about it. But you might want to stop off at the fire pit first. Laz is giving Bubba a hard time."

"About what?" I turned to her, curious.

"Everything. You know how he is when it comes to cooking." An overly dramatic sigh escaped her lips.

"Yeah. But I was hoping he'd be a team player today."

"Like that would happen." Sophia glanced at her watch. "The bride will be here in thirty minutes. We need to get back over there. Don't want to miss it."

"I wouldn't miss it for the world." Reaching for my purse, I took one final glimpse in the mirror, then said, "I'm coming, I'm coming." I adjusted the hat on my head and sprinted down the stairs.

Less than three minutes later, I found myself at the edge of the fire pit, where—true to Sophia's words—Bubba and Uncle Laz appeared to be having it out. Glancing down at the pot of beans, I couldn't quite figure out what all of the shouting was about. They looked fine to me. Great, even.

"I told you those beans weren't going to be fully cooked," Laz argued with a look of pure stubbornness written on his face. "But would you listen to me? No!"

"But sir, they're fine," Bubba said. He gave them another stir, and we all hovered over the pot, staring down. "And they'll go on cooking throughout the wedding, so there's still plenty of time to get 'em softened up before they're served at the reception. Trust me."

"Trust you, my eye." Under his breath, Laz muttered—in Italian, of course—something about the fire not being hot enough.

What happened next will be forever seared in my memory—pun intended. I watched, not quite believing it, as Uncle Laz reached for a container of charcoal starter. To my great horror, he pointed it at the hot coals just as Bubba leaned in to stir the pot of beans.

I'd just opened my mouth to shout "No!" when a monstrous burst of flame shot up, followed by an immediate cry of pain from Bubba. He jumped back, nearly knocking the pot of beans from its hanging position. Immediately, he bent over at the waist and released a wail unlike anything I'd ever heard before.

At the sound of his voice, Jenna came running from inside the wedding facility with a punch ladle in hand. She took to screaming at Uncle Laz, whose eyes filled with tears. On and on she went, the ladle flailing as she lectured him on his carelessness.

Bubba rose, and we caught a clear glimpse of his face, black as coal. I'd never seen such a strange and terrifying sight. He repeated "Oh!" several times over, then prayed aloud, imploring the Almighty for help.

I needed to do something. Quickly.

"Are you okay? Should I call for the paramedics?" My breathless words must've frightened him speechless, because my splendiferous chef simply shook his head and stared at me like we'd all gone mad. He began to pace back and forth, back and forth, not saying a word.

Seconds later, D.J. and Armando came running from inside the building.

"We saw it all from the window," my brother exclaimed. "Should we call 9-1-1?"

"No, don't!" Bubba put his hand up in the air, as if he'd had enough of this nonsense. "It's not as bad as it looks. Just give me a minute. Please."

Then the strangest thing happened. He reached up with the back of his hand to wipe the soot from his face, particularly the area around his eyes, which seemed to be bothering him the most. When he brought his hands back down, we all gasped in unison.

Bubba's eyebrows were missing.

19

Turn the World Around

There are those moments in every life where you hope—or
even pray—you might be dreaming. Moments where everything you *think* you've just seen was not real at all. As I looked
back and forth between D.J. and his charred younger brother,
I felt sure someone would wake me up, would tell me this
was all some horrible nightmare.

Instead, reality stared me in the face. As I gaped at our
eyebrow-less chef with his sooty face and scorched apron, I
realized I wouldn't be waking up anytime soon. And I wasn't
sure I'd want to anyway.

Earline, who'd been happily setting up her keyboard until
the accident, appeared at Bubba's side with a look of horror
on her face. She began to cry out as if she'd been the one
injured. Then, with a bona fide Mama Bear expression on
her face, she turned to Laz, looking as if she might very well
put an end to his cooking days forever.

You could've heard a pin drop as she opened her mouth.

"You . . . you . . . you . . ." The anger in her voice caused an unfamiliar vibration. I'd never heard this particular sound before. Hoped I never would again. "You are . . ."

She closed her eyes, drew in a deep breath, and slowly counted to ten. Then her lips began to move in what I took to be a prayer. This went on for a while, so I eventually decided to join her. I closed my eyes and ushered up my request too, that Earline Neeley would not choose this particular moment— just two hours before the Boot-Scootin' wedding—to shred Uncle Laz to bits. With her words or otherwise.

Now, I'm a firm believer in prayer, but what happened next astounded even me. Earline's face softened, bit by mesmerizing bit. The deep creases in her brow and the irrefutable slits of anger between her eyes eventually dissipated. Within seconds, she'd morphed into the kindhearted, charitable Earline Neeley once more. She looked at my uncle, patted him gently on the arm, and very quietly said, "You are one of God's children who simply made a mistake."

Laz, likely overcome with relief, began to weep and to plead with the whole group of us for forgiveness. "I didn't mean to hurt anyone," he said between sobs. "It was just my lousy, stinking pride. I let it get in the way . . . and look what happened. I could've killed him. I could've . . ."

I couldn't hear the next few words through the wailing.

Now, Italian men are known to be emotional, no doubt. But I'd never—repeat, never—seen my uncle in such a state. And as he melted down on us, the most unlikely of people moved in to comfort him—Dwayne Sr. and Earline.

"Don't fret," Earline said after shushing him. "I'm sure Bubba's going to be all right. He's been through worse than this." Smiling all the way, she lit into a story about some accident he'd had on his bike as a kid.

"Yeah, I'm fine." Bubba nodded, but I could still see the pain in his eyes.

"Coulda happened to anyone," Dwayne Sr. added, slapping Laz on the back. "Why, I've got some barbecue stories that'll singe the hair right off your head."

"Save 'em for another day, darlin'," Earline urged. "We've got to figure out what to do with Bubba right now. He's lookin' a little overbaked."

At these words, the whole group of us turned to stare at him. Through the smears of black soot, I could almost make out his face underneath. Didn't look too bad. Except for the missing eyebrows and the newly formed blisters, of course.

Jenna, who had never come close to publicly expressing her feelings for anyone—even David, her almost-fiancé—began to weep uncontrollably at this point. She threw herself into Bubba's arms, and he wrapped her in a loving embrace.

Good-bye, David. It's been nice knowing you.

"Stay calm, everyone," my father instructed. "We've got to keep our cool." He turned to look at Bubba, then reached into his pocket for his cell phone. "You're sure you don't need medical assistance, son? I've got 9-1-1 on speed dial."

"I'm sure." Bubba's eyes glistened, but no tears erupted. "Simply feels like a bad sunburn. Really, I'm just stunned more than anything. I'm sure I'll be fine after I get cleaned up a bit."

"Well then, let's get him to the house," Mama instructed. "I know exactly what to do."

She'd just turned to lead him to the Rossi homestead when the sound of sirens began to shriek in the distance. They drew closer, then closer still. I looked around at the group, astounded. "Did someone call the paramedics?"

215

When I got a "no" from everyone in attendance, concern set in.

"Doesn't sound like an ambulance to me, anyway," Joey said. "Sounds more like police sirens. Those are patrol cars."

"Patrol cars?" I echoed.

"Yeah. A whole slew of them, from the sound of it." After analyzing the sound another second or two, he added, "And I'd wager there's a fire truck in the mix."

A lump the size of a golf ball filled my throat as I imagined the what-if scenarios.

Less than a minute later, the wedding facility was surrounded by police and firemen. They swarmed us like flies on honey. My heart flew into my throat as an officer called out, "Who's in charge here?"

I looked around for the nearest bush to hide behind but finally decided to fess up. "I . . . I am." I gingerly raised my hand.

The fellow's dark uniform was intimidating enough. So was his six-foot-plus physique. But that stern look on his face really put me in my place.

"Ma'am, we've received a complaint from a neighbor that you've got a fire going on the property." He pointed to the fire pit. "You're in violation of city ordinance. That fire will have to be extinguished, and I'm going to write you up."

"You're giving me a ticket for . . . a campfire?"

"Yes, ma'am."

"Wait just a minute, officer." Uncle Laz stepped up and pulled a piece of paper from his pocket. "I have a letter from the city, giving permission for this fire. We applied for the permit over a week ago."

He opened the paper, and the officer read it, then gave a nod. "I see."

One of the firemen turned to give Bubba an odd look. "Sir, are you in need of medical care?"

"No, I, um . . ."

"Are you sure?" The officer gave each of us a suspicious look.

"We'll take good care of him, I promise." Mama took him by the hand and turned toward our house.

"Well then, have a nice day."

"Keep a close eye on those flames," one of the firefighters advised. "If the wind picks up, you'll want to extinguish it right away."

The policeman gestured to the other officers, who'd positioned themselves à la S.W.A.T. style, and they all relaxed. I wish I could've said the same thing about the Rossis and the Neeleys. From the looks of things, it would be a long while before any of us relaxed again.

As Galveston's finest left the premises, Mama led Bubba to our house, with Earline, Rosa, and Jenna following close behind. I started to follow them, but Sophia stopped me. "Bella, leave it to the others. You just go on with things like nothing ever happened."

"Like nothing ever happened? Are you kidding? Last night our bird stole Mr. Neeley's hair, and today our uncle catches Bubba on fire. What's next? Is Aunt Rosa going to poison the wedding cake and blame it on Earline? Is Armando's girlfriend's father going to show up with a shotgun and take us all hostage? Will Pop decide we need some sort of sports tournament in the middle of the reception? Or maybe we'll just all get arrested for starting a bonfire."

"It's a fire pit."

"Still. I'm beyond humiliated." I spouted a litany of my more recent failures, not the least of which involved ordering eighty boots from a total stranger.

Sophia listened intently for the first couple of minutes, then stopped me. "Maybe you are humiliated. And maybe you've been through the wringer. But that doesn't change the fact that you're also a professional wedding coordinator whose bride just pulled up in the coolest-looking limousine I've ever seen."

"Sh-she did?" Sure enough, from the side lawn I could just make out the pickup-style limo as it pulled into the drive. Three minutes earlier and they would've found patrol cars lining the property. Thankfully, the timing had worked in my favor.

Sophia dabbed at my eyes with a tissue and did a quick touch-up of my hair using her fingertips as a comb. "Now, you go say hello to that bride and act as if nothing has happened. Don't you dare let Sharlene suspect anything has gone wrong. This is her day. She deserves perfection. And don't worry, we'll keep things quiet out here."

And so I did just that. With professionalism taking hold, I dried my eyes and approached Sharlene and the bridesmaids, where I dove into a lengthy oohing-and-aahing session over how they all looked. Then I led them into the wedding facility for some photos before the big event.

Joey met us in the foyer with camera in hand and a completely relaxed expression on his face. Within minutes he had several great shots. In that moment, I was reminded that we—the Rossis—had done this before. Weddings, I mean. Oh, not themed ones, but weddings were weddings, just the same. We were professionals. Sure, I hadn't been the one in charge, but everything always came off without a hitch.

Mostly. Every family member had his or her place, and we worked like a well-oiled machine. Surely we could go on this way, now that I'd stepped behind the wheel. Right?

Within minutes the groom and groomsmen arrived. They were ushered into a different area for their pre-wedding photographs. Then, in what seemed like the blink of an eye, guests began to trickle in. I couldn't help but admire the abundance of Western wear. And the boots! Wowza! Talk about a feast for the eyes. I could only speculate, but based on all the signs, we had an exciting night ahead of us!

Armando and Nick flew into gear, serving as valet parkers. One by one, the beautifully draped chairs in front of the gazebo filled with happy, carefree guests, never knowing, never suspecting, the calamities that had taken place in that area less than an hour before. I overheard several people commenting on the smell of the barbecue and the authenticity of the rugged Western decor, which helped to put my mind at ease.

Thankfully, a beautiful evening breeze blew in off the gulf, creating the perfect temperature for an outdoor event. We couldn't have ordered up a better night to pull off this shindig. The traffic on Broadway was light in comparison to most Saturday nights. And the neighbors were all safely tucked in their houses. Many of the guests commented on the perfect weather and the perfect ambience, and I even heard a couple say they couldn't wait to tell this person or that about the amazing wedding facility they'd stumbled into.

A few minutes before seven, Bubba reappeared, wearing his apron, which Aunt Rosa had somehow salvaged. It would be difficult to aptly describe what our poor barbecue chef looked like. He'd almost returned to his former glory—albeit glossier. I recognized the scent of aloe vera, which my mother had liberally applied to his toasted cheeks and forehead. The tip of his crimson nose would surely heal in time, though it had already started to blister. And the lips would probably take awhile too. But those eyebrows . . .

I tried not to gasp as I observed the area where Mama had strategically penciled in fake eyebrows in a shade that didn't quite match Bubba's real hair color. Close, but no cigar. Still, I would never breathe a word to Bubba, and I hoped no one else would either.

Sophia drew close and gave him a scrutinizing glance. "I think Mama did a pretty good job, don't you?" she whispered.

"Well, she's the makeup queen, I'll give her that much." I sighed. "But they don't look real, Sophia. Admit it. Even Mama's not that good."

Sophia squinted and gave our well-done chef another pensive look. "They're a little dark."

"And a little thick," I said in a strained whisper. Turning to Earline, I tried to gauge her reaction to this most recent catastrophe. She was too busy playing beautiful music on the keyboard to notice, but I felt sure she'd have something to say later on. Hopefully something humorous. After watching her transformation earlier this evening, I had no doubt the woman walked and talked with God daily. Only someone with a close relationship to him could possibly cool down that quickly. And authentically.

I gasped as I glanced at my watch. Five minutes to seven. No time to fret over Bubba's eyebrows now. I needed to head back inside to prepare the bridal party for their entrance.

Something told me I should start with the guys. I found the groom looking pale and shaky as Patti-Lou pinned on his boutonniere, which she did like a pro. After giving a few words of encouragement and instruction, I headed off to find

Sharlene and her jittery bridesmaids. When I'd seen them last, they'd been in a flutter, touching up makeup and tidying up loose hairs. Now I found them sitting silently as they listened to every strain of music coming from the piano outside.

"Ready?" I asked, gazing into the bride's fearful eyes.

She nodded, then came to me for a quick hug. "I can't thank you enough," she whispered. "You've given me the wedding of my dreams, Bella."

I wanted to say, "Don't count your chickens before they're hatched," but I resisted. I simply nodded and whispered, "You're worth it," then turned my attention to the bridesmaids for my final speech. "I'm headed outside. Remember to listen for your cue."

As I stepped outside to the gazebo area, I marveled at how beautiful everything looked. The decorations were perfect. With all of the boots and flowers, the rusty wagon wheels and Texas stars, the whole area might've stepped out of an old Western.

I stood in the back, waiting for the musical cue that would usher in the groom and groomsmen. As the music shifted and the groomsmen took their places, D.J. slipped into the spot next to me and leaned close.

As the music shifted gears once again, I found myself distracted. Over the next several minutes, I watched the wedding unfold like a beautiful orchid opening just once for a brilliant burst of glory. Everything about the service went just as planned. The groomsmen looked amazing in their black Western suits lined up across the front. And the bridesmaids! They glowed with anticipation as they made their entrances up the aisle one by one. The yellow rose bouquets with red, white, and blue ribbons dangling underneath looked just right against their floor-length soft yellow gowns. Sharlene had been right—once again. *Okay, Lord. I get it. I'll take my brides at their word from now on.*

Then came the moment we'd all been waiting for. As Earline began to play "The Wedding March," Sharlene made her way up the aisle on her father's arm. She'd chosen the most beautiful white wedding dress, with Western flair, of course. The tea-length gown had a tapered eight-point skirt with fringed hem, which gave everyone just the right view of her exquisite white cowboy boots. Or would they be called cowgirl boots? Hmm. I'd never thought of that before. I glanced down at my feet, trying to settle the issue in my mind.

Turning my attention back to the bride, I admired the lace trim on the vintage dress. And that hat! She wore a white cowboy hat with a veil attached to the back. I'd never seen anything so unique—or appropriate.

Once she reached the gazebo, memories of Guido's most recent performance fluttered through my mind right away. I glanced up, double-checking. I knew I had nothing to worry about, of course. The bird had been quarantined to Uncle Laz's bedroom . . . probably for the rest of his life.

During the ceremony, I found myself caught up in Pastor Higley's beautiful message about God's view on marriage. At some point, D.J. slipped his arm around my shoulders and pulled me close.

"I've been meaning to tell you something all evening," he whispered.

"Oh?" *That your parents plan to sue us over Bubba's eyebrows? That you have every intention of skipping town the minute this wedding is behind you? That you wish you'd never stumbled into my life in the first place?*

"In all the chaos, I forgot to mention that you look amazing in that outfit." He winked, and I melted like butter.

"R-really?"

"Yep. You're the real deal, Bella. Half cowgirl, half—"

"Mental case?"

"No." He grinned and pulled me close for a quick kiss before whispering, "Half perfection."

"Hardly."

Still, hearing him speak the word suddenly put everything in perspective. Somehow these Neeleys could see beyond a person's flaws. They could even see beyond mistakes. They were walking, talking examples of godliness.

I swallowed the lump in my throat and listened as the pastor continued.

"Love is patient. Love is kind," he quoted. "It does not envy, it does not boast, it is not proud. It is not rude, it is not self-seeking, it is not easily angered, it keeps no record of wrongs."

As I listened, I turned to look at D.J. once again. Thank goodness he'd seen fit to forgive my quirky family members for all of their flaws of late. In so many ways he epitomized this very Scripture.

"Love does not delight in evil," Pastor Higley continued, "but rejoices with the truth. It always protects, always trusts, always hopes, always perseveres. Love never fails."

The good pastor might as well have been talking about the man with his arm wrapped around me. He'd already served as protector that night at the restaurant. And I now saw him as a trusted friend as well. But there was more. I'd fallen in love with D.J. Neeley from Splendora, Texas, and my life would never be the same.

Gazing up at him, I noticed the tears in his eyes. "You okay?" I whispered.

"Mm-hmm." He placed a gentle kiss on my cheek and pulled me closer.

The service came to its rightful end, and Earline began to play as the wedding party was dismissed. The bridesmaids and groomsmen exited as couples.

I'd been waiting for this part all evening. Each groomsman had a white Stetson positioned at the end of a row. As they walked out, they snagged their hats and, in chorus, hollered, "Yee-haw!"

I couldn't have put it any better myself.

20

In the Chapel in the Moonlight

After the bride and groom said their "I dos," Pastor Higley released the crowd into the reception hall for appetizers. The wedding party remained in the gazebo area for pictures. Joey, a consummate pro behind the camera, managed to get some great shots in record time. I'd never been prouder of him.

As we wrapped up, Sharlene looked my way with joy beaming from her face, then hollered, "Let the party begin!"

Yes, let the party begin! After the events of the past few days, I was ready for a boot-scootin' hoedown. Oh, if only I could relax and enjoy it like the others. If only I didn't have to worry about my caterers catching the building on fire, or D.J. fainting from fear as he took the microphone in hand. If only I didn't have to fret over broken chafing dishes or the number of trash cans we'd set out. If only I didn't have to wonder if we'd prepared enough appetizers or adjusted the AC to properly accommodate such a large crowd. *Then* I could have fun with the others.

I drew in a deep breath and heard the Lord whisper, "You *don't* have to worry, Bella. Do the things you need to do and leave the rest to me."

Ah. What a happy reminder. All of my fretting wouldn't accomplish anything anyway. Right? Might as well just have a good time and trust the Lord.

Once everyone was inside, the festivities began. Guests filled their plates to the brim with brisket, beans, potato salad, and more. I'd never seen so many contented people or heard so many compliments on the food. Bubba, Laz, and Jenna worked in tandem to serve the guests. After the eyebrow incident, my uncle had certainly learned his lesson.

I managed to sneak a bite of the brisket and had to admit it was truly amazing. The sauce had a zip and a zing to it, and the meat was so tender it practically melted in my mouth. And those southwestern beans! They were perfectly seasoned with just the right amount of brown sugar and sausage. And the texture? Primo! Man, Bubba really knew his stuff. Surely he'd even win over Laz, his toughest critic, with tonight's food.

Finally the awaited moment came. D.J. gave my hand a squeeze as he headed off to morph into a deejay. I whispered a silent prayer that his nerves wouldn't get in the way. I watched in awe as he opened the floor to the bride and groom for the first number. "Ladies and gentleman, our happy couple will now dance their very first dance as husband and wife." After less than a minute of watching him in action, all of my former worries faded away.

Oh, that voice! That beautiful, deep, mesmerizing voice! Just the sound of it and my breath caught in my throat. I was swept back in time to that first phone call where he'd won me over, sight unseen. And I still swooned every time the boy opened his mouth to speak. He'd reeled me in, and there was no turning back.

And now, as the melody of "Could I Have This Dance for the Rest of My Life" came on, I caught the eye of my handsome cowboy deejay. He winked at me from across the room, putting me at ease and causing my heart to flutter all at the same time. *Oh yes, D.J. Neeley. I'd like to have this dance . . . for the rest of my life.* In that moment, as my eyes locked in on his baby blues, everyone else in the room faded into the background. It was just the two of us, decked out in our cowboy/cowgirl attire, ready to dance the night away.

After the bride and groom finished their dance, D.J. called for Sharlene's father to take the floor. The misty-eyed oilman swept his daughter in his arms, and they danced to a song called "I Loved Her First." I'd never heard this particular song before—no great surprise there—but the words brought tears to my eyes. For a moment I could picture my own wedding, my own father-daughter dance. Surely my pop would blubber like a baby from start to finish. Likely, I would too.

Next came the mother-son dance. Cody and his mama enjoyed some laughter and a few tears as "Mama, Don't Let Your Babies Grow Up to Be Cowboys" played overhead. My thoughts shifted to my someday-wedding again. If I married D.J., he and his mama would be the ones dancing right about now. A mixture of feelings washed over me, and I found myself searching for Earline through the crowd. When we made eye contact, I waved and she winked in response. My heart did a little dance of its own as I realized just how much I admired her already.

As the music ended, the crowd stirred in anticipation. D.J. grinned as he made the announcement. "Ladies and gentlemen, we'd like to open the floor to all of our guests. C'mon and grab a partner, and let's get this show on the road!"

I'd never seen Patti-Lou move so fast. She snagged Mr. Billings by the hand and pulled him onto the dance floor. Not that he seemed to mind. Within seconds, they were two-stepping in tandem. The bride and groom knew all the right moves, and so did Dwayne Sr. and Earline, who danced as if they'd been doing it all their lives. Maybe they had. Maybe I was the only one who'd never learned the dance. I had to wonder if perhaps I'd spent my whole life one-stepping when I could've been two-stepping.

Out of the corner of my eye, I peeked at D.J. Maybe one of these days he could catch me up on all I'd missed. For now, I needed to two-step my way over to the punch table to see why Mama and Rosa had let the bowl go empty.

Over the next hour, I watched D.J. work the crowd. Turned out that deep twangy voice of his was a favorite, not just with the bride and groom but with everyone in attendance. Sure, Armando did a fine job managing the soundboard, but D.J. was the real star, calling the dances as if he'd been deejaying all his life.

I watched, awestruck, as Sharlene, Cody, and all of their guests did the "Waltz across Texas," line-danced with aban-don, and two-stepped like pros. I couldn't help but laugh as Rosa tried her hand—or rather, her feet—at the "Cotton-Eyed Joe." And the schottische that followed reminded me of one of her folk dances. She was actually quite good at it. Even Uncle Laz joined in, cane in hand. They'd found their com-mon ground—not in Frank Sinatra or Dean Martin music but in country-western. Go figure.

Of course, the night wouldn't have been complete without the addition of "Boot-Scootin' Boogie," which the groom had selected as one of his personal favorites. We all laughed as folks formed long lines, dancing as a group.

At 10:30 we brought the dancing portion of the evening to a close with an announcement from D.J. "Folks, it's time for the bride and groom to cut the cake."

I drew near to the beautiful cake, which Rosa had spent hours making. After Sharlene proclaimed it the most beautiful cake she'd ever seen, she and Cody did the usual bride/groom thing—smeared pieces of it all over each other's faces. Then Mama and Aunt Rosa served up hefty slices for the crowd. After that, speeches were given and toasts were offered.

I found myself getting misty-eyed as parents of the bride and groom took the microphone to speak words of love over their now-married children. How interesting to imagine what my mama and pop would say when their turn came. It's likely my mother—who would no doubt outshine the bride in appearance—would tell the crowd that she'd wasted twenty-nine years praying for a good Italian boy for her daughter. Pop would probably tell a couple of embarrassing stories, including the one about my misshapen head.

Suddenly, I could hardly wait.

As the evening wore on, several people from Sharlene's family made a point to thank me for my hard work. I heard everything from "This is a beautiful facility" to "I've never seen such a flawless wedding."

Little did they know.

Little would they ever know.

What happened at Club Wed stayed at Club Wed. No one would be any the wiser. Other than the Rossi and Neeley clans, anyway.

I paused to think about that. For the first time, our two families had something in common. We'd been through the fire together. Literally. And we'd come through it without a trace of smoke in our hair.

Well, most of us.

I prayed those events would unify us, but only time would tell. I scarcely had a chance to ponder this thought before Earline approached and took my hand. "I can't begin to tell you how proud I am. You have a real gift, Bella." She gazed into my eyes with both tenderness and depth.

"Oh?"

She gestured around the room. "You're an amazing wedding coordinator, but there's more to it than that. You know how to keep things going, even when the pressure's on."

"Trust me, only the Lord can do that. If it were up to me, I would've stayed in bed this morning after that fiasco last night. And today . . ." I shook my head and closed my eyes, wishing I could somehow will it all away.

"Oh, but it's been so much fun. The good and the bad. And think of the stories you'll have to tell your children. Even the not-so-good things are conversational." She offered up a wink before walking away, and I found myself standing alone, pondering her words. Children? Did the woman mention children?

At 11:30, the pickup-style limousine returned to the front of the wedding facility to pick up the bride and groom. As she brushed by me, Sharlene reached to squeeze my hand. "It was a dream-come-true wedding, Bella," she whispered. "I'll never be able to thank you enough."

"It was my pleasure." I tried to push away the tears, but they fell anyway. It truly had been a dream come true. For both of us.

The bride and groom climbed aboard the limo to head off to a five-star hotel on the beach. Tomorrow morning they would leave for Jamaica. Or was it Cancun? I couldn't remember. Not that it mattered. No, all that mattered right now was the fact that we'd done it! We'd actually pulled off a country-western themed wedding, and everyone seemed thrilled with the results.

After the reception hall emptied, the Rossis and the Neeleys hung around to clean up the facility. I could hardly believe the mess.

"You all really don't have to stay," I said as I watched Earline clear one of the tables.

"Well, shoot." She smiled at me. "What are friends for anyway, honey? Might as well stay busy. And besides"—she gave me a wink—"it gives me a chance to get to know you better. And your family."

I wanted to hug her right there on the spot, but resisted. Instead, I offered up a warm smile and worked alongside her, clearing tables and washing dishes.

We worked together for quite a while. I scraped food off plates. Pulled centerpieces from tables. Dismantled the chocolate fountain. Poured out the rest of the punch. Tossed dirty tablecloths in a pile in the corner. In short, I undid everything I'd spent hours doing in the first place.

As the clock struck midnight, I remembered the decorations in the gazebo. Grabbing a box, I headed outside. The chairs were now empty, but the tiny white Christmas lights we'd added to the lattice trim twinkled merrily. I stepped inside and started boxing up the decorations.

Just minutes into my work, I heard a familiar deep voice. I looked up to see D.J. standing beside me.

"Hey." I gazed into his eyes.

"Hey back." He took the box out of my hands and set it on the ground.

"What are you . . . ?" I gave him a curious look.

As he drew nearer, I could feel his breath against my face, warm and inviting. "We've both been a little busy," he whispered in my ear. "We never had a chance to dance."

"Oh." For a moment I thought I might be dreaming. Underneath the stars and the twinkling gazebo lights, the two of us seemed more like characters from a fairy tale than weary wedding planner and faux deejay. Still, there was no disputing the fact that God was up to something very real here, and I certainly didn't want to miss a thing.

"Would you do me the honor?" D.J. extended his hand, and I smiled all the way down to my toes as I slipped into his arms.

With the scent of barbecue lingering in the air and the soft shimmer of lights dancing all around us, we danced inside the gazebo to a country tune that only the two of us could hear. Then, when the music drifted off to the stars, D.J.'s lips met mine for a kiss that set off bona fide fireworks.

Thankfully, this time no one got burned.

21

Baby, It's Cold Outside

D.J. and I spent several minutes in the gazebo in each other's embrace, then headed back inside to join the others. We passed Patti-Lou on the way, her arms loaded with things that needed to go back to her flower shop. D.J. offered our help loading them into her van, but she shook her head. "Are you going back in the reception hall?" she asked, sounding a little breathless.

"Yes," I said with a nod. "How come?"

"You might want to put on your boxing gloves first." She disappeared into the darkness, and I turned to D.J., confused.

"So, do we or don't we go in there?" he asked.

"My pop raised me to face trouble head-on, so if there's a problem, we might as well confront it."

"Together." He kissed me once more, sending tingles all the way down to my toes, then we walked hand in hand into the hall.

I gasped when I saw Tony DeLuca and Bubba having it out in the corner. My ex was pushing Bubba in a taunting sort of way while muttering something about cowboys.

I sensed D.J.'s tension mounting as he observed all of this, but he managed to stay calm. Wish I could've said the same for Jenna. She approached Bubba and Tony with fire in her eyes.

"Back off, Tony. Leave him alone." The mama-bear sound in her voice surprised me. This was twice in one day I'd seen Jenna rush to Bubba's defense.

Of course, Bubba had been through a tougher-than-usual day. I gazed up at his now-blistered face and noticed the eyebrows had, for the most part, sweated themselves down into his eyelids. Not that he could help it. He'd worked hard from sunup until sundown. Still, his dribbling eyebrows reminded me of a woman's flowing mascara after she'd had a good cry. Only higher.

But Tony . . . well, Tony was another story altogether.

I gave my handsome ex a stern once-over. What was he doing here, anyway? He hadn't been invited to the wedding, and I didn't recall seeing him earlier in the evening. That meant he must've shown up while D.J. and I were out in the gazebo. Likely Tony's sour attitude had something to do with my budding relationship with D.J. In fact, I'd be willing to bet my boots on it. But why show up randomly, after midnight, no less? To pick a fight, perhaps?

Sure enough, as we entered the room, Tony shifted his gaze to D.J., and his fists clenched. Goodness, I'd never seen my ex in such a state. There might just be a shoot-out at the O.K. Corral if someone didn't intervene.

Thankfully, my father stepped up to the plate. "There's nothing to get all worked up about, Tony. Take a step back and cool down before I take that punch bowl over there and dunk your head in it."

Tony stepped back, but I could see a vein in his neck bulging.

D.J. glanced my way, then looked back at Tony, likely trying to figure out what, if anything, to do.

"What are you looking at, cowboy?" Tony demanded, turning to D.J.

Yikes. Where were my big brothers when I needed them? They would've handled this with ease, but it appeared they'd already left for the night.

D.J. gave Tony an odd look. "Excuse me?"

Tony squared his jaw, then drew nearer to my hunk-of-a-cowboy, muttering, "You think you're quite the man, stealing my girl away from me."

"Stealing your girl away from you?" D.J. crossed his arms at his chest and stared Tony down. "If she wanted to be with you, she would be with you."

Raising my arms, I began to rant. "We broke up months ago, Tony. It's over. Caput. In fact, it was over long before that, but I just didn't have the courage to tell you." Should I add that I hadn't shed a tear? That the only reason I'd hung on for so long was to make my mama happy? That I'd never felt as safe in his arms as I now felt in D.J.'s? That his kisses didn't set off fireworks and his eyes didn't twist my stomach into knots?

Nope.

"So this is what you want?" Tony thumped D.J. on the chest. "This hick? This backwoods hillbilly? You think he's going to take care of you the way I could?"

D.J. flinched, and for a moment I thought he might take Tony out right then and there. I had no doubt he could do it, I just didn't care to see my ex's blood smeared on the reception hall floor. Not right after we'd mopped it, anyway.

From off in the distance, I saw Earline's eyes widen. I half expected her to come shooting across the room and give Tony a piece of her mind, but she kept quiet. Miraculously, so did D.J., though I felt sure it must've taken every ounce of strength in him not to react.

Out of the corner of my eye, I saw Patti-Lou return for another load of floral supplies. She observed the goings-on between the guys and scurried out almost as quickly as she came. I didn't blame her. If I could've run from the place, I would have.

Instead, I gathered up my courage and decided it was my turn at bat. I spoke to Tony with forced bravado. "For your information, D.J. has more refinement in his little finger than you do in your whole body." A sudden burst of anger spurred me on. "In fact, he's every bit the man I'm looking for. No offense, Tony, but there's just no comparison." *So there.* I wanted to stick out my tongue, but manners prevented it. Well, manners and my mama, who watched all of this with a look of horror on her face. For once I was glad I couldn't read her thoughts.

I glanced at Tony. His jaw tightened as he muttered, *"Moglie e buoi dei paesi tuoi."*

"What's that supposed to mean?" D.J. asked, crossing his arms.

"Figure it out." Tony's eyes flashed with an odd mixture of pain and anger.

D.J. turned to look at me, likely hoping I'd offer the interpretation. But how could I? Tony's words, "Marry a woman from your own neighborhood," wouldn't make things any better. No, the only thing that would improve the situation now would be a strike of lightning from heaven, landing squarely between my ex and D.J. That would probably be enough to send Tony running. Maybe. I'd never seen him in this state before.

Bubba mumbled something about Tony being lower than a snake's belly, and Earline smacked him with the back of her hand—Bubba, not Tony. Seemed she still wanted her boys to mind their manners, even under the direst of circumstances.

Tony, on the other hand, lost his manners the minute he heard the words slip out of Bubba's mouth. For the second time in twenty-four hours, I watched something in motion-picture-quality slow motion. Tony turned and lunged at Bubba, fists clenched. In the distance, I heard Jenna call out, and I thought I recognized Aunt Rosa's voice as she cried out for three or four major saints.

None of those things stopped Tony, now a raging bull. Though Bubba stood nearly a foot taller than him, Tony's balled-up fist met Bubba's right eye with a solid punch. The smack echoed across the now-empty wooden floor of the reception hall. Jenna let out a shriek, then went on the attack. I flew into action, pulling her off Tony.

He stepped back, a look of pride on his face as he saw the marks he'd left behind on Bubba's already scorched face. "Now what are you going to do?" he taunted.

The words "turn the other cheek" flitted through my mind. If Bubba Neeley followed the biblical rule—which was more than likely, especially with his mama present—Tony would continue to pummel him until someone cried for mercy. Not that my five-foot-seven ex could really do much damage to Bubba. Knowing Tony, however, it wouldn't stop him from trying.

Oddly enough, Sophia intervened. She rushed to Tony's side, whispered something in his ear, and stepped back. For the first time, I noticed tears in her eyes, and it stopped me cold. *Conspiring with the enemy, Sophia? We're going to have words later.*

In spite of whatever she'd said, Tony didn't back down. He squared his shoulders and tipped his head back to look up into Bubba's eyes. "Now what are you going to do . . . cowboy?" There was something about the way he said *cowboy* that jarred me. *Cow*-boy. Like Bubba was more cow than boy.

Miraculously, all six-foot-four inches of Bubba Neeley stood stock-still. His jaw couldn't get any tighter, and his breaths—through his nose—were coming harder now, a sure sign he was trying to calm himself. There was no doubt in my mind Bubba could've squashed Tony like a pesky cockroach with no trouble at all. But would he? And if so, would anyone really blame him?

From off in the distance, Aunt Rosa began to pray aloud in Italian. Uncle Laz joined her, and within minutes their voices created a musical sound. Earline began to pray too. In English, of course, with a bit of a Holy Ghost gospel twang. After a few minutes of prayer, she directed her words at the devil, commanding him to flee in Jesus's name. Within seconds my mama linked her voice in chorus, and then the others followed suit. Before long, what had started out as a barroom brawl had morphed into a full-fledged prayer meeting.

I half expected Bubba to start singing "Just as I Am" and extend an invitation for Tony to give his life to the Lord. Instead, he grabbed a handful of utensils, flashed a crooked smile Tony's way, and tipped his hat as he headed for the door. "I always hate to leave a party early, but it's time to go. Besides, I'm feeling about as welcome as a skunk at a picnic."

"Wait, Bubba! I'm coming too!" Jenna glared at Tony, then took Bubba's hand, and they marched out the door together.

The rest of us stood like stones, unable to move. The tension in the room was so thick, I thought it might suffocate us, and the heat didn't help. After whispering a prayer that Tony would come to his senses, I glanced at Earline.

"I suppose we should get on the road," she said, giving my mother an apologetic look. "It's been a long day."

I'll say. Your son has been scorched by my uncle and accosted by my ex.

Likely I'd never see Earline Neeley again after tonight. Or Bubba. Or—my heart flip-flopped—D.J. Would the entire Neeley clan head for the hills, convinced the Rossis were nothing but trouble?

"It's a long drive back to Splendora, and we've got an early morning tomorrow." Earline took her husband's arm. "Church, you know. Pastor Higley's been preaching the most amazing sermon series. He started with taming the tongue and went on from there to teaching about self-control." She gave Tony a pensive look as she added, "A lesson we could all stand to learn."

She and Dwayne Sr. said their good-byes, then left the rest of us alone to deal with my angry ex.

Uncle Laz broke the tension by belching. He rubbed his belly and mumbled, "I need an antacid. Too much barbecue."

Apparently that was all Aunt Rosa needed to hear. She and Laz slipped out the back door.

"Yeah, I think my work here is done." Sophia gave Tony a sad look, then hurried from the room.

The field was narrowing. Pretty soon D.J. and I would be

left alone in the room to deal with Tony. Perhaps that was for the best. Surely I could calm this hot-tempered Italian down with a few cool words.

My parents stood off in the distance, probably wishing they could bolt too. Sure enough, they quickly bowed out, claiming Pop's lactose intolerance had kicked in, and we stood—the three of us—in an awkward triangle. Again, I noticed the look of pain in Tony's eyes. He looked like an injured puppy. Well, an injured puppy ready to bite the ankle of anyone who dared come near.

Looking up at D.J., I whispered, "Would you mind? I need to speak to Tony alone."

He gave me an "are you sure you want to be alone with this guy?" look, and I nodded. Tony wouldn't lift a finger to hurt me.

D.J. exhaled, and I could sense his frustration. "I'll call you tomorrow."

I nodded and watched as he walked away, then turned to Tony, trying a softer approach.

"Tony, look . . . I know this is hard. And I never meant to hurt you. I hope you know that. I still care very much about you."

His jaw flinched as I spoke those last few words, but he didn't respond.

"It's not in my heart to hurt anyone. But I can't force something I don't feel. And I don't want to spend the rest of my life with regrets, wondering if I made the right decision."

At this, Tony's head dropped, and he sighed loudly. "You don't love me, Bella?"

Man. He had to ask such a pointed question? No, I didn't love him. And no, I never would. But saying it aloud made it seem so . . . hurtful. "Tony, you're going to make some woman a wonderful husband someday. I . . . I'm not that woman. There's a part of me that will always care for you"—he looked at me with hope in his eyes, but I shut him down with my closing remarks—"but just not in the way you're hoping."

The words "in a brotherly sort of way" flitted through my mind, but I didn't say them aloud. Still, they rang true. Tony was the sort of guy who'd fit right in as part of my family. Just not as my husband. Maybe my parents could adopt him, but I'd never—repeat, never—take him back as a boyfriend or potential mate.

In spite of his earlier antics, I offered my now-deflated ex a warm hug and sent him on his way. He left with his gaze to the ground and his heart in his hands.

I meandered outside and found Patti-Lou, who worked to load up the last bits of floral stuff into her van.

"Hey, girl." I took a few steps in her direction, and she turned to me with tears in her eyes. "Whoa. What happened? Besides the obvious, I mean."

She shrugged. "I gave it my best shot, but I don't think I'll ever hear from him again."

Ah. Mr. Billings.

"How do you know?"

"Just a feeling I get. This always happens to me. I meet a really great guy, and then . . ." She sighed. "He's gone. Usually forever."

Wow. What an uplifting night this was turning out to be.

"Don't worry about me." Patti-Lou waved a hand in my direction. "I'm okay with being single. It's a terminal condition. In my case, anyway. I've reconciled myself to that fact."

She disappeared down Broadway in her van, but her words lingered in the air behind. They seemed to swallow me up like the night air. As always, I had to wonder if my single status would ever change. Were Patti-Lou and I destined to be in the same boat forever? Was my singleness a terminal condition too? After a night like tonight, D.J.'s family would likely encourage him to head to higher ground. Find someone with a less nutty family and a less volatile ex-boyfriend.

The very idea of losing D.J. brought the sting of tears to my eyes. A pain I'd never before experienced gripped my heart. Now that my cowboy deejay had boot-scooted on home to his condo at the edge of the gulf, I had to wonder if my chance for happiness had drifted out to sea.

22

Which Way Did My Heart Go?

The morning after the wedding, I slept in late. When I finally awoke, every square inch of my body ached. Even my toenails cried out in pain. I didn't realize until now just how many hours I'd spent on my feet over the past couple of days, or how many things I'd lifted, moved, or cleaned. One thing was clear—all of that work had finally caught up with me.

Swinging my legs over the side of the bed was tough enough. But attempting to step down? Near to impossible. My knees didn't want to bend. For that matter, neither did my back. Even my brain hurt, especially when I paused to think about D.J.'s rapid departure. He'd promised to call, but would I ever really hear from him again after Tony's shenanigans? I sat in queasy silence for a moment, realizing I'd had too much barbecue last night. Better not to mention it to any of the others, especially Rosa. She'd be offering to rub olive oil on my belly, her homemade cure for stomachaches.

Just as my toes touched down, I heard a rap on the door. I managed a feeble, "Come in."

Sophia stepped inside, fully dressed and looking like a prom queen. I hated her. How dare she? My sister was practically perfect in every way.

She plopped down on my bed with an apologetic look on her face. "Hey, Bella. You going to church today?"

"Yes. If I can just get my body to unfold, and if this queasiness passes."

She laughed, then gave me a sheepish look. "I'm going too, but I have ulterior motives."

"Oh?" I gave her a curious look.

"I need to pray for forgiveness."

"For what?"

She sighed, then peered at me with damp lashes. "I'm so sorry about inviting Tony last night without asking you first."

"Aha. So you're to blame." I'd never been one to hold back my thoughts where my sister was concerned, so I plowed ahead. "I just don't get it, Sophia. I thought you liked D.J. Why would you sabotage me like that?"

"Oh, I do like D.J.!" She offered a convincing nod along with a bright smile. "He's great. His whole family is. And I think you two are perfect together. And I wasn't trying to sabotage you at all, I promise."

I stared at her, confused. "Well, why bring Tony into the mix? Didn't you realize things would turn out the way they did?"

"Well . . ." My sister's cheeks flushed, and for the first time a niggling suspicion settled in.

"Don't tell me you're . . ."

"Do you hate me, Bella?" She gave me an imploring look.

244

"I didn't mean to fall for him. I've been fighting it for months. But I've had the wildest crush on Tony for ages now."

"Ew."

She sighed. "I know. It kind of grossed me out at first too. Falling for my sister's boyfriend."

"Ex-boyfriend."

"Yeah." Her gaze shifted to the ceiling, then back down again. "But to be honest, I liked him even when you were still dating."

"Double ew."

"I tried not to." Her eyes narrowed, and I thought I saw a glistening of tears. "You have no idea how hard I tried. Didn't you ever notice that I made excuses not to be around on the nights he came for dinner? And that time you invited me along on your date to Moody Gardens, I told you I had an appointment?" After I nodded, she sighed. "I lied. I spent that afternoon at the restaurant, drinking three large caramel mocha macchiatos."

"Yikes."

"Yeah, I was up all night. You know what caffeine does to me." She gave me an imploring look. "Oh, but Tony does the same thing to me, only worse. I can't sleep when I think about him. I feel like I'm on a high when he's around, and I have this huge, plunging feeling all the way to my toes when he's gone. I'm . . . addicted, Bella. And I can't help it."

"I understand that particular addiction, trust me." My heart had taken a pretty big plunge last night when I realized D.J. had left. And I certainly understood the staying up all night thing too. I'd hardly slept in the two weeks since meeting him.

Sophia continued, oblivious to my thoughts. "After you broke up with Tony, I hoped . . ." Another sigh escaped, and

I understood in an instant what she'd been trying to say all along. She'd been hoping Tony would turn his attention away from me—and toward her.

Well, this certainly explained why none of her dates ever seemed to work out. How could they, when she'd given her heart to another?

"I need you to forgive me." She looked at me with misty eyes. "I promised myself I'd never let a man come between me and my sister."

"Sounds like a song."

"I know, but I really mean it. He's . . ." She stammered over the words. "He's . . . not worth it. He'll probably never even figure out I exist, but you . . ." She reached to take my hand and gave it a squeeze. "You'll be my sister for life. So please forgive me."

"I'll forgive you on one condition." I eased myself to a standing position. "When you and Tony are married and have half a dozen children, I still want you to work for me at the wedding facility. I plan to be in business for years to come, and I can't do it without you. And you'll have to ask me to be your maid of honor . . . even if it's a little weird." I shivered, thinking about just *how* weird it would be.

"Oh, Bella!" Sophia lunged into my arms, almost knocking me down. "You've got it. And wouldn't Tony and I make beautiful babies together?" She clasped her hands together and giggled. "Sophia DeLuca. Has a nice ring to it, doesn't it?" Extending her left hand, she looked at the empty ring finger. "Someday. I know it's going to happen. I just know it."

A starry-eyed look replaced her once-sensible expression, and I shrugged. Maybe Sophia and Tony would end up living a happily-ever-after life, but would I? After last night, I highly doubted it.

Sophia sashayed out of the room, leaving me alone with my thoughts.

As I showered, I reenacted the wedding. Sure, the cleanup had presented some problems, but the actual wedding and reception had come off without a hitch. With God's help, I'd done it! I'd pulled off my first real themed wedding. And the bride and groom left for their honeymoon content. Really, that was all that mattered. Right?

Of course, there was that one little incident that involved Bubba's eyebrows. And the police. And of course there was Bubba's black eye to consider. But if you didn't factor in all of those things, the night could very well be considered a success.

A wave of satisfaction washed over me as I reveled in the possibility that I wouldn't drive our family's business into the ground. In fact, the more I thought about it, the more I looked forward to the next wedding—a medieval extravaganza. Knights in shining armor. Ladies-in-waiting. What fun I'd have working with the bride-to-be. Not that I really knew much about the Renaissance era. Hmm. I'd better spend some time researching over the next couple of weeks.

Oh, but right now all I wanted to do was relax. Take a deep breath. Thank God for all he'd done . . . and then fig-ure out a way to express my regrets to D.J.'s family about Tony's actions.

I spent the next couple of hours in church with the Rossi clan. Seated in the pew, I praised God for his many blessings and asked him to mend any broken fences between the Rossis and the Neeleys. Reverend Woodson spoke on overcoming obstacles, a lesson I needed to hear. And looking at his boots reminded me that I had a little business to take care of when

I arrived home: the Lanciottis. I needed to get them back into their rightful owner's hands.

Later that afternoon—after Rosa's traditional Sunday afternoon lunch of spaghetti and meatballs—I stood in the front hall, humming "These Boots Are Made for Walkin'." I found the lyrics applicable, since more than a dozen pair of boots had disappeared over the past week or so. Everyone in the Rossi family had claimed at least one pair. Mama found a pretty pair with fringe. Rosa had taken the orange pair, claiming they made her run faster. Armando, Nick, and Joey had each settled on a pair, and Uncle Laz . . . well, once he'd sworn off the Lanciottis, he'd settled on a plain pair of worn brown boots, claiming they were the most comfortable things he'd ever put on his feet.

I had to agree. The pair I'd selected for the wedding ended up being just the right fit. Maybe I'd been won over to the other side after all. Still, I couldn't keep the Lanciottis. I had to track down the owner. Had to tell her the truth.

Turning my sights to my email, I located the original email from the woman who'd sold me the boots. I located her name—Victoria Oldenburg—on the receipt. Found her address as well. And it didn't take much work on my part to locate her phone number.

With nerves kicking in, I punched in the number. She answered after the second ring with an abrupt, "Hello."

"Mrs. Oldenburg, this is Bella Rossi from Galveston. I'm the one who purchased the boots from you on eBay a little more than a week ago."

"That's *Ms.* Oldenburg," she countered in an all-too-serious voice. "And there's no refund or exchange, so don't even bother to ask."

"Oh, no, ma'am. I'm not calling to get my money back or

because I'm unhappy with the product. Quite the opposite."
I went on to explain that I'd located a pearl in the midst of
the oysters I'd purchased from her. "There's a pair of boots
here worth thousands of dollars."

She snickered. "The Lanciottis."

"You . . . you knew about them?"

"Of course." The tone of her voice changed as she continued. "Brian was always keen on expensive things. He used
to brag that he was the only man in Lubbock with boots like
that. Ya know, he was probably right, but I always hated to
hear him carry on about it, especially in such a public way.
He sure was a prideful man."

All this talk about Brian in the past tense made me wonder if he'd gone on to that great boot maker in the sky. But
I couldn't just come out and ask, could I? "So, you meant to
sell them to me for twenty dollars?"

"Yep. Serves him right."

Okay, now we were talking about him in present tense.

The not-so-happy Ms. Oldenburg went on to share far too
much information about her ex-husband—how he'd left her
for a pretty young thing named Missy who worked at his office. How he'd neglected to return home to pick up his things
before marrying Missy and building a mini mansion on the
outskirts of town. How she—the first Mrs. Oldenburg, not
the second—had sold off all of her ex's possessions on eBay
to get even. How she'd laughed when the sale of the boots
had gone through.

The woman's enthusiasm grew as she told the story, but
mine did not. In fact, I felt sicker by the moment. "So, you're
telling me I purchased something that didn't actually belong
to you?" I asked when she finally paused to breathe.

Her voice took on a defensive tone. "Hey, all of the women's boots were mine. I wanted to get rid of any evidence of my former life. And I had every right to sell the others. Brian left his stuff here when he took off. Possession is nine-tenths of the law, you know."

Okay, well, I'd heard that one before. I could almost envision the neighbor kid with my pop's prized basketball in his hand. "But does he know what you've done?"

"Yeah, he knows. That's between us. You just enjoy those boots now, honey. And if you know anyone who might want to buy a Ford F-450 Super Duty for pennies on the dollar, let me know." After a guttural laugh from the now-infamous Ms. O, the call ended.

I held the phone in my hand, flabbergasted. As I looked around at the boxes, the truth registered. I didn't have just a houseful of boots. I had a houseful of *stolen* boots. Brian's boots, to be precise.

Had he mourned their loss? Did he want them back? Only one way to know for sure.

I got back on the Internet, looking up the address for Brian Oldenburg. It took nearly an hour of work on my part, but I finally reached him. I quickly explained the predicament, and for a minute, I thought the fellow might cry.

"You . . . you've got my Lanciottis?"

"I do. Where should I send them?"

"And the others? You have all the others?"

"I do, but I've used quite a few of them." I further explained the situation, and he responded with, "You can keep those. No problem. But I'd do anything to have those Lanciottis back. And there was a pair of snakeskin boots I was partial to. Oh, and a goatskin pair that's worth a pretty penny. I'd like to have those three back. Don't give a rip what you do with the others, especially the ones that belonged to my ex-wife."

There was something about the way this fellow said the word *ex-wife* that caused my skin to crawl. Sounded so . . . final. So bitter. What was it with these two? Surely they'd loved each other once. Right?

After giving him my address, he agreed to have UPS come by to pick up the three boxes and to cover all costs related to the shipping. He also offered to reimburse my $800.

"You don't have to do that, Mr. Oldenburg," I argued. "I feel bad enough already. Trust me."

"Don't be silly. I'm happy to do it." He laughed. "I can't wait till I run into my ex-wife at the racetrack wearing those Lanciottis. It'll be worth every penny."

Hmm. At once I thought of one of Aunt Rosa's famous sayings: *Non si puo avere la botte piena è la moglie ubriaca*— you can't have your cake and eat it too. Sure looked like Mr. Oldenburg was gonna try.

I hung up feeling a bit nauseous. What would drive a couple to such lengths? Surely they'd once been a happy duo, facing each other at an altar to exchange "I dos." Likely they'd been addicted to each other in the same way Sophia had described. Now they met at the racetrack to argue over who got the boots? And if the former Mrs. Oldenburg had been this vengeful about cowboy boots, how had she treated their poor children? If they had children.

I tried to put the whole thing out of my mind but found it difficult. What was wrong with couples these days?

These troubling thoughts stayed with me as I considered my line of work. I loved the wedding biz. Loved it. Loved making the plans. Loved pulling off a great event. Loved the look of pure joy on the bride's face. Loved watching the couple ride off into the sunset for their happily ever after.

Only one problem—I'd never really taken the time to think

through the happily-ever-after part. What happened to my wedding couples after the big day? Would Sharlene and Cody still be blissfully happy a month from now? A year? Would they always feel the joy, the elation, or would the problems of life eventually kick in?

I sighed. The Oldenburgs might as well have kicked me in the shins with those boots of theirs. They'd certainly knocked the wind out of my sails.

My thoughts shifted to D.J. once again, and my heart took a plunge in the way Sophia had so aptly described just this morning. Why hadn't he called? Was he avoiding me? Had that incident with Tony been the nail in my proverbial coffin?

My gut twisted at the very idea, and I had to admit, I was addicted. D.J. Neeley was my caramel mocha macchiato. Only now he'd gone missing. Would he forget about me? Cast me aside like a worn boot? Would he move on to someone new and build her a mini mansion on the outskirts of town?

Determined not to let these questions get me down, I focused on my job—planning happily ever afters for everyone but me.

23

I've Grown Accustomed to Her Face

The following morning I awoke to the shattering of glass, followed by Aunt Rosa's shrill voice. Stumbling from the bed, I made my way to the window to peer outside. After rubbing the sleep from my eyes, my gaze shifted to the lawn, where I saw Rosa with the broom in her hand. *Oh no! Not again!*

She sprinted across the yard, her floral bathrobe flapping in the breeze. A couple of foam curlers bounced onto the grass as she rounded the corner. Once again the Burton boy was on the bristly end of the broom.

Swinging open my window, I heard Rosa shout, "And don't let me ever catch you doing that again!"

I shot out of bed and raced down the stairs, my eyes still sticky from sleep. Precious followed on my heels, her shrill yapping likely waking everyone in the house, including Guido. From the kitchen I heard him squawking, "Go to the mattresses! Go to the mattresses!" Still, none of this made sense.

What had the kid done at this time of morning to get Rosa all riled up?

Pushing propriety aside, I swung the front door open and stepped outside in my shorts and T-shirt. At that very moment, the Burton boy raced past the front steps. He paused long enough to holler, "Help me, please! She's gonna kill me! Do something!" He wasn't playacting this time around. I could read the terror in his eyes.

Now, I knew Aunt Rosa didn't have it in her to hurt anyone, but I could see how easily this could be misconstrued. She did have that wild-eyed look, after all. And her Italian phraseology let me know she wouldn't stop until she caught the kid.

My, how that woman could rant. And I had to admit, after years of listening to my aunt's temper-induced shouts, I now knew more saint names than the pope. It appeared one or two of them—saints, not popes—might just be on the Burton kid's side today. He made an abrupt turn toward his home, managing to make his way across the street and onto his lawn. Once there, he stopped cold, panting. Instead of his usual taunting, he disappeared into his house.

Rosa appeared from the side yard, dragging the broom behind her. She looked winded but otherwise in fine shape. "I'll . . . get . . . him . . . next . . . time."

"What did he do?" I reached out to give her a hand up the front stairs onto the veranda.

"Broke . . . into . . . the . . . house."

"W-what? When?" This revelation put a whole new spin on things.

"Just a few . . . minutes ago. I found him in the kitchen . . . stealing food."

"Stealing food?" None of this made sense. The Burtons

were millionaires, for Pete's sake. Why would the kid need to scrounge for food?

"I caught him . . . in the act," Rosa continued. "And when he saw me, he took off. Dropped a loaf of garlic bread on the floor . . . And he slammed the back door so hard the window broke. That's when I took off after him." She doubled over and took a few deep breaths.

"Wow."

The word had barely escaped my lips when a UPS truck pulled into our driveway. I saw the puzzled look on Eugene's face when he caught a glimpse of Rosa and me on the veranda in our pj's. He ran his fingers through his thinning gray hair, then finally took a few hesitant steps in our direction. Something on the ground caught his eye, and he paused to reach down and pick up a couple of pink foam curlers. With a smile, he offered a shy "G'morning ladies" as he gave them to Rosa.

"Not exactly good." Rosa proceeded to tell him about the day's rocky start, and then invited him inside for a cup of coffee and some cinnamon rolls. He willingly agreed. In fact, I observed a bashful smile nudging at the corners of his lips. Hmm. Very suspicious.

As we all stepped into the front hallway, I noticed Uncle Laz inching his way down the stairs, one hand on the banister, the other clutching his cane. He took one look at Eugene standing next to Rosa, and his expression tightened. His gaze shifted once again to the stairs.

"Morning, Lazarro," Eugene said with a polite nod.

My uncle gave him a brusque "Hello" but didn't look up.

I paused to watch the interaction between the three of them, noticing that something about this just felt strange. I'd known Eugene for years, but I'd never noticed the sparkle in Rosa's eye when she looked at him . . . until now.

Suddenly it all clicked. All of the times she'd paid him special attention. The glasses of tea, the food . . . Did my aunt have a crush on the UPS guy? If so, did it not matter that she'd greeted him in her robe and curlers? And why did my uncle care? Were his feelings of animosity toward Rosa so strong that he didn't want to see her happy at all?

Laz grunted and shuffled off to the kitchen behind my aunt and the UPS guy. Looked like Rosa wasn't the only one who'd awakened on the wrong side of the bed. I couldn't remember when I'd seen my uncle in such a state. What had happened to my family? Was everyone falling to pieces in front of my eyes?

Oh well. Nothing a hot shower and a cute summer outfit wouldn't fix.

Determined to shift my thoughts in a more positive direction, I went through my usual morning routine, prettying myself up more than the norm in the hopes that D.J. would call and want to see me.

Once I'd approved of the reflection in the mirror, I headed back downstairs, intrigued by the sound of voices raised in anger coming from the back of the house. I made my way to the kitchen, where Mama appeared to be chaperoning Rosa and Laz while sweeping up bits of broken glass from the back window. She glanced up with a warning look in her eye, so I kept my mouth shut. As always, my aunt and uncle were going at it like two alley cats, only this time they had an audience. Eugene sat on a nearby barstool, watching the interaction with a puzzled look on his face.

"Whose business is it if I want to hang pictures of Sophia Loren in the restaurant?" Laz directed his words at Rosa, and his eyes flashed with anger. "She's Italian, isn't she? And it's an Italian restaurant. I can put anything in my restaurant I want to put in my restaurant. No woman is going to tell me what to do."

Whoa. I really had to clamp down on my tongue at that one.

The strangest look passed over Rosa's face. Was that . . . jealousy? Just as quickly, she said, "Well, of course, Lazarro," pasted on a forced smile, batted her lashes, and offered Eugene another cup of coffee and a cinnamon roll. I'd never seen her this flirtatious.

Wait a minute. Was this all some sort of act meant to ruffle Uncle Laz's feathers? If so, it appeared to be working. Laz gave Eugene the evil eye, and our flustered UPS guy suddenly decided he needed to get back to work. He grabbed the boxes of boots and headed off on his way. I had no doubt he'd ask for a different delivery route next time.

Eugene had no sooner left the room than Rosa erupted in tears and ran out of the kitchen. Laz muttered, "Women," then reached over, grabbed Eugene's cinnamon roll, and took a bite, his eyes still flashing with anger. Off in the corner of the kitchen, Guido—who until now had remained quiet in his cage—erupted in a song that sounded strangely like "Amazing Grace." In between verses, he hollered, "Wise guy!" a couple of times. Mama looked at me and sighed.

After a couple of minutes, Laz rose to his feet and headed to the back door. When it slammed behind him, I looked at my mother and asked the obvious. "What is going on between those two?"

"This time, you mean?" She rolled her eyes. "This war between them has gone on too long. It's giving me an ulcer. Sometimes I wonder if merging my family and your father's under the same roof was a good idea. My stomach can't take it."

My gaze shifted to the back door, then back to my mother. "Today's battle was different though. Did you notice?"

"Yes." Mama shrugged. "But who can figure them out? I don't know where Rosa got her temper. She's nothing like me or my other sisters. And Laz . . ." She grinned. "He might be your papa's brother, but they're worlds apart in attitude. I wish he could adopt some of your papa's kindhearted ways."

"Kindhearted ways, eh?" My father ambled into the kitchen dressed in his running shorts and a T-shirt.

He leaned down to kiss my mother on the ear, and she giggled, then whispered, "Cosmo, not in front of the children."

That was enough to propel me from my seat. With newfound energy kicking in, I headed out to the backyard, where I found Laz working in his garden. I'd spent hours with my uncle in the yard in years past. Surely he would find nothing suspicious about me joining him now. I made my way through vine-ripened tomatoes, squash, lettuce, pepper plants, and mounds of basil, where I caught a glimpse of Laz standing next to his fig tree, giving it a far-too-serious look.

I drew near and spoke a gentle "Hey" to warn him of my presence.

He turned and grunted.

So much for the gentle approach. "Laz, what's going on? Really. You're not yourself lately. I miss my old Uncle Laz."

Another guttural sound erupted, and he turned to snatch a basket, then headed to the tomatoes. I followed along on his heels in much the same way I'd done hundreds of times over the years. He reached the first tomato vine and snagged a couple of ripe tomatoes, tossing them into the basket.

"Laz, c'mon. What did she do to make you so mad?"

"Crazy old woman." He went back to work filling one basket, then a second. Before long, we were working on our fourth. Together. And though I tried to bring up his problems with Rosa, he dodged me at every turn.

Looking to change the topic, I asked him about his garden back in Italy, the one he'd grown up tending. This shifted him into a wistful conversation that brought tears to his eyes. Over the next several minutes I heard all about his teen years working alongside his papa in the garden. I could see pain in his eyes as he mentioned his father's death, and pride when he talked about how he'd helped his poor mama raise the younger children over the following years.

"Your papa was just a little thing when our father died," Laz said. "Maybe seven or eight. And he needed a father figure." My uncle squared his shoulders. "I had to be that father figure. I washed dishes at a restaurant till all of the children were grown. And when Cosmo moved off to America, leaving the rest of the family behind, it nearly broke my heart."

"Why did he come to the States?" I asked.

Laz's expression shifted to a smirk. "It's funny what love will do to a man. Your mother grew up just a few streets from us. But her family moved to America when she was just fourteen or so. Nearly ate Cosmo up. He was smitten."

"Wow." I knew they'd loved each other since childhood but had never known the specifics.

"She was a beauty queen, your mama. And such a sweet little thing. Cosmo never forgot her, even after her papa took her off across the waters. As soon as he was old enough, he sold everything he had to get the money to move to New Jersey. Said he'd follow her to the ends of the earth . . . and he did." A smile teased the edges of my uncle's lips. "Your papa never could think straight when it came to your mother, that much I can say for sure."

"Nothing much has changed then." Still, this news put a whole new spin on things. I had no idea my father's sole purpose for coming to America was to follow my mother. He'd always told me he came to find a better job and a new life.

"So, did you know Rosa back then?" I asked.

Laz grunted his response. "Know her? Who didn't?"

"Was she pretty like my mama?"

This time Laz answered with a snort, and I decided to call it quits right there. Enough talking about the family.

Something about the mention of Rosa's name must've convinced Laz our tomato-picking time had ended. We carried the too-full baskets into the kitchen and put them on the counter.

Rosa looked up from loading the dishwasher, a stunned expression on her face. "What's this?"

"You know." Laz gave her a stern look, then left the room, claiming they'd done without him far too long at the restaurant today already.

Rosa turned to me, obviously flabbergasted. "Does he not see that I was on my feet all weekend? He thinks this is the perfect day to make gravy?" She muttered something under her breath about men, then took to scrubbing the tomatoes. I left her to her own devices, ready for my second shower of the day. As I made my way to the stairs, I passed my parents in the living room. They sat together on the sofa, reading. Mama's head rested against my father's shoulder. Funny. I'd never paused to consider just how in love they still were after all these years.

I thought about their relationship as I showered and dressed again. That's what I wanted. What they had. A real happily ever after. The kind that was willing to risk everything, to travel across oceans, cultures, and time. I wanted someone to follow me to the ends of the earth, and vice versa. And more than anything, I wanted a shoulder to rest my head against.

I wanted D.J.

My heart twisted. I wanted my caramel mocha macchiato. My knight in shining armor. My deejay. But would I ever see him again? If my father could follow my mother all the way from Italy to New Jersey, why hadn't D.J. Neeley picked up the phone to call me?

The phone works both ways, you know. The thought flitted through my mind, but I pushed it away. He needed to be the one to make the first move, not me. Right?

Minutes later, dressed in yet another great outfit, I crossed paths with my sister as she headed upstairs. I could tell from the too-pink cheeks that she'd been in the sun. "Water park," she managed as she bounded past me. "Deany-boy and Frankie. Got to shower."

"I understand."

I continued on my way downstairs and then into the kitchen to help Rosa. It didn't seem right to leave her alone with the gravy making. Thankfully, I found my mother standing at her side. Together they peeled the freshly blanched tomatoes and put them into giant saucepans on the stove.

"How many jars?" I asked, opening the cupboard.

Rosa surveyed the tomatoes with a skilled eye. "Probably twenty-five."

I pulled out the jars and lined them up on the counter, then settled onto a barstool to watch them work.

Mama stirred in cans of tomato paste to enhance the flavor of the fresh tomatoes, then Rosa sautéed onions, garlic, and olive oil. This was the part I loved best. The smell captivated me and made me hungry. It also reminded me of Uncle Laz and his story about growing up in Italy. Perfect time to hear the other side of the tale.

"Tell me about your life when you were girls," I encouraged them. "In Italy, I mean."

"What do you want to know?" Mama turned to me and shrugged. "I moved when I was still young, so my memories are limited."

"Mine aren't." Rosa smiled. "I can tell you anything you like."

"Oh yes, Rosa has wonderful stories." My mother sighed, then turned to her older sister. "So tell us."

My aunt continued to work, not missing a beat. "What do you want to hear?"

"Tell us about when you were in the convent," Mama said.

I almost fell off the barstool at that one. Convent? I stared at my aunt in disbelief. She'd never married, that much I knew. But, a nun?

Rosa gave me a sly grin as her story began. "There was the most beautiful little convent near our home. I always heard the sisters singing and felt so compelled to join them." She drew in a sharp breath. "You must understand, I always knew I wasn't like the other girls in my village. Certainly not like your mama here."

"What do you mean?"

She shook her head. "I was never pretty. Never had a figure. And in our area, the pretty girls all married young and had lots of babies. Me . . ." She sighed. "I knew it would never happen. So I needed a different plan."

"Rosa!" I'd never heard such blunt words.

My aunt turned back to stirring, though I thought I saw tears glistening in her eyes.

"Someone broke her heart," my mother whispered. "But she doesn't like to talk about it."

"What's to talk about? It's in the past." As Rosa turned to fill a couple of the jars with gravy, she dabbed at her eyes, then forged ahead. "Anyway, I got this idea the Lord was calling me to be a nun. I wanted to serve him, of course. So I told our mama I wanted to go."

"What did she say?" I asked.

My mother turned to me, her face beaming. "Oh, let me tell this part. I was really young, but I remember how proud Mama was. To have a daughter enter the convent was such a special thing. Our mama made sure everyone in the village knew, and she even threw a party the week before Rosa left home. Everyone was there."

"Yes, Mama was overjoyed. I know she was very proud of me." Rosa's expression hardened a bit. "Besides, it saved her the trouble of having to explain her spinster daughter to the other villagers."

"Rosa!" Mama looked at her, clearly stunned.

"How old were you again?" I asked, trying to steer the conversation in a different direction.

"Seventeen. Your mama was little bitty, like she said. So it broke my heart to leave her and the others behind. But I had to do what I felt was right."

"So, what happened?" I leaned forward on my barstool, completely enraptured.

"They changed my name. I wanted to be Sister Maria Sophia, but they had other ideas. So I became Sister Angelica."

"Angelica. Angel. How beautiful."

"And how unlike me." Rosa chuckled. "I took a lot of

ribbing over that back at home. But to answer your questions, I scrubbed a lot of floors." She lifted her skirt and showed off her callused knees. "And said a lot of prayers. And, well . . ."

"What?"

"Got in trouble with the mother superior. A lot."

Why didn't that surprise me?

"She told me I needed to get my temper under control. That God was getting mighty tired of wrestling with me, and she was nearly as tired."

"Oh?"

Rosa shrugged, then filled another jar with gravy. "Couldn't say for sure what I was mad at. Maybe just the fact that I didn't fit in. I was different, like I said. No boys ever looked my way. So maybe I thought God would reject me too. I was hardfisted toward him, just in case. Problem is, putting up walls between yourself and God isn't the best idea, especially in a convent. They tend to frown on that there."

At this revelation, my heart completely melted. Mama gave me a "don't say anything" look out of the corner of her eye, and I clamped my mouth shut before asking anything too personal. Still, I had to wonder what had happened to cause such rejection in a woman as young as seventeen.

"There's nothing worse than feeling different. Like a square peg in a round hole." Rosa pointed to her pudgy midsection. "Or in my case, a round hole in a square peg." Feigning a smile, she added, "But one thing was for sure, God never called me to be a nun. After only two months, the sisters sent me home. Said the Lord would use me in another capacity."

"They gave you an honorable discharge?" I teased.

"Hardly." She winked. "But while I was there, I discovered

my love for cooking. I think the sisters put on a lot of weight when I was in the kitchen."

"Aha." It was all beginning to make sense now.

"So when I got back home, I helped Nano and Nana in their restaurant." Her face glowed as she wrapped up the story about how she'd worked for her grandfather and grandmother. "By the time our papa made the decision to move to the States, I was doing really well for myself."

"So you stayed behind."

"Yes." She paused with a reflective look on her face. "So what if people never saw me as pretty in the traditional sense? They seemed to find value in what I did when I was in the kitchen. And that was enough for me, I suppose."

"Oh, but Rosa . . ." I reached over to embrace her. "You're valuable to God, regardless. It doesn't matter what you look like or even what talents you have. He cherishes you. You're beautiful in his sight."

At these words, her eyes brimmed over. She shook her head. "I'm sorry, Bella, but that's too much to imagine." She and Mama continued their work filling the jars. We shared a little more small talk, but I could tell our real heart-to-heart had ended.

This bothered me for the rest of the day. Had she really not figured out that God found her valuable simply because she was his child? What could I do to convince her?

24

I'd Cry like a Baby

On Wednesday afternoon, I decided to call Jenna. I hadn't really talked to her since the wedding and needed to see where things stood with the whole Bubba-David scenario. I walked out onto the veranda and settled into a wicker chair to make the call.

When Jenna answered, I almost didn't recognize her voice. She sounded like she'd been crying. Ironically, that didn't stop her from giving the usual spiel.

"Want to share a pizza with a friend but can't settle on the topping?" Jenna sniffled. "You're keen on pepperoni, he's got his heart set on Canadian bacon?" Her voice cracked, and I felt sure tears weren't far off. "Why not try our Simpatico special," she choked out, "a large hand-tossed pizza, split down the middle with your choice of toppings on either side. Now you can both be happy . . ." She dissolved into tears, then tried again. "Now you can both . . . be . . . happy . . . for just $14.95."

"Jenna, are you okay?"

"Oh, Bella! Is that you?" A sob erupted from her end of the line. "Can you come over here? I need you."

Heavens! Could the week possibly get any stranger?

I arrived at the shop minutes later with Precious tucked into my purse. I'd neglected my poor little doggie of late and owed her a trip to town. Of course, I'd lectured her all the way over to be on her best behavior. Hopefully she would comply.

As I walked into the restaurant, I realized the reason Jenna had asked me to come. David—her sorry-to-see-you-go boyfriend—sat at the counter, a washed-out look on his face. I drew near with fear and trembling. Hadn't I been through enough this week already? Did I have to watch the unraveling of my friend's relationship with her boyfriend? Why this? Why now?

"David." I took the seat next to him and offered a practiced smile.

He turned my way with the saddest look on his face. "Oh, hey Bella. How are you?"

"Good." I started to add, "And you?" but stopped myself short, afraid I wouldn't like the answer.

Jenna turned to me with a pleading look in her eyes. "I told him I couldn't help it, Bella," she said. "I didn't mean to fall so hard for Bubba, but I just couldn't help myself."

"Bubba." David repeated the name, a look of disbelief on his face. "Who has a name like Bubba?"

"Someone who's kind and generous and wonderful." Jenna leaned her elbows onto the counter and sighed. "Oh, David, I think you'll really like him. He's a great guy. And you two have so much in common."

He quirked a brow, as if to ask the obvious. "Like what?"

"Well . . ." Her eyes brightened. "You both like to fish."

"Keep going."

"And . . . well, you both care about me!"

I'd have to remember to talk to Jenna later about proper protocol for ditching a boyfriend. Her current approach left something to be desired.

With my pup dozing in my purse, we spent the next half hour sharing a Simpatico special and convincing David he would be better off single than with someone whose heart just wasn't in it. Though he seemed heartbroken, I had a feeling he'd bounce back pretty quickly. He didn't seem the sort to wallow in his grief. At least not for long.

As I left the restaurant, my cell phone rang. I recognized Patti-Lou's number at once and smiled. She always knew just what to say to cheer me up. I answered with a boisterous "Hey, girl," ready to shift out of depression mode.

"Hi, Bella." She sighed.

Oh no. Not you too. "Patti? What happened?"

After a brief pause, she explained. "It's Bob Billings. He's never going to call. He was just toying with my emotions. He doesn't care about me. Sometimes I wonder if anyone ever will."

"Hold that thought. I'm coming right over."

I hung up the phone and started to pray. If I'd known the day was going to end up centered around broken relationships, I would've prepped myself. Packed a box of chocolates, maybe, or at least some tissues.

Five minutes later I marched into the flower shop, ready to do business. I could hardly believe Patti-Lou's appearance. She'd pulled her bleach blonde hair back into a messy ponytail and wore no makeup. Her T-shirt looked wrinkled. Very suspicious.

"What did that man do to you?"

"What *didn't* he do, you mean?" Patti-Lou dabbed at her red-rimmed eyes. "He hasn't called, Bella. Not once. I gave him my number, but . . ."

"Is that all?" I groaned. "Patti, it's only been a few days. His daughter just got married. It's likely he's off on vacation or sitting somewhere with a fishing pole in his hand. Don't give up the ship."

I pushed aside my own concerns about why D.J. hadn't called me since the night of the wedding and focused on my friend. She went on to talk about her pitiful love life, and I came back with my usual, *"Finché c'è vita c'è speranza."*

"Where there is life, there is hope," she responded with sadness in her voice. "I know, Bella. But it looks like I've been putting my hope in the wrong things. I need to figure out what God wants for me, not what I want for myself, and that's going to take some time."

"I understand. Trust me."

She paused, then looked over at me with tears in her eyes. "That's why . . . that's why I'm retiring."

"You . . . you're what?" A thousand questions went through my mind at once. "Why?"

Patti-Lou paced the store as she spoke. "I can't do it anymore. I've put together my last wedding bouquet. I've pinned on my last corsage. I've decorated my last centerpiece." A sob erupted, startling me. "I—can't—do—this—any—more. Period."

Well, that I understood. Still, I had to do something, and quick. I couldn't lose Patti-Lou. Not now, when I needed her so desperately. And she clearly needed me as well.

"But, you can't retire. You're *far* too young for that. And you have to make a living. How will you do that if you give up the shop? Be logical."

"I'm moving to Montana to live with my sister."

"Montana?" I practically squealed the word. "Are you kidding? You're moving from the balmy Gulf of Mexico to the frozen tundra?"

I dove into a lengthy explanation of the winters in Montana, but Patti didn't seem to hear a word. "It couldn't be any colder up there than it is right here, right now." She sniffled. "Every man I fall for has a heart made of ice."

I spent the next ten minutes convincing her to use this trip to Montana as a vacation, nothing more. "You'll feel so much better after you've had some time away," I explained. "Then, when you come back, you'll see things in a whole new light."

As the conversation drew to a close, I did something I rarely did these days. I offered to pray with her. Out loud. Hand to hand. Heart to heart. I dove in, ready to do business with the Almighty. My passionate words being lifted up to the throne room surprised even me. Where had they come from?

As we ended our prayer time, Patti-Lou promised to call me once she settled in at her sister's house. I gave her a few details about the upcoming medieval wedding just to tempt her. We'd need flowers, after all. Lots of them. Surely she could see what an important role she played in the lives of young couples in love. That should be enough to keep her on the island for years to come. Once she got this grieving spell behind her, anyway.

I drove home in a stupor. When I reached the house, only one thing sounded appealing—tossing myself onto my bed for some one-on-one time with God. Having my little heart-to-heart chat with Patti-Lou had opened up a can of worms. I couldn't stop thinking about all of the crazy, chaotic events that had worn me down over the past few days.

Hmm. Maybe I'd better make a list of all the things I'd

been trying to handle on my own, things that would be better off in God's hands. I started with my love life and went from there. Before long, I'd scribbled down twenty-three things and had somehow veered from the original topic.

Glancing down at what I'd written, I wondered if maybe the things on my list were really important enough to bother God with. Sure, he wanted me to stop trying to control every facet of my life. And he longed for me to give him my anxieties. However, he probably didn't care that my brothers left the toilet seat up or that my father mowed the lawn in his running shorts. I scratched through the last few things on the list and focused on the big stuff at the top. Clearing the air, spiritually speaking, was always a good thing, especially on days like today when clouds loomed overhead.

After spending some time in prayer, the phone rang. I groaned, hoping it wasn't someone else needing relationship advice. To my surprise, I saw D.J.'s number. *Well, it's about time you called, mister. Just see if you can pretend I don't exist and then call me up after four days.*

Wanting to play hard to get, I waited until the fourth ring to answer. Then, I tried to sound nonchalant with my opening. "Hello?"

"Bella, I'm so sorry."

At the sound of his deep, hypnotic voice, I melted like a block of ice in the sun.

D.J. rushed to get his message out, his words tumbling so fast I could hardly make sense of them. "The morning after the wedding, I got a call from my boss that his brother's house in Brenham had a serious mold problem. He said he'd pay me triple my hourly wage if I'd go up there and take care of it. I had to remove the Sheetrock in three rooms and replace it, then texture and paint."

"Wow."

"Yeah, so I left in a hurry, and I know you probably won't believe this, but I left my cell phone at my condo."

A wave of relief as mighty as the gulf swept over me. He hadn't forgotten about me!

"I couldn't remember your cell number, so when I got there, I looked up the wedding facility's number and used the house phone to call you there. You didn't answer. I left a, uh . . ." He chuckled. "Well, a long message. I was hoping you'd listen to it before someone else in the family heard it."

"You called the wedding facility?" I slapped myself in the head. "I haven't checked my voice mail since the day of the wedding." I could hardly wait to listen to the message. What had he said? I giggled, thinking about how I planned to march over there the minute I finished this call to find out.

"I have to tell you something." He paused, and fear wriggled its way around me like a sweater on a hot day.

"W-what?"

"I need you to know that I'm crazy about you."

"You . . . you are?"

"I am. It's killing me to be away. I have to see you." He explained that he'd just arrived home and needed to shower first, then the tone of his voice softened almost to a whisper. "I want to stand in the gazebo and kiss you under the stars. I want to two-step with you across the dance floor. I want to watch your mother paint on Bubba's eyebrows and listen to your aunt and uncle fight over Dean Martin and Tony Bennett."

"It's Frank Sinatra," I corrected him. "They argue over Dean Martin and Frank Sinatra."

"Okay, whatever. Whoever." D.J. laughed. "In case you

haven't figured this out, I'm dying to see you. What are you doing tonight?"

"Tonight?" I forced back the chuckle that tried to escape and put on my most serious voice. "Well, I don't know if I'm available. I'll have to have my people call your people, and we'll see if it can be arranged."

"Ah. Speaking of your people and my people . . ." He explained a plan to get our two families together on Saturday for a Fourth of July celebration. I agreed, on one condition.

"No matter what happens—no matter what crazy schemes my family cooks up—you will look at me as an individual. Don't judge me because of my kooky family."

"Kooky family?" He seemed surprised by my words. "Bella, I love your family. And they're no crazier than mine, trust me."

"Really?"

"Mmm, yeah. And wait till you see them all together in Splendora. I guarantee you, it's going to be a day for the history books."

We spent the next few minutes whispering words of endearment in both directions. If his phone message was anything like this, I could hardly wait to hear it.

When the call ended, I felt giddy. Lighthearted. Serene. And though I had my doubts about the merging of our two families on Neeley turf, I knew one thing—this Fourth of July would indeed be a day for the history books.

25

Return to Me

The Rossi family has always been particularly fond of the Fourth of July. As immigrated Americans, the older Rossis enjoyed celebrating this one in style. So when we received the invitation to take the Rossi clan to Splendora on Independence Day, I wondered if Mama and Rosa would play along or if they would insist on sticking with the status quo.

Earline's invitation left little wiggle room. Bring the whole clan, kids and all, she said. She even went so far as to invite the dog. I could almost see Precious in Splendora now, barking at people's heels and digging up Earline's azaleas.

Thankfully, my parents were thrilled. So were Rosa and Laz, who had resorted to silent glares as their only form of communication. Nick agreed to come along with Marcella and the boys. Joey asked if he could bring a date—Norah, the woman who'd so recently put a spring in his step. And Armando . . . well, Armando, in his usual whipped-by-every-wind style, had headed back to Houston for the day, likely to stir up more trouble with his ex-girlfriend. Sophia opted to come with us, but I could read the sadness in her eyes. Surely she wouldn't ask to bring Tony along.

On the morning of the Fourth of July, the whole Rossi family packed up goodies for the day ahead. Rosa had baked, of course. Enough to feed a small army. And Marcella, always the creative one, had come up with a beautiful red, white, and blue corsage to offer D.J.'s mother as a thank-you for having us. Using one of the leftover Texas-themed bandanas from the wedding, I created a little sash for Precious to wear. She didn't take to it but finally stopped trying to chew it off. Laz left the CD player running so that Guido could get his daily dose of "Taming the Tongue."

We'd just finished loading everyone into the vehicles when Aunt Rosa's voice rang out. "Wait, Cosmo! I've left something behind." She scrambled out with Uncle Laz on her heels.

Sophia looked at me, bug-eyed. "You don't think she's going to wear that costume again, do you?"

I shuddered at the thought of it. Not everyone dressed like the Statue of Liberty on the Fourth of July, but Rosa found it a necessity. Sure enough, minutes later she appeared on the veranda, completely decked out head to toe as Lady Liberty. And Uncle Laz . . . well, not to be outdone, he showed up behind her wearing his Uncle Sam getup. They shot daggers at each other with their eyes, then headed to the car. Before we knew it, we were ready to roll.

It took three cars to get the entire Rossi clan to the Neeley home. My sister and I chatted all the way, talking about life, love, and new fashion styles. We arrived at 11:00, just as the temperature gauge in the Lexus registered 102 degrees. I couldn't imagine grilling hot dogs and hamburgers in this heat. Might not need a grill after all. Just toss 'em on the pavement and let the sun do all the work.

As we pulled into the driveway, my gaze shifted to the mob of people scattered about. In lawn chairs. In hammocks. Under a newly constructed tent. On the front porch. They filled every square inch of space, eating watermelon, drinking lemonade and tea, and gathering like flies around Bubba's smoker. There were several tables set up as well, and many of the guests played dominoes. Chickenfoot, perhaps?

And the children! I'd never seen so many. Whose kids were these? D.J. had said they were inviting family and a few friends. Who had this many friends?

From across the lawn, a large dog that looked more like a horse than a hound came bounding our way. The monster put both feet up on the window of our car, and Earline called out, "Get down, Bruiser."

Rosa let out a little cry. "They've sicced the dogs on us!" she hollered. "Everyone freeze!"

We did just that, until D.J. snagged the hound and held him at bay. I did my best to calm Precious down, but she insisted on baring her teeth at the beast. We climbed from our cars, and I prayed the day would go well. Oh, if only we could make up for the other night! I fanned myself and prayed for a miracle.

After getting the dog calmed down, D.J. headed my way with a grin. I melted into his arms—"melted" being the key word, what with the temperature being so high. As he held me close, I gazed up into his gorgeous baby blues and whispered, "I'm so glad to see you."

He responded with a kiss on the forehead. "Not as glad as I am to see you," he whispered in my ear.

In spite of any past problems, Earline welcomed us with

open arms. She took one look at Aunt Rosa in her Statue of Liberty costume, and her eyes misted over. "Oh, thank you for the reminder," she said, brushing away a tear. "Lady Liberty always makes me cry. Why, all I have to do is see a photograph and I'm a blubbering mess."

"Me too!" Rosa gave her an admiring look, and I realized they'd just crossed an invisible line into true sisterhood, one that defied all geographical limitations. The Statue of Liberty didn't care if you hailed from Galveston or Splendora. She didn't care if you'd come by ship from foreign shores. Her flaming torch welcomed one and all to a land free from persecution and shame.

I guess I had a lot to learn from Lady Liberty. I could barely get my head wrapped around the cultural differences between D.J.'s family and mine. Surely the walls would come down—in time.

"My great-grandparents came to this country from Scotland in the 1800s," Earline explained. "They told my grandmother a story about seeing the statue for the first time, how overwhelmed they were. They'd always dreamed of a new life in America." She cleared her throat. "Look at me. I'm an old fool. Getting all sentimental over a holiday."

"It's not foolish at all." Rosa embraced her, and they shared a special moment, then my aunt turned to the flowers in Earline's garden. "Oh, oh!" She made her way from flower to flower. "It's just like my garden back home!" She began to explain—in her native tongue—that the Neeley property with its vibrant colors reminded her of the area behind her childhood home in her small Italian village. I'd never seen my aunt so happy, or so animated.

And my mama . . . she politely followed behind as Earline showed off the yard, but I knew she didn't really care to spend much time in the sun. Surely the makeup she'd spent all morning applying would be running down the sides of her face if we didn't do something—and quick.

Thankfully, Earline ushered us inside before I could give the matter much thought. Getting inside meant climbing over the dog, who'd now taken up residence on the front door mat. Precious yapped the minute she saw him, but I did my best to keep a dog fight from breaking out.

Within minutes the ladies found themselves inside the seventy-three-degree trailer while the men—minus D.J., who tagged along on my heels—stood perched in front of the barbecue pit in the front yard.

"Do you like sweet tea?" Earline reached for the pitcher, then started putting ice in plastic cups.

As I nodded, D.J. leaned in and whispered, "Be warned. It's not sweet tea, it's glucose tea."

"I heard that." Earline gave him a stern look as she filled our glasses. "And you're from the South, boy. We drink our tea sweet in the South."

"Yes'm. Just wanted to give the ladies a heads-up, after you-know-what happened with you-know-who."

Well, if that didn't get my curiosity up! I gazed back and forth between D.J. and his mama until she finally explained. "Sister Jolene neglected to tell me she's a diabetic. We had a little . . . um . . . incident the last time she came for a picnic. But she's fine now. Just fine. We prayed her through."

"Well, I'm not diabetic, so we're in the clear." I took my glass of tea and drank it down in a hurry, then handed it back, ready for more. "I've gotta have more of that glucose tea."

Earline smiled and refilled my glass. "There you go, honey bun. You're a real Southern belle at heart, aren't you?"

Bella. Belle. "Yeah, I guess I am."

"Well then, you'll love the ice cream I'm making. It's peach." As she went on to describe the delectable taste of the homemade ice cream, my eyes wandered to the window. Looked like another car was pulling up. I turned back to Earline, and she glanced outside.

"Well, praise be! It's Pastor Higley and his beautiful wife, Nelda." Earline fussed with her hair. "I must look a fright." She turned back to us for our approval, and we nodded in one accord. "I hope you don't mind a crowd," she said. "But I told the folks in Sunday school, 'Anybody who doesn't have anybody can come.' Likely half of Splendora'll be here within the hour. We usually have a packed house on the Fourth."

I looked around the yard, trying to figure out where we'd possibly squeeze in our new visitors. D.J. glanced my way, probably wondering what I thought of adding more people to the fray. I must admit, it all seemed a little overwhelming. But I loved the Neeleys, and anything that made them happy made me happy. Besides, getting to know D.J.—his world, his friends, his traditions—could only serve to make us closer.

We ventured outside to add our voices to the ever-growing chorus. After the pastor and his wife visited with us for a few minutes, they meandered off to see about Bubba's cooking abilities. I turned my attention to a beautiful little girl with dark curls swinging back and forth in the tire swing. Her gleeful squeals filled the air. Behind the swing, someone had set up a Slip 'N Slide for the kids, along with two blow-up swimming pools. The younger kids splashed around in the tiny pool, their mothers standing by, and the older ones— upper elementary, at best—tossed horseshoes.

Deany-boy and Frankie played shy for the first half hour or so, but eventually they started tormenting the girls with a couple of tree frogs they'd found in the field on the side of the trailer. I was glad to see they were fitting in. Now if I could just relax and do the same . . .

At 1:00, just after consuming more hot dogs and hamburgers than anyone should be allowed by law, I heard a couple of familiar voices. Turning, I found the trio of "sisters" approaching. I took another sip of my sweet tea and braced myself for their arrival.

"Yoo-hoo!" Jolene called out to me. "I remember you, you pretty little thing. You came to visit us at church a couple of Wednesdays ago. Aren't you D.J.'s girl?"

"Hush, Jolene." Bonnie Sue swatted her on the arm. "It's not polite to ask folks if they're dating." She flashed a winning smile as she turned to face me. "But you are, aren't you? It'd be a shame not to, what with both of you being so pretty and all."

I almost laughed aloud. I'd never considered myself pretty and certainly never thought of D.J. as such. Handsome, yes. Pretty? Hmm. Maybe. He did have great lashes, though. And awesome cheekbones. And the best hair I'd ever seen on a guy, sawdust or not.

Yep. He was pretty.

"You two are going to make beautiful babies together," Twila said, looking more than a little dreamy-eyed. "I can just see them now."

"Ooo, me too," Jolene crooned. "They'll have his wavy hair, I'll betcha. And look at this!" She reached up with a fingertip to trace my cheek, a gesture so personal it startled me. Her big blue eyes widened. "I declare you're freckle free. Not a jot or a tittle. Surely your babies will be spot free and wrinkle free!"

I wasn't sure how to take that, but I offered a weak "Thank you."

My mama drew near, her jaw dropping as she took in Jolene's robust peaches-and-cream complexion. "Oh my." My mother—never one to stay silent long—just stood in awe, staring.

"What, honey?" Jolene's brow wrinkled. "Have I got something between my teeth?" She jabbed a fingernail between her two front teeth, then turned to Twila for examination.

"Clean as a whistle," Twila said.

They turned back to my mother, whose cheeks flashed crimson. "I'm sorry," she said. "It's just . . . your pores! They're spectacular."

"Oh, I know!" Jolene's face beamed. "And I work hard to keep them that way."

"Do you exfoliate?" my mother whispered.

"Oh, hon, of course. I discovered the joy of exfoliation three years ago and never looked back. It's so . . . so . . . cleansing. Almost spiritual."

I laughed so hard a mouthful of sweet tea came shooting out—unfortunately, all over Sister Twila, who turned to me, flabbergasted.

"I'm sorry." I giggled. "Just couldn't help myself. I can't believe you're talking about your pores."

"Oh, honey." Twila dabbed herself with a napkin. "At our age, we have to. And in the summertime, in heat like this . . . why, if I let things go, I'd have pores the size of pinto beans."

Thank God I hadn't taken another sip of tea. I would've lost it for sure.

"You should try living on the coast." My mother fanned herself with an empty paper plate. "It's so humid. Sometimes I wish I could live up here in the country."

I turned to her, stunned. "You do?"

"Yes." She swiped the back of her hand across her cheek. "Your father and I have talked about it dozens of times."

"You have?"

"Of course." She nodded, a serious expression on her face. "My face would look ten years younger, I guarantee. And my skin wouldn't be so oily. It's so hard to keep the T-zone clean when you live on the coast." She ran her finger from forehead to nose, then from cheek to cheek. "I'm always perspiring."

"Glistening, honey, glistening." Jolene patted her on the arm.

"Country living is so good for the body and the soul." Bonnie Sue turned to my mother and asked the most dangerous question one could ever ask another woman. "How old do you think I am, hon?"

Now, I knew my mother to be rather blunt, so I shuddered at her potential answer. When she came back with "Fifty-two?" relief flooded over me. In fact, my heart soared with joy. *You go, Mama!*

"I'm sixty-five on Tuesday," Bonnie Sue said with a prideful look in her eye. "I haven't changed one iota since I was fifty, and I don't mind sayin' it's clean living and exfoliation. There's no better combination."

"Why, that practically rhymes," Jolene said. "Exfoliation . . . combination. I'm going to embroider that on a sampler and hang it on my wall."

"And I don't know about the rest of you," Bonnie Sue continued, "but I've found the most heavenly moisturizer."

"Oh?" My mother looked her way, looking very interested.

"Bag balm," Bonnie Sue explained. "I use it on my face and my hands. Feet too."

"Oh my, yes. My fingers used to look a sight. Quilting, you know. But you see how pretty these hands are now?" Twila said, extending her hands. When we nodded, she said, "Bag balm. Every night. And I sleep with tube socks on my hands after I rub it in." When my mother responded with a sour expression, Twila quickly added, "Clean socks, a'course."

"Of course." We all nodded.

"Does anyone have a slip of paper?" my mother asked, her eyes wide with excitement.

Earline sprinted into the trailer and returned a few seconds later with a notepad and pen, which she handed to my mother.

"What did you call that moisturizer again?" Mama asked.

"Bag balm."

"Hmm. I don't believe I've seen that at Nordstrom's. I'll ask my beauty consultant."

"Nordstrom's?" Twila laughed. "Oh, honey! You need to go to the feed store to get udder cream."

"Feed store?" My mother paled. "Udder cream?"

"I hear tell they're sellin' it at Walmart now," Jolene threw in. "You might try there."

The expression on my mother's face as she processed this latest information was priceless. I couldn't blame her for being stunned. In our neck of the woods, women turned to Botox and collagen injections, not bag balm. To Mama's credit, she scribbled down the words *udder cream* in her notepad, then looked up with a polished smile.

My mother then gave Twila a solid once-over. "I do hope you'll excuse me for staring, but you have the shiniest silver hair I've ever seen. What is your secret?"

"Mane and Tail."

"M-mane and tail?" My mother scribbled down *main and tale*. "Do you mind if I ask—"

"The feed store." The three sisters spoke in unison. "Horse supply section."

"Well, forevermore." My mother shook her head as she continued to scribble. "Who would have guessed?"

The trio of sisters went on to share the rest of their homemade beauty secrets. Turns out, Crisco was a great makeup remover and even treated psoriasis and eczema. Jolene showed us her elbows as living proof. Hemorrhoid cream worked wonders for wrinkles around the eyes. And Bonnie Sue swore by kitty litter mixed with half a cup of water as a face mask, though she was quick to add we should buy the unscented kind. Twila ended the conversation with her suggestion for the ideal facial peel—Pepto-Bismol.

I'd never seen my mother write so fast. When we finished, she closed her notepad and tucked it back into her purse, then stared at me with a joyous expression. Who could blame her? She'd stumbled across a gold mine of beauty secrets, and I had a feeling they'd cost far less than the things she routinely purchased at the Clinique counter.

Jolene leaned over and whispered, "Did you get all that, honey?"

"Got it," Mama said with a nod.

"Well then, we have nothing left to teach you." Jolene gave her a playful wink.

My mother offered profuse thanks for their expertise, and I could tell she meant every word.

As we stood discussing what we'd just learned, a fellow in his early sixties with an extended belly and a winning smile joined us. He nodded at the group and offered a "Howdy," then turned his gaze to Twila.

After a quick "Hey, Terrell," she looked the other way.

Earline happened by with a tray filled with cookies. "Ice cream will be done in a jiffy, ladies. But for now, have a couple of Rosa's homemade fig cookies."

"Made with figs from Uncle Laz's tree in our backyard," I threw in.

Twila turned up her nose at them. "Honey, you know I'm watchin' my waistline." After a second's pause, she reached to snag two cookies and added, "And it's gettin' easier to see every day."

The women laughed, and Terrell whispered, "Have another one, honey. Might just slow you down enough I can finally catch you."

Twila turned all shades of red and nearly choked on her cookie. After Terrell left, she whispered, "Heavens. That man's been after me for the past four years."

"Not interested?" I asked, nibbling on a cookie.

Again her face flushed pink. "Oh, more than interested. Just like to play hard to get." She fanned herself with a cookie. "A girl's gotta be careful, you know. Don't want to jump into something 'less the Lord gives me the go-ahead."

"At least Terrell's a good guy," Jolene said with a sigh. "Remember Cotter Puckett, that fellow who fancied marrying me and moving me off to Cut 'n Shoot, away from my friends and my church?"

"I remember that fellow," Bonnie Sue said, fanning herself. "His engine was runnin' but nobody appeared to be driving."

"He was a sure sight better than that Frank Peavey fellow who chased me around," Jolene said. "He told me I was the only one for him, but I caught him making eyes at Glenda Jamison up at the Sack 'n Save."

"Speaking of Glenda Jamison . . ." Bonnie Sue's eyes narrowed. "Don't you think it's a shame, all those women having surgery to make themselves bigger?"

"Heavens, yes." Twila fanned herself once again. "Now me, I just did it the natural way." When we all turned to her, she smiled and said, "Coconut cream pie."

The women all had a good laugh at that, then dove into a conversation about men these days—how so few of them were what they called *bona fide*. I turned my attention to locating D.J. and finally caught a glimpse of him in the side yard, playing with the kids. One of the little girls squealed with delight as he pushed her in the tire swing. He happened to look my way and gave a little wave. My heart fluttered.

"Oh no, look there." Jolene sighed. "Just look at that boy. He's got it bad for you, Bella."

At her words, I felt as if a hundred butterflies had been let loose in my stomach. I could hardly stand the joy as I watched him from across the lawn.

"He's bona fide," Bonnie Sue said with an affirming nod. "No doubt about it."

Oh, D.J. Neeley. You're bona fide, all right.

All of the women chimed in their agreement, including my mother. I gazed at her, curious. Did she really think D.J. Neeley was God's ideal for her daughter? Better even than Tony? From the look in her eyes . . . yes.

Several minutes later, Earline informed us that the peach ice cream was done. She dished up hearty bowls of the stuff, and I took a hesitant bite, not knowing what to expect. D.J. joined me just as a dollop plopped off my spoon and onto my blouse. I scooped it up with the spoon and ate it, then licked my lips. "This stuff is delicious."

"I think you were made for country living, Bella." He winked.

"Ya think?"

"Yep. And Precious too." He pointed at the dog, who'd taken a spot on the porch, curled up next to Bruiser.

"Uh-oh." I giggled. "Looks like she's got a crush."

"She's not the only one." He slipped his arm over my shoulders and drew me near, planting a little kiss on my nose. Just as quickly he stepped back and put his hands up. "I know, I know. No PDA."

"Oh, but this is different," I argued, leaning in close. "We're in the country now. You can kiss me all you want in the country."

"Better watch what you're saying, Bella." He set aside my bowl of ice cream and kissed me on each cheek, then tenderly on the lips. I slipped my arms around his neck and leaned my head against his for a moment. Then, after a small child whizzed past us with a water balloon in her hand, we shifted gears. We grabbed our bowls of nearly melted peach ice cream and retreated to the porch swing.

We sat alone at first but were eventually joined by a passel of children I didn't know while the last of the ice cream was consumed. Pretty soon D.J.'s parents joined us on the porch, followed by most of my family. As the afternoon sun tilted farther and farther to the west, casting an orange glow over the Rossi and Neeley clans, we enjoyed some family time together, swatting flies and talking about how fast the summer was flying by. Before long, the last bits of daylight crept over the horizon, and evening shadows wrapped us in their embrace.

As the colors of the sky faded to gray, Earline said, "Bubba, you ready for your solo?"

He groaned and said, "Mama, do I hafta?"

"Well, a'course. It just wouldn't be the Fourth of July without hearing you sing."

After a deep sigh, he rose from his chair and moments later began to sing. The words that flowed forth took my breath away. I'd heard "I'm Proud to Be an American" dozens of times at patriotic events, of course, but never like this. Bubba's rendition had us all in tears by the end of the song. After the last stanza, he took his seat, and a quiet "Wow" rose up from the crowd.

Mama, being Mama, apparently had one of her brilliant-beyond-brilliant ideas. "Bubba, I don't know if I've mentioned it, but I'm a sponsor at Galveston's Grand Opera."

"Oh?" I noticed the hesitancy in his voice, like he knew what was coming.

"The opera is holding open auditions for *The Marriage of Figaro* in a few weeks. You've got to audition. You have the most beautiful voice."

"But I only sing country-western songs," he said. "Don't know nothin' about opera."

"For now. But your pitch and tone are excellent, and I feel sure you could be trained to sing opera." I could hear the intensity in her voice as she said, "Besides, it's a comedy, so you would have so much fun doing it. Would you . . . would you at least promise to pray about it?"

After a moment's pause, he responded, "Well, sure. I guess it won't hurt to pray."

"Never does," Earline said with a hint of laughter in her voice. "Never does."

After that, we all grew silent. I pondered Bubba singing on the stage at the historic opera house. Though I never would have considered it until now, I had to admit the idea held considerable appeal. Hopefully to Bubba as well.

Dwayne Sr. finally announced the time had come for fireworks, and the crowd shifted back to the lawn, where we watched the men at work.

"Boys and their toys," Earline whispered in my ear. She slipped an arm over my shoulder as we watched them together. I leaned against her, and a feeling of warmth settled in my heart— one that had nothing to do with the weather—until the first loud boom rang out. Earline must've felt my shudder, because she looked at me and laughed. "Scared of the fireworks?"

"A little." Mostly, though, I just worried that someone might get hurt. I watched as the older kids played with sparklers. Round and round the sizzling, crackling lights spun, dancing against the night sky. The smaller children put their fingers in their ears as the firecrackers began to pop in rapid succession.

When Earline released me from her embrace, I settled into a lawn chair between my mother and my aunt, who'd finally changed out of her costume and into a skirt and blouse. I couldn't help but notice Laz as he kept a watchful eye on Rosa, particularly when there were other men around. The strangest curiosity rose up inside me as I observed him. One minute he acted like he couldn't stand her, the next he guarded her like the Secret Service.

Hmm. I wonder.

A bottle rocket blazed across the sky, interrupting my ponderings. It provided just the right splattering of light to watch as my man—my bona fide man—lit another one and pointed it heavenward. Pride tingled through me—the good kind, not the bad. Leaning back against the lawn chair, I closed my eyes to dream a little dream about D.J. Neeley.

Before long, the words to a country song found their way to my lips. And funnier still, against the sound of laughter, fireworks, and sparklers, I was pretty sure I heard the angels chiming in.

26

Everybody Loves Somebody Sometime

The two weeks after the Fourth of July passed like a whirlwind. D.J. and I settled into a comfortable but happy routine, one that gave us plenty of time together in the evenings after a hard day's work. He loved Aunt Rosa's cooking, sure, but he enjoyed spending time with the entire Rossi family even more. Go figure. Before long, he became a permanent fixture around our dinner table. With each passing day, my heart grew all that much more attached to his. Unlike my relationship with Tony, I didn't even have to try. No, the feelings I had for D.J. Neeley were bigger than anything I could've conjured up. Only the Lord could have done something this remarkable.

Those same two weeks brought other changes to the household. Uncle Lazarro and Aunt Rosa actually held a couple of civil conversations with each other. In fact, I was pretty sure I caught Rosa blushing when Laz looked at her once. As for the others . . . Nick and Marcella headed off on vacation to the Texas Hill Country with the boys, Sophia informed me she'd given up on her infatuation with Tony DeLuca, and Armando moved back to Houston because he'd fallen for his ex's cousin. Bada-bing, bada-boom. The more things changed, the more they stayed the same.

Not that I wanted things to stay the same. Oh, no. I'd almost grown accustomed to the shifting of sands, the turning of the hands on the clock. In fact, I rather liked the fact that I seemed to have passed from one stage of my life to another. What was it Earline had said the day of the wedding? "Trust God for a new season." And that Scripture passage she'd given me—the one from Song of Solomon—ran through my mind each morning as a new day appeared. "The flowers appear on the earth; the time of the singing of birds is come."

I truly felt like singing now. The Lord had unlocked the key to my cage—symbolically speaking—and with wings unclipped, I soared free. I spread them wide and flew to places I'd never gone before. My heart, now no longer bound by fears and frustrations, was finally ready to love. Finally ready to move forward.

God had done such a work—not just in my heart but at the wedding facility as well. Club Wed saw an influx of customers after the Boot-Scootin' extravaganza. Turned out Sharlene and Cody had done more than sing the wedding facility's praises. After returning from their honeymoon, they actually sent a handful of new clients my way. Between that and our latest ad in the *Houston Chronicle*, I began to see a steady climb in business. With my nerves now behind me, I settled into my position as manager, paying particular attention to the upcoming medieval wedding. I dreamed of ladies-in-waiting and knights in shining armor. Funny how each dream morphed into one about D.J.

On a Thursday afternoon in mid-July, I arrived home exhausted from the heat and a hard day's work. The steady stream of calls and visits from new customers kept me hopping, and I ached to crawl in bed for a nap before dinner. Convinced no one would care, I decided to do just that. Less than ten minutes after falling asleep, however, my cell phone rang. Groaning, I grabbed it to check the number. A 406 area code? Where in the world was that?

I answered tentatively, wondering if perhaps word about the wedding facility had spread that far. I recognized Patti-Lou's voice at once.

"Bella? Can you hear me?"

"Barely." I did my best not to yawn, though everything within me longed to.

Her voice cut in and out. "I'm at . . . sister's . . . mountains . . . reception . . . bad."

"Um, okay." I forced myself awake and tried to play along. "When are you coming home?" Surely by now she'd had her Montana adventure and was ready to hit the beach again.

"Oh, Bella! I met . . . man . . . handsome cowboy . . . married."

"W-wait!" I couldn't stand this! What did she just say? "You met a man?"

"Yes."

"A married man?" Surely not. I forced my sleepy brain to engage, wondering if I might be dreaming this. I'd had stranger dreams in recent weeks, no doubt about that.

"I'm . . . married."

"You're married?" I could hardly believe it.

"*Getting* married." She giggled.

"B-but, you've only been there two weeks. How could you . . . ?"

"Such . . . God-thing."

I sighed, then made up my mind not to ask another question. She proceeded to tell me—in fragmented sentences—about the man of her dreams. How she'd flown all the way to Montana to meet him. How their eyes had met across a crowded room, just like in the old song "Some Enchanted Evening." How he played the drums at her sister's church. How he owned a strip mall in Missoula and had the perfect space for her new flower shop once they returned from their honeymoon cruise to Alaska.

I listened closely, not wanting to miss any more than necessary. At the first lull in the conversation, I asked, "But, what about the shop here?"

"That's why . . . calling," she said. "Want to give your family . . . dibs."

"Wait. Dibs? As in first dibs? You want us to buy the flower shop?"

"Yes." She went on to explain that it was the perfect solution. That Galveston needed the florist business to continue.

"I'll talk to my parents about it," I promised. "But I have no idea what they'll say."

When I ended the call, I leaned back against the headboard, enthralled. *Patti-Lou's found someone. She's getting married. And she's living . . . in Montana.* My mind could hardly take it in. I would miss her terribly. And, man! Losing the florist shop. What a blow to the business. Would my family really be interested in taking it over?

I leaned my head back against the pile of plush pillows, determined to sleep a few more minutes before approaching

Mama with the idea. After a while, I finally gave up. Might as well get this over with.

As I swung my legs over the side of the bed, I heard someone singing. Sounded like a worship song of some sort. Kicking off the covers, I padded barefoot to Uncle Lazarro's bedroom door and knocked. After giving it a minute, I realized he must be gone, so I inched the door open. I found Guido in his cage, warbling a pitchy song. The minute he laid eyes on me, he shifted gears and spouted, "May the words of my mouth be acceptable. May the words of my mouth be acceptable." Over and over again he repeated the same verse.

I could scarcely believe my eyes or my ears. Laz had done it! He'd actually made some progress in reforming the bird. Guido looked up at me, and I could almost sense him smiling. Wow! Looked like God had really done a work on the bird. He'd had his "come to Jesus" meeting, just like Laz.

Suddenly I could hardly wait to talk to Mama. Between Patti-Lou's happy news and the bird's encounter with the Lord, we had some partying to do!

Minutes later, fully dressed, I located my mother in the living room, reading her Bible. I hated to interrupt her but couldn't resist the temptation. I decided to start with Guido and shift to Patti-Lou afterward.

"Can I ask you a question about the bird?"

"Sure." She looked over with a wrinkled brow. "Wait. What's the deal with the cowboy boots and jeans? This is the third time this week."

"Oh, I dunno . . ." I stared down at my feet. "They're really comfortable. Don't know how I lived without them for so long."

"Mm-hmm." She grinned, then asked, "What about Guido?"

"Did you know that he's—"

"Singing praise songs?" She smiled. "Yes, I heard him attempt 'Amazing Grace' this morning. Not bad, but he changed keys a couple of times."

"Actually, I was referring to the Scripture I just heard him quote."

"Ah." She nodded. "You can thank Earline Neeley for that. And your uncle, of course. He jumped right on board with her plan. He played those 'Taming the Tongue' CDs nonstop, you know, starting the day of the wedding. And now he's making Guido listen to the Bible on CD."

"Really?"

"Yes, but we almost lost him in Leviticus and Numbers. Laz ended up skipping right through to Deuteronomy, I think."

After a chuckle, I admitted something that had been weighing on me. "You know, Mama, I had my doubts about that bird. I'm ashamed to admit it now."

Mama rested her Bible in her lap, then looked at me, her eyes narrowing. "Why are you so surprised, Bella? You've seen God do some pretty amazing things over the years."

After a shrug, I decided to come clean. "I think I'm just trying to figure out how he works—God, not the bird."

My mother laughed, then looked at me with a twinkle in her eye. "If you get that figured out, let me know. In the meantime, just trust him. He's got things under control, even the things we can't see. Or maybe I should say *especially* the things we can't see. Oh, and speaking of miracles . . . you might want to take a peek inside the kitchen."

"Oh?" I shuffled my way into the kitchen, the pointed toes of my boots leading the way. I could hardly believe my eyes when I saw the Burton kid eating one of Rosa's homemade garlic twists. She stood next to him, reading something from a piece of paper. To her left, Pop's basketball sat on the countertop, with the skateboard nearby.

At first I pretended to go about my business. I snagged a soda from the fridge. Popped it open and poured it over a glass of ice. Grabbed a cookie. Settled onto a barstool. Watched Rosa and the boy, hoping one of them would eventually offer up an explanation. Instead, the kid kept chomping, pausing only to mutter an occasional "This is really good," at which point Rosa would hand him another twist and smile.

Finally, I could take it no more. "So, what happened?" I stared them both down. "The lawsuit's off?"

"Lawsuit?" Rosa laughed and clasped her hands together at her chest. "There was never a lawsuit. Right, Dakota?"

Ah. So he has a name. He's not just "the Burton kid" after all.

I looked at the kid for his response. He shrugged, then spoke with a full mouth. "I thought my letter sounded pretty good, though, didn't you?"

She nodded, then handed him another chunk of bread.

"Wait a minute." I felt my blood begin to boil. "You wrote that letter?"

He shrugged and muttered a hesitant "Yeah."

"Your dad didn't write it?"

Dakota flashed an impish grin. "Nah. He doesn't even know about it."

I stared him down, my temper rising. "You're telling me your parents aren't mad at us?"

"Nope." He took another bite. "In fact, I heard my mom say she was wondering why none of the neighbors had stopped by to welcome us to the neighborhood." He flashed a sly smile. "Maybe you should do that. I feel kind of sorry for her. She's looking a little lonely."

"I'll do that." *After I strangle you!*

"Her name is Phoebe, by the way. And my dad's name is Bart."

"But, what about the police?" I asked. "Who called them the night of the wedding?"

Dakota raised his hand, then turned back to his food, not even flinching.

"You've got to be kidding me. You led us to believe—"

"Yeah, I know, I know." He looked up at me with a broad grin, likely meant to win me over.

"He wrote the most wonderful apology letter." Rosa shoved the piece of paper my way, and I stared in awe when I saw he'd written it in both English and Italian, just as she'd demanded.

"How in the world did you . . . ?"

He shrugged and took another bite, then spoke around the mouthful of food. "I went to one of those translator sites online. It's pretty cool what you can do on the Internet."

"Yeah, like figure out how to word a lawsuit letter."

"Oh, I didn't get that from the Web." He grabbed a glass of tea and took a swallow. After wiping his mouth, he explained, "I just borrowed one from my dad's office. He's a lawyer, you know."

I counted to ten silently before responding. "Yes, I know. Apparently you'll make a good one too. Someday."

Shrugging, he said, "Maybe," then shoveled another piece of bread into his mouth.

"So, um . . . what won you over?" I asked. "Did Rosa wear you down?"

"Yeah, but not like you're thinking." He paused, and I could read the embarrassment in his eyes.

"Oh?" I turned to my aunt.

"It was the bread," she explained.

"I just couldn't take it anymore." Dakota sighed. "It almost killed me. Every day I'd smell that garlic bread baking, and before long . . . I cracked."

"Aha."

"Couldn't take it anymore. Had to get some or die trying."

"That explains what happened the other morning."

"Hey, I can't be blamed for that," he said. "She left the back door unlocked when she took the trash out. I was just following my nose."

Rosa patted him on the back. "I forgive you for everything, Dakota. On one condition."

"What's that?"

"Tell your parents they're invited to our house for dinner tomorrow night. I'm making manicotti."

When he nodded, she turned to me and whispered, *"Cane che abbaia non morde."*

Dakota looked up at me, a worried look on his face. "What does that mean?"

"She says 'the dog that barks doesn't bite.'"

"Huh?" His face contorted.

"Basically, your bark is worse than your bite," I explained. "She's saying you're a pushover. She thinks she had you the whole time."

"Ah." He nodded and tore off another piece of bread, shoveled it in his mouth, and said, "Maybe she did."

"Would you like to help me cook dinner, Dakota?" Rosa asked. "We're having chicken parmesan and fettuccini tonight. I can teach you how to make the Alfredo sauce from scratch if you like."

His eyes widened, and he nodded. "Sure. Why not."

I left the kitchen with my drink in hand, marveling at what the Lord had done in such a short period of time. He'd saved the bird, restored Rosa's relationship with the neighbors, and found Patti-Lou a mate. And a cowboy, no less!

If God could do all of that in an afternoon, I could only imagine what adventures the evening would hold!

27

You're Nobody
Till Somebody Loves You

Later that night, Rosa served dinner—not in the kitchen as usual, but in the dining room. With Deany-boy and Frankie at church camp, this was an adults-only night. And we were an even-numbered group, what with Sophia being away on a mystery date. She'd had a couple of those lately but wouldn't spill the beans about who she was seeing. I secretly wondered if she hesitated to introduce him because her heart was still given over to Tony. Only time would tell.

Pop took up residence at the head of the big table with Mama to his right. Laz sat at the other end. D.J. and I took our places to Mama's right. Joey and his new girlfriend, Norah, sat across from us, their faces beaming. They had that "we're just so happy we found each other" look. I understood all too well. Likely D.J. and I still had the same look on our faces. Down a little farther, Marcella's face also glowed as

Nick—in an uncharacteristic way—pulled out a chair for her. Something about that just felt . . . fishy.

Stranger still, as soon as my aunt finished carrying in bowls of food, my uncle rose and pulled out her chair. Pop coughed—probably to keep from saying something about it. I bit my tongue as well. As Rosa took her seat, we all held hands to pray. My father's voice trembled as he thanked the Lord for his family and for all of the many blessings of late. I gave D.J.'s hand a squeeze under the table, realizing just what a blessing he'd been in my life. *Thank you, Lord! You've been too good to me!*

After the prayer, I looked up, and my breath caught in my throat as I noticed something more than a little unusual. Rosa. She was wearing makeup. Not just a little lipstick. That would've been strange enough. No, she wore blush, eye shadow, and even a bit of mascara. And she'd done something different with her hair. I must've stared a bit too long because she caught my eye and gave me a little wink. I thought I heard my mother whisper the words, *"Finché c'è vita c'è speranza."* I mouthed a silent "Amen to that" in response.

Within seconds the table came alive with conversation. Rosa passed the fettuccini to my pop. He scooped a hearty serving onto his plate and started to dive in when my mother gave her usual warning. "Cosmo, take your pill."

"Oh yeah." He shuffled off to the kitchen to find his lactose intolerance pills. Upon returning, he kissed my mom on the forehead and proclaimed her to be a lifesaver.

Then the feast began. Of all the meals my aunt cooked, I preferred chicken parmesan and fettuccini Alfredo best of all. Something about the creamy parmesan. And her Caesar salad was the best. D.J. seemed to like it too. Of course, he'd learned to love most every sort of Italian food.

As we ate, Joey and Norah told us all about their day at Moody Gardens. Afterward Laz went on about how Bubba had become a permanent fixture at the restaurant, then Rosa talked a mile a minute about "that precious boy from across the street who only needed someone to show him the love of the Lord."

I kept a watchful eye on Nick and Marcella, who occasionally joined in, but more often than not spent the meal staring at each other and smiling.

Finally I could stand it no longer. I stared at my sister-in-law until she finally looked my way.

"W-what, Bella?" Her cheeks flushed.

"Something's up."

"Oh?" Her gaze shot to Nick, who shrugged and grinned. "What makes you say that?"

"You two are up to something," I said. "Are you plotting to move away and leave the kids with us to raise or something? What's all the grinning about?"

"Well . . ." She looked at Nick once more, and they both grinned ear to ear. "We, um . . . we do have an announcement." The minute my mother started panting, she quickly added, "We're not moving away from the island. Don't worry, don't worry."

"It's nothing like that," Nick said. "We're staying in Galveston for sure."

"What then?" I asked.

Marcella shrugged. "We're looking at a new house. A bigger house."

"Bigger?" Pop laughed. "That house is plenty big enough for the four of you. And the market's not good right now. You should wait till interest rates go down." He went off on a tangent about the current economy, but Mama and I looked at each other, understanding Marcella's full meaning. There could be only one reason they needed a bigger house.

I hated to interrupt my father but couldn't help myself. "Y-you're having a baby?"

When Marcella nodded, the ceiling blew off the room. Well, close. Rosa began to sob—in a good way—and shared the news with any and all saints who might be listening. Mama promptly proclaimed the baby would be a girl and started verbally decorating the nursery. Laz countered by saying the baby would be a boy and that he would put him to work in the restaurant. Pop brought up something about the cost of sending a child to college. D.J. beamed ear to ear and offered congratulations to the happy couple. And Joey and Norah raised their glasses to offer a toast. Seconds later, we all joined them.

"To the baby, and to the happy parents!" Joey said.

"To the baby, and to the happy parents!" we all echoed.

The conversation around the dinner table really took off after that. The voices layered on top of each other, creating a rhythmic motion in the room, and I found myself caught up in it.

After the meal, D.J. and I retreated to the swing on the veranda. The evening breeze off the gulf caught us in its embrace, and I smiled as I pushed a loose hair out of my eyes. As we settled onto the cushioned swing, D.J. turned my way and whispered, "There's something I want to tell you."

"What? Did Aunt Rosa hurt your feelings with that comment about your brother's dog? I told her not to mention it, but she—"

"No, Bella, listen."

"Are you worried about what Laz said about your brother showing up at the restaurant so much? 'Cause if you are, you can relax. He really likes Bubba now. I know, because he told me that—"

"Bella, stop." D.J. pulled me near, and I leaned my head against his shoulder and relaxed. "I want to tell you that . . . I love you."

My heart shot straight up from my chest to my throat, and I barreled to an upright position. "You what?"

"I love you." He ran the tip of his finger along the edge of my cheek. I leaned into his palm and tried to slow my racing heart. *He loves me!*

I felt like a shy schoolgirl as I whispered, "I love you too." Oh, the joy that flooded over me as those words escaped. I'd held them captive for weeks, and now they were free to dance, to sing. D.J. leaned close, and my heart swelled as he traced my cheek with kisses. Seconds later his lips met mine, and we shared a kiss for the record books. I could practically see the sparklers now.

A stirring from inside the house drew us apart, and D.J. smiled as he gazed into my eyes.

"I knew I loved you from the moment you fainted at the wedding facility. I can't believe it took me almost a month to tell you."

"The minute I fainted?" He nodded, and I slapped myself in the head and muttered, "Crazy."

"When did you know?" he asked, drawing me close again.

"Hmm." After a pause, I responded, "I knew I loved you the minute I saw your cowboy boots ambling up the driveway at Club Wed that first day."

"Oh? You have a thing for cowboys?"

"I do now."

He leaned over to kiss me again, but we stopped short when the front door opened and Nick and Marcella walked out.

My brother gave me a pretend stern look and said, "No PDA."

When I shifted my gaze to Marcella's soon-to-be-blooming belly, he shrugged and said, "Hey, we're married." They disappeared down the front steps and into their car.

As we leaned back against the swing, a beautiful breeze off the gulf swept over us. I could almost taste the salt in the air. Or was that love? Funny, all of my senses now ran together.

The stars twinkled overhead as D.J. and I rocked back and forth. The wind slowed down a bit, and the air eventually hung heavy around us. Our quiet conversation morphed to peaceful silence. We sat on the swing so long I could barely keep my eyes open. In my dreamlike state, I thought I remembered D.J. saying, "I love you." Had I only imagined it? My eyes grew heavy, and I drifted away on a cloud where angels nibbled on spoonfuls of peach ice cream and chased each other with water balloons.

"Hey, wake up, sleepyhead." D.J. nudged me, and I forced myself awake.

"W-was I sleeping?"

"Mm-hmm." He yawned and stretched. "But it's okay. I really need to go anyway. It's getting late, and I've got to be up early. I've got that renovation job in the morning, remember."

"Yes, I remember." D.J. Neeley was great at renovating things. Look what he'd done to my heart, after all.

We said our good-byes and shared three or four more sweet kisses before he headed off on his way. I practically crawled up the stairs, exhaustion taking hold. The only thing keeping my brain engaged was the memory of D.J.'s words: "I love you."

I whispered them again, just to remind myself. As if I could ever forget. Through the drowsiness, I somehow made it to my room and dressed for bed. I'd just snuggled under the covers and started to drift off when a memory surfaced. Patti-Lou. The flower shop. I'd completely forgotten to talk to my mother about it.

If I don't do it tonight, I'll never remember tomorrow.

My parents' door was open, and I saw Mama sitting on the edge of her bed, dressed in a white nightgown. She looked over at me with a smile. "Bella. What's up, honey?"

"I meant to tell you this earlier and forgot." I went on to tell her about Patti-Lou's thoughts concerning the flower shop—that our family should buy it from her. It made no sense, of course. We were all far too busy to take on any new projects. Surely Mama would shoot down the idea in a heartbeat.

Ironically, she did just the opposite. "What a positively fascinating problem," she said. After pausing to reflect, her eyes lit with excitement. "And you know who would be perfect to run it? Marcella."

"Wow." The idea hadn't occurred to me, but I could almost see it. Marcella was very creative and loved working with her hands. And she'd helped Patti-Lou out on more than one occasion. But, running a store? How would she do it while expecting, and with the boys underfoot? Would she even be willing to give it a try?

As my mother gave an explanation of why Marcella would be the ideal person, she reached over and grabbed a jar from her bedside table. I almost choked when I realized it was udder cream. She opened the jar and worked it into her face in tiny circular motions, never missing a beat in the conversation. After finishing with her face, she slathered the cream on her hands and rubbed it in. Pausing from her chatter, she looked up at me with chagrin.

"What?" I asked.

"I need some of your father's socks. Do you mind?" She held up her greasy hands and grinned.

"Um, okay." I walked to his dresser and opened the top drawer, looking for a pair of white tube socks. I found none. Instead, I came up with a pair of black trouser socks. "What about these?" I held them up.

"Hmm. Not sure."

I carried them over to her and helped her slip them over her hands and arms. Unfortunately, they kept sliding down to her wrists.

"I know!" I went back to Pop's drawer and located his sock garters. Turning back to Mama, I added, "You're gonna need these." I tossed them her way, and she snagged them like an Astros outfielder.

My father chose that minute to exit the bathroom, saying, "Imelda, have you seen my hemorrhoid cream? I—" He glanced at me and turned all shades of red as he realized I'd heard every word.

I shifted my gaze to my mom, who gave me a sly wink. Aha. For some reason, the knowledge that she'd stolen his hemorrhoid cream made me feel like laughing. Fighting to hold it together, I pointed at my pop's blue boxers and white T-shirt and said, "Hey, we match."

Pop looked at me with a puzzled expression. "Bella, do you mind if I ask what you're doing in my drawers?"

I looked down at my boxers and said, "These are mine, actually."

He groaned, then pointed to the dresser. "No, I meant what are you doing in my *drawers*." He walked over to the dresser and peeked inside, then looked over at Mama, staring at the socks on her hands. "Is nothing sacred anymore? A man has to hide his socks from his wife?"

"Oh, Cosmo, don't fret." Mama gave him a flirtatious smile. "Just wait till you see how pretty I'll look in the morning. Then you won't mind sacrificing a pair of socks to support the cause of beauty."

He took a few steps in her direction, helped her fasten the sock garters on her arms, then planted a tender kiss on her forehead. "You're beautiful right now." A moment later, he sniffed the air, a suspicious look on his face. "What *is* that smell?" Glancing down at the udder cream, he shook his head and said, "I don't even want to know," then walked back into the bathroom, mumbling something about his hemorrhoids.

"I'm sorry you had to hear all of that, Bella," my mother said, "but a woman's gotta do what a woman's gotta do. Before you know it, I'll be eighty and won't look a day over fifty." She nodded as if that settled the whole thing, and I chuckled in response. If I looked half as good as my mother did in my early fifties, I'd be thrilled.

At that moment Rosa popped her head in the door. She had a puzzled look on her face. "Imelda, I can't find the Crisco," she said. "I need it for the pies I'm baking tomorrow. It was on the second shelf in the pantry. Have you seen it?"

"Seen the Crisco?" My mother fanned herself with her sock-covered hand. "Why, I haven't baked in years. You know that." When Rosa left the room, Mama gave me a wink and whispered, "It worked like a charm to remove my makeup. But don't tell, okay? I'll buy some more at the grocery store tomorrow."

Heavens, no, I wouldn't tell. My mother's new beauty secrets were just that—secrets.

"You know, I've been thinking." She paused and looked at me with a serious expression. "I'd like to use the reception hall at the wedding facility to throw a little welcome-to-the-neighborhood tea for our new neighbor across the street."

"Dakota?"

"His mother, silly. That poor woman probably thinks we're all just awful." Mama went on to explain in detail how she planned to remedy that over the next few days. I had a strong feeling Mama and Mrs. Burton were going to end up fast friends. Before long, Mrs. Burton would be a sponsor of the Grand Opera, just like my mama. And who knew—she might even end up helping at the wedding facility.

My mother released a lingering breath. I could tell she had something on her mind, so I said, "Out with it, Mama. What's up?"

The most curious look passed over her face before she finally spoke up. "I've been wrestling with this for days. Actually, ever since our conversation awhile back."

"Conversation? Which conversation?"

"The one about Rosa joining the convent." Mama paused, then sighed before saying, "I guess there's one thing I should tell you."

"Oh?"

Mama looked around to make sure no one was listening. "Remember how I told you someone had broken her heart?"

"Of course. How could I forget?"

"What you don't know is . . ." Mama drew a deep breath, then continued. "The boy who broke her heart—the one who wouldn't look twice at her when she was a teenager—was your Uncle Laz."

"W-what?"

She nodded. "From what my parents told me years ago, Rosa had had her eye on Lazarro from the time she was twelve or thirteen. We were neighbors, after all, and we went to the same church and the same school. Laz even worked in our family's restaurant for a while, washing dishes. But that boy . . ." Mama shook her head. "He wasn't the nicest kid in town. In fact, he was quite a troublemaker, from what your father tells me. He'd make the Burton boy look like an angel."

"Wow." Hard to imagine.

"When Laz found out Rosa had a crush on him, he turned his attention to another girl to make a point."

"Oh, poor Rosa!" My heart broke at this revelation. Made me want to head over to Uncle Laz's room and give him a piece of my mind.

"And Laz, um, ended up marrying that other girl two years later," my mother added.

I gasped. "Aunt Bianca?"

"Yes." Mama nodded. "And then, after some time had passed, Laz and Bianca came to New Jersey to live near us. Your papa was thrilled to have his brother back in his life, of course. And I was too. Both of them, actually." A little sigh escaped as she said, "You know, I always loved Bianca. And she never knew about Rosa's heartbreak. We never said a word."

"So what happened?" I crossed my legs, ready for the rest of the tale.

"Rosa was back in Napoli, making a name for herself as a cook," Mama explained. "And, as you heard her say, she did pretty well. She ran her own restaurant for the last twenty years she was there. Everyone in Napoli knew her, and she was written up in the papers because the place always did such great business. There was even some talk of her doing a show on television. A cooking show, of course."

"Wow." This latest news registered slowly.

"Then my parents passed away, and Rosa was truly alone. I knew how difficult it must have been, so I asked her to come and stay with us. But it was pure coincidence that I made the suggestion just a few days before your Aunt Bianca passed away. I certainly didn't mean to . . ."

"Oh man." I got it now. Uncle Laz—the very person Rosa had avoided for forty-plus years—lost his wife just prior to Rosa's arrival.

"They were forced together under the same roof," Mama said. "I could tell it was hard on Rosa at first, but Laz had given his heart to the Lord by then and treated her better than I expected."

"So what happened between then and now?" I asked. "Why all the bickering?"

Mama smiled. "Oh, I have my theories. It's one thing to live in the same house with someone you care about. It's another thing to live in the same house and not be able to share your real feelings."

"Real feelings?" I stared at my mother, dumbfounded. "Are you saying . . ."

"I can't be sure, of course." She shrugged. "But all the signs are there. And you know what I always say, Bella. *Il tempo guarisce tutti i mali.*"

"Time heals all wounds," I echoed. "So do you think Laz will come to his senses? He's pretty stubborn."

"I think so," Mama said. "But it might happen quicker if we agree to pray about it for a while. What do you think?"

"Of course!" After pausing to think through this information, a new resolve kicked in. I shared my thoughts with a smile. "Mama, here's what I think. If God brought Pop all the way from Italy . . . if he brought D.J. all the way from Splendora . . . then I have to believe he's big enough to bring Uncle Laz all the way from the backyard to the kitchen to find Rosa."

Mama winked, then reached to hug me as she whispered, *"Finché c'è vita c'è speranza."*

Our voices blended together in perfect unity as we both echoed the familiar words: "As long as there is life, there is hope."

28

That's Amore

July sweated its way into August, and before long, our Galveston summer prepared to roll itself back out to sea. Mama put together a beautiful tea for the neighborhood ladies to welcome Phoebe Burton to Galveston on the first Saturday of the month. Meeting the woman in person put a whole new spin on things. In every way she was her son's opposite. Quiet, unassuming, polite . . . I could find no flaws in her.

Of course, there was that one little thing about her being Presbyterian. Rosa hadn't taken that news lying down. Me? Well, I couldn't help but chuckle. The Lord, in his own unique way, continued to expand our horizons.

The changes in my parents and siblings were undeniable, as was evidenced by our first annual family photo day on the third Thursday in August. Mama entered the living room dressed in a denim skirt and blouse ensemble that tied in nicely with her new cowboy boots. She offered a smile before sitting next to me on the sofa.

"Why did Joey pick the hottest day of the year to take family photos?" she asked as she checked her appearance in her compact.

"I think he's just anxious to get a photo with Norah in it," I said. "Do you blame him?" He'd had her name tattooed on his arm, for Pete's sake. The two rarely spent any time apart.

A smile teased the edges of Mama's lips. "I have it on good authority we'll need to hire a real photographer soon."

"Oh?"

One of her finely plucked eyebrows elevated slightly. "Well, he can't very well take the pictures at his own wedding, can he?"

I gasped at this news. "Are you sure?"

She nodded and whispered, "I've seen the ring," then put her finger to her lips.

"B-but they've only been dating for several weeks."

"Honey, when it's the right one, you know it. You could date six weeks or six months or six years, but eventually you would end up at the altar." She gave me one of those "you get my real meaning, right?" winks, and I smiled. I got it. And yes, I knew D.J. Neeley was the one. But we weren't in a huge hurry, for sure. No, we were having far too much fun getting to know each other. And each other's families.

Still, I had to wonder how many weddings Club Wed would see in the next few months. Bubba and Jenna were pretty much inseparable these days. Every time I looked into my best friend's eyes, I saw wedding rings floating around in there. And then there was the upcoming Patti-Lou bridal extravaganza, way up in Montana-land. Sadly, I would not be able to attend. And, of course, the medieval wedding. I'd already been making plans for our happy bride and groom.

"Just look what God has done," I whispered, looking around. In two months' time, everything had changed. And the Lord was all to blame. Every good and perfect thing that had happened in my life lately came from his hand. I'd never been more grateful, or more aware of his presence in my life. Sometimes I wondered what I'd ever done to deserve such goodness.

Several minutes later, the living room filled with the whole Rossi clan. I had to laugh when I saw my family members in their cowboy gear. Pop even brought a lasso just for fun. And the boots! I chuckled as I thought about how the Lord had provided boots for one and all, and even paid me back for them. Mr. Oldenburg's check had arrived soon after he received the Lanciotti's, along with an emotional thank-you letter. It took some doing for me not to fret over the ex-Mrs. Oldenburg. I'd been praying for her instead. Unfortunately, I always found myself humming "All My Exes Live in Texas" as I prayed. Hopefully I'd be able to let go of the song in time.

"Hey, look at us," Armando said, gazing around the room with a grin on his face. "We're the Beverly Hillbillies."

"More like the Thrillbillies, what with all the drama in our family over the past few months," Joey said.

We all got a good laugh at that one. Still, looking around the room at all of the denim, button-up shirts, and hats, I had to admit Armando was right. The Rossis had morphed into the Beverly Hillbillies. The twenty-first century version anyway. With Precious cradled in my lap, I concluded I must be Elly May. And Rosa, with her hair curled up in a knot on the back of her head, could almost pass for Granny, if you factored in a few extra pounds. Nick looked a bit like Jethro Bodine today, and Pop . . . well, in his current getup, he could almost pass for Jed. My family was every bit as nutty as the original TV cast, but just as lovable too. Perhaps even more so. My heart swelled with joy as I realized just how much I adored every person in the room.

D.J. arrived at the last moment, looking a bit winded. The sawdust in his hair reminded me of our first meeting. These days I wouldn't recognize him without it. Nor would I change a thing about him. I loved his deep twangy voice and his smokin' baby blues. I adored his tall, handsome looks and the amble in his step. Best of all, I loved him. Loved the goodness shining out of his eyes. Loved the way he credited the Lord for every good thing in our relationship. Loved the fact that his family had fallen head-over-heels for mine, and vice versa.

My heartthrob cowboy settled in next to me on the sofa, and Joey did a head count. Realizing all parties were accounted for, he adjusted his camera one last time and joined us for the first photo. Then the second. Then the third. By the time we got to the seventh or eighth, we'd taken to doing some funny poses, including a great one of the whole family line dancing together. I could hardly wait to see that one in print. Likely Mama would enlarge it and hang it on the entry room wall.

Not that I minded. No, this boot-scootin' family photo had been my idea, and a good one, if I did say so myself. Still, I had to wonder what the photographs would look like after the next wedding. Could I talk the guys into dressing up as knights in shining armor? Looking around at the smiles on their faces, I could almost imagine it.

We'd just finished the last of the photos when the doorbell rang. Precious started yapping, which sent Guido into his rendition of "Amazing Grace." Thank goodness we'd finally had his wings clipped, otherwise he might've taken flight across the room.

I sprinted to the door, and when I opened it, I couldn't help but gasp. Earline and Dwayne Neeley stood there, fully decked out in motorcycle gear. Behind them in the driveway stood the most gorgeous Harley Davidson I'd ever seen. Shiny red and black, it glistened in the sunlight, putting off a glare that nearly blinded me.

"Y-you bought a motorcycle?" I stepped out onto the veranda, stunned.

"Mm-hmm." Earline giggled. "Isn't she a beauty?"

"We've been wanting to buy one for years," Dwayne Sr. said. "Don't know why we didn't do it sooner. It's been great for both of us." He tipped Earline backward and gave her a passionate kiss.

Whoa, you two! Watch the PDA!

I kept my focus on the bike. The big, beautiful, shiny bike. I could hardly picture D.J.'s parents on the back of it, but apparently they'd ridden it here from Splendora.

"Take a look at this." They both turned around at the same time, revealing the emblem SHADE TREE BIKERS—HITTING THE TRAIL FOR JESUS on their backs.

"Wow." I hardly knew what to say. "So where are you headed?"

"State park on the west end of the island," Dwayne Sr. explained. "We're camping out tonight. Not sure what tomorrow holds. We're gonna take this one day at a time."

"Good idea." Not just for their beach trip, but for their lives.

"I've got a pretty good idea the Lord is calling us into the motorcycle ministry," Earline said. "We're praying about it, of course. But you never know what new roads he has for you unless you open yourself up to the possibilities."

"Well, amen to that!" I gave her a huge hug, realizing she meant those words as much for me as for herself.

Within seconds, the whole family joined us on the veranda. Nick's boys took one look at that bike and started running toward the driveway.

"Don't touch it, boys," Nick called out.

"Nah, let 'em touch," Dwayne Sr. said with a crooked grin. "No harm in that."

After several more minutes of the Rossis and Neeleys oohing and aahing over the Harley, I saw Dakota approaching from across the street. The kid's eyes widened when he saw the bike. For a minute I thought he might try to climb aboard. Instead, he turned to Frankie and Deany-boy. "You guys wanna shoot some hoops?"

They shrugged and Frankie said, "Sure," then they disappeared around the side of the house.

As I watched them, my heart practically sang. Oh, what progress could be made with time.

Mama ushered us back inside, extending the photo invitation to our guests. "We've got to take one more picture with everyone in it."

"Dressed like this?" Earline pointed to her leather jacket.

"Oh, trust me, you'll fit right in."

They tagged along behind us, joining in the fray as Joey snapped one last photo. Afterward Rosa invited us into the kitchen for thick slices of homemade cheesecake with raspberry topping. Laz followed on her heels, even offering to help fetch the plates and forks. As I reached for plates and silverware, I was pretty sure I caught him looking at her out of the corner of his eye. She offered him a shy smile in response.

As soon as they'd finished slicing up the cheesecake, he turned to her. "I, um . . . I'm working on a new menu for the restaurant. I wondered if . . ."

"What?" My aunt glanced up at him with a mixture of curiosity and fear in her eyes.

"Just wondered if you might want to help me, is all." He gazed at her with what could only be described as tenderness—the Lazarro Rossi version, anyway. I wanted to dance a little jig. Wanted to kiss my uncle on the forehead and thank him for finally seeing the light. Wanted to take each of them by the hand and walk them into the sunset. Instead, I joined the others at the table and left the two to their own devices.

Mama's eyes glistened as she made an announcement. "Cosmo and I are dying to go to Europe next spring." After a pause, she added, "We've been planning it for ages but didn't feel comfortable leaving until after Bella got the wedding facility running smoothly." Her face beamed as she looked my way. "And things are going so well, I'm ready to book our flight right now."

Earline crooned, "Oh, honey! I've wanted to see Italy all of my life." She giggled. "Couldn't you just see the two of us at the Coliseum? And the Vatican? And Tuscany! I hear tell it's beautiful up there."

"Oh, it is," Mama agreed. "I spent my childhood in Italy, you know."

"Yes, I remember you telling me." Earline's face had a dreamy-eyed expression. "All of my life I've dreamed of floating down a canal in one of those little boat thingies."

She sighed, and Mama gave her a pensive look. "Why didn't you tell me you wanted to go to Europe? You two must come with us." She grabbed Earline's hand and gave it an excited squeeze.

"Do you really think so?" Earline asked, looking stunned. "You'd be okay with us taggin' along?"

"Okay?" Mama clasped her hands together. "Why, I think it's a perfectly wonderful idea. Don't you, Cosmo?" After an affirmative reaction from my father, she turned back to Earline. "You know what I'm going to do? I'm going to teach you Italian before we go. You'd be a natural."

"I would?" Earline chuckled. "Well, go figure."

Mama began to explain—in Italian—just what made the language so beautiful. Within seconds she'd transported me all the way from Texas to Napoli. Hmm. Maybe I should go on this vacation with them. Or, better yet . . . I looked at D.J. out of the corner of my eye, and an idea took hold. Maybe one day we could honeymoon in Italy.

Hey, a girl could dream, couldn't she?

Mama and Earline began to talk about some spa in the south of Italy that my mother had read about online. "It's in an indoor cave," my mother explained. "And you won't believe how wonderful it sounds." She listed the spa's amenities—a Turkish bath, a Jacuzzi, and massage therapy.

Earline practically drooled. "Oh, honey, that sounds divine. A real honest-to-goodness spa. The closest I've come in Splendora is Cut Loose, where I get my hair done. Well, that and the Fancy Fingers nail salon in Porter. They've hired a new eyebrow plucker, you know."

"Ah." Mama nodded. "Girl, you're long overdue. There's nothing like a good facial at a deluxe spa to put a new spin on things. And speaking of facials, Bella, have you ever seen my skin look better?" Mama pointed to the areas around her eyes and hands. "When I think of all that money I spent on expensive creams, it makes me cringe. All I needed was udder cream. Amazing."

"Amazing," Earline and I echoed in tandem.

I had to admit, she did look better. In fact, we all did.

Something about meeting the Neeleys had put a healthy glow on every face.

The women dove into an extensive conversation about beauty products, and the men went back into the living room to talk about motorcycles. Another knock at the door interrupted our chatter. No one budged, so I finally offered to answer it. I opened the door to the mailman, who held an Express Mail envelope in his hand. I took it, thanked him, and headed back to the kitchen.

Mama looked up from the conversation and pursed her lips. "What is it, Bella?"

"Something for Laz."

My uncle turned his attention from Rosa and took the letter from me. I watched as he examined the return address. Suddenly his eyes lit with recognition. "This has to be from Sal. It's from Atlantic City." He opened the envelope and smiled as he read the letter. "Looks like Sal is doing better. He's asking about Guido."

"Time to send the little prodigal home?" I asked.

Laz shook his head. "No, not just yet. Sal still has a long road ahead of him but should be home by the fall. We'll figure out a way to get Guido back then. But that's a good thing because I need the extra time. I've got to figure out a way to get Guido's feathers to grow back. And he's only halfway through the Old Testament CDs. He won't hear a full-out salvation message till he hits the New Testament."

"You've got to get him through the gospel of John if you're going to stand half a chance," Earline said.

They lit into a conversation about the best salvation Scriptures, then put together a focused plan of action. If they had their way, Guido would be able to pray the sinner's prayer within a month. I still couldn't get over the fact that he'd made so much progress already. And it seemed to be rubbing off. Even my dog was in better spirits these days.

The room filled with fun-loving conversation once again, and I celebrated the fact that the Lord had truly done a work in our two families. They were more than getting along— they'd become one.

Suddenly D.J.'s face lit up, and he rose to his feet. "Oh, Laz, I keep forgetting to tell you something." When my uncle looked his way, he said, "I've come up with a name for the barbecue pizza."

"Oh, wow." I gazed at D.J. in surprise. In all the madness, I'd nearly forgotten.

"You found the right Dean Martin song?" my uncle asked, drawing near.

"I think so." An embarrassed look crossed my handsome dee-jay's face. After a moment's pause, he said, "Bamboozled."

"What?" we all said in unison.

"What does bamboozled have to do with barbecue pizza?" Laz asked.

D.J. shrugged. "Well, here's my take on it . . ." He gave me a shy glance. "The idea occurred to me when I realized I'd been bamboozled. From the day I first met you and your family, I've been . . . changed. You've knocked me off my feet. All of you."

"In a good way, I hope," I said.

"In a very good way." He reached for my hand and gave it a squeeze. "But that feeling you get when life throws some-thing unexpected at you—that's the same feeling I got when I heard about the barbecue pizza. It's different. Not what I was expecting. And when people eat it, they'll be—"

"Bamboozled!" Uncle Laz clasped his hands together at his chest as if in prayer. "I love it!"

"Yeah." D.J. looked over at him with a shy smile. "Really?"

"I think it's perfect," Laz said. "Now, to come up with the perfect pitch." He headed off to the other side of the kitchen, where he and Rosa began to jot down ideas for a phone message to entice customers.

I gazed at D.J. with new admiration. "Wow. That was pretty clever. And I can't believe you remembered."

"Remembered? Are you kidding? I've spent hours on the Web. I could name any song Dean Martin ever sang. Try me."

We spent the next ten minutes doing just that. I was finally convinced he'd memorized Dean's entire repertoire, so we shifted gears. He gave me that now-familiar "come hither" look, and I quirked a brow. "Come with me?" he whispered.

"Sure." I followed him through the crowd of people to the back door.

Once outside, he led me to the back of the house, where we sat together on a bench near my uncle's garden. The landscape looked a bit dried out and barren. Still, it was quiet.

D.J. gave me a gentle kiss on the end of my nose. "I just needed to get out of there for a minute," he admitted. "I want you to myself. Is that selfish?"

"No way."

He slipped his arm around my shoulder, and I gave him a tender kiss.

"So, I have a favor to ask." I reached up with the tip of my index finger and traced D.J.'s cheek, loving the feel of the stubble under my fingertip.

"A favor?" His brow wrinkled. "What? You want me to come up with a tofu pizza? Something with a quirky name?"

"Nah." I laughed.

"What? You don't think I can do it?" He gave me a playful frown. "I think we've already established that I'm a jack-of-all-trades. So if you need me to take over your family's restaurant or help Marcella at the flower shop or maybe learn how to make coffees, I'm your guy."

"Oh, you're my guy all right." I offered him a playful wink. "But I really just wanted to ask you to deejay the next wedding."

"Is that all?" He laughed, the relief evident on his face. "I thought it was going to be something scary."

"Well, there is this one little thing . . ." I bit my lip, trying to work up the courage to tell him.

"What's that?"

"You, um . . . you have to wear tights."

"Say what?" He paled. "You want this good ol' boy from Splendora, Texas, to wear tights in public? Like little girl lacey tights?"

I doubled over in laughter. "No. They're more like leggings. Part of a medieval costume. You've seen the guys at the Renaissance festival, right?"

D.J. shrugged. "Yeah, in pictures. But I've never—repeat, never—worn tights, and I never plan to."

I shrugged. "Well, think about it. Stranger things have happened, you know."

"Um, yeah. They have. And most of them over the past few weeks, if memory serves me correctly." D.J. ran his fingers through my hair, and I rested my head against his shoulder. "Bella, you've done something to me. I can't think straight anymore."

"I hope you mean that in a good way."

He chuckled before responding, "I do. You've brought me out of my shell. I was perfectly content to spend my days building things with my hands, but you . . . " He smiled. "You've got me building things with my heart."

"O-oh?" I stared up into his gorgeous blue eyes, mesmerized.

"Yeah." His breath felt warm against my ear as he whispered, "I've got plans, Bella Rossi. Plans that include you. I hope you're up for 'em."

"I . . . I . . ." A lump formed in my throat, and I couldn't finish.

"Don't get any ideas that you're gonna run off and break my heart," he added. "You're my girl now."

"Yeah?" I teased.

"Well, sure." He wrapped me in his arms and whispered, "Possession is nine-tenths of the law, you know."

Indeed, it was. And right now D.J. Neeley possessed my heart, every square inch of it. Might as well put a SOLD sign on that property. He'd captured me, and I'd never be the same.

Sure, we had our differences. He was a little bit country. I was a little bit Italian. But oh, mama mia! What a delicious combination!

Sister Twila's Beauty Secrets

For soft, wrinkle-free hands, Twila recommends bag balm (commonly known as udder cream). Apply liberally on hands and feet at bedtime, then cover with socks.

To clear up those annoying wrinkles around the eyes, Twila and the other full-figured sisters suggest dabbing on hemorrhoid cream. Voilà! Wrinkles disappear!

Wishing you had soft, bouncy hair? Mane and Tail (located at all trendy feed stores) will do the trick. It'll put the "giddyap and go" in your hair—and your step!

Sister Twila loves to use sugar mixed with a bit of olive oil as a facial scrub. Be sure to rinse with cold water afterward. (According to Twila, a woman can never be too sweet.)

Worried about cellulite? Twila understands! She recommends you rub used coffee grounds on problem areas. (Warning: folks are liable to ask, "Where's the coffee?" in your presence.)

Looking for a great makeup remover? Crisco is the best! Twila also recommends it to treat psoriasis and eczema. She'll be happy to show you her elbows as proof of its effectiveness. Crisco also bakes up a great piecrust.

If you're like Twila, you love a great face mask. Unscented kitty litter mixed with half a cup of water is the cat's meow!

Twila can't say enough about her favorite facial peel—Pepto-Bismol. Apply liberally, allow to fully dry, then peel away for soft, luscious skin.

Struggling with dark circles under your eyes? Twila has the solution! Try raw potato slices. They're loaded with potassium, the perfect antidote for tired, puffy eyes!

Twila recommends that all you women, young and old, apply liberal amounts of sunscreen before going outside, whether you live on Galveston Island or elsewhere.

Finally, Twila's best beauty secret of all—water! Be sure to drink eight to ten glasses per day to keep your skin and your body hydrated. Here's Twila's rule of thumb: If you're 130 pounds or less (and frankly, she doesn't know many women who are), drink 64 ounces a day. If you're heavier than that (like most gals), Twila recommends you drink half your body weight per day in ounces of water. In other words, a normal-sized woman (say, Twila's size—approximately 200 pounds) should drink 100 ounces of water a day, and so on. Twila is quick to add that you must memorize the location of all restrooms at local shopping centers before adopting this practice.

Acknowledgments

Though I've been writing for years, I truly feel the Weddings by Bella series is a first in many ways. Through this wacky tale, I was able to share both my love of weddings and my love of comedy. And what fun to have such a lively cast of characters! Bella and her quirky family members boot-scooted their way into my heart!

To my editor, Jennifer Leep—thank you for falling in love with this story. You get my writing voice, and it shows in the way you constantly encourage me. What a blessing you are!

To my agent, the awesome Chip MacGregor—I can never thank you enough. You believed in Bella, and you believe in me. Thanks for finding the perfect house for my comedies! Here's to many more years—and projects!—together.

To my copyeditor, Jessica Miles—girl, I appreciate you so much! You added that extra sparkle to my words. (Here in Texas, we call that a "spit shine.") You're a true word-smith!

To my critique partners, Kathleen Y'Barbo, Martha Rogers, and Linda Kozar—you are the wind beneath my wings.

Thanks for taking the time to read through my story and offer critique. I value your input so much! And thanks for laughing in all the right places.

To my Lord and Savior, Jesus Christ—only you saw the personal struggles leading up to this book. You finally swung wide the door for me to write the kind of story I'd been aching to write all along, and I'm so grateful!

To my readers—praise the Lord and pass the pasta!

Janice Thompson is a Christian freelance author and a native Texan. She is the mother of four grown daughters, three beautiful granddaughters, and a brand-new grandson. She resides in the greater Houston area, where the heat and humidity tend to reign.

Janice started penning books at a young age and was blessed to have a screenplay produced in the early '80s. From there she went on to write several large-scale musical comedies for a Houston school of the arts. Currently, she has published over fifty novels and nonfiction books for the Christian market, most of them lighthearted and/or wedding themed.

Working with quirky characters and story ideas suits this fun-loving author. She particularly enjoys contemporary, first-person romantic comedies. Wedding-themed books come naturally to Janice, since she's coordinated nearly a dozen weddings, including recent ceremonies and receptions for her four daughters. Most of all, she loves sharing her faith with readers and hopes they will catch a glimpse of the real happily ever after as they laugh their way through her lighthearted, romantic tales.

When *Hollywood's* most eligible
bachelor sweeps into town,
will he cause trouble for *Bella*?

Don't miss book 2 in the Weddings by Bella series,
coming in January.